A Moonserpent Tale

A Moonserpent Tale

Rosemarie Montefusco

This is a work of fiction. The characters, events, settings, and dialogue are inventions by the author. Any resemblance to actual events or persons, living or dead, is coincidental. No identification with actual persons, alive or deceased, places, or incidents is intended or should be inferred.

ISBN – 13: 9798766900832

Dedicated to the memory of Dorothea M. Rothgaber, who continues to shape everything.

And to Bella, who once mentioned she wanted to read to this.

And to Matt, who would only keep it alive.

Contents

Part One

Part Three

Part One

Chapter One

Of Witches as Couriers

A raina tripped over a piece of driftwood sunken in the sand. She caught herself in the stumble, but not before the corner of the spell book poked her cheek. As she rubbed away the sting, she checked that afternoon's harvest to see if any of it had fallen from the basket on her arm. It was all still there—withered, weak, and hardly substitutes for the plants that would hold some hope of stifling fever.

On returning to their round stone cottage, she found Kerikan asleep with her spectacles barely holding to her face. They teetered with the old witch's slow, raspy snore. Araina deftly lifted them away to examine just how badly they had been bent. Not as much as the day before, though still such a waste, the young witch thought. Despite being too weak to read on her own, Kerikan would continue to place the things on the end of her nose as if they were required to hear her grandniece's reading. Araina caught her great aunt's scrutiny as she gingerly corrected the frames.

"I expect they'll snap next time. Then you'll not have them when you actually need them."

"They're no more worth the worry or work."

The old witch's pale assurance hindered Araina's warning, "...They really can't take another twisting." She placed the spectacles on the nightstand and returned to the harvest on the table. "There's not an un-blighted stem of blue flag through all the estuary. So I thought the next best thing would be if I use some of the dried hyssop and mix that with—"

"My Araina. No more worth the worry."

The hoarse reiteration slipped below the sea breeze from the cottage windows. Araina lifted her eyes to it and away from the basket of next-best-things.

"Mind your gazing. You idle as though you are done," the dying woman, who suddenly no longer sounded like one, prodded.

"Done with what, Aunt Kerikan?"

1

"Things in need of doing. Lessons. Tasks." Her insistent tone had atrophied little in the few weeks it had been away. Araina was no less accustomed to it.

"Am I ever done with those?"

"Not those. Gone like the leaves and roots. Dying and dead. You've others, beyond me and here, but not you and where you'll go."

"Go?"

Kerikan sighed, slow and rough. "I would only keep waiting to send you. If ever. But it seems I cannot do otherwise. We must work with the you that we have. Time over ability. But then, whatever else have we done? Now, empty the cloaks out of the chest."

"It sounds like your fever's back up. What if I tried some—"

"Shush. How'm I to get you started if you talk over and through me? Go on," Kerikan urged.

The young witch looked at the revitalized steadiness over her great aunt's face and moved to the foot of the bed. She raised the lid of the cedar chest with a creak and proceeded to drape lace shawls and embroidered cloaks over its edge, prompting the old witch to scold, "You waste time! Toss them to the stone."

With a sigh, Araina bundled the remaining garments and let them drop to the sand-scattered floor. She looked to Kerikan for further instruction.

"On the bottom there, you see? Lift that up."

Araina saw the gap to which her great aunt referred and placed her fingernails between the notched boards. Waiting within the hidden cavity was a small case carved from rosewood. Araina lifted it over her head to meet with Kerikan's view.

"Be careful if it suits you! Now, bring it here."

The little box was presented at her bedside.

"Open it."

Araina dragged back a chair, sat, and uncovered a tiny flute, primitively formed from what she would have guessed was crystal—a quartz of violet, smoke, and blue.

"There you are," Kerikan greeted it. Before Araina could think to bring it to her lips, she was warned, "Don't. You'll break it."

"For what use is it then?"

"For you to take with you."

"Wouldn't I be more likely to break it if I'm taking it somewhere? And…to where am I taking it?"

"Keep it in that box. Show it to no one. Say nothing of it until it arrives at the same place you're taking the spell books."

"Which spell books?"

"Those." Kerikan lifted her sunken eyes to the highest shelf. "The last two nearest to me."

"How'm I to take them if I'm not allowed to touch them? They are on *that* shelf," Araina countered.

"Touch any and all of them, but only after you've delivered those two. You may open neither. You will give them to a friend of mine. He's expecting them."

"And where is he?"

"In the tower of the ruins. It's beyond the market, through the wooded border. They are to be placed in his hands, by you. Tell and show no one else."

"Could you not just send them with that red-tail? It still comes and waits every morn—"

"Flawless nonsense. I know you can wander your way through a tangle of trees. There is nothing more to this than that, my Araina. You know what you need to carry and where."

"And as for the when?"

"They and you will go after I. Soon as you've a full day's light to start." The old woman's rasp returned with the reminder of why this was passing between them. Araina almost forgot the spurring of it all until she saw that urgent little spark leave Kerikan like the wick-held glow of a snuffed candle.

"I've never gone that far..." Her gaze traveled the cluttered shelves and portrait-dotted walls. "And then, after..."

"Anchors and harbors are useful things, my Araina, but a ship cannot be guided by its anchor. And what need of ships that never leave harbors?"

"And what of witches as couriers?"

"At these times, as they are, we work with what we have, as we are. And so you as you are. Witch, courier, or otherwise."

Kerikan stopped breathing with the late day breeze. When the sun left the rocks where the harbor seals used to bask, her body was shrouded and placed upon a narrow raft. Araina sent it beyond the inlet's low breakers and watched it disappear, and somewhat faster than dreaded and expected. The hard work of it was a comforting weight—one only apparent through its dissipation. The witch pulled her feet from the sand and shook away its clinging grains before reentering the cottage.

The chair at Kerikan's bedside was dragged back and served as a means to the formerly forbidden summit of the overcrowded bookshelves. Araina carefully pulled the two from the many, keeping each of their thick covers tight to the mass of pages. It was an unnecessary precaution as both were sealed with ornate puzzle locks. She studied them briefly, confident she could have bested them with some time and trial, but obedience conquered their lure. The locked tomes remained as such and were gently rested on Kerikan's bed next to the flute in its box.

The witch crossed the kitchen and moved to her bedroom. She tossed her sketchbooks, pressed-pigments, and paintbrushes from the lid of a woven trunk. After a rummage, she retrieved a bundle of cloth, unwrapped it, and revealed a misericorde. A sliver of her reflection was shown in its blade. After looking up to confirm the whole of it in her bedroom mirror, it stole her for a moment—a presence as solitary as ever before.

Kerikan was gone, certainly, but that was the last and greatest parting of a recent many. There were no more crickets sounding from the dune grass at night, no moths swirling over it, or bats dashing after them. Even the raccoons, Araina's evening beach-combing companions, were fewer and fewer until the witch walked alone in search of scant medicinal plants—rather than curious little things in the sand.

That same stout and fertile frame, held in olive skin and a lousewort dress, felt so much frailer than it appeared in the glass. Her hazelnut mop of slow twists and waves, all but slipped free of a hasty braid, obscured her deep and close-set eyes. The only thing that seemed un-tussled, un-sunken, and un-exhausted was that infamous nose—the one that prompted Kerikan's visiting friends to say, "Unmistakably a Moonserpent. Un-missably a Crest child" every time they saw it. In observing all the last few weeks had left of her, it occurred to Araina that she might be the last living, moving thing, not only in that cottage, but also upon its seashore. She looked back to the dagger and rewrapped it in the cloth.

It was tucked in a woven sling bag and rested below a slate-filled purse, a pairing of flint and fire steel, the two spell books, and the flute in its box. As she closed the bag, a startling pain shot from her left palm. Araina examined it closely, looking for a forgotten burn or burrowed thorn. She found no visible cause for such a sudden and harsh pressure. A rinse of cool water from the pump provided no avail. She pushed and picked at her skin with her thumbnail. The motion uncovered nothing, nor did it worsen the pain—even when she dug at it, harder and fiercer. Still, there was nothing.

Araina could only ignore it and considered what remained to carry or address. There was the sailboat—far enough onshore but still at risk of drifting away in a late summer squall. She went on digging at her palm as she stepped out into the setting sun and pushed her little vessel up to the cottage walls. The sting raged on with a maddening urgency to be free.

"What is that?" she growled.

Araina looked to her toes and retrieved a black scallop shell. Snapping it in two, she dragged one of the shards across her palm with a sharp compulsion. The thin cut released a slow stream of blood. Though the pain rolled away with it, no clear cause was uncovered. The witch bathed her sliced hand in the saltwater and sighed her thanks to be rid of the sting and perhaps better able to face the morning.

Salt spray and first light served to remind Araina who and where she was, and that the stark silence throughout the cottage was to be expected. She tossed the weight of hair from her face and dropped her feet to the floor. She shed her nightgown, quickly laced the center of her stiff-seamed tulitiere and the sides of her knee-knickers, then lowered the lousewort dress back over her head. Perhaps it was not the best attire for whatever lay beyond the market, she considered as she tied its bow at her back, but surely it made more sense than a freshly cleaned or less comfortable dress. It seemed no more or less suitable than anything else she owned.

From the shelf above Kerikan's bed, she took the apple-shaped jewel box and lifted its stem. Buried below the old witch's turquoise charms and the young witch's first pairs of earrings, was the Moonserpent seal ring. Araina slipped it on the center finger of her right hand. She tapped it against a jar of rosaberries before they were placed in the sling bag, along with the last of the bread, a wooden canteen, and a spare dress and set of undergarments. Lastly, she tethered her hair with a wide ribbon and slung the bag's strap over her form. Left with nothing more to gather or face but the front door, she opened and walked through it, then stood—captive to the familiar sea.

That little sailboat could still be pushed back down the sand, into the waves, and beyond the inlet, she dared to think, and quite easily with no one to question or scold her—no one to know she had a task unfulfilled. The measure of its peril and merits, compared to a trip beyond the market, was cut by a scratch of talons over roof tile. The red-tail hawk waited above the door.

"That's right," Araina exhaled to herself and then looked up to inform, "There'll be nothing today. Or after. You needn't come here anymore. I imagine the hunting must be better elsewhere."

The hawk blinked at her once and flew off.

After watching its ascent to the estuary trees, Araina's eyes fell to the small copper star dangling above the doorway. Kerikan insisted that it be placed there some years ago—to catch energy gone adrift, or so the old witch explained, "It must go somewhere. It's first to touch you and last to leave you. And when it goes adrift, something must catch it. Why not us?"

Araina reached up and removed the little star. She cleared old spider silk from the black ribbon and tied it around her neck—more to remind her the door could only be so far away for so long. She fiddled with it a moment and trekked on with the tide at her back.

Chapter Two

Odd Sorts

Beyond the estuary and a thick of woods, spots of rooftops finally shown between the trees. An amalgam of voices and faint music told of the market's proximity. Araina fast found herself in the mix of it—the awning-topped shops, stands, and parked carts, traveling merchants, soldiers, resident townsfolk, and the many creatures they raised, sold, and kept. The witch was at once overwhelmed and enticed by the crowded sounds and smells. They roused sense memories of the few times she accompanied Kerikan there. During every visit, she felt and kept separate. As she was informed then, Drudgenwood was friendly to, though not a place for, Crestfolk. Araina saw no reason to defy that, particularly as she was there alone and only to pass through—and free of delay. On surveying the sunlight reflected in high windows, it occurred to the witch that the latter could be a problem; it was much later than she anticipated.

Three racing children muddled her pace on the road. A fourth and the smallest trailed the others before stumbling to a halt. She stared up and squeaked, "A witch!" Araina looked at the girl in her little yellow shift and pinafore—a long stain of pink trickled down its center. Her voice sparkled with her gaze. "Do you do magic?"

With a tenuous smile, Araina responded, "…Not quite."

"Doba!" an older boy called back. "Don't stand in the middle of the road, toad!"

"Don't call me toad!" She started after the boy. "Bye, witch!"

Araina's smile held as she turned, only to be struck, with the rest of her face, by a plank reaching from a passing cart. It knocked her to the dirt. On lifting her hand to her throbbing forehead, she was grasped and hoisted by her wrist, then pulled by it below the overhang of a shop.

"Are you alright, miss?" a uniformed man asked as he released her arm. Araina pushed the hair from her face—the ribbon holding it back had fallen away.

"I-I. Yes. Th-thank you, sir." She lifted her eyes to him, first seeing his red and black jacket, its brass buttons, and series of emblems. The brim of his cap shaded his face to a neatly trimmed mustache.

"Mustn't stand in the middle of the road like that, miss."

"I'm sorry. I see that now." Araina's cheeks flushed. She went on rubbing her forehead—more for the sake of hiding behind her arm.

"Is your home near?"

"No. I-I'm traveling through."

"Through? Through to where?"

"…East, well, northeast. Beyond the wooded border." Araina slowly lowered her hand and adjusted the strap of her bag.

"I'd advise against that, miss."

"Oh? Why is that?"

"Begging your pardons, but someone who can't keep on her feet in town doesn't belong anywhere east of its borders."

"I'm afraid I have little choice. It's a very important matter."

"Important or not, anything in that direction is, well… Seems that knock to your head has kept you from thinking clearly. There." He pointed down the road. "That's the inn. You'll have better hold of your senses after a rest. Come, I'll escort you to get a room before they fill—"

"Thank you, sir. Perhaps I'll do that, but I can manage without an escort. Thank you."

"Very well then, miss."

After a tip of his cap, he converged into the passing crowd. Araina again surveyed the suggested inn. Its wide roof reached above most others. She quickly inhaled and took a step, only to have her path interrupted again.

"Have the witches stepped forth from their strange hidden work? Have these wars of ours rapped at their doors? Has the blood and the bad measured up to their worth? Have they decided what they're hiding for?" A young man sang and strummed his trubizar, smiling as he circled her.

"For what reason they are hiding, or rather, why they are hiding," Araina corrected before amending, "Though neither would suit the rhyme, would they? Wait, what do you mean hiding?"

"Hiding and biding, time lost to idling. Busying with spells and charms. Stalling and spinning their strings and yarns. But war is not far, and despite history and lore, neither witch nor warlock can ignore it much more."

"Wars aren't any knowledge of mine."

"If not wars, what then? What of the time that you spend? Moving east and wielding no sword?"

"I don't suppose you would know anything about traveling that way?"

"'Fraid east is no more of my knowledge than war is yours," he explained and ceased his strumming.

"So you're not unlike the Crestfolk of which you sing."

The minstrel laughed lightly. "Here and there, in my own little way. So what is not war and yet lies to the east?"

"I expect the answer is met on arrival."

"Well, may it be a satisfying one to have you traveling against the advice of a Svet Hagen major."

"Is that what he was?"

"Indeed. And now that you know it, you should also know their officers are too chivalrous to be of any help to ladies, witches or otherwise. But witch or lady, I'd not discard his advice. Spend the night off the road. Odd sorts are about."

"Odd sorts?"

"Oh, they're not hard to spot. All the easier to stay out of their way. And all the more reason to ease into traveling despite the guidance of the world-worn. Best to be well-rested if proving them wrong." He resumed his strumming with his loose rhyme.

"I suppose there's little sense in moving through the dark."

"A wise thing to suppose, lady-witch. Luck in your travels, north, east, or otherwise."

He tilted his trubizar, prompting Araina to notice a small tin cup suspended from its neck. She reached into her sling bag, freed two slates from the purse within, and dropped them into the cup.

"Generous *and* lovely," he declared. "You'll do just fine in this world."

Araina blushed and turned away, following the sinking sun to the inn.

The windows of its lowest level were made of amber glass set in latticed iron. Before its wide doors, plank walk, and stable posts, a gently swinging sign read: *Monworth's Spirits & Inn.* Araina stepped up and over to the entrance, and just as she reached for one of the handles, it turned and out stepped a large, bearded man.

"Ah, you the new one? Bit early, isn't it, girl?" he blustered.

"Beg your pardon, sir?"

"I haven't hired you?"

"I don't believe so…"

"Then you'll be needing work?"

"Not currently, but I was told that rooms are available here. Would you happen to—"

"And fine rooms they are. Look 'bove your head there." He gestured at the sign. "That's me. Monworth." He looked at Araina suspiciously. "You alone, girl?"

She checked over her shoulder before answering, "...I am."

"Why would you be traveling alone during days as these?"

"I—"

"Thought so when I saw ya. Not hard to see now. A witch, ay? Reckon you come from the old midwife's."

"I have, sir."

"Can ya tell me something then, girl? Have your folk gone and used up all the plants? Do you know why the damn things're half-dead? Can't afford to hold my stock. Stillers charge a fortune cause the rye ain't what or as much as it should be. Not a bit of juniper suited for beggar's gin. Wines'er better for polishing goblets than filling 'em."

"I wish I knew," Araina answered through Monworth's continued probing. "Are there any rooms left for the night, sir?"

"Charge eight a bed. Bolts're down at midnight. Be in before then."

Araina counted slates from her bag and dropped them in his hand.

"Haven't got a key on me. One'a the girls'll have it when supper's up. 'Nother hour or so. Wouldn't be too late in the gettin' it. Not the most fitting place for a young lady with all the Hagens and other sorts about."

"I see. Thank you."

She watched him turn off into the alley and considered simply waiting upon the plank walk to get a key as quickly as possible and hide away until morning. Though with some light left and the streets quieting, an ideal time to explore Drudgenwood Market took shape.

The merchant stands and shop windows appeared better stocked at a distance and in her few memories. The fruits and vegetables on offer were small and sickly, especially for the season and prices. A loaf of bread was priced nearly as much as her accommodations for the night. She was hoping for more choices among portable comforts—seeded buns or honeyed almonds—but was only able to procure a few apples and a pouch of roasted pumpkin seeds. Her most enthused purchase was a jar of borage-butter—less a provision than souvenir—which the merchant boasted would clean and smooth all curls, even those so thick and free as found upon the head of a witch. Araina, eager to put the pleasant-smelling salve to the test on her return to the cottage, could not resist.

With the road's torches aflame and most shops shuttered, she walked back to the inn. The glowing amber windows suited the layered voices reaching from their panes. A few horses were bound to the posts—their red saddle blankets bore Svet Hagen insignia. Beyond them, a passenger pigeon of great girth was perched and snoring on the rail above the water trough. Araina had never seen one so large. His peculiarity was furthered by the tiny pack strapped over his rotund body. Perhaps a carrier dove, she wondered before stepping up to the doorway.

The witch entered the light of chain-hung lanterns, iron sconces, and a deep stone fireplace. Several cauldrons simmered and steamed on its hearth. A massive hunk of meat sputtered from a hanging spit. It was quickly coated with brine by a young blonde woman, who gave it a hard twirl with the ladle's handle. She then spun, gathered scattered tankards at the nearest table, and traversed a maze of patrons to return to the bar, where she smoothly refilled a row of more tankards. They were set before laughing soldiers, grousing old men, and one pale ogre with a wide clearance around him. He hunched silently over his ale, which sat in his grip like a pounce pot.

A dwovish woman carried a tray scattered with empty bowls, carved spoons, and coins. Her limited stature provided unique advantage for navigating the clustered crowd but not for lifting the tray up to the bar. After steadying it, she gestured to a table in the center of the room. An acute dread tightened her tired face. The blond barmaid commiserated with half a glance and loaded the tray with three overflowing tankards.

She smoothly collected the coins and passed them back to the dwovish woman. "Steady on, Alice. Purse strings get looser with everything else."

Alice sucked in a breath and carried the tray to two more pale ogres. Their forearms nearly covered the table and also obscured an elf. The trio and their game of cards amounted to quite a sight for Araina. As with the ogres, she had never encountered but only heard of elves—that they no longer lived this far west and seldom had business with anything exceeding their size. This elf, however, looked more than at home behind his smirk, ardently worn as if he was twice the size of his brutish opponents. It seemed an eccentric confidence, for he only just surpassed the height of the playing cards themselves.

Araina broke her stare and looked for Monworth. Clusters of Svet Hagen soldiers in their red and black made it difficult to distinguish one body from another, especially as caps were hooked on sconces, rested on chair backs, and amidst messes of bowls and yet more tankards, rather than atop heads. The witch, barely clear of the inn's threshold, wanted to be away from all of it. Her appetite had disappeared and nothing seemed more desirable than a room key and the door it would lock. To her relief, Monworth finally appeared behind the bar. He began talking to the barmaid as she struggled to uncork a bottle of wine. Araina drew a bracing inhale of smoke, grease, and ale-misted air, then rushed over.

"Excuse me, sir? Sir?"

"You're very late for work, girl," he grumbled.

The barmaid beside him rolled her eyes and continued to battle the cork.

"Begging your pardon, sir. We spoke earlier. I paid you for a room," Araina stated.

"That so? How much I charge you?"

"Eight slates."

"Eight, eh? Must've been in a good mood. Margret, we got any other girls staying?"

The barmaid quickly scanned the room and answered, "Doubt for the whole night."

"Give the witch the top'a the hall. Take her up when you're done. Mind your distractions in the doing of it." Monworth hoisted an empty keg over his shoulder before exiting through a side door.

"Just be a few minutes, miss," Margret assured through her ongoing struggle to uncork.

"Been a few dozen!" one of the soldiers yelled with a grin.

"If only you kept as sharp a count of your tab," she retorted.

Araina extended her hand with a smile. The bottle was eagerly surrendered with the corkscrew still stiffly poking from the top. The witch gripped, finagled, and bested it with a glassy pop, earning a drunken cheer from some of the onlookers. She returned the corkscrew and bottle to the barmaid.

"Thanks for that! Nice technique you have."

"You're welcome. I'm just used to stubborn corks."

After filling and distributing a line of goblets, Margret looked at Araina. "We don't see many witches in town anymore. Just the old midwife now and again."

"My great-aunt."

"You're from the shore then. Why are you staying here?"

"My route was longer than I thought and I didn't want to travel in the dark."

"Can't blame you. It's gotten worse."

"Has it? Do you know if that's true going northeast?"

"I just know what I hear from my brother and the other soldiers, and whatever merchants still come through that way. Which, come to think of it, aren't many."

"…I see. When I mentioned it earlier, an officer strongly advised I avoid it."

"That's not surprising."

"Do you know anyone who might provide some guidance? And without too many warnings or questions to precede or follow?"

"What'd you say your name was?"

"I didn't. It's Araina."

"Oh, like the sand flower?"

The witch nodded.

"Well, Araina, if I had to send you to one of these cads…I think Thomas would be the one to ask. Dirt on his boots is still fresh enough to tell something of the wider world. Hey, Tom. Tom!"

A young man at a nearby table dropped his head over the back of his chair, wearing a mirthful, upside-down grin.

"You called, my golden-haired angel?"

"He shouldn't give you a hard time. Don't let him give you anything else. Oh, here's your key. Room's right at the top of the stairs." She produced a small key from an apron pocket and handed it to Araina. "I can still show you in if you wait for me to get a break between bellows and belches."

"Thank you, but that's quite alright. I think I can find my way up the stairs at least. Thank you again, Margret."

"And you, Araina."

The witch navigated to Thomas's table, where he and another soldier chortled over the rims of their tankards. Before she could make an introduction or inquiry, he asked, "So Margret thinks we'd make a match, huh?"

"I beg your pardon?"

"Oh, she loves a game. Always trying to throw me off." Thomas lifted his view to see Margret toiling away, searching for any trace of eye contact. "I'll not be bested so easily, my sun-crowned goddess!"

Margret briefly glowered back and flicked a rag off her shoulder, quite clearly in his direction.

"She said you'd have some advice as far as traveling east." Araina's statement reclaimed Thomas' attention and that of his comrade.

"You don't want to go that way."

"Why would you want to go that way?" the other soldier added.

"It's less that I want to and very much that I must. I'm looking for a tower beyond a wooded barrier, northeast, near ruins." She only broke eye contact to check her left palm, which, for half a moment, she swore was stinging again. "Is there a road I follow? Or maybe a trail that goes in that direction?"

"Would you call what's left of that march a trail, Hal?"

"Who knows what it looks like now. We were barely single file through those woods a month ago. Barrier's End. Might be easier as a lone trek, though I wouldn't want to be in that place alone. The shortest cutoff still takes three, maybe four days, and that's if you stay straight on as you can. Not easy to do anymore. Think you've got Crest grounds past that."

"That's it then. I can't thank you enough, gentlemen," she said.

Thomas laughed. "You shouldn't thank him at all for an answer like that."

"It's just helpful to know more of what to expeeccc—" Araina gasped as liquid ran down her back.

"Nice one, Earl! Now I gotta order another drink!"

The witch turned to see the source of the spill. The elf, standing at an overturned tankard, chuckled heartily. His ogre companions joined in boisterously. Thomas and Hal brusquely left their chairs.

"Apologize to the lady, elf," Thomas demanded.

"Mind your business, human. Ain't like I stained your dress." The elf and his company resumed their laughter.

Thomas unsheathed his sword and Hal followed. Both ogres dropped their cards and stood, leaving Araina precious few seconds to drop to the floor as their fists flew and knocked the soldiers off their feet. Everyone else in the tavern jumped to theirs.

Araina unfroze long enough to crawl past the tables before they slid and flipped with the force of brawling bodies. She almost managed to stand until a bottle flew and crashed above her head, sending her to her knees again. All sense of where the staircase could be was utterly lost. Her next best escape, the entrance, was a short though treacherous crawl past stomping boots and below a rain of glass and wood shards. Still not on her feet, she parted, then fell through the doors.

Claiming great gulps of night air, she frantically rose and stumbled across the plank walk. Her fingers rushed across the sling bag to feel for the corners of both spell books and the rosewood box before they shook bits of broken glass and splinters from her hair. The fray past the windows only seemed to grow. After looking up and then down the dark road, it appeared Araina would simply have to wait for it to subside.

She sat on the planks and felt the damp fabric against her back. The ale-scented bother was punctuated by a sudden crash through the window—made by the elf, who tumbled out into the road. He gave his head a shake and brushed amber shards from his tunic and trousers. After a quick check of the little purse and dagger sheathed on his belt, he caught sight of the witch.

"Nice night, eh, sweets?"

Araina finally noticed his voice, touched with a northern accent and surprisingly burly—not squeaky or thin as she would have expected of an elf. His lack of headwear also defied their depictions in tales and illustrations. He instead bared a round head of close-cropped, bark-brown hair and pointed ears. Stubble crossed his wide chin and jaw, thick neck, and that unwavering smirk.

"Ain't gotta be shy, sweets. Ain't gotta stare neither. Never see my sort before? Seen my share'a witches."

"I…"

"Witches, warlocks, folk comin' and goin' to that tower some ways from here."

"You know about that place?"

"Ain't been inside but know how to get there."

"Is that so?"

"Wouldn't call it the easiest stroll. Ain't bad as they say though, provided ya know where you're goin'."

"I would imagine."

"Couldn't help but hear ya might be headin' that way. Lucky you, runnin' into me. You're gonna need a good guide. Not to brag, sweets, but ya found the best. Ready to go when you are. Once we work out'a price, 'course." His offer was flourished with a wink.

Araina only turned an ear toward the inn. The clamor was starting to fade.

"So whatcha say?" he prompted.

"I'll manage, thank you."

"You ain't sound too sure 'bout that. Look at ya. Ain't even wearin' shoes."

"Never been much of a problem. My feet are quite tough."

"Heh, if ya say so, sweets. Should ya change your mind, it's handy to know who to ask for." The elf presented a tiny square of paper.

Araina took it and squinted to read: *Den Handkey - Freelance: Anything.*

She raised an eyebrow. "…Thank you."

"Well, got'a feelin' they're done pourin' for the night. Nice talkin', sweets. For your sake, hope ya ain't wrong 'bout your feet."

He winked once more and pulled a kerchief from his belt purse. With it knotted over his hair and the points of his ears, he hopped to the plank walk and climbed to the rail where the passenger pigeon went on snoring.

"Hey Pidgie, c'mon! Snap to!"

With the elf's demand and settling onto the bird's back, Pidgie awoke and blinked his little orange-ringed eyes.

"Onward!" A jab of Den's knee followed the command and pushed the pigeon to flap and force his heavy body to the end of the rail. Araina stood as they plummeted, expecting to hear a telltale thud, but the two took off into the night sky and were fast out of sight.

Her attention quickly fell to the approach of soldiers. Araina slipped away toward the alley and watched as they entered the inn and returned carrying unconscious or injured dwoves and humans. Ten of them grunted through their dragging of a limp ogre, who was rolled down the plank walk and into the road. Still more men exited, some limping, others rubbing their arms and necks. The procession only ended when a booming voice confirmed, "That's the lot of them."

Monworth dusted off his hands and returned inside. Araina quickly followed after to see the shambled state of the inn. Margret swept broken glass while the other barmaids cleared scattered tankards and wiped splatters of ale and stew from the walls. Araina, cautious of her bare feet on the littered floor, knelt down to gather some of the larger pieces of a broken bottle.

"You don't need to do that. We get it cleared faster than you'd think," Margret assured.

"Does this happen often?"

"Depends who's in town. Gets bad when squads move through. They destroy it now and then, but that's why they pay first. 'Course it helps that the town's best craftsmen are also the biggest drinkers. They rebuild whatever we ask for a free pour on the regular. That window might be a problem though." Margret sighed and looked at the hole created by the elf. "I think the glazier left a few weeks ago."

"I noticed a lot of dark shops," Araina stated.

"They go south as food prices go up. It's hard to trade for anything when the crops are so bad. You haven't been here in a while, have you?"

"Not for years."

"Why not?"

"Aunt Kerikan never saw much reason for me to come into town. Not when there was so much to be done. She did the shopping. Though I expect it was mostly just to drop in on old friends."

"Kerikan... That's right," Margret said brightly and began righting chairs. "She was my grandmother's midwife, for my mother and all my aunts. She helped deliver babies all through town, even at the palace."

Araina nodded slowly. "That was her."

"*Was* her?"

"She passed very recently. That's the reason I'm here. I'm taking care of one last thing she wanted me to do. Requires a bit of travel."

"I'm awfully sorry to hear that. I thought witches lived almost forever. She wasn't that old, was she?"

"No. Not for a witch. It was strange." Araina added a broken chair leg to a growing pile.

"Well, you're very brave to've come this way on your own with things as they are."

"I wouldn't say that. I'm honestly beyond ready to turn around."

"Well, hopefully tonight'll be the most lively part of your travel."

"I hope you're right. Speaking of that, I should probably get some sleep for an early start."

Margret nodded. "Left plenty of water for the basin if you want to wash up."

"Thank you." Araina turned in an attempt to see the stain down her back. "By the way, are elves and ogres regular visitors here?"

"Seen lots of strangers this summer. It's like the sellers gone south. The worse the crops and wars get, the stranger the folk that pass through. 'Course, they always stop for a drink. But don't let that worry you. We're locked up for the night and the room's all yours."

"Thank you, Margret. Goodnight."

"G'night, Araina."

The witch climbed the stairs, felt for the key out of the sling bag, and unlocked the first door. Its edge crashed into the footboard of one of the four beds, paired on perpendicular walls of the tiny room. A small table with a basin and pitcher waited below the single window. Araina placed her bag down and locked the door behind her.

After filling the basin and washing her face, she thought to try some of the borage-butter—if only to be sure all the glass was cleared from her hair. She smoothed it through, enjoyed the light scent, then rinsed it as the merchant instructed. Following a wring of her dripping twists, she removed her dress and soaked the stained portion in the basin.

As she fast discovered, every one of the beds offered the same lumpy, sack mattress. The unyielding, coarse choice upon which she finally settled still could not repel the drag of the day. Before it fully claimed her, the warnings she received rang through her brain. Over the layers of her recollection, a preternatural voice growled, "Path gone."

Araina opened her eyes with a start but found no earthly source. She quickly fell into a weighty, dreamless slumber.

Chapter Three

Diversions

A sharp, dusty stream of sunlight ignited the russet and maple of Araina's irises. She exhaled the musty staleness in her throat and dragged back her tresses to better receive a swell of hastened sounds—raised and urgent voices over footfalls, hoofbeats, and straining wheels. She rose from the bed, crossed to the window, and widened the partially opened shutters.

A shuffling, shouting mass of people led, loaded, and trailed carts. Their animals followed, as did children too grown to be hoisted on shoulders or sat among possessions in rolling wagons. In observing it all, Araina caught the eye of the previously encountered minstrel where he stood at the roadside. With a rich smile, he nodded up to her, as if offering some sort of approval. Araina then realized she was standing before the window in only her tulitiere and knee-knickers.

She ducked below the sill, grabbed the sling bag, and threw her spare dress over her blushing head. After lacing its bodice, she lifted the lousewort one from the basin and wrung it out—briefly breaking the room's stagnation with the cool scent of the borage-butter. As she shook, then folded the dress back into the bag, a hurried knock and voice called, "Araina? Are you awake?"

"Margret?" Araina unlocked and opened the door to see the barmaid. Her shoulders and eyes held a distraught tension. In her shaking hands she offered a small, cloth-wrapped bundle.

"Bread and cheese. Don't let Monworth know I gave it to you. I've come for your key."

"You're too kind. You didn't need to— W-what's going on?" Araina exchanged the key for the bundle, trying to keep pace with Margret's rushed movements.

"Vexhi broke the western line. Couldn't hold them back...at Shoda." Her voice broke and her eyes began to well.

"What do you mean? I don't understand."

19

"They're on the march this way. My brother was fighting there. I don't know if he... I don't know how he'll be able to..."

"I-I'm so sorry. I—"

"You're a witch!" Margret abruptly recalled.

"I—"

"That means you could use cards, or stones, or tea...or something. You can see if he's still alive, right? I-I have some tea I've been saving... I could get it right now. Does it need to be special witches' tea?"

"Oh, Margret. I'm afraid it doesn't work that way. The people you see offering such things, they aren't really Crestfolk. That is, they're not... They aren't actually witches. And those things aren't witchery."

"...You mean they can't tell—"

"No. No one can. I'm sorry."

"I don't know what to do. Maybe I should stay behind and..."

Araina sighed. "Margret, I can't tell you what happened or what will. But if there's one thing I can say, as far as being a Crest witch, it's that you don't stop when you have a direction or purpose. No matter the plan, the path guides the end." She swallowed hard and fiddled with the star at her throat. "At least that's what a lot of older Crestfolk would say. It's all I've to rely on myself. But you should go where you'll be safe and not alone."

"You could come south with us. Or back to the shore?"

"I'm afraid that's not... I can't. Not yet. Thank you very much for the bread and cheese, and everything else."

"Just take care of yourself out there. Will you come visit when this is all over?"

"I will. I'd like to meet your brother. Maybe I'll see him on my way."

"You'll tell him I went south?" Margret pleaded, seeming to take Araina's dark joke as a type of assurance.

"Of course." The witch smiled.

After a quick farewell, Araina was left to gather the last of her things and descend into the dark tavern. The silence was only broken by the patter of her bare soles across the floor and the noises beyond the walls. She let herself out to confront them.

Keeping clear of the push and steady in the opposite direction, Araina only stopped to fill her canteen at the town's fountain. Through a slow drink, she watched a man remove the cloth awning from his shop and then fold it away. She continued beyond emptied stands and was greeted by windows shuttering, locks clicking, and soon nothing but a slow wind made audible by the eerie calm.

She came to the outer grounds of Drudgenwood Palace, recognizing it from two or three visits well-over a dozen years ago—when she was presented to old women in shining silk dresses and lace shawls with facetted beads. They would catch sunlight when the women plucked climbing flowers from the walls and placed them in Araina's curls. There were sighs, murmurs, and hums full of concerned softness that deepened faraway looks from Kerikan. The faint recollection of their sentiments was no better decipherable to a grown Araina as she looked through the crumbled border and spied bare shrubs and fountains empty but for curled leaves. She turned away and proceeded along the dirt.

The climb of the morning sun fed an invigorating, then aggressive heat. It rode Araina's shoulders while the road below her feet narrowed into a path. It soon trickled into a faint trail, closed in by coarse yellow grass, which was lost at the rise of another hill. Thick woods lined the horizon just beyond. At the sight of it, Araina recalled her console of Margret and words regarding plans, paths, and ends, which prompted her to curse her own attempt at comfort. She adjusted the denting strap of the sling bag and descended the slope into the dark trees.

It swept over her all at once, the misty light cutting through the twisted and bare boughs, the dense sugary smell of fungus and rot, the snap of branches in the distance, and strange clicks she could not trace to any insect she knew. From the view on the hill, she thought this dense wooded mass, dreadful as it appeared, would have meant cooler air, but Barrier's End was hot and stagnant—and yet creeping, almost oozing. Not a few steps in and it surrounded her with altered, starved, and lurking things. She found herself somewhere in the middle of a grasping dance between predator and prey—and expected a fight to maintain her separation.

"If going through is all that matters, simply go fast," she uttered to herself and hastened her steps—which soon slowed to traverse a fallen tree, a sudden drop in the land, and tangle of roots claiming what she hoped was a path. "Alright then," she panted, freeing her ankle from a coil of dead vines. "Perhaps pace is less important than perseverance."

* * *

Barrier's End made it easy to lose the day. The sharp cuts of sunlight at its perimeter merged into a strange gleam, like light shown through pine resin. Araina developed a hatred for it, not only for the way it enhanced every ominous crevice and twisted shadow, but for how it robbed her of all sense of time. It could have been noon, dusk, or any hour in between. Her appetite was no better indicator—the wood's sour smell tainted the very thought of food. She wondered if there was any hope for acclimating to it as she stopped to drink from her canteen. Beyond her swallow and the sodden seal of the cork, a faint rhythm became audible.

Araina tucked her hair behind her right ear and then her left, straining to determine the sound's source. It grew closer—a bird's wings, flapping dense and fast through the trees at her left. Though too cloaked in haze to identify, it was clearly due her direction. Finally, it came into view. It was a passenger pigeon— the passenger pigeon with the elf gripping the straps of his pack. They nearly collided with the witch, missing her head by an inch before disappearing into the low boughs. A thin branch knocked the elf back. He bounced once before rolling onto his stomach and before Araina's feet.

He lifted his face from the dirt and righted himself with a jump. Araina parted her lips to react, but in an instant, he bolted to her ankle and climbed up to her knee. She gasped and grabbed for him as he crept around to her calf and clung. He only just escaped her frantic fingers as a new commotion neared. In an instant, Araina was encircled.

A large company of gnomes, dwarves, and woodland trolls tromped through the brush on hogs, raccoons, and weasels. The riders boasted makeshift blades, clubs, and the odd farming tool. A dwarf on a small boar drove his way forward and halted to inquire, "Seen an elf?"

Araina felt Den's body cling and tremble behind her knee.

"An elf, you say?" she asked.

"Ah hah. Must've passed."

The sense of perspiration not her own and her recollection of the previous evening, made her want to unpeel the elf from her leg and drop him to the dirt. And yet, the confrontation urged caution in doing anything for or against anyone's favor. The most preferable outcome, she concluded, was to be rid of them all—whether they be brandishing weapons or clinging to the hem of her knee-knickers. The easiest route to that, however, was less apparent. She had already played dumb and anything but maintaining that denial could lead to further questions and delays—perhaps even assumptions of alliances.

"All I've seen pass was a mourning dove. And I only noticed it since these woods are so dreadfully barren. I'm sure if an elf passed, I would have remembered. But, no. I've encountered nothing of that nature."

"A dove?"

"Or perhaps it was a passenger pigeon…"

"Ah hah. Which way?"

Araina limply pointed to a parting in the trees, opposite the direction Pidgie had flown.

"Sure about that, witch?"

"Quite. Again, it was the first living thing I've seen in this awful wood all day. All the more reason I'd like to be on my way out of it. If you don't mind, gentlemen, I'll say good afternoon and fruitful hunting." With her lie, a clammy breath of relief rippled across her skin. It made her grit her teeth, which she relaxed to ask, "Oh, should I happen to come across an elf, would you tell me why finding this one is so important?"

"Gaming debts," the dwarf answered.

He and his cohorts left her path and pressed down a slope between the trees. After they cleared from sight and earshot, Araina hobbled behind a tree, pulled the elf off her leg, and all but dropped him to the ground.

He immediately declared, "Bunch'a leach-saddles don't know what they're talkin' 'bout or who they're messin' with! They're lucky ya held me back, sweets—hey, wait up! What's the rush?" On his tiny legs, the elf somehow managed to keep up with Araina's hastened steps. "Ah, that's right. Headin' to that witches' place. Nice time and spot to run into me again. Woods get much tougher just'a few miles on, but then, you're on'a lousy path anyhow."

Araina slowed as she bypassed a series of large rocks and dodged a low hanging branch. "What's wrong with this path?"

"Nothin' if ya like spendin' a week here. But, if ya ain't got that kinda time, which from the looks of it, ya ain't, you're gonna wanna turn off this way. Cutoff up ahead. Good one too. Two days, free and clear."

"Cutoff?"

"Already told ya. Gone through here before. Even if I hadn't, I can get a nice high view. Speakin' a' that. Hey, Pidgie!"

The elf whistled overhead. The passenger pigeon flapped from the stripped canopy and landed upon the ground. Araina creased her brow at the both of them.

"Gonna be honest with ya, sweets, looks like this place ain't treatin' ya too nice. Ya look lonely…and sweaty. So, tell ya what. For that bit ya did me back

23

there, lemme help ya make up the time I cost ya. An' then some. I'll show ya the best shortcut you're gonna get here. Won't charge ya nothin' neither. Maybe ya share'a couple crumbs with us. For that, I get ya outta here safe, sound, and quicker than any empty-skulled, swill-suckin' soldier says it takes. Two days. Sound good?"

The crease in Araina's brow sharpened, then was sighed smooth as she turned to the thickening shadows and shifting light—gone from a sickly, resin-filtered haze to a waxy grey. The decline of a second, or perhaps third, set of eyes on a much shorter trail lost its articulation.

"You can honestly get me to Crest borders in two days?"

"Get ya there for breakfast, day-after-tomorrow."

"What about your pursuers?"

"Ain't no nobody pursuin' me now, thanks to your sneaky witchy thinkin'. But hey, if they catch up, got me a nice hidin' spot." He winked.

"If they catch up, I've suddenly found you and was in the process of turning you over. Understood?"

"Alright, ease off, sweets. Not somethin' we even gotta worry 'bout."

"One more thing."

"Thought ya were in'a hurry."

"No more sweets."

"Huh?"

"My name is Araina."

"Ya mean Ariana?"

"No, not Ariana. Ah-rain-aah. It's Araina."

"Ain't that a flower or somethin'? Thorny one, right?"

"Yes. This way, was it?" She nodded to the narrow path he suggested.

"That's it. So how'd ya get stuck with a plant's name?"

Araina walked on without an answer and with the close tow of her new company.

Chapter Four

Company

D en's prattle spurred Araina to wonder if the assurance of a shorter journey was worth the companionship. She could find no complaint about Pidgie, but the elf carried on regardless of her responses or lack thereof. He came to the topic of gnomes—and his very specific grievances with them, as well as the people who confused them for elves.

"Even when those idiots ain't got those stupid hats on, they still got those mangy beards. And let's say ya come across a gnome that's shaved the thing off, 'cause it's fulla lice or gnome-fleas, they still ain't even close to an elf. Fatter, stupider, and if ya ask me, uglier. Ears curved like turds. No offense."

Araina huffed a bristled sigh. "I just thought gnomes were taller."

"Feh, by a hair, maybe. Hey, what ya stoppin' for, sweets?"

"It's Araina. I'm stopping to make camp. This is a half-decent place for a fire and I need to gather kindling while I can still see."

"If you're scared'a the dark, just say so."

"I'm not. But without a lantern, I don't see navigating this place by night."

"If ya say so. Me and Pidgie could do with supper anyway."

Den looked at Araina expectantly, trying to catch her eye as she gathered broken branches and curled leaves. She dragged a small fallen bough into the center of their tiny clearing and cracked it in two below her foot. The halves were then crossed and surrounded with kindling. A few quick strikes of the flint and fire steel sent sparks into the pile. Araina held her hands before them and, through a smooth motion and thick exhale, drew up flames. Den's astonishment rose with the blaze. Its glow revealed his tiny impressed grin.

"Heh, almost forgot 'bout that."

"Forgot about what?"

"The whole witch thing. What else can ya do?"

"I…"

"Can ya put fire out the same way?"

"I can push it and part it." She lowered a hand into the fire and spread her fingers, repelling the flames on each side. "Depending on the amount of it, that may be enough to snuff it, but I can only send it in another direction." She withdrew her hand, the flames peaked after. "I can't simply make it disappear."

"Can ya teach me that, sweets?"

"It's Araina and probably not. Fire-raising is very elemental witchery, but you need to learn the essences and laws of fire, and then…how can I explain it? How to influence it. It's basic but it's not quick. And, if an elf were to attempt it…well…"

"Well what?"

"Well, the trial and error portion of it might be a bit severe for someone of your…stature."

"Feh! Lemme tell ya, my stature comes in handy for more than ya think! Look at you, clunkin' your big head 'round low trees while your legs're still too short to keep much'a stride."

"And yet the back of one makes a suitable hiding place, does it not?" Araina rejoined. "Do you suppose that search party's gone far? I wonder how well a shout would carry through these bare trees."

"Heh, point made. Doubt it'd reach 'em though. By now, they're stuck in the worst'a this mess and won't be clear'a it for days. And I'm just havin' a bit'a fun, swee—erraina. So now that we got'a fire, what ya got to cook over it? Was part of our deal, 'member?"

"It was, wasn't it? Though you did say crumbs, not a hot supper. I've some bread and cheese, though nothing to cook it on or in, unless you want to hunt for a rock to do as a hearth or a stick to do as a spit."

"Too much hassle. Cold'll do Pidgie and me just fine. Pass it here, swee—."

"I told you—"

"Alright, alright. I ain't gonna be callin' ya Araina all the time. Stuffy name. Thorny plant. A-rain-ee-aahh. A rainee-ahhh ha! That's it! Rainy!"

"Rainy?"

"It works. Kinda moody."

"Moody?" The witch sighed. "It's better than sweets I suppose."

"Now, how 'bout that bread and cheese, Rainy?"

Araina unwrapped the bundle gifted by Margret and handed a torn bit of bread and crumble of cheese to Den. She ripped another corner of the crust and placed it before Pidgie, who happily proceeded to dent it with his dark beak. Though the portions given to Den were nearly half the elf's size, he finished both without pause. Araina tore off her own share and chewed it slowly, watching the fire.

"Nothin' better for a good night'a sleep than cheese," Den declared on the tail end of a belch. He settled back against Pidgie's girth. "Night-night, Rainy. Give'a yell if somethin' tries to eat ya, rob ya, or whatever else has ya so scared'a the dark."

Araina sighed her exasperation across the spout of her canteen and tonelessly bade, "Goodnight."

She pulled the sling bag close and rested her head upon the folded dress and underclothes within. Her focus fell beyond the meager circle of firelight until her eyes refused to stay open.

In one movement, Araina threw herself upright and sat wide-eyed, unsure of what dream could have woken her so fiercely and yet been so easily forgotten—and whether her sleep had lasted hours or minutes. She swallowed past a hot crowding in her throat. The shallow wound across her palm began to throb. As she squinted at it, she heard something rush through the leaves and darkness behind her. With a strained twist, she found nothing.

On her knees, she inched over to the fire and dragged it up, sending the light beyond the small clearing. It caught a pair of eyes in the distance. With their stare, it became clear they were not simply reflecting the fire, but blazing with a light of their own. They kept Araina frozen and half-wondering why neither Pidgie nor Den had reacted to the far-reaching flames—and if they remained at her opposite. She had no opportunity to check or call for them as the eyes and their owner charged forth.

In an instant, the massive creature leapt and pinned the witch to the ground. Its claws began to draw blood from her shoulders. She could still scarcely perceive its visage beyond its muzzle—a wolf, or some otherworldly version of one. Its lush fur was red and its body hulking. Though the fire burned but a reach away, breath steamed hot from its snarling mouth. Too late Araina remembered the dagger in her bag. Regardless of its reach, the unrelenting claws suppressed any action, near or remote. She strained to kick or wriggle free but her body would not obey her fear or fury.

All forces within her silenced when the wolf asked, "Is it yours to claim?"

Araina's initial shock was lost to further incredulity as the deep growl was recognizable.

"You'll not say?" it went on. "We could take the throat then. Soon, soon, soon." The wolf lowered its jaw below her shuddering chin. "There. Below and over. What will it sustain once spilled? We won't find out until you are righted, will we?"

The wolf retreated, freeing her to lift her shoulders from the ground and grip the wounds. "Obedience your compass, Moonserpent. If then, cease your spilling."

Araina discovered the flow of blood from her shoulders had stopped. Instead, the slash across her palm spilt red.

"That," it growled "Choice stolen. Love and sand."

The witch recovered a shriveled version of her voice. "What are…what…"

The wolf drew in again, close enough to tear out her throat, and expelled another steaming breath at her neck.

"Path gone. Press on." Through its snarled command, it snapped and dragged her down.

Araina cried out. When she felt only the rough impact of the forest floor, her eyes opened wide and found nothing—no wounds on her throat or shoulders, no flaring eyes in the shadows, or searing jaws at her neck. The fire was low, just strong enough to illuminate Den and Pidgie. Both remained undisturbed and deeply snoring. A scan of the trees only revealed a small change in light, telling that dawn would soon break. Araina curled into herself, shook, and whimpered, but could not bring up tears.

It's because I've not mourned. I'm going mad because the tears are stuck. I just have to get back and they'll come. I just have to do as she asked and then get back. I can sort it out there. It will make sense at home.

Her breathing slowed as such notions seemed safe to trust. She followed them to sleep.

Chapter Five

Tolls and Exchanges

Incited by a tug at one of her tresses, Araina woke with a start.

"C'mon, Rainy! We're losin' daylight." On observing the witch's sunken, darting eyes, the elf proceeded to ask, "Rough night? Looks like ya went back to town and had'a few drinks. Ya didn't think to invite me?"

The witch sat up, rubbed her face, and felt moisture over her left eye. On pulling her hand back, she found her palm was bleeding again.

"What happen? Cut yourself or somethin'?"

"A day or two ago. It's just healing on its own time…apparently."

She took the edge of her sleeve at her elbow, and without the aid of her reflection or any water taken from her canteen, wiped the blood from her face as best she could. She wobbled to her feet, shook out her hair, and brushed dirt and bits of leaves from her dress.

"This way?" She picked up her sling bag.

"What, no breakfast?"

"You said it yourself, we're losing daylight."

Den blinked back, dismayed.

She sighed, rummaged through her bag to retrieve the pouch of pumpkin seeds, and extended, "Alright, here."

"How'm I supposed to carry those? Bit'a an armful."

"You'd think for how little you can carry, a few seeds would be more than enough of a meal."

"Don't they teach humans 'bout anythin' 'sides humans? That ain't how elves' guts work. Notice how I been keepin' up with you? We move as fast as humans, we eat as much as humans. And carryin' ain't 'bout weight but shape."

Araina poured out a handful of seeds for herself and chewed through his explanation. As she returned the pouch to her bag, she tore off a large piece of bread, which she then halved and extended to Den and Pidgie. The elf accepted and ate it even faster than his supper.

"What about the cheese?" he prompted.

"It's for the next clearing. This way then?"

"Uh huh. Hope ya can keep your path if I die'a starvation 'fore lunch."

"I am going to take that risk," Araina decided and walked on.

With the day's heat, the gnats became ravenous, though they only seemed to have a taste for Araina's blood. Den and Pidgie traveled on unperturbed while she swatted and puffed them away. The land at her feet lowered, then loosened. Though there were fewer jutting rocks and fallen boughs to cumbersomely traverse, the path became mucky. Araina had to rely on low branches or split trunks to drag her ankles from sludgy pockets of earth. As with the insects, her companions remained untroubled, with Den on Pidgie's back and Pidgie able to progress in short flights and long hops through the tangle overhead.

"Tell me this is as worse as this gets," she pleaded.

"Oh yea, much better just ahead," Den replied with a smirk.

"It is?"

"No, we're headin' to the swamp. Gets worse the closer ya get. But if ya want the truth don't tell me what to tell ya."

"Fair enough," Araina acknowledged between labored breaths. "Why are we heading into a swamp?"

"Because you wanted fast and fast ain't easy 'round here."

"How much slower is easy?"

"Ain't no easy. Maybe *easier*. Ain't worth it though. 'Least double the time. Maybe triple. Eh, why even ask, Rainy? The path you're on's the path you're on. Gotta admit, you ain't doing too bad considerin' ya got no shoes. What's with witches and no shoes?"

"The less you wear them, the less you need them."

"So you go trompin' through the snow with nothin'?"

"No, I wear boots in colder seasons."

"Probably should've brought 'em with ya for this."

"I would've done a lot of things had I expected this. And I imagine this would be a slog in anything, especially if you're not riding on a bird's back," Araina's statement wobbled as her mud-slicked toes gripped for balance on a jutting root.

"Couldn't tell ya from up here. Ain't ya worried 'bout a jetsamadder takin' off your toe?"

"Not presently. When was the last time you've seen any snake, let alone a jetsamadder?"

"Ya don't see jetsamadder. Only feel 'em, as they're bitin' through your toe. And the less snakes I gotta deal with, the better. Good riddance."

"I miss seeing snakes. So this swamp up ahead, I'm guessing it and this…*path* leading to it, are why soldiers have to go around the long way?"

"Uh huh."

"Then how are we supposed to bypass it?'

"*We?*" Den looked over his shoulder and down at the witch as she pulled her foot free from a particularly stubborn siphon of earth.

"How am *I* supposed to bypass it?"

"Depends on how much solid ground's been swallowed up. Used to be a good leap would get'a human across. You're probably gonna need'a little help though."

"Help from whom? Or what?"

"We'll see what's on offer. Smell that? Means we're close."

"How could I not smell that? If it means we're nearly there, I suppose that makes it a little less terrible."

"Heh. You're funny, Rainy."

Rocks began to emerge from the mucky soil and serve as stepping stones. Twisted tree roots reached up, their beds of dirt seemingly suctioned or swept away. The litter of the forest floor that so hindered Araina's steps was somehow eroding and revealed better footing. Looking up from her cautious traversal, she saw where the black muck pooled and appeared to flow. The thickest of its miasma hit her soon after. She choked and nearly lost footing as her eyes began to sting and water.

"Den," she coughed.

"Huh?"

"How—" Araina choked again and pulled the end of her sleeve over her mouth. Though the fabric was generous, it kept her face fixed to her elbow. She dropped it and remembered the cloths wrapping the remaining bread and cheese from Margret, the dagger, and the last of the loaf from the cottage. She tore a bit from the dagger's bundle and held it over her nose and mouth. "How do I get past *that*?"

"Eh, humans are so sensitive in the worst ways. Ain't ya ever smell a forest eatin' itself? Give it a minute, you'll get used to it."

Through her squinting view, she continued to survey the rank river of sludge. The only interruptions in its filmy surface were jagged sticks and rotting sheets of bark. There were no means of support or connection to the opposite side. The impassable sight before her shot curses throughout her brain. Den caught her narrowed eyes beyond the cloth crumpled to her face.

"Whoa, what's that look for? Told ya fast wasn't gonna be easy."

"I wouldn't call this fast either." The edge of her tone was little dulled by the cloth. "You said you knew your way through. You said you'd guide me out of here. You know I can't fly! Go on then! How'm I to get past this? Freelance nonsense! I should've just—"

"Ease up, Rainy. I said ya'd need some help. Pretty sure I know where to find it."

Without another word, Den and Pidgie left their low branch and flew to the other side of the sludge. They turned off into the trees and out of sight, leaving Araina alone and fast wondered how long she would remain so.

She briefly considered the likelihood of abandonment. It weighted her stomach more than the stench. Crossing the swamp through her own designs and devices was daunting, but the thought of traveling backwards was even more dreadful. As she remembered where she slept and her encounter in the darkness, the witch was scarcely able to look over her shoulder. She instead looked around her feet and began to catalogue materials that might be useful for a raft. With another gauge of the wretched, dense flow, the notion of anything floating and faring on it for very long was quashed. Nothing took shape in its stead before the now-familiar flapping pulled her attention. Den and Pidgie landed on a root beside her.

"Ain't got anythin' to worry 'bout, Rainy."

"Is that so?"

"Took care'a your little problem." The elf confidently tipped his chin to the swamp. Araina saw nothing.

"Care to explain how?" she droned.

"Nah. You'll see in'a minute."

Den kept his little eyes forward while Araina's fell on him, their patience dwindling fast. After several long minutes, what appeared to be a floating log came into view. It was skippered by an odd creature who looked to be mostly long tangles of hair—parted only by a round nose, pair of thick hands gripping a paddle, and set of bulbous, hairy toes. He steered his crude canoe through the sludge, eventually wedging the vessel between two rocks near Araina, Den, and Pidgie.

"Cross?" the creature asked.

Araina could only assume the question was directed at her.

"Yes...please."

"Pay. Cross."

"Pay? Oh, of course. What's the price?" She reached in her bag to retrieve her slates.

"Hair," he answered.

"Hair?" She looked at the creature and then to Den.

"Wants some'a your hair," the elf clarified.

"Why?"

"What's it matter?"

Despite the elf's shrug and dismissal, Araina's wary stare held.

He sighed. "Dunno if ya noticed the lack'a shops, Rainy, but Lem here ain't got much use for money. He sees somethin' useful or just appealin', that'll do. Guess those tendrils on your head'er doin' the trick for 'em. Take it as a compliment."

"Couldn't I give you something else? Wouldn't you rather some food? I have some apples. Some cheese maybe?"

"Hey! Don't go givin' away the cheese!" Den interjected.

Lem shook his head, or at least appeared to from under his tangled mop. "Hair."

"What will you do with it? Use it for spells?"

Araina's interrogation sparked Den's laughter. "Lem look like some kinda warlock to you? Probably gonna use it to floss 'is teeth and toes or hide under his pillow and pet it 'til he falls asleep. C'mon, this is takin' too long...same as your hair."

Araina looked at the lengthening sunlight on the trees. From the back of her neck, she pulled a strained ringlet over her shoulder and pinched a few inches from the end. She crouched and presented it to Lem.

"Will this do?"

Lem disembarked and hobbled toward Araina. Though his own mop blocked all but his nose, mouth, and chin, he leaned in for a closer look and reached toward the offering. Araina withdrew slightly.

"More," he urged.

The witch reluctantly pinched higher. Lem nodded with a pleased grunt. His hand disappeared and reappeared holding rusty clippers.

"I'll take care of that part, thank you." She reached into her bag for the dagger. She grit her teeth and sawed through the lock with the old blade. It was then surrendered it to Lem, who confirmed his delight with another grunt. He tucked the twist away and returned to the canoe, leaving space for Araina to board.

The vessel wobbled as she cautiously knelt to its hull and gripped the sling bag. Lem pushed from the rocks with his wide hairy feet, then furthered the distance with the oar. Den and Pidgie passed overhead and perched at the opposite side. The voyage, though sluggish and somewhat serpentine, was thankfully short. Araina fought the impulse to leap ashore the moment the crude bow touched what could scantly be called solid ground. She instead reached for a length of tree root and pulled herself to the steep bank.

"Thank you very much, Lem." She attempted to smile through a drawn though gracious exhale, thinking that it might be advantageous to leave a favorable impression for the return journey. Lem showed little interest in such propriety and simply pushed away, steering the canoe downstream.

"Enjoy that hair," Den called as he and Pidgie swooped in. Araina glowered and stepped toward what seemed to be a small path through the trees.

"Through here?" she curtly asked.

"Uh huh, that way." Den chuckled. "C'mon, quit worryin'. Can't even tell whatcha cut. Shoulda gave 'em more, if ya ask me."

"I didn't." Araina quickly pressed forward, pushing branches out of her path. "How do you know what he will or won't do with my hair? And why didn't you mention that you knew someone who lives here?"

"I know sorts everywhere and anywhere." Den nudged Pidgie to follow the witch once again. Araina slowed her steps and looked at him pointedly. "Who are you?"

"Huh? Whatcha mean? Already gave ya my card."

"No. Just who are… What made you want to help me through here?"

"What'd ya hit your head or somethin'? I owe ya for savin' my skin yesterday."

"No, before that. Night before last. You offered to guide me through here even then. Do you just wait around, hoping to lead strangers through swamps after starting brawls in taverns?"

"Heh—hey! *You* were the one who started that business. Little witch making sloshed soldiers all uppity. Feh, soldiers. Shove 'em in a uniform, boss 'em around, and that makes 'em think they're in charge of anyone ain't dumb enough to do the same."

"Well, since you're clearly not that sort, what are—"

"Whatever I want. Depends how bored I am, if there's any money to be made, and if I'm in the mood for it. Easy to get it off humans, though they're pretty boring...'til ya find one that's outta place. That can get interestin'."

"Like me?"

"Uh huh, like you. Too bad you ain't as interestin' as ya look."

"I'm not sure I mind that."

"'Least that's one thing so far. Witches still ain't as boring as regular humans. What'd your folk call 'em? Landos?"

"Landers."

"That's it. But would it kill witch folk to not be so...stuffy?"

"What about elves?"

"What about 'em?"

"Are they more interesting than Landers and not so terribly serious as Crestfolk?"

"Eh. Ain't spend time with elves if I can avoid it, which ain't hard to do these days or in these parts."

"Why?"

"Why what?"

"Why do you want avoid elves?"

"I'd say that's the end'a question time," Den muttered.

"I don't think you get to end question time with a question. I think you have to end it with an answer."

"I don't gotta to do nothin'. How 'bout you quit askin' me this and that and just say *thank you Mr. Handkey for gettin' me 'cross that swamp* in that pretty little voice'a yours. Ya know, the one ya used when askin' for directions from brass-blinded, chipped-tooth, rot-breathed soldiers. After that, ya can hand me some cheese. Been waitin' for hours."

Araina stopped and looked at Den as he and Pidgie crossed over to the next branch.

"So you like talking, just not about yourself. Or rather, who you are." She reached in the sling bag and began to unwrap the cheese.

"Uh huh. Now, I'll take 'least half'a whatcha got there and Pidgie'll need more bread." The elf extended his hand.

Araina slowed her unwrapping. "You never spend time with other elves. There's no Mrs. Handkey?"

"Why? Ya proposin'? Ya ain't quite my type. And ain't ya kinda old to be unmarried yourself? Now, as ya were. Cheese, please."

His smirk descended to something guarded as it was irritated. Araina, deciding she would push it no further, was about to oblige his demand, but saw his hand was no longer flung forward to receive it. He instead looked at the back of Pidgie's head, lost behind his little eyes.

"I apologize," she stated. "Maybe your manners are starting to rub off on me. And you are right, I'm not terribly interesting. You, conversely, stir some curiosity. I've never met an elf. But I've also never known a life so…untethered. One that lets you do as you please and when."

"Don't sound like much fun. 'Specialty hearin'' it said in such'a posey-nosed way."

"Well, it affords few opportunities to be bored, at least." The witch shrugged.

"Only so ya don't go askin' me again, there *was* a Mrs. Handkey. An' some kids. Gone now. Ain't sure why ya care. But no, I ain't spend time 'round elves, seein' as there ain't any elves I wanna see."

"…I'm sorry."

"What for? 'Less you burnt down our forest. And if ya did, sorry ain't gonna cut it. Heh. You ain't no soldier though. If anythin', your little fire trick might'a come in handy." He took the chunk of cheese from her before reminding, "What 'bout Pidgie's bread?"

Araina silently fulfilled the request.

"So where's Mr. Witch?" Den asked through his chomping.

"There's no Mr. Witch, nor has there ever been. I'm not quite twenty, after all."

"So? Should've a couple brats by now."

"Not for my sort. That comes later, if at all."

"Whatcha mean?" With the belched question, Den and Pidgie had both finished their food and resumed their fluttering pace along Araina's trek.

"It's different with Crestfolk. We don't marry so early and we don't have as many children as Landers. There's a lot to teach and to learn. Families tend to stay small, especially in my Crest," she explained.

"What's with that? So you're *of* somethin', right?"

"Yes. My Crest is Moonserpent. So, Araina of the Moonserpents."

Den burst with laughter as he observed, "Is that ever a hoity-toity mouthful. Heard'a few of 'em but none like that."

The witch could do little to stifle her smile and blushing. "Well, be what it may, it's not surprising that you've not heard of it. It's an old Crest but a very small one now."

"Don't that just make you special."

"Not unless I live up to it." Her buoyed cheeks fell.

"Oh no? That fire thing ain't enough?"

"Far from it. But, apart from getting beyond these woods, I'm not sure how much any of that still matters."

"Must be a load off."

"One would think. How much longer now?"

"Early tomorrow, if ya plan on stoppin' for the night."

Araina looked at the haze, stretching pale over the trees, and submitted, "As much as I'd love to do otherwise, it looks as though that will be necessary."

"If you say so, Rainy o' the moon snakes."

"Before *that* name starts to stick, should I mention its origins are with sea serpents and not snakes?"

"Nah, ya shouldn't."

"Fair enough."

Before the sickly daylight faded into grey and then darkness, Araina collected firewood and kindling, and again drew flame from a spark—though Den was considerably less impressed as a repeat spectator. She cleared rocks and brush from the place where she would settle and offered slices of her apple to Den and Pidgie before biting into it.

"Whatcha got 'sides apples? Any more bread?"

With the elf's inquiry, Araina took note of the remains from Margret's bundle. She passed it to him.

"That it?" he asked after devouring it. Pidgie's gingery eyes seemed to be asking the very same.

"I have rosaberries and more pumpkin seeds. And a little more bread."

"More bread? Pass it over."

Araina's hand shook slightly as she unwrapped the loaf carried from the cottage. She tore it into three portions, surrendered two to Den, and held the last— weighing the thought of rewrapping and returning it to her bag.

"Where'd ya get this one?"

"From home. My great-aunt's recipe."

"Damn good. She's gotta make me s'more."

"She died very recently. I know how to make it though."

Araina looked into the fire. As her teeth sank into the crust, her senses left all else behind and attempted to create an impossibly perfect memory of aroma, taste, and texture. Then it was gone. Not long after, Den slipped into a steady snore, soon joined by Pidgie's. Araina strained to listen above the rhythm while she felt for movement in the darkness and dense air. Before yielding to her falling eyelids, she pulled the fire to see what could be caught beyond the labyrinth of trees. Nothing glowed or growled. It was enough to let her settle for sleep.

Chapter Six

A Task Fulfilled

Though she was anything but rested, Araina was quick to find her feet, shake off what dirt and dried muck she could, and be free from Barrier's End and ever again experiencing it for a first time. After complaining of a seed and berry breakfast, Den led them through the remaining miles, beyond the sour haze, and finally to a field of pale golden grass. Hard shapes of grey erupted from the ground, the largest of which was a great reaching tower.

"Didn't believe I'd get ya through, did ya?" the elf asked as they trekked through the blades.

"There's some distance between disbelief and doubt. Although, you did say you'd have me here for breakfast and it's well after lunch."

"Feh, suddenly you're good at keepin' track 'a meals."

"Regarding that, I suppose you'll be off to your next opportunity?"

"Uh huh. Just gotta wait for one to show up."

"Well, if you're going back toward town and you don't mind waiting a bit, I wouldn't say no to a shortcut in the opposite direction."

"How long ya gonna be?"

"I have to take care of something important but I don't see it taking too long. How about I do what I need to do, and if something better comes along before then, I'll find my way on my own? Otherwise, I can give you a few slates for the return trip."

Den tilted his head from one side to the other, as if rolling the options to-and-fro between his pointed ears.

"Gonna share whatever food they give ya?"

Araina acquiesced with a sleepy nod.

"Alright. If you're outta there 'fore I get bored, why not?"

* * *

The distant shapes defined into structures. Though mostly ruins of a once grand palace, odd barbicans, battlements, and smaller towers remained and served as anchorage for cleavers, five-leavers, and multiflora—somehow growing lush. Rising far above it all was the hexagonal keep that Araina spotted from the horizon. As she approached the gapped outer walls, she spied people moving about the former courtyard. Small groups were seated in the grass and on fragmented steps. Their jewel-tone frocks and tunics were like wildflowers poking through rocks. A few among them wore uniforms of black with a wide stripe of deep green fabric running the length of one sleeve.

Caught in her distant survey, Araina barely noticed Den and Pidgie soar past her head and land upon the remnants of an iron gate, well-within sight.

"No, Den, wait," she hissed and chased after.

"Feh! Soldiers here too. Can't get away from 'em."

"Keep your voice down. I—"

"What? Thought ya were supposed'a be here."

"I am. I think. But I'm not sure how—"

"Hello," a small voice greeted at her back. Araina turned and met with a dark-haired girl.

"Oh, hello."

"Welcome!"

"Thank you…"

"You are welcome. Are you a moon…a moon-something…"

"Moon snake?" Den chimed in to assist.

Araina's countenance momentarily sharpened at the elf before she smiled and sought to confirm, "Moonserpent?"

"That's it! Are you a Moonserpent?"

"I am."

"Grandpa saw you from upstairs. You're supposed to follow me." The girl's voice descended into a whisper as she added, "But I'm not supposed to let anyone else know."

Araina crouched down and met her hushed tone. "I see. To where shall I follow you?"

"Inside."

"Alright then. You lead the way."

"Hey, Rainy—" Den pushed to interject, hardly curbing his volume.

"I'll meet you here when I'm through."

"*If* I'm still here."

Araina responded with a halfhearted wave as she was led through the remnants of an archway and crossed into the boundaries of the ruins. Her newest guide took her toward the keep in silence. The sensation of stares from the distance spurred her to think of how dirty and worn she must have appeared, especially to people dressed so brightly and beautifully. The sight of their airy fabrics, blossom-dotted braids, and curious, clear-eyed glances made her thankful to be led swiftly out of view. On reaching a large, stained-glass paneled entrance, the girl veered off to a smaller door behind vine-crawled gates, through which they passed into the cool darkness of a stone stairwell.

Araina followed up flights and over landings, then through a long, sunlit passageway. Opposite the windows, intricate tapestries were hung between painted doors and spiraling, colored-glass sconces. Her steps slowed so she could observe the ornamentation and catch her breath after such an ascent. Dreadfully thirsty and tired, and now with her task at a foreseeable end, every moment and movement seemed weighted. Finally, they stopped before a pair of indigo doors.

The girl rapped upon one and called, "Grandpa? She's here. The Moonsna…" then looked to Araina for guidance once again.

Before she could provide it, a voice through the door answered, "Moonserpent. Please show her in."

"Grandpa's in there."

"Thank you." Araina smiled to her little guide, who fast departed—clearly happy to be done with her errand.

Left alone before the doors, a sudden trepidation pulled at the witch's stomach. It radiated to her hand at one of the ornately curled handles. She eased it forward and let herself into a huge study.

Multiple landings kept reaching bookcases, heavy desks, and tufted armchairs and chaises. There was scarcely a trace of wall not covered by rows upon rows of shelves filled with books, tools, contraptions, and artifacts. A wall of windows and several large paintings were the only vertical surfaces that remained unobscured. A sudden sting cut through the witch as she recognized one of the portraits.

A shining frame kept an image of Kerikan, a much younger version, dressed in a billowy layered gown. Her rich, still-cocoa-dark curls flowed below the weight of a twisting circlet. In one hand, the not-yet-old witch held a small bouquet of motherwort, yarrow, and fenugreek. The crook of her opposite arm cradled a thick book. Along its edge, a silver quill waited in the deft curve of her fingers. Her eyes carried a sagacious and serene countenance—one Araina had seen seamlessly transform into impenetrable sternness, perplexed exasperation, and pure disappointment. The portrayal so held Araina's senses that it almost made her forget how she came to view it, until she realized she was being watched from one of the landings.

"Oh, forgive me, I-I…"

"Take all the time you need with her," a slim young man offered with a smile. "She's why you're here, after all." He stepped down to Araina's level and added, "And please pardon me for sending my granddaughter to fetch you. I was eager to meet you the moment you arrived, but I saw fit to keep our meeting secret, or rather, private for now."

He sat in one of the four armchairs that circled a low table. Araina stood silently as one question tripped over another and then another.

"Ah, but it's been quite the journey for you, hasn't it?" He left his seat and walked to a cart with a green glass teapot. A matching cup was filled and placed on the low table. "This will do you quite a lot of good. This tea helps the lungs to fully fill. Which I find very useful for easing words that will not flow."

Araina cautiously approached and sat in the armchair before the cup.

"Thank you." She fought to drink as slowly and politely as possible, though her thirst allowed her little propriety. Her host was quick to fill the cup again.

"I understand your path has been less than friendly," he stated.

"Well, it—"

"And yet here you are. That's why I must insist you tell me whatever you need, whatever I might provide to ease you, and without any delay for etiquette, Araina."

"Thank you. You-you already know my name."

"Of course."

"Oh…I wasn't sure whether I'd be—"

"Well, I knew I'd be more likely to see you than Kerikan, considering her most recent letters. I couldn't be exactly sure when, naturally, but we've been keeping a lookout over the last few days. I have to say, when I woke this morning, I had a feeling about today. And here you are." He replenished Araina's tea yet again and smiled with an odd familiarity. "Please, as much as you'd like, my dear."

"Thank you." She strove to suppress the tension creasing her brow and the curiosity-driven route of her eyes over the young man's form and asked, "Aunt Kerikan sent you letters?"

"Indeed. It was, well, it's one thing to gather it and another to read. That is, when she told me what'd be coming. Sadly, it was not as much of a shock as it should have been. Not with all that's come to pass. But that's why you're here, isn't it? Oh, I am so delighted you're here. It's something to finally see you. And not just for what you carry, but after so much she's told over so many years. And to see you, hear your voice... It's beautiful. Simply beautiful."

"I-I... Th-thank you. I do beg your pardon, but, how did you come to correspond with her?"

"I can hardly remember a time when we hadn't. It feels as though it's been most of our lives."

He met the witch's perplexed expression. After a long moment, he dropped into the back of the chair, shaking his head with abashed laughter.

"Forgive me, Araina, forgive me. You would think, going through this day after day, I couldn't possibly forget. But it's the afternoons that lose me. They make it feel so natural. It's then that I am most free. And what you must think... When I said my granddaughter..." He continued to laugh heartily. "We've all grown too accustomed to it. Oh goodness, how can I explain?"

Araina's flummoxed face held no answers. The young man batted the tips of his long fingers together and looked at the teapot for a moment before turning back to her.

"Spats between warlocks can be ridiculous things. Utter foolishness. It's so easy to lose sight of where offense was given and taken. It fast becomes about pride. It's not any concern for you though, my dear, but it is an explanation for my appearance."

He briefly left his armchair and the resiliently confused witch to reach to a shelf. From its scattered collection of objects, he selected an hourglass, turned it over, and placed it on the table before Araina.

"We all age with sand, well, sand as a placeholder for time. It's a suitable placeholder in the way that a moment may be no more noticeable than a single grain among so many others. A spell could upset that. A spell could cause one to age, in appearance, far faster than a normal course. It's as if a much greater quantity of sand were to move in place of a few grains. A pinch, or a spoonful, possibly. In other words, a year in a minute, or a decade in an hour, or a lifetime in a day, but only in appearance. And perhaps, the most interesting factor of such a spell, would be the cyclical nature of it. To start and end each day as a lifetime, and to repeat it in as reliable a manner as this sand would again fall through an overturned glass. Could you imagine such a spell, Araina?"

"I suppose I could imagine it. Though I didn't know spells like that existed outside of theory. To affect another's physical form so drastically…"

"Sometimes it simply takes an adept rival to put a theory into practice. It's all in the convincing of the target. And of course, a bit of trickery to bend the natural workings of that target's body, which can be done through ingestion, inhalation, sound… But never mind the details, my dear. I'm simply trying to explain why someone appearing only years older than yourself would have a grandchild. I have many of them now. I don't know how much Kerikan has shared with you about her old friend Tanzan."

"Tanzan of Marido?"

"An absolute honor to finally meet you, my dear, or more fittingly, Araina of the Moonserpents."

Araina searched the young man's face and her mind for the details of the portrait hung in the cottage. She knew little about him beyond a mix of wryness and esteem kept by Kerikan. And though he was among many names suspended between myth and memory, before and during her great-aunt's midwifery, she knew they corresponded, but little else. As Araina worked to recall those uttered reflections when a message would arrive or leave on a bird's leg or breast, she could not deny those small essences that anchor a person and a life to a face— even as it takes on history and pain. Araina wondered how it would happen to her own face as she studied portraits of her mother, father, and grandparents, and then Kerikan's presence over her nineteen years. Now she tried her best to do it backwards and inquired, "What is the purpose of such a spell? That is to say, how does it benefit the warlock who cast it upon you?"

"Apart from it being terribly draining for me, it mostly speaks to his abilities. It's something I could correct and counter over a week or so, as he's challenging me to do, but I've been extremely distracted, Araina. I've been waiting for either another letter from your great-aunt or a delivery from her lovely grandniece. I take it that must be why your shoulder there looks quite strained by your carry. The weight of that spell book, certainly. And then there is the key."

"…Key?"

"Did she not mention the key?"

A dire concern surfaced with his question. Araina felt a flush of heat over her body as she fought to remember any instruction involving a key, and further, wondered why he had referred to only a single spell book.

"She didn't…"

Rather that meet with Araina's troubled expression, again, he laughed.

"Why does that not surprise me? You poor young woman, she told you to bring me two spell books, didn't she? I'd further guess that she forbade you from opening them and gave the sense that they are the most ruinous of secret things?"

"She did."

"And those locks didn't tempt you in the slightest? Not one for puzzles?"

"I rather enjoy puzzles, but—"

"But not to such a level that you would betray her wishes. Of course not. Now then, let's help you fulfill your task, Araina."

Tanzan extended his slender hand. Araina reached into the sling bag and handed him one spell book and then the other. He slid the hourglass away and placed the books side by side. Araina moved her teacup to provide ample clearance.

"There wouldn't have been all that much harm in you opening them, and I shall show you why."

Through a series of intricate movements, he shifted the overlapping components of the lock with his fingertips. The first spell book was unsealed with a tinny snap. He turned back the cover, picked up a portion of pages and let them fall away. They were blank.

"This book keeps a great many things, but they are well-hidden. And not by cypher or riddle, but by appearing to not even exist. For what is the best way to keep a secret? Give no indication there's a secret to be kept."

Araina leaned in and looked at the pages as Tanzan let them drop. They were thicker, rougher, and more primitive than any sort of paper she had seen before.

"You may touch them if you wish," the warlock offered.

She lowered her fingers to a page and turned it with reverent caution. With its textured emptiness, she felt almost deceived. She subconsciously rubbed her left palm, unsure if she even wanted to learn what the other kept or did not.

"You can see how this particular book might be so right for keeping secrets. This one is less suited for such a purpose." Tanzan went to work on the next lock. "Because as I mentioned, it is less a book than a key."

With the lock snapped and the book's cover opened, a cavity in the pages was revealed. It held a vial of dark liquid. He raised it against the wall of windows and shifted its contents. "Or rather, the keeper of a key."

Araina squinted at the vial, then Tanzan—she could swear he had aged, just slightly—and quietly observed, "I'm afraid that doesn't appear to be a key either."

With a laugh, he gently returned it to the second book's cavity. "No, it doesn't. That's why it's perfect. You did a splendid thing carrying these here, Araina. Positively splendid."

"I'm glad. It was simply what she asked. And that was all you were expecting?"

Tanzan leaned back into the chair's dense cushion and looked at her. "What is amiss, my dear? I sense there is something more sapping your voice than satisfied curiosity or relief at a task fulfilled."

"I-I'm just thinking about the journey back, I suppose." Her attempted smile was fast overpowered by dejection.

"We mustn't have you setting out so soon. You shall rest for a night or more. There are far too many people who will insist upon meeting Kerikan of the Moonserpents' grandniece, daughter of Jekea and Captain Mirran, granddaughter of Ceroiade and Baval, and Elandine and Rliac—"

"I can't imagine why. A rest does sound quite nice though," Araina confessed. "If you wouldn't mind, a friend…my guide, he may still be waiting for me. I should let him know I intend on staying a night."

"Oh, you did not mention you had a traveling companion."

"An unexpected one. I didn't think it wise to have him follow me in since Aunt Kerikan was insistent I kept the spell books quite hidden. Oh, there's also a flute—"

"That's very wise. You should alert him of your plans. But please, invite him for a meal and rest as well."

"That's very kind of you. I should warn you though, he has quite an appetite."

"We've plenty to share here."

"Thank you." Araina rose from the armchair—rather thrown by the sudden lightness of her sling bag.

"Before you depart, will you answer me this? Is it your hand or your throat that pains you more?"

She nearly gasped to answer, "My hand."

"If you return here, we can explore why that cut will not heal."

Araina looked at her palm and Tanzan again, frozen in his offer.

"How—"

"All in good time, my dear. For now, off you go."

Chapter Seven

Accommodations

Araina dashed down stairs and across landings to inform Den of her plans and return to the study for answers, but as she approached the stairwell's lowest entry, she was intercepted by a middle-aged woman in a yellow cotehardie.

"Good afternoon, Araina," she intoned with such dignified poise it was almost intimidating.

"Hello…"

"I am Trinera, a key keeper here. I will show you to your accommodations."

"Oh, I-I…thank you. It's nice to meet you. I was just told by Tanzan that I should speak to—"

"The elf?"

"Yes."

"He's made himself at home in the kitchen garden. I believe he's playing a game with some of the children. Would you like me to show you where you'll find him?"

"Oh…I see. Thank you."

Trinera led her through halls and eventually outside to a stone landing. Down its stairs, plots of herbs created a patchwork of colors and scents. The mix kept several that Araina would have given anything for just days earlier. Skipper butterflies and bees worked at their blooms, carrying out a scene that seemed like a memory. She could have watched them for hours, and nearly knelt down to do so, until she heard Den. He and Pidgie were seated upon a bench before a small audience of children.

"Alright, since you rolled'a four, that's the new chance. Bets in the middle— Oh, hey, Rainy."

The elf and his attentive crowd briefly looked up at Araina's approach, then dropped their eyes back to a series of lines drawn in the dirt, piles of small stones, and a pair of crude dice.

"I see you've made some new friends. Or perhaps students? ...Or marks?" Araina inquired.

"This is what some'a us call fun, Rainy. Should give it'a try one day. Ya take care'a your business?"

"Most of it."

"That mean ya headin' back?"

"Not quite yet. I thought I'd stay the night and take care of a few more things. A meal has also been offered."

"Was hopin' to hear that. Alright, kids, keep it goin' while I get some grub. Don't look so defeated, freckles. Ya ain't outta the game yet. C'mon Pidgie."

With Den's parting, the children let out a collective groan but continued rolling the dice and placing stone wagers.

"So how did you come to teach children hazard, or tail, or whatever that was?" Araina asked along their walk to the garden's entrance.

"Listen to you. So ya heard'a a game or two, huh? Was gettin' ready to take off 'til I saw some soldiers playin' on the other side over there. Wasn't 'bout to join that game, so I got my own goin'."

"Wonder if their parents will appreciate that."

"Relax, Rainy. These folk ain't seem anywhere near as stuffy as you. Think I like it here," Den declared as they reached the landing where Trinera waited.

"Trinera, this is Den Handkey and Pidgie. They led me through Barrier's End," Araina explained.

"A pleasure, gentlemen. Please follow me to your accommodations."

With their entry into another stairwell, Araina was quick to ask, "Afterwards, would it be possible for me to return to Tanzan's study? I believe he had something more to—"

"You'll have an opportunity to meet with him after you've taken some time to refresh yourself and have a proper meal," Trinera stated on their ascent.

"I see. He did make it seem as though—"

"Proper meal's just the sorta opportunity I was hopin' for."

With Den's boisterous interjection, Araina could not deny the rolling pang in her stomach. She further considered her appearance after such swampy travel and that a chance to bathe, eat, and rest should not be refused or postponed. Still, her hand seemed to burn, her throat throbbed, and everything within her wanted to know not just the cause, but how Tanzan came to recognize it. Lost in the pondering, she failed to track just how many flights they climbed before a door was opened to a small but inviting room.

Within was a generously dressed bed, a dark-wood writing desk and scoop seat, a nightstand, narrow wardrobe, mirror, and a tapestry depicting the ancient sea serpents for which Araina's Crest was named. Silver threads accented their slick, twisting bodies and crescent-shaped tails.

"You'll see a dressing gown there and there are other garments in the wardrobe. They are all yours to wear while we have your things laundered," Trinera explained.

"Thank you. This is all so much. I honestly was just hoping to continue speaking to Tanzan. Please don't let us be any more of an inconvenience. Certainly not past tomorrow."

"We're not inconvenienced in the slightest, nor will we be tomorrow, or past that.

"Good to know. How 'bout you take a break from bein' in such a rush, Rainy?" Den suggested as he Pidgie made themselves quite comfortable upon the pile of pillows. "How long 'til supper's up?"

"Not long," Trinera answered. "Araina, you can trust that your arrival means a great deal to Tanzan, but he has other engagements to which he must attend. Please, let me show you to the bath."

"I'm just a little confused. He did say—"

"Please, Araina. The bath is just this way," Trinera prompted again and gestured to the periwinkle blue dressing gown hung from the wardrobe's doors.

Araina attempted a gracious smile and gathered it into her arms. She lowered the sling bag to the stone and turned to insist that Den not touch anything. Instead, she found him facing the wall—already asleep along with a gently snoring Pidgie.

She turned and followed Trinera down the hall to a room of white stone. An oblong, tile-lined pit waited in the center. Leaves and petals floated upon the steaming water within.

"You can leave your things here. I'll have them added to the laundry. I'll return shortly to show you to supper."

Araina thanked her again and was left alone in the quiet, fragrant room. She undressed, lowered herself in the water, and sank to her chin. As her eyes fell shut, she imagined the dirt of Barrier's End drawing away like smoke caught in the wind. She ran her fingers over her bare arms and legs, feeling the sting of briar scrapes and gnat bites against the raw slash of her palm. She could swear it was wider and longer.

With a deep exhale against the water's surface, she went to work on her tresses. Dead leaves and bits of bark joined the bobbing petals as she picked them free. Though the sweetly infused water and the rolling clouds beyond the window gave her every reason to stay, bask, and simply breathe, Araina could not let herself have any of it. As soon as her skin felt smooth and she could pull her fingers through most of her waves, she was out of the bath, in the dressing gown, and back on her way to the room.

A gentle push of the door sprang Den from his slumber.

"Haah?" he groaned and slurped. "Supper ready yet?"

"I've not gotten any word. Why don't you wait for it in the hall? Get out, please."

"Huh? What for?"

"I need to get dressed."

"Ya think I'm gonna lift my head from this pillow to peep at you? Pfft. Don't flatter yourself."

"Until you've washed, your head shouldn't be anywhere near that pillow, nor should any other part of you."

"Feh! I'm still fresh as a daisy." Den sat up, stretched both his arms, and took a deep whiff of his armpit. "A manly daisy. Whadda 'bout Pidgie? He don't offend your haughty little sensibilities or that bumpy witch's nose 'a yours?"

"Not in the slightest. He gets to stay. You however…"

Araina widened the door and prompted his exit. The elf grumbled and slid down the bed's quilt to the floor. A brisk latching snapped the moment he cleared the threshold.

From the wardrobe, Araina selected a simple summer dress with an embroidered draw below the bust. She laced her undergarments and stepped into it, trying to keep the fabric clear of her damp hair. Before she could think to braid, twist, or bun it, a gentle knock fell at the door. Trinera waited on the other side with Den at the ribbon-trimmed hem of her skirt. His boot sent a quick beat over the stone, as if driving a march to the waiting meal.

"Supper is served," Trinera informed. "Will your companion be joining us, Den?"

"If she's done playin' dress-up."

"I was referring to your passenger pigeon."

"Pidgie? Nah. 'Long as it's up to him, he don't do much once that sun starts goin' down. That's a bird for ya."

Trinera proceeded down the hall, tailed by Araina and Den. "We have community meals in the great hall, especially when we have guests. But Tanzan thought it would be better for you to take supper in a quieter space."

"Will he be joining us?" Araina asked.

"He tends to dine alone in the recent weeks. I believe he prefers it that way due to his condition. He's also been taking more time to reflect on the news of your great aunt. He did mention that he may make an appearance."

"I do hope that he will."

"Naturally," Trinera said through a stubbornly genial smile, then nothing more through their descent into and passage through more hallways. Araina could not tell if the rolling compression in her stomach was a sudden swell of hunger—rising with a waft of warm spices—or simply a pang of dread at the thought of moving from one welcoming amenity to another, without answers and perhaps without end. Before the notion could grow, her focus fell upon a table just beyond a pair of doors.

A huge dark wheat boule breathed its heat across a polished knife and cutting-board. Beside it were wedges of cheese, a stone pan of roasted tomatoes and peppers covered in zarmen seeds, and a small tureen. The steam escaping its lid joined that rising from a plate of broiled flounder over dark greens, and a bowl of long rice mixed with slices of sweet potato, elle bean, king's root, and split-stem herbs. Pewter pitchers held wine, tea, and water. Though the table was long and its offerings generous, just two places were set.

"Please." Trinera gestured at the seats. "Help yourselves."

In a blink, Den scurried up the chair leg and onto the table's surface. He began tearing at the boule and the cheeses. He then wrapped his arms around the handle of a serving spoon and dropped a spilling helping of rice upon his plate. In the short moments it took Araina to push in her chair, Den had already finished a quarter of the eager portions. She tried to pay him no mind, filled her goblet with tea, and plated a serving of flounder and tomatoes and peppers. She dared to check for Trinera's reaction to her shameless dining companion. The woman's refined countenance revealed nothing.

"You folks got any beef or bacon?" Den asked through a mouthful.

"I'm afraid not," Trinera answered.

Araina leaned toward the elf. "Crestfolk don't raise meat the way Landers do. Animals are only eaten if they are hunted or caught wild."

"So if I wanna steak or slice'a roast, I gotta go back to town? Feh. Better fill up on cheese then."

Araina rolled her eyes. All displeasure drowned below a perfectly seasoned wedge of tomato. Its flood seemed instantly nourishing. Whether it was owed to her first hot meal in days or the first unblighted, fully grown food she had tasted in months, was no clearer than it was enrapturing.

"I see sustenance has exceeded the sum of its parts," Trinera commented, apparently noticing the veil of bliss fall over Araina's face with a bite of flounder. "Though I understand the ingredients alone have become scarce beyond our walls."

"They have. Quite scarce."

"But ya can still get beef out there. Bit pricey now," Den interjected. "Don't see what's so great about plants for eatin' 'Less you're feedin' a cow or pig. These ain't bad though."

"Perhaps we can procure some pheasant? We may also have elk in the larder."

"That's not necessary," Araina was quick to assure. "My guide is always free to be on his way, in search of beef or whatever else he wants. These tomatoes, they're grown here?"

"I will arrange for you to see it tomorrow."

"Thank you. That would be lovely. That is if—"

"Yes?"

"Well, I'd hate for anything to interfere with my meeting with Tanzan, whether tomorrow...or this evening."

Just as Araina broached the subject again, the doors parted with a creak and a shadow was cast over the floor. It disappeared in an instant. Trinera had no reaction, making Araina wonder if she imagined it.

"Have you tried the soup? It was prepared especially for you."

Trinera gestured at the tureen and an empty bowl beside it. Though it seemed an odd offering on a summer evening, Araina could not find words polite enough to decline. She instead lifted the lid, took the ladle, then stopped as the aroma struck her. It was Kerikan's recipe, or so the scent claimed—and flawlessly. Dark green stems of frog wand, whole leaves of beggar's bay, tiny noodles, and specks of infused oil swirled in a cloudy broth. It belonged in a blue glazed bowl, waiting for her on the cottage table with every first true snap of autumn—when the windswept cheeks and noses of little wandering witches became a bit too rosy.

Araina swallowed past the lump in her throat and tried to steady her hand as she ladled a shallow serving into the bowl. Feeling Trinera's eyes upon her, she leaned forward and let her hair fall to obscure her face. She slipped her finger in the bowl's handle—thankful that there were no spoons to reveal the tremor of her hand—and brought the soup to her lips. They would scarcely part to allow the broth to touch her tongue and flow down her throat. It was stinging, enveloping, and perfect—like a slow, snuffing embrace.

Araina lowered the bowl to the table and removed her shaking fingers. Behind the cover of her still-drying tresses, she touched one cheek and then the other. Her skin remained dry and hot—not a trace of a tear to be felt.

"I think we've come quite close to perfecting that recipe," Trinera declared.

"I can tell. Thank you. I don't think I could eat another bite. Thank you."

"If it's anything like 'er bread, I'll take some."

Den looked at Araina and then his empty bowl. She quickly filled it and covered the tureen. Though she half-wondered how the elf would manage to drink it—whether he would lean over the rim and slurp or somehow tip it to his mouth without drenching his body—she simply wanted to retreat from the aromas, the lack of answers, and the strain required to remain cordial through it all.

"There's nothing more we can serve you, Araina?"

"Nothing. Thank you."

"Very well. On to your meeting with Tanzan."

"I ain't done eatin' though," Den asserted.

"You are welcome to dine as long as you wish, Den. Tanzan is to meet with Araina alone." Trinera turned to Araina as she briskly left her seat. "Shall I escort you?"

"Or—or direct me. I'm sure I could find my way."

"I shall show you to the correct stairway."

Chapter Eight

Illuminations

U p flights and across landings, the witch eventually came to the same window and tapestry-lined passage—this time lit green and amber by the glass sconces. The eerie glow tempered her eagerness to a simmering apprehension. After knocking at the indigo doors, she rubbed her left palm through the pitting stretch of seconds that preceded footfalls. A crisp click sounded from the lock and freed the doors to drift, revealing shifting shadows. Araina timidly widened the clearance and entered.

A pair of lanterns crowning the fireplace, a low-wicked hurricane lamp upon the table, and flickering reflections in the windows were her only means to navigate the study.

Tanzan sounded several decades beyond his afternoon self as he instructed, "Sit down." The curt insistence quashed whatever urgency remained of Araina's questions. She found the seat opposite his and lowered herself to its edge. Little of the warlock was visible through the shadows cast by the wingback chair.

"Did you enjoy your supper?" His inquiry, though flat, was baiting.

"It was very…generous. Thank you."

"Quite restorative, no doubt."

"Quite."

"So you had the soup then."

"I did."

"Simple in all the right ways," he declared, as though tasting it in that moment. "Only weighty in how nourishing it is. Kerikan would give it to women before and after delivery. For fortification to face what lay ahead and the hours, days, and weeks to follow. Did she ever explain how she came to perfect it?"

"No."

"She didn't talk much about that part of her life, did she?"

"Not very much. Not with me."

"But you do know why she was so renowned?"

"I...I know she was the midwife to most of western Drudgenwood. For Crestfolk, and the old royals, middling-sorts, poor folk. That's why we lived so near Landers."

"Quite a unique way for a Crest witch to grow up, wasn't it?"

"I don't know that I considered it such. I was most always kept on the shore."

"To be a Crest midwife who serves Landers is also unique, but that wasn't solely the reason for her prestige. Your great-aunt was extraordinary for other reasons. Do you know what they were?"

"Not particularly. Only that she's...that she was quite known."

"Did you know she had never lost anyone in her charge? Neither mother nor child. Not in all her years of midwifery."

Araina kept silent as Tanzan leaned toward her, revealing a face now creased and vaguely dour.

"Could any other midwife say the same?" His tone slipped into a slow depth that seemed heavier than his age alone. "Although, there's one exception. Isn't there?"

Araina stared back. Her palm throbbed and her throat began to thicken. Something solid yet jittery took hold of her core and leaked into her limbs.

"Yes. One." Her answer flickered with the glass-kept flames.

"Your mother."

The witch faintly nodded.

"The only one she lost." Tanzan's gaze briefly fell to an unseeing stare, then returned with a pointed scrutiny as he added, "And it was a great loss. Jekea was a truly remarkable witch. Expected to live up to and beyond so many exceptional Moonserpents before her. Still, the loss was more than that for Kerikan. But then, to her, Jekea was more a daughter than a niece. Perhaps even something more than a daughter. Something beyond kindred, almost a pure budding or root of all come before. But try as Kerikan did, immaculate and skilled as she was, your mother would not live."

He slowly shook his head before returning his chin to the bridge of his fingers, then went on, "And yet, you were kept that day. Ordinarily, that would be some solace. But no. Instead, a tether. To the loss. To the anomaly. All that remained of an extraordinary young witch. Gone, but for Araina. Or rather, the arainas. She expressed it as such. All gone but for the arainas. They bloomed the very next morning. Oddly late, so many days after the equinox. Hence your name. Did she ever tell you that?"

Araina did not answer over her clotting breath. Tanzan was not stayed by it.

"All that was left of her work from that day would be you. Though, it was not a coddled or elevated place, was it?"

The witch stiltedly exhaled before rationing, "I-I had nothing else with which to compare it."

"Is any comparison required? Surely not when hope becomes expectation and then…utter disappointment. Every lesson, every task, every moment of study and practice, Kerikan was sharp in seeing your shortcomings, wasn't she? After all, you were not only a Moonserpent, a new life in a fading Crest, you were the link to a loss. The loss. An opportunity to salvage something, at first. But then, alas." He sent a spindly sigh across the smoke and shadows. "And what does that expectation do? What happens to a child when she becomes increasingly aware, as she grows, that it's ever-present, and that she never so much as nears what she was to be? Does it drain and defeat? Does it fill and fortify? To what does it amount, Araina?"

His questions bit, not only in their mounting force, but their pertinence. Araina found she could answer none as they swirled, and spiraled, and summoned so many others.

"All because of a loss come too soon. All because, try as Kerikan did, she could not save a woman who was not supposed to die so early." Tanzan's unceasing stare became curious as it was confrontational. "My, that rings familiar, doesn't it?"

His words slowed and hung, like a key turning in a rusty lock that was then left to simply droop in place. A hiss of heated anger and cold cavernous grief created a small storm in Araina. As if he could sense its rising, Tanzan leaned and slowly slid the hurricane lamp further down the table, sending her tensed face into shadow.

She took little notice, swallowed past the hardness in her throat, and finally responded, "Not entirely."

"Oh? And why not?"

"Aunt Kerikan wasn't an anomaly." Araina buried her stinging, shaking left hand into the grip of her right. "Not for me. As you've pointed out, and as she clearly told you, I-I've only ever failed. Her passing was a failure, but not any…not anything unique. Only a great one among so many others."

She squeezed and scratched the flesh of her palm, trying to soothe away the sharp pressure. It would not yield.

"And where does that great failure, among so, so many others, leave you now? What is left to salvage from it? Only a link to yet another loss?" the warlock prodded.

Araina fell silent again, caught between the searing pain in her hand and his words, firmly anchoring her reality.

"But then, a link for who?" he pressed. "What purpose is there beyond that? What remains, Araina?"

"I was told to carry the books. And…"

"And now?"

"I…"

"What remains, Araina? What was it beyond constantly striving to prove your worth to a woman who would only ever see what was gone? Other than blindly longing for the familiar, what part of that would you have back? What remains for you? What remains *of* you…beyond a link to losses that are now tethered to no one, except to you? And then what? You must uncover an answer. For without that, alas."

Araina parted her lips and froze. She was absorbed by a new sting—hot and buzzing—this one centered in her larynx. It was like a spark popped from a fire, but rather than cooling on landing, it grew, and caught, and began to push a panicked impulse. It spread to the back of her skull, rode the curve of her jaw and under her eyes, and then diffused over the whole of her form.

She looked at Tanzan and saw a small smile cross his face. To see such an expression in response to her pain and alarm would have seemed a type of madness or malice, but it held no trace of dark satisfaction. Instead, it was wonderment. Only then did Araina realize a soft light had been cast over her clenched hands and the dark fabric covering her lap and breasts.

Mouth agape, she startled backwards in her chair. The light was indeed emanating from her throat and moved with her body. As she reached to touch it, she discovered the slash across her left palm was releasing a steady flow of blood. The witch's chin bobbed and shuddered, grasping for explanations like air.

"It's quite alright, Araina," Tanzan delicately assured while panic stretched the witch's eyes. "It's alright. In fact, it's wonderful. I will explain. For now though, I want you to take that awful, crowded ache and send it out."

"O-out? What?" she gasped.

"No questions yet. While we've got your throat alight, send it out. Here…" Tanzan rose and moved to her. "I think it will help if you stand."

Araina clumsily followed, causing the light and shadows to convulse with her motion. She kept her left hand curled to stifle the further spilling of blood to the floor and the borrowed dress. It was all for naught as Tanzan took her wrist and raised her arm. He then stepped back.

"I know that hand must hurt terribly, my dear. Do something with it. Send it out. Through that wound."

Araina looked to him, then to her hand over her head. For a moment, she was distracted by the thin ribbons of red rolling to her elbow, but she soon learned the described action began to assert itself naturally, almost insistently.

It was, at first, disturbing, as though she could deliberately push blood through her vessels. Her insides tightened and strained. Then, the feeling subsided. Whatever crowded her throat began to drift and disperse. It went dark as it followed a raw path to her left hand. Her fingers spread with its new convergence. A small sphere of light appeared. It balanced itself above the bleeding slash.

Araina slowly lowered her arm and looked upon it, silent and aghast. The little light gave off no heat, no sensation, no sound, no scent. And though it did not touch her, it moved as though an extension of her. She flattened her hand, pulled back her thumb and it grew—further illuminating her surroundings and a joyful but wordless Tanzan.

"Perfect," he whispered. "It's…perfection, Araina. Now, when you're ready, and before it takes too much of you, call it back."

"Call it back?"

"Yes. It's yours to reclaim. You should be able to…fold it away. Call it back, within you."

She looked at Tanzan's gesture, then back to the little shuddering star over her palm, and carefully began to bend her fingers inward. The light dwindled down, never allowing itself to be touched. It shrank until it was no more and shadows took hold of the study again.

Suddenly aware of her weakened legs and center, Araina almost toppled back into the chair. From the cradle of its dense stuffing, she worked to feed and empty her lungs. Tanzan crossed behind her and lit a lamp, followed by several candles. He returned with a handkerchief, which he pressed to Araina's bleeding palm and left for her to limply hold in place. A crystal decanter and pair of small goblets were placed upon the table. The first was filled and set before Araina—who still appeared too depleted to lift it. After filling his own, he settled to face her and took a slow sip.

"Before I answer your questions, permit me to apologize. I was only capable of orchestrating all that caused you frustration, and sadness, and turmoil because it was essential. Casting is only born through quiet and lasting pain. And summoning it forth, that usually requires some provocation. I'm relieved it took no more than it had and I gained no joy from my role in helping it surface. I cannot say I regret any part of it, however. Look at where we are."

"W-what... What happened?"

"Casting, my dear. You are able to cast."

"Casting? B-but casting takes a lifetime of study."

"No. No, no, no. Perhaps you're thinking of helix glow? Or something from the dawn dwelling studies? But no. What you've done is casting. Doloris Lucerna as it's sometimes written. A lamp of pain. To think that it can simply be obtained through study is foolish. If it were a matter of that, it wouldn't be so rare. Casting has everything to do with circumstance and how it is kept and carried. It is ache stored and transformed in just the right way. It has to go somewhere. And so has gone yours."

"I—"

"Indeed, Araina, you can cast. And as you undoubtedly see, it will drain, somewhat. But as you become accustomed to using it instead of only carrying it, it will be all the more manageable and useful."

"Useful?"

"Yes," the warlock affirmed with a laugh. "In addition to reducing your reliance on candles and lanterns, it's physical force. It just happens to be luminous. Quite useful through either attribute, I'd say."

"You mean that it's—"

"As arrows to the archer, stones to the onager, so is luminous energy to Araina of the Moonserpents. Rather exciting, no?"

The witch moved the bloodied handkerchief from her palm and looked at the wound—now beginning to clot. It appeared no more extraordinary or comparable to a bow or catapult. She closed her fingers and tucked her hand into her center.

"But what do I *do* with this?"

Tanzan laughed again. "Draw it forth and let's get better acquainted, shall we?"

With her arm limply extended and her hand uncurled, Araina hesitantly breathed forth a small sphere of flickering light. Her eyes, first incredulous and then curious, clamped on it.

"What happens if you hold it out before you, almost as if to push or toss it away?" Tanzan proposed.

Araina eased her palm sideways and still the little ball of light maintained. She turned it again so her opened hand faced the wall, illuminating the towering bookshelves and paintings.

"Now, toward the fireplace. Send it into the stone," Tanzan instructed with an eager smile.

"Send it?"

"Yes. Cast it out. Remember, Araina, it is as arrows to the archer, though there's no bow to bend. There is only you and your illumination, and whatever you choose to do with it. Let's see what that old stonework makes of it. You needn't be shy, my dear. There's a reason this keep is solid among ruins."

Araina dragged her lower lip free of her teeth and teetered out of the chair. With an exhale and a smooth spread of her fingers, she hesitated, tensed her arm, and then flung the light away. It sped, silently, swifter than she could follow with her vision. In half an instant, it hit the back of the fireplace. Small chips of stone flew from the dent as the light dissipated.

"I'm so sorry!" she cried out.

With an impressed chuckle, Tanzan lifted himself from the chair. He took the lamp from the table and inspected the damage.

"Nothing to apologize for, my dear. That was quite…impactful. Come, see for yourself."

The witch joined him by the hearth and observed the notable depression and border of white dust where the stone met her light. Araina raised an eyebrow.

"I can see not using candles as much, but I can't imagine why I'd ever need to do something like that."

"Well, we can talk more about that tomorrow. For now, let's treat this little ability of yours very much like the book and the key and keep it between us." Tanzan gestured her back to her seat and settled into his. He looked at the portrait of Kerikan in the low light. "With regards to that delivery, I must say, I'm not sure I'd have made the same omissions as Kerikan. But then, informing you of what you carried would also require telling why you had to do so. I suppose it would have been much to ask of her and of you at such a time."

"Is that not something you can do at this time?" Araina suggested.

"I'm afraid, my dear, apart from so many other hindrances, my time to do so is growing short. …For now. If I were to begin, I want to ensure I'd be able to finish. And my shifting state aside, it's not yet clear if I can, well… A few things are not yet clear. But that is also a state that continues to shift." The warlock refilled his goblet.

Araina looked at the skin of his hands—stretched thinner as he raised the spirit to his lips—and asked, "What is it like when it starts over?"

"When my time ends to start anew?"

She nodded.

"I cannot tell you how it appears," Tanzan answered after another sip. "I sat before a mirror once, hoping to see it in full, but it was a blink and I'd gone from frail as a pile of branches to a squirming infant in a robe." He weakly smiled. "Trinera may be better able to tell you. She's here when it happens. Ready to keep me from getting into too much trouble crawling about this mess. I've no doubt it's amusing, perhaps nearly as much as it is draining."

He exhaled across the rim of the goblet. "And before I come any nearer to that transition and I leave you to some much-needed rest, permit me to tell you, that the resilience of your great aunt's aliment was not found in any shortcomings on your part. Whether I am newly born or decrepit, I know I wouldn't gain much rest until you'd been told that, my dear. Particularly after all with which I've confronted you. Know that her passing was no failure of yours. Not in any sense."

Instead of the cold, dense clog in her throat, an honest grip of grief settled in its place. The sadness felt pure—almost comforting in its clarity. Araina finally began to feel tears well in her eyes.

"If not my failing, then what?"

"Kerikan's dying would be unusual in any other time. But in ours, it wasn't terribly surprising. Look at what you had to work with to simply quell a fever. Hardly so much as a sprig of yarrow. Have you wondered why that is?"

Just as soon as they surfaced, Araina's tears were stayed by curiosity.

"Of course," she answered.

"It is no single blight nor failed harvest. It is not an early frost nor late spore. Everything about our world's failings has been summoned."

"Summoned?"

"In a way. Whether it was wanted or even expected, I cannot say. But it's come about because the laws of our world are not nearly as immutable as we need them to be. The wondrous, countless, constant little happenstances that enable everything, the laws that set seeds to grow and mountains to rise, that are sure and true, and yet ever-changing, can all be bent and undone."

"Undone?"

"Indeed." Tanzan emptied the goblet with a final sip. "That process appears to be underway. It's as though death has been called aloft to tear at the seams and the binds…and all that lives and finds order within. That's why every cure you mixed, with what little you could forage, couldn't do much for Kerikan. And why Kerikan herself seemed to wilt so."

"But *why* is this happening? You said it's a process?" The witch's brow tightened.

"The answers are complex as the questions are pressing, but I'd dare not cause wonder or worry that might steal any more sleep from you. I've no wish to give you more to ponder or grieve tonight. I've only told you what I have so you may know, none of it was yours, Araina. That was not an expectation you could have met. Please know and keep that. And further, find ease in what I say now. What you have brought is of consequence. Things that have been undone can be set right. And things that have not, can be preser—"

A firm knock at the door stole Tanzan's words and startled a befuddled Araina.

"Without fail. That will be Trinera now. Will you let her in, my dear? My goodness, you do look quite…well, you look as I expect you'd look after such a telling. Take solace in what I've said. And solace in knowing that there will be more answers for new questions, but with a new day."

Araina lifted her lower lip and rose from the chair. She crossed the study, parted the doors, and met with Trinera, who smiled subtly.

"It appears as though you're past due a rest," she observed and stepped into the study. Araina could only manage a heavy nod as she moved into the hall. "I've some tea left for you in your room. It will help you find sleep."

"…Thank you."

"I'm sure you'll need no assistance finding your way back in the dark."

Before Araina could respond, Trinera bade her goodnight and closed the doors.

Alone, the witch held her left hand open but still guarded at her chest. She called forth a small sphere of light and looked at its warm cast over the tapestries and stone walls. She then folded it away and navigated by the dwindling glow of the colored-glass sconces.

Chapter Nine

Legacy and Possibility

Araina remembered reaching her room, taking notice of Den and Pidgie asleep on the windowsill in a gathering of the drapes, and drinking the tea left upon the nightstand. She did not remember changing from the blood-dotted dress to a linen chemise or climbing into bed, but that was in what and where she lay when light appeared beyond her weighty eyelids. She parted them, expecting to face an intrusively early dawn, but instead found the pierce of the red wolf's gaze. It hovered over her, clear and sharp, while darkness had taken all else.

"Tears and yet we are here. Throat uncrowded. Never clear. Still here. Always here. To carry and obey," it growled, breathing steam. Then it lowered itself, covering Araina's body with a crushing sensation of heat and density. As she winced, her clamped eyes were again challenged by light. She met it with a gasp and saw only the sunlit room. Den and Pidgie were also absent.

On regaining her breath and bearings, she rose and selected a dress from the wardrobe. She slipped into and laced it before the mirror. After a small, whistled exhale and another quick affirmation of solitude, she opened her left hand and permitted a spark of light. She stared into it and then its reflection. Some of its flare was lost in the morning, which had also transformed answers and ends into more questions. She folded away the glowing sphere.

While she attempted to match the initial inviting arrangement of the quilt and pillows, she strove to recall whether she had bothered to make her own bed at the cottage and stumbled through the echoes of Tanzan's interrogation. Though his motives were thoroughly revealed, what remained at the seashore was not. A slow roar of hunger pulled her from the spiral. Perhaps breakfast would be easier sought than the next direction—or would at least fuel it—she thought and decided the room where she and Den took supper seemed as good a starting point as any.

A waft of baking dough, toasting millet, brewing coffee, and sugary aromas with traces of spice met her in the lower hall. She parted the doors and poked her head within the cozy dining room, where she spied a small spread of cloth-covered canisters and baskets, stacked plates, and a kettle shallowly sputtering within the fireplace. Beyond it, a door opened and out stepped a young man—though not young enough to be Tanzan at that time of day, or so Araina calculated. His face and voice confirmed that he was someone she had yet to meet. He greeted her by name, nevertheless. "Good morning, Araina."

"Good morning…"

"Sage."

"Good morning, Sage."

"Good morning." His nod and smile were of equal vibrance as he relayed, "I was told to find you here and that you'd likely be looking for your friends. They've eaten and gone out. They did tell me…that is, the elf told me, to say they'd run into you later. The pigeon didn't have much to say."

"Oh. Thank you."

"I was just dropping off some shallots. They've got quite the supper planned for you." With his mention of a meal, Araina's stomach released an audible grumble, which then prompted Sage to suggest, "You should have something to eat before we head to the conservatory."

"The conservatory?"

"Yes. Trinera said you wanted to see it and Tanzan insisted you do."

"I did? He did?"

"Here." Sage lifted a cloth from one of the baskets, revealing a pile of large and densely seeded cakes. "They're filled with almonds and honey. They'll keep you well-sated. Oh, and I never start a day without at least one of these." From the pocket of his azure tunic, he uncovered and handed Araina a large aureolin apple.

"Just off the tree. Coffee or tea won't travel as well, but that's not a worry. There's plenty where we're going. Tea at least. I hope that's alright."

"Yes, either's fine. At the conservatory?"

"Yes. Well, the tea's at my cabin, just nearby. Don't forget your…" Sage raised the basket again.

Araina thanked him, selected the topmost seeded cake, and delicately inquired, "Did Tanzan say why he insisted I see it?"

"No. Just that he did. Received word to show you earlier this morning. C'mon, it's a mostly flat path. You should have no trouble breaking fast as we go. That's usually what I do back and forth each day."

He grabbed the empty crate at his feet and led Araina through the door into a kitchen. Instead of proceeding toward the noise, heat, and savory wafts mixing just beyond a pillar, Sage took her through another door, into a passage of cupboards and casks, and then outside to the yard of herb plots.

"I always like to cut through here," he explained as they came to another door. Though it appeared to lead into a new portion of the keep, it opened to a lush path of green. The stone beneath their feet was ebbed away by moss. The former walls were only irregular columns reaching up to incomplete arches and parilla-climbed rafters.

"This must've been quite the castle once," Araina pondered aloud.

"Must have, but anyone who can tell us for certain is long passed."

"Could it have been from the Kyloade Wars? Or when Drudgen was last conquered?"

"I'm not sure. History isn't my strong suit. Don't forget about your breakfast."

"Thank you." Araina took a bite of the apple. "I must admit, I thought I'd save the cake for the cup of tea you mentioned."

"An idea sound as it is popular." Sage tapped at his pocket where his own share was kept. "It's not far now."

They reached a thick of trees, their boughs alive with birds. Araina's bare feet dragged in the moss as she abruptly halted—the entirety of her attention caught the glint of a newly spun web. A rotund orb-weaver tidied the center.

"Everything alright?" Sage asked at the cease of her footsteps.

"I-I'm sorry. It's been so long since I've seen one. I've missed them so. I'd watch them pull every strand, set every spoke... I just... I wondered if I'd ever see one again."

"I've heard things are very different from where you've traveled. I only know it from the hard work to keep what we have. Especially now that we're supplying vittles and medicinals to much of the Svet Hagen, in addition to our own folk."

"You're feeding that many people? How?"

"You'll see just up ahead. And don't worry, there are more friends like her as well."

Their trail widened to a clearing. Within, a massive structure of stone, iron, and reaching walls of glass was centered. Great clusters of green shown beyond the panes. Still more glass and iron formed a converging roof with an opening in its center. As she squinted through the reflected sunlight, Araina could faintly see an intermittent passage of insects. The impressive glass building was sharply contrasted by a quaint wood cabin a short walk away. Gentle waves of heat breathed from its clay chimney.

"So what's first then? Tea or the conservatory?" Sage asked.

"I don't know if I can choose."

"Since you can't seem to take your eyes from it, let's start with the conservatory."

He led her around the glass walls and parted its door to rows and rows of plants. Basins and troughs held just about every herb and edible crop Araina had ever known and others she had never seen. They bordered short and robust shrubs with berries and dense tangles of fruiting and flowering vines. Every few yards, a tree erupted from the array, also bearing blossoms, nuts, and fruits. Their branches supported narrow trellises of interlaced reeds, through which more vines climbed. The vast interior was hot and alive with sound. Below the hum of insects darting near and far, a slow rhythmic trickle chimed through the dense air. Thin chains were suspended from curved rafters overhead, dropping down into the planting beds and carrying thin streams of water.

An awestruck Araina toured the tidy maze of growth—only realizing her mouth was agape when a honeybee nearly flew into it. Sage silently returned the empty crate to a stack and let her wander.

"H-how…how've you managed all this?" she inquired.

"It's a lot of elements come together and much love from many of us. It's just you and I now, and our flying and crawling friends." Sage followed the path of a flittering ladybug with a smile and continued, "But I'm only one conceiver and caretaker. There are many hands and hearts in this."

"It's amazing." Araina's view kept falling to thick beds of growth—leaves and stems for which she had desperately searched over recent weeks. Almost as if to mock all her time spent wondering whether they still existed, they crowded one another before her eyes. The witch's astonishment turned to something sour in her stomach. She lowered her face so her hair would obscure her tears.

"Araina? Are you alri—"

"I am. I'm sorry. It's just, to see them right here. I could have saved…or helped her with a fraction of this. Or at least, I could have made it easier. I could have made it less painful. At night, when the worst of it would… Usual failings or not, this would've—"

"Oh, Araina. This, what you see here, this is just a shutter in a storm. A storm it sounds like you've been weathering for some time," Sage gently assured.

"It would have been enough. It's keeping everyone here fed and alive, isn't it? And now an army?"

"Well, two. Our own troops have filled the barracks again. And, it's feeding them for a time. But this is also running out. This shouldn't exist. It should be in the ground. I'm not sure why Tanzan would've wanted you to see this if it would upset you so."

"Oh, there must be some reason." The witch sniffled and huffed a short laugh before sighing. "If there's nothing else he wanted me to see, then I should probably go back. I have to decide what I'll... Where to start..."

"Wait, you've been promised tea. At least have a cup and collect your thoughts," he offered.

Araina nodded her acquiescence. They left the conservatory and moved to the cabin.

The small dwelling kept Sage's bed, a few cabinets, and shelves of books and small clay instruments. A trubizar hung on the wall. A cushion-tied rocking chair was opposite a small hearth and fireplace, where a stone kettle rested on a trivet over its embers. In the center of the space, a chest functioned as a low table where a woven cloth, pair of clay mugs, and a little round honeypot waited.

"You can take the chair there. I prefer the floor, even without guests," Sage offered.

"Thank you, but I'll join you there as well." Araina lowered herself before the chest as he retrieved a wood-corked canister and pinched out a few large leaves.

He crushed and dropped them into the mugs before filling each with steaming water while he remarked, "I wonder if Tanzan should have given you more time. You did just arrive, didn't you?"

"Please don't worry. And please forgive me for reacting so. I'm glad you showed me this. Truly. It's beautiful and unfathomable for all it must require. But the more I'm here, the more I wonder where I'll begin back home. I've never known it the way it will be."

"Then why not stay here for a time?"

The surface of Araina's tea rippled against her exhale. "I don't know if this makes sense, but it may be harder to stay in a temporary loveliness than a lasting emptiness. Even if empty, it is lasting. And I didn't expect to miss the ocean quite so soon. It's still beautiful. Perhaps because I can't see what's below its surface, or rather, what's no longer below it. Home is still home, I suppose."

"Hmm. Well, the seashore aside, maybe once you meet more of us, you'd feel at home here. Then it could be lovely and lasting, or at least, not empty. It's not just the few folk you've met in the tower. Most of the families have their own cabins nearby. You could stay and help us care for the conservatory, and the plots, and then there's the dairy, the aviary, the fishing and hunting grounds. All of it needs extra care now."

"It's generous of you to suggest it. I shall consider it. Thank you for the tea and for coming to collect me and show me this."

"My privilege and pleasure, though I wonder if Tanzan thought you'd gain something else. You're off to speak with him?"

"If permitted. Our conversation was cut short last night. I should see if he wishes to continue it. Or if it matters." Araina took a final sip and rose from the floor.

"I find a good talk with him sprouts perspective. Maybe it will help, as far as what you decide is next."

"Depending on what that is and if I don't get a chance to see you before I—"

"Oh, I'm sure we'll see one another. And if you do return home soon, I'll make sure you have everything you need to keep your strength up for the journey."

"Thank you again, Sage."

"You are welcome, Araina."

Through the broken wall and into the yard of herb plots, Araina found Trinera waiting on the stone landing. Her voice and stance were somehow queenlier than the previous day.

"Salutations, Araina."

"Good morning."

"I trust Sage provided you with breakfast?"

"He did. Thank you. I finished it on my walk back."

"Those cakes are always exquisite this time of year. Late summer honey has such character to it. Our hives work as diligently as the rest of us, as you've now seen in part. What did you think of our conservatory?"

"It's beyond impressive."

"Tanzan has been eager to hear your thoughts on it."

"I see. ...I was hoping to speak with him."

"That's fortunate. He's waiting in his study now. I'll escort you."

"I'm sure I can find my way—"

"I insist." At Trinera's polished intonation, Araina's ascent to the landing slowed. Her loftiness held when they entered the now-familiar stairwell. "Sage has accomplished much in very little time. So too has everyone responsible for the growth there."

"I can only imagine the effort."

"Yes, but we rise to meet these difficulties. We've all our parts to play."

"You seem to do quite a lot yourself, if you don't mind me saying."

"Key keepers always do, but my day does not start and my nights do not end with that. My duties have only shifted since your arrival."

"Oh. My apologies for the disruption."

"You mustn't apologize for something you've not caused. Many of us felt it best if I looked after you myself."

"Oh."

"And I know it's not been unappreciated."

"You've been more accommodating than I could say, thank you."

"And yet you look as though you are eager to be on your way."

Araina silently cursed the melancholic pall that must have been clear as any feature on her face. Trinera made no immediate demands for an explanation or excuse and only stated, "I hope you'll consider staying in our company. We're holding a small banquet tomorrow. There are some who would very much like to meet you."

"I—"

"Before you accept or decline, please, wait until you've spoken with Tanzan."

"Just the same, I don't think I should…at the very least, I-I've not brought anything appropriate to wear to such a—"

"That will not be a problem. We've used the measurements from your laundry to prepare something."

Trinera eased open one of the study doors, leaving no opportunity for question or response—only entrance. Araina warily obeyed.

Inside, she again looked at Kerikan's portrait. She considered her great-aunt's portrayal upon the canvas compared to the old witch in her last days—her reduced, slack, and sallow form before it was fully shrouded—and then the exasperation so often worn otherwise. Araina narrowed her eyes at it. Even if she would have been so indulgent to ask a portrait, aloud, just how much that woman knew of what was built up within her, and whether the luminous result would have finally been impressive enough, her great-aunt's image appeared far too elevated to grant a clear and simple answer. The imagined confrontation was interrupted as Araina felt a warm, wet sniffing at her hand and then an urgent nudging of it.

A large herding dog insisted on her attention. She knelt down, eager to give it, but ceased her petting a moment to look into the dog's eyes.

"This isn't some other part of it, is it?" she dared to inquire. "Are you a dog at this day or hour for some reason, Tanzan?" Behind her, another nearly identical dog joined the other's pursuit of affection. "Or two dogs, perhaps?"

"My apologies, Araina, and no, as you can see, I am here and neither Aradia nor Usil. That's quite enough, you two. Go on and settle or it's downstairs. Go on," an adolescent Tanzan commanded. The dogs withdrew and found their resting places on the rug below the windows—though not without a few parting licks to the witch's face.

"Those beasts get very excited when they meet someone who appreciates their gift for distraction. The more important the work, the more they intrude. I've recently kept them out of here for obvious reasons. Speaking of such, have you revealed anything about your ability?"

"No. Although, last night, Trinera led me to think that she may have some sense—"

Tanzan laughed heartily. "Well, yes. She would. Did she mention that we're having a special supper tomorrow?"

"She used the word banquet."

"That does sound a bit elaborate, doesn't it? I hope it hasn't discouraged you from partaking."

"Lovely as it sounds and hospitable as everything has been, I thought it best if I return home sooner rather than later."

"Oh dear, whyever for? I thought you would have been all the more eager to spend time with us upon seeing just the conservatory. There's so much we've yet to show you—"

"Everything here is very impressive, it's just…" Araina looked at the sprawled dogs, thankful to have them to set her eyes upon instead of Kerikan's portrait or the ever-changing Tanzan. "Well, it-it's difficult to know that things I tried so hard to find were here. Simply growing. I have to wonder, then, if it would've mattered. If it would have changed anything. If it would have meant not facing…" Her words slipped into a low sigh. "And that aside, I can't help but think, perhaps you've some purpose in having me see these things. That you might be trying to conjure something else out of me. And your question of what remains is still—"

Dismay leadened Tanzan's youthful face. "On the contrary, Araina. I'm not attempting to conjure a thing. I am instead offering something."

"Offering something?"

"An explanation. An ongoing one."

"...For?"

"For what we spoke about last night."

"About this process you said was underway?"

He gestured her to an armchair. Araina hesitantly accepted.

"I did not have you visit the conservatory to evoke anything from you. I did it mostly because I needed a bit of time this morning. I needed my own questions answered, permissions granted, and assurances that a proper explanation could be given. And indeed, I was hoping it would encourage you to extend your visit so that such an explanation could be provided at a more...digestible rate."

Tanzan stopped to observe the sheen in Araina's maple eyes and the depletion darkening the skin around them. He sighed.

"But you've fulfilled your task. And I will only share explanations that you have interest and will to hear. Otherwise, we will make every provision for your return journey. I can arrange an escort and you may leave within the hour, tomorrow, in a month, whenever you wish. If, however, you decide otherwise, that choice begs a warning."

"A warning?"

"Yes."

"What warning is that?"

"A warning that all will be different."

"I'm afraid that's already come to pass." Araina said through a weary smile.

"Oh, I do understand why you say that, my dear. But, heavy and strange as it all feels to return to that shore, to be a witch alone, you only know the whisperings of why you face that. You don't yet know the underlying shouts. And you still have the option to keep it as such."

To Tanzan's surprise, the witch's smile lifted to a laugh.

"Have I said something funny, my dear?"

"No, no. I'm sorry. It's just nice to be *asked* whether I'd like to learn something. Especially something that might be difficult to know. With Aunt Kerikan, it wouldn't've been a question, but an instruction."

"Well, her methods were her methods, weren't they? For what you can now do with a motion of your hand, I suppose we have them to thank for that. What little consolation that may be."

"I still couldn't say." Araina's voice slipped back into a forlorn luffing. "I know your aim was to help me rouse that ability, but I suppose my eagerness to return home, strange as it will be, is because that's where I'll have to create answers to question you asked. I honestly don't know what remains there without her. Or of me. Warnings aside, will that be helped by the explanation you're offering?"

"I can already affirm, there is much that remains of you, Araina. Your seashore is another matter. Along with all other places."

"Will that be any less so, if I choose the option of not knowing?"

"I would wish that. But it is both impossible and too late, for its consequences have brought you here."

"Then what choice is there?"

"Some comfort of ignorance, while it lasts, or devastating but definitive understanding all at once."

"Again, what choice is there?"

Tanzan nodded and walked to a chest in the corner. A lock clicked, a hinge squeaked, and he returned with the two spell books. They were set before her and their puzzle locks were conquered once again.

"Your great aunt Kerikan had a memory and gift for research that was immeasurable. It was as though she could dowse wisdom out of books by opening them. She could then apply that wisdom as though she had conceived it. And further, her work as a midwife enabled her to gain trust from generations of families, Crest and Lander alike. Through such bonds, she acquired an extensive body of resources and knowledge. The greatest result of which is represented here."

Tanzan pressed his fingers to the covers of both books. He moved one aside and opened the other, again revealing a mass of blank pages.

"There is a study rooted in a special sort of understanding. It holds a theory that everything living and moving through our world converges into a path. And along that path are significant concentrations that link to and also underpin it. All that's born, breathes, and evolves is governed by one or more of these interconnected concentrations."

Tanzan opened the second book, lifted the vial from its cavity, and placed it upon the table.

"Now, this core theory has given way to others. The most significant, is that it's possible to access these concentrations. The theory holds that this can be done through earth-rooted materials. They've been called many things. I think touchpoints is the simplest way to describe them, as they can be touched, held...and changed. The interlinking path of these points is most often called the Meridian's Reflection. To map it would lead to each point. And such a route holds unfathomable value. But of even greater value, are the workings that can potentially manipulate it all."

"Manipulate it all?" the witch echoed.

"Yes. All that is."

"All that— So, by this theory, everything that is, could be...altered?"

"Yes. Altered or undone. Through the touchpoints."

Araina, her brow thoroughly tensed, challenged, "Why would someone want to do that?"

"It heartens me to hear you ask it, my dear. But you must remember, not all think as Crestfolk do. The idea would be to bend or undo in attempt to create something else. But of course, it's unimaginable to properly account for all that entails. All the complexity. Even our folk, for all we seek to uncover and keep of this world's deepest workings, could not accomplish it. Nevertheless, every few centuries or generations, the tale of these touchpoints and the Meridian's Reflection is rekindled and spread. They are inevitably subject to a bounty."

"A bounty for information on them?"

"A bounty for the actual touchpoints, through the details of the Meridian's Reflection. Usually one or a few Landers find some mention buried in a legend. If they've the right pairing of hubris and resources, they seek them out. To very limited degrees of success, until recently."

"Recently? But you said theory, and then tale, and then legend, Tanzan. This doesn't really exist, right? None of this is possible, is it?"

"For ages, it wasn't clear. Most Landers dismissed them as our whisperings. And there are Crestfolk who doubt them as well. Such a notion has been thought too fragile, orderly, and simple to ever explain, let alone birth and foster the beautiful chaos that amounts to all that sets order to the world and also fuels perpetual change. But there were Crestfolk who thought otherwise. Your great aunt, your grandmothers, myself, and a few of our long-passed mentors, friends, and rivals, there were many of us who thought it worth an exploration. We studied and studied, sometimes as a matter of sport. And always as a matter of getting to the depths of this world, as all Crestfolk would seek to do. And then, she pieced it together."

Tanzan pushed the blank book toward an increasingly guarded Araina. He lifted the stopper from the vial. An earthy, coppery scent wafted from the black

73

liquid as it clung to the severe, needle-sharp tip. He brought it before the first page and let the liquid drop. It sat as a bead upon the stark, aged paper.

"The heat from one's breath should be enough. Go on, Araina, breathe upon the page."

She stared a moment, inhaled, and slowly eased air from her lungs. As the warmth crossed the thick surface, the bead of liquid spread and streamed into lines upon lines. The movements of Kerikan's quill darkened in place.

"It is a sight to see it again," Tanzan dreamily remarked. "Within these pages, Kerikan provides the working of each touchpoint and the means to access them, for whatever ends."

Araina squinted, then blinked at a steadier, tighter version of her great-aunt's familiar handwriting and the thought of what it was said to hold.

Tanzan let her breathe and slowly recoil from the page before he continued, "As I said, your great aunt was renowned for much, but only at the very end of her life did she learn her true legacy had become relevant beyond a theoretical history. The changes that drove her death, along with so much else, were a horrific confirmation that someone had stumbled upon at least one touchpoint and untethered it from its place."

"But that can't…Tanzan, that…it can't be… *That's* the reason? For all of—"

"That is why there is no potency left in what few plants you could find. That is why Landers are so mystified by the failure of their crops and livestock. That is why our work is feeble, and why your home will not be home for much longer. It will instead dry up or flood with caustic, barren tides when some misguided attempt at utilization or exploitation is carried out."

"That can't be…"

"It is, my dear. It's in motion."

"But yesterday… Yesterday, you said, what has been undone can be set right. You told me so I could sleep. Did you just say that so I could sleep?" Araina demanded.

"No. I also told you that because, for now, it is true. The laws accessed through the touchpoints cannot be fully changed without the proper arrangement, a collective one. Nor can they be accessed without the workings in this book. Their connections are strained, but they have not yet unraveled."

"But how do you know that?"

"If otherwise were true, it would be *quite* apparent. I doubt we'd be breathing, let alone speaking to discuss it."

"So having this book, th-this book and key…means that everything that's needed, it's all here?"

"Not all of it. Kerikan had not yet mapped the Meridian's Reflection."

"Then how will—"

"I've since taken care of that. Not alone, but with some special resources and connections of my own. Who would get to that first was a friendly competition your great aunt and I had for some time. One I was late to finish. Very late. But not too late. There was enough time for me to inform her and her to send you here with her work."

"But how do you know for certain no one besides the both of you had all this? You said someone stumbled across a touchpoint and caused all this mess. How do you know it was an accident?"

"Because *no one* could have what Kerikan uncovered over all those years. No one has her abilities. I cannot imagine it being done in less than ten lifetimes with anything short of who she was and what she collected. But you are bright to question that, Araina. There are those who will try, even as the consequences are wrought upon all that is living. That's why we will use this book and key, and a few other advantages, to prevent that. We will then restore what has been undone."

"Where does one even begin?"

"Touchpoint by touchpoint, until there are no more to be unearthed. And then, we reclaim whatever has been taken."

"How will you know from whom must they be reclaimed?"

"There are very few over the whole of this world who have the armies, alchemy, and the assets. It's not difficult to conclude. There's a reason why Vexhi march and conquer so steadily these days. There's a reason why Svet Hagen counter to hold land and dwindling resources. But for the time being, that's only a detail. Only an obstacle in a long path ahead. We've our first steps and considerable advantage, in large part because of what's on this table."

"And then what? You collect and then reclaim, and then…you said even Crestfolk couldn't hold hope of altering them properly."

"Indeed. Which is why we seal them, through the same workings that alter them. Instead, we bind them untouched and invulnerable to hands, bounties, or hubris. To be unmovable from and of soil."

"How is that done?"

"It's all here, Araina. It's witchery. It's in this book, defined by this liquid, brought by you. That is why you are owed thanks with Kerikan. Yes, it's your

Crest that has people here eager to meet you, but that alone is not the reason for a banquet."

"I just carried them. That's no comparison to—"

"She's no longer with us to thank."

"Please don't rely on me as her placeholder, Tanzan. Clearly, you know that I—"

"We'll rely on you for no such thing. Besides, it's unnecessary. You've a place of your own, not one to hold for her. After all, these resources were not of much use to us had they remained at your cottage. The same is said of you."

Araina shrank back from his statement and sat rigid in the plush armchair. As she looked at a newly energized, quickly maturing Tanzan, she recalled Kerikan's briefly sustained renewal and the instruction that her finest cloaks and shawls be tossed to the cottage's sandy floor.

"What do you mean?" she uttered.

The warlock smiled at the swirl of inquiry and dread in her eyes. "Oh, it's little more than a whim, my dear. Well, a bit more than just a whim. Let's call it a possibility. You've brought quite a lot of that with you. I want to see, that is, a few of us want to see, if whims and possibilities might amount to a sturdy idea. Maybe even a wise approach. That's how we ended up with all this in the first place. But there's much to confirm, yet. And to assist with that, someone is waiting to meet you."

"...Because I'm a Moonserpent?"

"While I can't speak for him, I doubt that's of much consequence, considering..."

"Considering what?"

"Who he is."

"And that is?"

"Someone you've as much reason to meet as he has to meet you, and quite regardless of your Crest. So you needn't feel any pressure, my dear. Now seems as good a time as any to call on him, but we'll save him steps and treat ourselves to a change of scenery."

Chapter Ten

Decisions and Orders

S ol had grown accustomed to unusual sights while living among Crestfolk, but the elf, watching him from atop a cracked column beside a girthy pigeon, was notable. On learning he had been spotted, the clearly perturbed elf climbed on the pigeon's back. Though they appeared poised to fly, they kept their vantage point. Sol paused, waiting for words from the onlooker, but only stares were exchanged. He then proceeded through the stained-glass bordered doors.

"Dunno what that one was. Moves like a soldier but where's the uniform? Ain't one'a Rainy's folk. Don't like the look of 'im," Den grumbled to Pidgie with a scowl.

Without lanterns to shadow and shorten its reaches and without the clatter of pewter, glass, voices, and song, the central hall felt like an entirely new place in the light of day. The soldier had tasted no equal to the grand meals served within, yet he preferred it as an echoey stone cavern that so defined the landing of his boots, until he stopped and assessed the advancing footfalls and a creak of a door hinge. In a short lapse, his hand moved to the sword at his hip. He let it fall away to link with his left behind his back and stood among the stretching tables, waiting for the two figures to move from their silhouetted approach.

"Solairous," Tanzan greeted. "My thanks for your coming so soon after being requested. I'm pleased to finally introduce Araina of the Moonserpents. Araina, this is Sergeant Solairous Ekwidou."

As he raised his head from a quick bow, Sol's visage, stately though scarred, gave Araina no feeling for the reception. The perfectly balanced blankness of it all was palpable, almost unnervingly so.

"It's nice to meet you." Araina smiled though gained nothing from it.

"Solairous has been staying at our barracks," Tanzan explained. "He joined us not long after a mission some distance south. I wanted him to meet you and share something unusual he encountered. Solairous, if you would be kind enough to enlighten Araina, I'd like you to recount what led you to our grounds."

"All of it?"

"What you told us just after your arrival." Tanzan gestured to the seats at the end of the centermost table.

With his eyes set on the surface, Sol's search for words slowly uncovered, "I don't know how familiar you are with battlefields. Fronts, specifically."

"Not very. But the front is where the opposing forces meet, correct?" Araina responded.

"Yes. In the last few battles, mostly near the front…well, there've been these strange…forms. I don't know that I should call them that. They're almost like shrouds, but also like ink. They move through the air and block out everything behind them. It's hard to describe."

"However you can, Solairous. I'd like Araina to hear how they move and what occurs,"

The soldier's dark eyes returned to his hands. Araina's view fell to them as well, then to his face, and back to his knuckles and wrists. Thick and thin scars crawled his skin. They slipped from under his sleeves. One ran from his right temple to his hairline, another crossed his cheekbone just below, while another one flanked his recently shaven chin.

It was briefly dented by contemplation as he explained, "They float and they move, until they…seep in."

"Seep in?" Araina asked.

"Eyes and mouths, mostly. Sometimes into wounds, if accessible. I thought they were something the Vexhi made. They have the strangest beasts at their disposal. But, these are different. They don't care which side you're on. They've gone into Vexhi the same as they do Hagens."

"And when that occurs?" Tanzan prompted.

"When they get inside a body, it goes dead. It still moves, for a few minutes, then they go dead. And then, they're gone. There'll be lines of dead soldiers without wounds. I thought, if they're not in the Vexhi's arsenal, your folk would be the sort to ask if they existed in nature or…something."

"You noticed something else about them, Solairous. About the light?"

Sol nodded and looked back at Araina.

"Seems less likely that it happens to anyone carrying lanterns. At least at first. But with enough time, and if there are a lot of them, even that doesn't matter. I've only ever spotted them at night, except once, in the daylight, at an…unusually hard clash. A slow end to a tough situation."

"The experience Solairous is describing is an encounter with what's been called an umbra," Tanzan elaborated.

"An umbra? So…a shadow?" Araina endeavored to clarify.

"It's not merely the absence or obstruction of light, my dear. They are presumed to be related to a specific role in our world, one of process and transition. It's been suggested that they are carriers. Possibly, collecting life from what has passed and guiding it elsewhere. It was astute of Solairous to wonder that they might be a natural mechanism. But one of which we should know nothing. One that should never appear or act without a natural or ordinary death. But that's not what you've seen, is it, Solairous?"

"No. These were soldiers on their feet, able-bodied and mostly unstruck, but they writhe and fall. You see one sink in, the body flails, and then they fall down dead."

"We've taken to calling them umbras, Araina, but they shouldn't have a name because we shouldn't know about them. They shouldn't be rising and working ahead of being called. But, per Solairous' accounts and a few others, that seems to be what is occurring. I have every reason to believe it's rooted in matters of which we've just spoken."

Araina kept deathly still but for her eyes. "So they would be stopped in the process of restoring everything else?"

"I think we have to trust that will be so. You sound fearful, Araina, though I think you might have little reason to feel such. I've asked Solairous to share these things with you, but now I will ask you to share something with him. I know I urged you to keep your ability between the both of us, but I'd like you to make an exception now."

"Here?"

"Yes. I only want him to see what's possible. Nothing more. Solairous, please pay close attention. Never mind the workings of it. Araina, if you please and when you're ready."

The witch curled her fingers firmly into her palm and left her chair. Her eyes kept down and clear of her onlookers as she moved several paces from the table. Her quaking palm was presented, and just above, a sphere of light took shape. The witch failed to absorb their reactions. She too stared into the illumination over her palm and thought to Sol's mention of lanterns and Tanzan informing her that any fear of what he called umbras was, for her, unmerited.

"Oh…no," she exhaled and finally looked up.

Sol's iron countenance had fallen away to a slow astonishment—below it, an instant calculation of what had felled comrades and foes alike and what this young woman held. It fast laid claim to the most unexpected, unusual of sights encountered since his passage into Crest borders. All stock he had taken of her when she moved from an approaching silhouette suddenly shifted. Tanzan looked at both of them and could not deny a smile.

"It doesn't end there, does it, Araina? Do you remember what followed after you asked what to do with it? There is a very large fireplace to your left, one even sturdier than that in my study. If you please."

Araina closed her eyes. The light quivered through her fingers. She thought to fold them, apologize, and walk away, but past that, she could picture nothing. She then thought how the pieces would fit when she sent that light into the stone, and beyond that, all the shadows and horrors into which she might be expected to send that same light. How the gap between another empty fireplace and an umbra would be bridged remained elusive as it was terrifying. Though the wondering chilled her, it swelled the light.

Araina inhaled, spread her fingers, and sharply tossed it forth—partly driven by the hope that no more of it would remain in her body. Just as before, it flew, faster than sight could hold it, and boldly crashed into the stone. It filled the dark cavity for an instant, drew up rock dust, caked ash, and shallow tremors, then it dissolved. She let her arm fall slack to her side and her eyes drop to the floor.

"Solairous, no one beyond these walls has witnessed what you have just now. Its very concept is unknown outside our borders. Araina, I've said little of what you can do, because, based on more recent happenings in our world, its significance is now very apparent. Now that you've some idea of that, there are considerations underway of which you should be—"

"You need me to fend off these things, don't you?" Araina snapped. Both Tanzan and Sol stared back in silence at her increasingly fracturing inquiry, "You're going to have me to do that, aren't you?"

"Araina, you are a witch, not a soldier. You are not given orders," Tanzan said.

"What then?" she asked, losing her breath. "Why else would you have me standing here?"

Tanzan slowly rose from his seat. "Because, you will be asked to make decisions. Decisions that cannot and should not be made without a full and honest view of—"

"You'll ask me to go out there? In battle? At the front?"

"Is that what you see yourself doing?"

"I didn't see myself doing any of this!"

"Solairous," Tanzan swiftly addressed the soldier with his eyes fixed upon Araina. "In your opinion and experience, do you find any use in fending off umbras, one by one, by throwing a witch into the frontline of battle? Would that be a wise approach under any circumstance, let alone to what we face?"

"No. At least not a sustainable one."

"What do you suppose would happen the instant Vexhi learned of what you've seen today?"

Sol's dark eyes went to work before he carefully answered, "There'd be an effort to capture. And...utilize."

"To be nothing but clear, Araina, sending you into battle would be a terribly useless and wasteful tact. Beyond that, the grandniece of my oldest and dearest friend will not be put in such a position. You are indeed going to be asked to use your abilities, but not in the capacity you're imaging or fearing. You're needed for something much greater."

"Greater? Greater than that?!"

"Yes. What you carry in your body is luminous. It can be used to beat back the essence of death risen too early, but that is simply an advantage. It's not your end."

"Then what is?"

"This is somewhat untimely... Before anything was asked, the intent was to further discuss..."

Tanzan sighed and looked away from Araina to Sol, whose robust blankness had all but returned, with the exception of a sharp and thorough certainty—mostly worn on the curve of his right cheek and in another divot in the scar beside his chin.

The steadily aging warlock muttered to himself, "I suppose it's a given." He looked back to the witch, made static before the fireplace but for her shuddering fists. "You already know what is required. We discussed it this very day. The touchpoints, uncovered, carried, and sealed. It needs to be done as quickly and quietly as possible, by someone who can move through Lander and Crest borders alike. That cannot be done with an army, it cannot be done with a squad, and it isn't done anywhere near a battlefield."

"But I—"

"And yet, it's not done alone, but with a guide who knows how to track and travel, and clear of detection. And with a survivor of umbras, one who knows how to separate them from ordinary shadows. And with a warrior, who can fight, fell, and outmaneuver the earthy forces that would hinder our movement."

"But even with all of them—"

"They're just one person. The one seated just there. We needn't more than pairs of rightly skilled hands and strong steps. And a decision."

Araina further tightened her shaking fingers, which did little to steady her voice as she countered, "Even with those things out there, and even with this light…there must be another who is better suited to this! You explained it to me yourself, Tanzan, why I'm able to cast. You said it was ache stored and transformed. Where are the origins of that but in shortcomings? Yes, she was sharp in seeing and stating them, but they are no less true! There is nothing of me as a witch but unmet expectations! What if this is to be my greatest? A link to a loss does not begin to—"

"Every Crest general and high priestess's prodigy of a child, grandchild, niece, and nephew have been suggested and considered. All of them immaculate in their studies and skills. They've met and surpassed every expectation. They're true naturals at countless aspects of witchery, but of what value is that in this?"

Araina did not respond or move but for her quivering.

Tanzan fixed a severe look on her. "We need someone charged with a task who will see it through. We need someone who fully understands, not only what might be lost, but what has been lost already. And if she has light at her fingertips, all the better. Not one of us could imagine how this would take shape, so how can we be sure whether there'd ever be such a thing as a perfect remedy? You and Solairous, arriving as you have and carrying what you do, simply make the most sense for what lies before us. And while we have you both, here and now, what we do not have is time. But it is a decision, not an order."

"How is it a decision? How is it anything but an order?!" The witch's left hand curled into an empty claw, almost flaring along with her questions.

"Because you can still say no. You can return home, just as you intended this very morning. Then, we will continue, with whatever remains for as long as we can, whether whims or possibilities come through, or until our slow death is complete."

Araina dropped her eyes from the warlock's. After a stilted stream of air, she proposed, "What if…what if I were just there for light? What if someone better, someone more proficient, would be the one to—"

"Because that is unnecessary. None of what's being asked is beyond you. You simply must decide."

The witch brought her hand to the star hung around her neck. Its former point of suspension fell vivid behind her eyes and the scratch of the red-tail's talons dragged through her brain.

Tanzan watched the quaking in her chin cease and tenderly offered, "The matter is pressing, my dear, but there is still some time for you to—"

Araina splintered his conciliation to contend, "It seems I cannot do otherwise."

In the sunlight beyond the stained-glass framed door, Araina stood and waited for the sharp tone to clear in her skull. It crescendoed with her answer, blocking out everything beyond Tanzan's smiling response, his hand upon her shoulder, and suggestion she go take some air. Sol followed after a moment, said scant words, bowed his head again, and left across the field.

Her ears eventually cleared as she watched the song sparrows poking at the grass. Their quick movements and the breeze shifting the tresses over her shoulders made all feel untethered. Everything in the world seemed in motion but for her form and being, now weighted by a purpose. She was thankful to finally be left alone with it.

"See, Pidgie, told ya she was gonna hav'ta come out sooner or later."

Araina turned and discovered Den sitting with Pidgie upon the ledge of a stained-glass panel.

"Hex-bile. I almost forgot…"

"Yea, figured ya could use a reminder." Den climbed on Pidgie's back and the two of them swooped to the ground, startling away the sparrows. "'Course, wasn't sure if you were waitin' for us to show up or just watchin' that bandit guy leave. Somethin' suspicious 'bout him."

"Solairous? He—"

"'Nother stuffy name. What'd he want?"

"Nothing. You know I came very close to saying that I'm almost glad to see you."

"But instead you're definitely glad to see me, right?"

"You're at least a change of tone."

"From the looks'a ya, you're overdue one. What ya been up to in there? Ya said ya ain't gonna take long and ya barely come outta there since."

"I should tell you now, this is going to take much longer than I expected."

"Whatcha mean?"

"I'll not be going back the way we came. Not for a while." Araina's voice disappeared into a strained exhale.

"Huh?"

"It's not important. But, you should probably be on your way. I've to go back inside soon. And, well, I don't want to keep you from any opportunities."

"None've come up." The elf shrugged. "Slow day."

"A day. Is that all it's been?"

"Uh huh. Sure ya didn't hit that big curly noggin'a yours? So you'll be here for a bit. That means they'll keep feeding ya, right? Figure that means they'll keep feeding us. An' beef or bacon aside, I ain't had food this good in a while."

"Things are different now. This isn't just a few suppers and I'm on my way for you to tag along… This…this is very different."

"Heh, what's goin' on, Rainy? You're pale as ale suds."

"It…it seems I've said yes to something. I don't know if I should have." Her eyes searched the horizon. "I don't know if it's something I can do."

"But someone asked ya to do it?"

"Yes. In a way."

"Ya didn't say, 'Hey, let me do it.'? Someone said 'Hey, Rainy, we want ya to do this,' right?"

"I suppose." She returned her view to the elf. "More or less."

"Then whatcha worryin' 'bout?"

"Many, many things."

"Eh, what for? If someone asked ya to do somethin' and ya mess it up, you ain't really the one who messed up. Person who asked ya did." His simplification hoisted Araina's right eyebrow.

"I don't think it works that way."

"Does the way I look't it."

"What if something goes wrong and someone else gets hurt? What if many do? What if messing up is because…because you're the one who messed it up and things go terribly, terribly wrong?" she countered.

"What if this, what if that," Den dismissed. "Too much wonderin'. Too much thinkin'. 'Less it's gonna decide your next meal, eh, ain't worth the trouble. Just look at it this way, if ya got someone like me and Pidgie, and we're in the air watchin' your back, then there ain't nothing to worry or wonder 'bout. Should see some'a the messes we get outta."

"I already have."

Decisions and Orders

"Heh. You ain't seen nothin'."

"I might have to agree. But regardless, I know *this* isn't as simple as that."

"Feh, humans always think that way. Take it from someone who found'a way over all'a your heads. No trouble stayin' ahead when you're over everyone else's. Just gotta get a higher view."

Araina furrowed her brow at Den's grin. The sight of him and the passenger pigeon just beyond her bare feet almost lifted a smile from her sigh.

She fiddled with the star strung from her neck and shared, "My great aunt once told me that just because something makes sense, that doesn't make it true. And even if something is true, it may not always make sense. That's because, true is always true, while sense is limited to you. I feel like your assurance is somehow in the mix of that."

"What'd I just finish sayin'? Humans make everythin' too complicated. Witches worst'a all."

"Regarding witches, and warlocks for that matter, none've asked you to leave yet? Or have you been lurking out of sight so none get the chance?"

"Huh? Ain't been lurkin' at all. Between lookin' for you, we've gone on'a tour of the place. Found our friends from yesterday's game, a lady gave us some pie and these little chewy berry things. Pidgie's been samplin' feed with these chickens we found. Big fat chickens too. Delicious lookin'. What'a waste. Anyways, what'd ya expect? I'm just supposed'a wait around 'cause you slept-in then disappeared?"

"Well, if they know you're here and they're still feeding you, I suppose it's fine if you stay. ...If you choose. But don't rest on when and where I go. I'm afraid I won't need to employ any guides in the near future."

"Whatever ya say, Rainy. Speakin' of feedin' us, get any word on lunch?"

Chapter Eleven

Starting Points

The spell book and vial waited at a desk nearest the wall of windows. Araina settled in the chair before it as a middle-aged Tanzan poured a cup of tea.

"We need you to retain everything you uncover over the next eight nights. I am certain this will help," he pledged and set down the steaming cup.

"Eight nights?" the witch asked after an inhale of the earthy vapor.

"Indeed. One for each law and one for the arrangement."

"Is there a reason why that must happen at night?" she inquired, gauging the heat of the tea with her lips.

"It was decided that the better part of your daylight hours should be spent taking some instruction from Solairous."

"Instruction?"

"Yes. Rest assured, I've made it quite clear to him that by no means is he to train you for anything close to combat, but he and others managed to convince me that you become familiar with some basic aspects of defense."

"Did he say what that would entail?"

"I imagine it will be only the most essential of lessons."

"You said others managed to convince you?"

"Indeed. You'll have opportunity to meet them at our little supper tomorrow. Now that you'll be with us for a time, you'll be able to attend and make acquaintance with the many who belong to our immediate community, including the Coven. That reminds me, we should set aside time to take a look at that flute."

"The flute, that's right! I—"

"She really didn't forget a thing, did she? Of course, it's not really a flute." Tanzan laughed.

Araina looked at the warlock with exasperated skepticism and asked, "Is it another key?"

He laughed again. "Not quite. Though, regarding the key, a single drop per page should be sufficient. A breath to follow should bring it all to life. I only remember so much of how Kerikan arranged it all, but I have every confidence she kept comprehension and digestibility in mind. What else would've been the point?"

"Well, knowing Aunt Kerikan… Should I read as I reveal? Or do I reveal and then read?"

"I think I'd choose the former. Or perhaps the latter? This is your task now, my dear. You'll find your own rhythm. I shall keep my distance but I'll not be far if you have questions. Aradia and Usil are also here to keep you company, though I don't know how much guidance they'll provide."

Araina looked at the lounging dogs and smiled. Only Usil responded with a full yawn and a lazy drop of his muzzle to his paws.

"Happy harvesting, my dear," Tanzan bade and moved to the other end of the study.

Araina turned to her canine company again. When they offered neither encouragement nor the distraction she would have so welcomed, the witch took a cautious sip of tea, lifted the vial's stopper, and began.

As each drop and breath conjured words, the desk keeping the book, the chair below her, the nearly empty cup of tepid tea, the rest of the room, and all else faded. The pages themselves were lost. Her connection with her being and senses separated. All that remained were the words.

The witch came to the first law and found something complex yet intuitive in its explanation. It was not a simple governance of a force or defined aspect of the natural world, nor was it segmented and stacked as it would be in a book or lesson, but it remained rooted in a logic. There was not a single thread to follow, but a branching and interwoven series of essential things—simultaneously born from and sustaining one another. The thought that someone would attempt or have any ability to unravel it seemed incomprehensible. That something greater could be created in its place was further unfathomable. The very notion overturned her rhythm of the drops, breath, and words.

Araina briefly lifted her eyes and found a thick fog. She thought it the result of staring at the pages for too long, until it thinned and revealed the portrait of Kerikan—without its frame and at an entirely different end of the study. Though attired and adorned in the same grand portrayal, the old witch was wilted as she was on her last day alive. Her cavernous eyes, doubting and desperate, were fixed to Araina.

As though the air and her voice were the same force, a warning rasped across the room, "You'll break it." It converged into a low growl and breath of sharp heat that rolled across the curve of Araina's left ear. With a gasp, she reconnected to her body and started upright, knocking the chair to the floor. Its thud woke Aradia and Usil and stirred Tanzan from his work.

"Araina? Is everything alright?" he called from across the study.

Mouth agape and breathless, the witch looked about the lantern-lit patchwork of surrounding bookshelves and the book upon the desk. A modest portion of its pages were turned and bolstered by black liquid—its reduction in the vial was just enough to note.

Araina craned her neck to confirm Kerikan's image was static upon the canvas. "Yes. Terribly sorry about that."

She righted the chair and blinked at the most recently darkened page. The final word upon it read, *Ecivy*. It kept her eyes until a shadow dulled its distinction. The witch looked up to see a now-elderly Tanzan.

After a survey of the page, he remarked, "We called that the tide law until she revealed its proper address. And it's so much more than that, isn't it?"

"It's almost too much. When you first explained it, I expected they'd be concentrated in a simpler way, as Landers do with their four elements or humours, and whatnot. But this is complex. Motion, and weight, and sustenance, and memory, and...some parts of water. And that's just the first few pages of it." Her eyes left Tanzan's and returned to the book. "Did she not give its name until the end for any particular reason? I probably would have started with that."

"The names are part of the workings that access them. The sounds across their unearthed surfaces are part of that process. Knowing Kerikan, she would have thought it best to keep that behind the knowledge of what they hold. After all, what use is a name without appreciation for what it calls?"

"To think, this is only one. And yet, it is making sense. Perhaps more than most witchery at which I've sat and stared but could not carry out."

"That is good, Araina. Very good. I had not a doubt. You too should be confident in your comprehension. And you must carry that confidence tomorrow evening."

"At the banquet?"

"Yes. But fear not, my dear. There's much support for where you sit and no question among those who proposed and finalized that arrangement. Bear in mind, you come at the end of a long consideration of many. I simply don't want any...opinions to make you question yourself. They are only that now. Opinions."

"Is it absolutely necessary that I attend? Wouldn't staying here and making progress be a better use of time?"

"There's plenty for both. There will be many friendly faces who've been eager to make your acquaintance since your arrival. And before anything else came to light, pardon the pun. That aside, it's as much to your benefit as theirs. The next week will not be easy. The comforts offered here will most certainly be difficult to maintain thereafter. All of us should enjoy them while they're available. Now, you've an early start tomorrow. Solairous requested you meet with him in the southern yard after your breakfast. He also asked if you've carried or have experience with any sort of weapon."

"Carried, yes. Experience...no."

"Well, a starting point, nonetheless. If it's that old long dagger, I would think it will do. Have it with you for your instruction."

Before Den or Pidgie stirred from their nestled place in the drapes, Araina had risen, dressed, brushed and braided her hair, and crept below the bed to retrieve the dagger. With its unwrapping, she twisted and turned her grip to gauge the weight and reach of the blade. A hesitant thrust out and down prompted laughter from the windowsill.

"This place under siege or somethin'?" Den inquired.

"Not that I'm aware."

"So ya just cuttin' off the rest of that mop?"

"I wouldn't have bothered to braid it then."

"Yeah, what's with that?"

"I thought it best to keep out of the way. I have an instruction after breakfast."

"So that's why you're swingin' 'round that butter knife. Finally, some entertainment." The elf lifted himself from the cushion of Pidgie's breast.

"Are you sure there's nothing else you could find to occupy yourself? Solairous will be there and you've made it quite clear you don't care for soldiers."

"I'll hold my nose. Be worth it to see what ya can do with that thing besides cut hair. Heh, don't go lookin' at me like that, Rainy. C'mon, don't wanna be late for your *instruction*."

* * *

After a meal and mugs of coffee so fine they could not be rushed, Araina, Den, and Pidgie were shown a narrow outdoor path to the southern yard. Through lines of spice-tone laundry and along vine-crawled wall remnants, they came to a field with a solitary tree. Sol waited at its trunk. In addition to the sword at his hip, a quiver of bolts was fastened to his belt, and a single-grip crossbow was slung on his back. Another quiver, filled with arrows, rested with a bow not far from his boots.

"Good morning, Solairous…or Sergeant Ekwidou?" the witch cautiously greeted.

"Just Sol is fine. Though I notice your folk tend toward formality."

"Some do, but not all, Sol."

"So these are friends of yours?" He tipped his view to the elf and pigeon as they landed in the grass near Araina's feet.

"Den Handkey and Pidgie," she introduced.

"Should I ask which is which?"

"And what 'bout you, huh?" Den pointedly dismounted Pidgie. "Nice try, dressin' like some thief. Too bad the thickness 'a that skull up there gives ya away as some kinda soldier. What's the matter? Too dumb or ain't dumb enough to pick 'a side?"

"For the time being I'm on the same side as your friend," Sol tepidly answered then looked at the witch. "Tanzan didn't mention we'd have any spectators, Araina…was it?"

"My apologies. He seems to think this will be entertaining. And yes, it's—"

"It's Rainy," Den interjected.

"It's Araina," she clarified and flintily eyed Den. "Please don't let him be a factor. He'll grow bored and be off soon enough."

"Heh, depends how much 'a a spectacle ya make 'a yourself, don't it, Rainy?"

Before she could counter or curse him, the elf returned to Pidgie's back and they flapped over to a wall remnant.

Sol reclaimed Araina's attention on observing, "I see you have a misericorde." He gestured at her side. She offered him the hilt. He raised and tilted the blade before his eyeline. "This is a bit broad for what it should be. Wager someone had this specially made. Ever do anything with it?"

"Nothing…decisive. It's only an heirloom, though it seemed better than nothing upon leaving home."

"It'll suit our purposes. You don't have a scabbard for it?"

"No. I don't know that it ever had one."

"We'll get one made before it's necessary." Sol extended the hilt, and as she took it, assessed, "So you're right-handed."

"Yes."

"We'll start with that. Let's see you make a fist."

The witch lowered the dagger to the ground and curled her fingers over her thumb. She held it as if offering something. Sol grabbed her hand and began to squeeze.

"Hurt?" he asked.

"A little."

"And now?" He tightly pressed her fingers into her thumb.

"More so," she confessed.

Sol lightened his grip and unfolded her fingers. He tucked them into her palm and latched them below her thumb.

"That's a fist. What you had was a soon-to-be-broken hand. They tend to be of little use. Yours is still in a good state." He took a step back and rolled his shoulders to broaden his chest, then prompted, "Go on."

"Go on?"

"Let's see you throw a punch."

"Yeah, Rainy, go on! Right in the jaw!" Den encouraged from his place on the wall.

"Your hand still hurt from when I squeezed it?" Sol asked Araina.

"Not particularly."

"Let's say it does. Settle the score, but preferably not in the jaw. Our heights might make that awkward."

"I'm not going to hit you," she protested.

"You're that strong, huh?"

"That's not what I said or meant."

"Say or mean whatever you want, but show me what you can do. Go on."

"I'm not going to hit you, Sol."

"How did you think this was going to work, Araina?"

"I don't know but I've never hit anyone."

"Then we really need to get started."

With fear of testing his patience winning over fear of causing him harm, the witch inhaled and extended her fist into the center of Sol's chest. Though it was like hitting densely packed sand and no more climatic, Araina withdrew and immediately stammered out a string of apologies before noticing Sol was smiling.

"Well, you've got something in that arm and you take instruction, eventually," he declared.

"Was that all you needed me to prove?"

"No. Think you can do that again, only faster?"

"I think so, provided I had to."

"Let's say that you do. Let's say you're in a situation that doesn't involve any convincing. Instead, you just hit someone because you have to. Make sense?"

"Depending on the situation, I suppose…"

"Well, let's say this is one of them and my hand is that someone. It's someone who's going to attack when and where you least expect it."

In a smooth, sudden motion, Sol sidestepped behind Araina. As she turned to follow, he made a full revolution, sending her into an awkward spin. His open palm swept around the other side. Araina closely spun to meet it with her fist. Sol dropped it with the strike and raised the other in a blink. Araina gasped but struck it down in turn.

"So we're working with a bit of strength and a few reflexes. Let's take them on the offensive. That means you're going to advance. I'm going to step back as you strike and you're going to keep me moving. Got it?"

"I think so."

"How many times have you hit me now?"

"Three."

"And I'm still in one piece. That means you can strike harder. Plenty of open land behind us, so we'll go as long as you've got. Your right to my left. Your left to my right. Ready?"

Araina nodded and answered Sol's stance.

His palm rose and she struck, one after the other, proceeding pace by pace, until they moved beyond any wall remnant or vine-covered step.

Once the blows of her knuckles faded, Sol told the breathless witch, "Your persistence is promising. Maybe it'll outlast your politeness. Again, heading back. This time 'til we reach the tree. We'll try an experiment."

He stepped behind her and turned. With a deep draw of air, Araina again advanced.

At the lone tree, Sol let her find her bearings and stooped to pick up the bow and quiver in the grass.

"What you did yesterday, with the light, you can do that anytime?" he asked.

"It seems so. I've only just learned I can do it."

"You don't know how quickly you can…loose it?"

"Not quite, but at least as quickly as you saw yesterday."

"What about your aim? Think you could hit an arrow out of the air?"

"I've certainly never tried."

"So this'll be a lesson for both of us," the soldier concluded.

He removed the crossbow from his back and the quiver from his hip. The one carrying arrows was secured in their stead. With the bow in his grip, he moved across the lawn.

"On the count of three, in this direction." He extended his arm across a perpendicular path from Araina. "See if you can knock it as it passes."

She readied her palm. Sol slipped an arrow, nocked it, and drew.

"One. Two. Three."

With the release, Araina summoned and sent her light straight through the air, missing the arrow. Before she could express frustration or otherwise, an incredulous shout burst from the wall remnant.

"What?!"

"Hex-bile," the witch hissed to herself. "Forgot about him again."

"What was— How'd you— Rainy!"

Araina slowly shut her eyes before looking over at the elf and coyly asking, "I'm sorry, did you say something?"

"What is that?! With the—with the light thing! Have ya been able to do that the whole time?!"

"Would you mind not shouting about it, please? And obviously not. I would've used it back in the woods."

Den dropped off the wall with a bounce, leaving Pidgie undisturbed in a mid-morning doze. Sol also moved to approach the witch.

"Guessing he only just learned you can do that as well?"

"Yes," she sighed.

"Rainy! You got lightning comin' outta your hand!" Den continued to shout.

She briskly crouched down. "Den, do you remember yesterday when I mentioned I said yes to something?"

"Uh huh…"

"Well, it has a lot to do with what you've just seen. And you need to stop shouting so."

"Is that a witch thing? Like that fire trick? Can they *all* do that?"

"No. And no…unfortunately."

"Do it again," the elf insisted.

"If you stop making a fuss, you'll see it again, but you must keep your voice down and you mustn't tell anyone about this!"

"Whom'I gonna tell? Pidgie? I just wanna see it! G'head." Den scurried across the grass to reclaim his vantage point. "C'mon then! Another arrow!" he called out with a grin.

"Doesn't look like he's bored yet. Think he'd be an easier target than an arrow," Sol wondered aloud.

Araina did little to hide her snicker, which slowed into a sigh as she declined, "Maybe if he wasn't so close to Pidgie."

"Another arrow then," Sol stated and turned to reclaim his position across the yard.

Araina took aim as he readied the bow.

The eighth arrow finally succumbed, scantly tipped out of the air. The tenth was a sure strike. After more hits than misses, and just as Araina's light started to flicker and drag, Sol had her take up her dagger. He unsheathed the sword at his side, revealing a blade that was almost pure white through its hold on daylight. Between the simple guard and crested pommel, the hilt was complexly wrapped to form a precisely tailored grip.

"Everything I show you will be about knocking a blade away. Tanzan's been quick to remind me, I'm not training you for combat," he remarked. "I mention it because of the look on your face"

"I'm sorry. It's an impressive-looking sword. Though I know nothing about them."

"Like that misericorde, this was a specialty craft. Made for a certain approach. A balance of slash and stab, contact and clear. Depending on the situation, as you put it."

"This isn't one of those, is it?"

"No." With his affirmation, the lesson began.

By midday, she learned how to push away several sorts of offensive strikes using the dagger's blade and guard, and with a promising degree of strength. As she centered her weight out of a parry, Sol caught her braid from its swing. Though he did not tighten his grip, Araina froze.

He let it rest across the crook of his hand and informed, "The women soldiers knot their hair or cut it so no one can get ahold of it."

"Understandable. Traditionally, witches keep it long."

"Well, for a witch, today was a good start," he declared and dropped the braid. "Might get away with your life in the right situation. We'll see if that can't be improved over the next week."

"Seems it'll be a rather full one. I'll be glad when this banquet is out of the way."

"Not looking forward to it?"

"Are you?"

"Your folk serve the best food and drink I've had in a while. Maybe ever. Nothing special to you though, huh?"

"That's not quite true. Though, for what the feasting may be, it's the folk that have me eager to be done with it," Araina acknowledged through a dense breath.

"Thought these are your folk."

"They are. Well, I'm not quite… It's just that Tanzan warned me to expect some scrutiny."

"What's that matter?" Sol shrugged. "Decision's made. You wouldn't be out here otherwise."

"I suppose. But still there's the facing of those who are questioning that decision, as well as those who aren't questioning it."

"Which ones've got more of your concern?"

"Both. Though, perhaps the latter. I wonder if they might be trusting things that aren't there. I'll take combat training over a room full of high expectations."

"Keep that in mind for tomorrow."

Chapter Twelve

Arrangements

After passing through the emptied laundry lines, Araina, Den, and Pidgie parted from Sol. Trinera hardly waited for them to pass the threshold into the keep before Araina was directed to the upstairs bath. Den and Pidgie opted for the pitcher and basin waiting in the room.

Following her scented soak, the witch was intercepted by two young women, introduced simply as Imari and Dionis, who said little as they led her to a room furnished with tufted settees, an upholstered dressing screen, and an overwhelming spread of jars, bottles, combs, brushes, pins, and picks. It seemed as though every tool and tincture had a part to play in sorting Araina's hair.

Dionis marshaled much of it in precisely layered braids and twists, pausing only when she reached the curiously cropped portion. The rest was set in ringlets down Araina's back and ornamented with sprigs of periwinkle. A feather was dipped in dark paste and grazed along her eyelashes while her lips were stained with a maroon syrup. A bowl of rosy powder was then selected from the arsenal, but after gauging the strong flush already claiming Araina's cheeks, Imari returned it to its place. Presented with a mirror, Araina uttered her thanks and remarked on their skill—and refrained from asking if they would also assist in removing it all once the festivities ended.

Trinera appeared over her shoulder, carrying a gown of frosted violet and a lavender chemise—made of such fine fabric it would have shown gossamer-sheer if not for its billowing layers. Araina carefully slipped within and stepped out from the dressing screen to be laced into the gown. Lengths of ribbon were worked in and out of the eyeleted panels, stiffening the fabric below the gathered bust and around the waist. The rest parted to reveal the chemise. Yet more lacing was required down the elbow-length sleeves, which ended in diaphanous drops of fabric nearly trailing to the floor—making her feel like some mix of damselfly and scissor-tail.

After surveying the cohesive effect of Araina's tinted, coiffed, and gowned appearance, Trinera proposed, "Perhaps you'd prefer some lace or a pendant for your neck?"

"If it's not unbecoming, I'd like to keep the star."

"It is not unbecoming. I'll let you return to your friends so that we may also prepare. I'll lead you downstairs after."

Back in the room, Araina found Den strutting before the mirror in his own ornate attire. An embroidered doublet, dark trousers, and polished boots were impressively scaled to his proportions. Instead of the brown kerchief, a fine blue cap topped his tiny round head. Pidgie was not formally dressed, much to Araina's disappointment. Though she so wanted to see the passenger pigeon in a little sash or miniaturized ruff, he was simply snoring in the light of dusk. The fluffing and landing of his feathers gave the witch some guidance for her own pace of breath against the gown's lacing. She finally gained a rhythm only to lose it when an opulently clad Trinera appeared and led them away.

Music and mirthful exchanges swelled with their descent. After far too short a passage, they arrived at one of many archways to the central hall. The crowd within floated like autumnal leaves caught at a river's edge. The brilliant hues of their finery were all at once deepened and haloed in the light of dangling lanterns and rows of candelabras. Tiny, twinkling glints fell over all of it, birthed from candlelight behind prismatic vessels, which were layered in fireplaces in place of flame.

Taken by the beauty and the overwhelming cacophony of sound, bodies, and movement, Araina was fleetingly comforted by how easy it might have been to be swallowed into it—out of sight and below notice. That notion unraveled when face after face gradually turned and looked upon Trinera and then Araina at her side. Glowing and heavy reverence was returned with Trinera's unassailably serene smile.

Her smooth nods and rise to the reception were uninterrupted as she explained, "You'll both be free to enjoy the evening as you wish, but for now there are some important introductions and seating arrangements. Den, Tanzan requested that you join him. Araina, you'll be seated with the Coven."

Though the pitting in Araina's center sharpened, she said nothing and went on discreetly attempting to observe the crowd without meeting any unfamiliar eyes. Her view caught Sol, who stood beyond the rows of long tables and among conversing soldiers. Though he was in a tailored uniform jacket, it was the only one in the room lacking a dark green stripe running the sleeve. Failing to reach his eye, Araina continued to search for Sage, Tanzan's granddaughter, even Imari and Dionis—any somewhat discernible face to which she could anchor herself. She remained adrift along the path to her seat, which she learned was among a dozen old women, all dressed in opalescent silks and jeweled in exquisite circlets, cabochon brooches, and swaying earrings.

"Araina," Trinera simply stated and fluidly departed to guide Den to his place-setting.

"So she wears the ring on her finger as well as the nose on her face. Funny how they either grow into or never out of it," the woman nearest Araina's left remarked.

"And there's that mane of tendrils upon her head. Stubborn in that set of kin. Though it seems they tried to batten it into itself," added the one beside her.

"Well, of course. You don't remember? We saw her in the gardens. Though she was quite a bit smaller then, wasn't she," asserted the one across from them.

"No. That was just a few years ago. This one's too old," another on the right objected.

"No, no, no. That was well over a decade ago. Nearly two. You forget how fast time moves now."

"She had short hair," yet another interjected.

"Yes, quite right. Don't you remember? Kerikan cut it after she broke too many combs in it."

"She's the same one?"

"Did you forget that hair grows?"

"Of course not! Why is she just standing there?"

"No one's told her to sit down. She's Kerikan's. She'll stand all night before taking seat without being offered."

"Oh do sit down, Araina. You've been invited to take on this dreadful business, you needn't wait to be invited to a table."

Araina, dizzy from trying to follow their exchange, cautiously fought with the gown to inch inwards toward the table. A seat in their midst did little to aid her comprehension as they continued.

"What would she make of all this?"

"Whatever it would be, she'd make it known. And louder than Tanzan, no doubt."

"Even when he confirmed the casting, I still didn't like it."

"Kerikan wouldn't have liked it."

"What are any of you talking about? Why would she have the pipe then? Kerikan did give you that, didn't she, Araina?"

Araina's stained lips parted but remained silent. She timidly nodded.

"Doesn't mean a thing. The old relic may not even work anymore. Either way, if she's carrying the book and key, so that should follow. Why wouldn't she keep them all together?"

"Oh, don't take everything that woman did as a given. You can't read a mind no matter how often a mouth shares its opinions. Especially from presumption, and based in your memory."

"What did you expect? She leave it back in that chest to wait for some better occasion?"

"What better occasion could there be?"

"Precisely my point."

"Well, what does it matter now? It's all been carried, so it'll all be used. How are you feeling about that, by the way?"

The young witch stammered, barely certain she had been addressed.

"Yes, Araina? Go on."

"I...I didn't feel I could say no. About the flute, I was wondering—"

"Well, of course not, you're Kerikan's. My own granddaughter is a gem. She'll be a priestess one day. She was nearly asked."

"I thought it'd be perfect for my great grandson. I still think so."

"Oh, he's not yet grown into the reach of his sleeves. And you forget about those shadows."

"Well, if not for them, he'd still be perfect."

"If not for them, half this room would be perfect."

"Have we not been through this enough? She is here, it is her, and it is done."

"Indeed."

"If you need any questions dispelled again, Trinera'll be looping back soon enough. The very same goes for you, Araina, as that flushed face shows you've sprouted wonderings in need of withering."

"Trinera? I thought it was Tanzan who—"

Araina's mention of the warlock was met with a round of cackling.

"Oh there's no question about what he wanted, and how quick he is to set things in motion, but Tanzan is Tanzan. Trinera settled it. There're the details and then there're decisions, and they lie with the Coven."

"I gather Trinera is more than just a key keeper," Araina presumed.

"Do not discount key keepers, my girl, but yes. She is also a high priestess, if that's what you're after. Just like the rest of us. It would've been said, some years ago, just as you're likely to become, but things didn't go in that direction, did they?"

Araina shook her head.

"So be it. As there are decisions, there are also directions, unexpected directions. We'll see what you do with them or what they do with you. Now, Araina, keep it low and let's have a look. We've heard enough about it. High time that we see it."

Araina leaned in, discreetly slipped her hand between the maze of crystal, pewter, and porcelain, and summoned light before the Coven.

A stretch down the same table, Den vaguely perceived Tanzan's maundering and Sol's occasional input. The better portion of his attention was set on whiffs of spicy and savory fare, until he was addressed by the warlock. "With that said, Den, has Araina explained that she'll not be returning west for a time?".

"Huh? Uh huh. Somethin' like that. Mentioned you folk're havin' her do a job."

"One might call it such."

"Just did. Hope you're payin' her decent. Seems pretty nervous 'bout it. But, eh, seems that way 'bout everything."

"She hasn't told you what the work entails?"

Den idly shook his head while his view held to the serving plates and bowls sluggishly working their way up the table.

"This big meal a regular thing or just somethin' to do with Rainy's new job?"

"Well, we—"

"Wait. This somethin' to do with those witch stones?" Den finally looked across the table. Sol's eyes shot to the elf, then swung to Tanzan.

"W-witch stones? You know of some type of stones, Den?" the warlock stammered.

"Stones or tablets. Somethin' like that. Been hearin' little dribs and drabs. Big talk in certain circles for the price they fetch."

"What…what do you know about them?"

"Not much. Some fellas say they're just'a trick to catch bounty-sniffers. Some say they're out there but ain't clear what they look like. Some don't care either way, not with the fortune ya stand to get from just the sight'a one. Meant to ask

Rainy about 'em, seein' as she's a witch and all. Kinda forgot 'bout it. Bounties that big an' details that slim'er usually just scavengers' ramblins."

Tanzan dropped back to his chair, mouth agape. Sol moved his focus from the elf and reached for his goblet. After a slow drink, he lowered it and turned it in place on the table. A few notions began to overlap behind his tightened brow.

Tanzan lifted his own goblet. "The margins are not as clear as we thought," he muttered along its rim before releasing an uneasy exhale. He placed the goblet back down. "I need her at those pages, Solairous. You'll have to move faster with your end. Three days. You'll depart the before the dawn on the fourth. Is that feasible?"

"Less time than I'd like. Today's pace was promising though."

"And the casting? Did she…"

"Hit a fair number of arrows."

"Heh, that was somethin' to see," Den chimed in.

Tanzan's view locked on the elf again. "So you're aware of that as well…" Dismayed, he turned to Sol, then pressed his fingertips to his forehead. Sol looked at Den, who appeared comparably perplexed by Tanzan's exasperation.

"So if you folks're sendin' Rainy somewhere, I'm still for hire, if ya wanna send 'er with'a good guide." Den tipped his chin at Sol. "Wait, they got you goin' too?"

The soldier looked back, unblinking, and after a long moment, asked, "That bird goes with you everywhere, doesn't it?"

"Doesn't *he*. And uh huh. Like it or not."

Sol leaned back and aligned with Tanzan's ear to propose, "From the ground, he's almost indistinguishable. Just a pigeon flying overhead."

Tanzan blinked his strained eyes and matched Sol's discreet tone. "I'm not seeing the significance, Solairous. You're suggesting…"

"Could be useful. There are worse scenarios for reconnaissance. If he's come with her this far and he knows what he knows, keeping him close might be better than the alternative."

Tanzan didn't immediately respond. The steaming platters and bowls now before them kept the entirety of Den's attention, leaving him unaware of the warlock's staring.

Finally, Tanzan explained, "The services of a guide would not be required, Den, but if you're interested in other work… Work that requires you continue with Araina and now Solairous…"

"Gotta be honest, I ain't a fan of his sort. Soldiers, I mean. If that's what he even is. But, eh, if the pay's right."

"Well, Solairous might not be what you'd know as a conventional soldier. And we can discuss your rate so long as we have your commitment. That means the utmost secrecy and limited details on where you'll be going and what your company will be doing."

"Like I said, if the pay's right. Ain't got much else goin' on 'sides samplin' your folk's grub." Den crammed an impressive quantity of potato in his mouth. "Lucky for you, and don't tell 'er I said this, I ain't mind Rainy all that much, 'least as far as humans go. That means I'll give ya a break. But you gotta pack us plenty'a food like this."

Tanzan slowly exhaled again. "Solairous, I expect you'll see Araina move from her seat before long. When she does, I'll need to speak with the Coven. I'll leave it to you to inform her of the new arrangements."

As though tipped by a counterweight, Tanzan rose an instant after Araina. She attempted to traverse a path between the tables, as inconspicuously her gown and nerves would allow, while Tanzan marched his way to Trinera at the head. The band also left their place settings, returned to their instruments, and resumed their playing. Others got up to dance, reunite with friends across the room, clear plates and pitchers, or put down new ones.

In the shuffle, Araina was intercepted. Some, as they told her, recognized Mirran and Jekea in her, others wanted to take the time to finally meet a Moonserpent, and still others wanted to ask of Kerikan's last days and the state of the western shore. She tried to conjure responses and steel her manners, even as her heart raced and the gown's lacing stifled her air. Before another string of eager questions devoured the last of her poise, a hand found her shoulder.

"Did everyone enjoy the first course?" Sage asked the tight orbit and was answered with enthused thanks. His smile broadened before he added, "Please excuse us for a moment," and veered her to the outskirts of the room.

"Thank you. Thank you endlessly for that." Araina's voice was as hoarse as it was gracious.

"You looked like you needed to be collected again. I'm due on my trubizar for the next song. Can I lead you to a hiding place?"

"I should prob—" Araina felt another hand on her shoulder, this one's touch was heavy and brief. As she turned, so did Sol's expression—from placidly aloof to slightly perplexed.

"Only me under all this," the witch assured.

With Sage's cordial nod and depart to join the band, the soldier said, "There've been some changes."

"What sort of changes?"

"The elf will be with us."

"You mean when we… You're serious? Oh, not that freelance-everything guide business again. Wait, I thought you know where we're—"

"He's not going to be a guide. Might be useful to have someone in the air. Mostly, he knows more than Tanzan likes."

"What do you mean?"

"It's not just your folk who are now actively looking for these things. We've got more competition than anticipated."

"What will that mean?"

"For now, that there's less time to get started. Three days."

"Three days? That's two a night, plus the arrangement," Araina tallied with her hand twiddling the ribbon around her neck.

"If it needs to cut into defense, so be it. We'll adjust."

"How can I go out there if I'm not sufficiently—"

"Three extra days wasn't going to take you from witch to warrior."

"It would've been three days closer." Her counter almost stirred a smile from Sol.

"But you're a witch, not a soldier, remember?"

"Will you make sure no one follows me or sees me leave? I have to get back to that book."

With his nod, Araina thanked him and gripped the gown to clear its hem from her toes. She hastened to the nearest archway as Sol obscured her path.

When an ancient Tanzan returned to his study, he found Araina at the desk, working in a linen chemise with a dressing gown draped over the chair back. Her hair, hastily removed from the braids and twists, resembled late autumn underbrush scattered with periwinkle petals. Usil and Aradia were a sprawling tangle amidst the witch's feet.

The warlock attempted to pass them and into his chamber, but just as he reached its door, Araina softly explained, "My apologies that I left without a word. Sol told me plans had changed. And please forgive my appearance. I couldn't work in the gown and I didn't dare take the book from this room."

"There are no apologies you could ever give for where you sit. And for your appearance, all that matters is that you appear here. Happy harvesting. And goodnight, my dear."

Tanzan left her in the low light, before the emerging words, and in the company of his snoring dogs.

Chapter Thirteen

Gone to Ash

Sage tucked the latest bundle of sprigs into the final pocket of an oil-coated canvas keeper.

"This last one will stave off hunger for quite a while. It will stifle pangs anywhere from hours to days. It's only a precaution. You'll have more than enough provisions and you should have opportunities to resupply. Though, I don't know if crops have become poor in the northeast. You already know you can't trust foraging. Just take care not to get them wet and they'll last for ages." He carefully rolled the canvas and tied it closed.

"Thank you." Araina attempted a smile as she accepted it.

"Much more to go?"

"I've all the laws and their markings, and how to draw them up. Then there's the sense for finding them. I've been assured that will be clear when I come to the first. It's hard to imagine it from words alone. Tonight is the collective arrangement and evocation, and then tomorrow is…it."

"It's just one foot in front of the other after that," Sage offered.

"I will try to remember that." She looked at him, then across the interior of the conservatory. "That first step feels impossibly far away and yet all too near."

"Perhaps a cup of tea in the meantime? To speed it along or push it back a bit?"

"You know I'd love to say yes to that."

"Back to it though?"

Araina nodded.

Sol could not match the currently teenaged Tanzan and Araina's shared focus on the old rosewood box, not in a study filled with so many unusual things. Even as the witch revealed the iridescent little instrument, the soldier was thoroughly occupied with the metal pendulums suspended over maps, odd contraptions with overlapping lenses, and complicated-looking devices with gears, cranks, latches, and metallic tiles etched with angular and curling symbols.

"I cannot tell you how your family acquired it, but I know it's been with your Crest for quite some time." Tanzan turned the flute before his eyes. "If it is what it's said to be, then it's very useful for a ritual of sorts. It's nothing to do with the touchpoints, but whoever makes use of this will be uniquely capable. At least that's the idea behind this little artifact. And if it can really do what's been said, it's best not to handle it."

"Forgive me for saying so, but that's not very specific. Can you tell me more about the ritual or what you mean by capable?" Araina asked as he returned it to the box and closed the lid.

"I'm hesitant to do so. While I've been told many things, I know little. But I will direct you to someone who can give you proper answers. She, fortunately enough, is someone you'll need to see anyway, which is what I've called you both up here to discuss. I shall show you on the map there."

They joined Sol on the upper landing. After retrieving and partially unrolling a series of maps from a pile, Tanzan selected one and spread it across the desk. Accounting for the warlock's reduced stature, Sol assisted in its flattening and holding.

"You'll see here, this is where the first point on the Reflection takes you. The land will sweep up, in a wooded step before the outer Noxprimma. And, as we spoke, you'll find the town and lake of Dekvhors. Once that first touchpoint is recovered, you'll need the remaining locations. That information will be awaiting you here." Tanzan tapped his finger upon a coastal town and dragged it back slightly.

"On the northeastern outskirts of Radomezen Port, you have friends waiting for you in an old Crest temple. Although, it's less a temple now and more of a small academy. Home to one of the most impressive libraries and researchers below this half of the sky. It's headed by Ceedly of the Drakheirs. She's the key keeper there and a brilliant archivist and historian. Your questions on that instrument are hers to answer, Araina. Most importantly, that destination will lead you to all others."

"But what of the touchpoint that's already been unearthed? How will I—"

"Recovering that one is not your worry. I will only say discussions between the Coven and Svet Hagen command have been underway for our common cause. Troops are preparing to rally at your back. They will recover what has been taken.

Gone to Ash

You will then assemble and seal them. Connected but entirely separate endeavors, my dear. Speaking of that…"

"I supposed the earlier I get to it, the better." Araina looked at the familiar desk.

"Solairous, let's leave her to it. I'd like to run through some further details with you and Trinera. You can also give us a final review of your provisions."

Tanzan rolled up the map and Sol followed him out of the study.

By sundown, Araina had all of it: Ecivy, Fiwrn, Mtolin, Yurkci, Weraln, Celuf, and Aqzim. She had their governances, their markings, the motions to evoke them from earth-borne things, and the scent and weight of air to know they were reachable—vented from an interruption in the Meridian. And finally, she had their joining and sealing in the form of the arrangement and names to bind them, unchanged. Unlike any other lesson taken from words upon a page, or instruction spoken or shown, this was the first to which she felt bound. The small hairs over her skin would not land—as though the knowledge had forced some primal, resilient alertness. It was terrifying and invigorating, shattering and solidifying. With a quivering hand, Araina dared to seek more.

She raised the stopper and let a drop hit the first of the few remaining blank pages. She exhaled across it but the drop would not spread. Instead, it rested, holding and bending the wavering light of the study. It bled slightly, shrank, and then dried, leaving only a stark, irregular dot upon the parchment.

Araina looked at it beside the heavy lines on the neighboring page. Her eyes grew weighted and her shoulders narrowed into her neck. She swept her head out of a droop and rose, trying to assert her consciousness. Stumbling in the low light, she reached one of the armchairs and struggled to keep her eyes open in the shadows. They grew thicker, so much so that Araina could not be sure whether her lids had fallen or if the candles had suddenly been snuffed. A tapping of claws upon the floor sharpened somewhere ahead of her and then across the rugs framing the armchairs.

"Usil? Aradia?" Her calls were met by a familiar layer of growls.

"Stolen, by flame, by pain."

"Please, tell me what you are," she whispered. "I know you are not a who."

"Trust gone blind."

"Are you grief? …Madness? Something else?" the witch asked through a tremor.

"By trust, by pain, by flame."

107

"Araina?" Another voice reached across the darkness.

She opened her eyes to the elderly Tanzan. Behind him, the fireplace snapped and flickered. Its light left little cover for wolves, deceased great aunts, or much else Araina would have anticipated.

"It seems you've fallen asleep, my dear."

"I…I think I remember getting up. And then…"

"But you've completed it. And you know all you've uncovered?"

"Yes."

"And you understand—"

"To reveal, arrange, and seal, by sense and scent, touch and motion, placement and words. It's as though my blood feels thicker with it. How she knew to write it that way… I feel I've never been without it."

"That is very good." Tanzan moved to the book upon the desk. Araina looked at the fireplace, wondering why it was alight on such a warm evening. She stared into it, feeling the heat upon her cheeks and forehead, until Tanzan returned and blocked her view. He held a small book with a woven cover and bit of charcoal.

"Could you draw the arrangement and write the sounds that seal it?" he requested.

Araina righted herself in the armchair and did as he asked. She handed her work to Tanzan, who examined it, smiled, then tore the page from the bindings and handed it to her.

"Now will you burn this, please?"

Araina looked back with unease but rose, and again, did as asked. She stood and listened to the paper hiss and singe away to ash.

"I trust you see the sense in doing so. We've lost the cover of a secret so hidden it didn't exist. Now it's plain as ink. That means it can be found. That mustn't be allowed to happen. Would you see that as sound, my dear?"

"Yes."

"Your markings upon that page were perfect."

"Thank you. I'm glad to know it."

"You've been asked for much in a small collection of days. Some of the greatest things asked of you have been to make one or two very large decisions. There's just one other you'll need to make before dawn. And then after, you will simply have to follow where it leads."

"What is it?"

Tanzan left her and her wary question by the hearth. He walked to the desk, closed the spell book, and handed it to her.

"Burn it," he stated.

"What?"

"Toss it into the fire."

"Absolutely not."

"That is what you are deciding then, Araina? You will leave us vulnerable?"

"No…" The witch tightened her quivering hands to the cover. "No, no, no. How can this even be a suggestion? No. Does the Coven know what you're asking of me?"

"They insisted this be done. I'm giving you the choice."

"H-how can that be? Tanzan, no. No. No, there must be a connection to these words. It cannot only be me!"

"Whyever not?"

"Because I am just—because what if…"

"If that is your thinking, and therefore your decision, you may place that book back upon the desk. We shall hide it away somewhere. Though I can't imagine a truly secure place that would be impossible to reach. Not if someone ultimately wanted it. And there will be a great many who do, and would destroy all else to get it. And then, everything we've worked for thereafter. It might require retaining defenses at the expense of more assertive offensives to recover what has already been taken."

"I see your point, but to trust—to put so much faith in…" Araina swung her head. Then she eased opened her eyes and lifted her view to the old warlock. Her voice fortified and darkened. "This is another one. Isn't it?"

"Another what?"

"An attempt to conjure something. My first step isn't out there. It's in here. And it's not even a step. It's a toss into flame. No. Why else would you or the Coven insist I do this? I would never be asked to do this if I were the only link."

"Is that what you believe?"

"It's just as you said. The best way to keep a secret is to never show there is a secret to be kept," Araina rushed. "I have to believe that this isn't the sole source…that I'm not the only link after this. I have to. If I don't, I won't be able to move from where I stand. And then, of what use is any of it?"

She turned to Tanzan, who gave neither encouragement nor skepticism in response to her words or her straining grip upon the book. Araina looked at the thickness of pages pressed between the covers and the dark traces around the edges—the convergence of her recent days and hours with those long passed by

Kerikan. The witch slowly removed her left hand from the book and took the weight of it in her right. With a toss, she gave it to the flames.

Part Two

Chapter Fourteen

A Broken Bowl

Araina didn't immediately recognize Imari and Dionis through the fogginess of sleep cut short and their tidy appearance in their Crest army uniforms—their hair braided and woven into immaculate buns above their dark collars. Their voices also seemed sturdier as they explained how the long bodice was specially woven to resist tears and fraying but would still be breathable for late summer travel, and how the wide and high-hemmed trousers, almost resembling sailors' slops, would permit uninhibited movement but still appear as a skirt—and not any sort of military garment conspicuous to Landers—and that these articles being a dull black would afford the best cover amidst trees and after dark.

Araina was less interested in the bison-leather sandals—a compromise in place of boots. They assured her that bare soles were one thing from the seashore and through a forest, and entirely another across rock fields and mountain passes. She was shown how to properly weave them around her ankles and promised they would soften with wear. Before letting her ascend to the study, they provided a belted scabbard to keep her dagger at her hip, a cloak for cover and sleep, and a thicker pack to keep all other trail necessities. She added to it the flute in its box and the canvas fold of medicinal sprigs. The woven-cover book with a torn page joined the amassing essentials.

"It will make a suitable field book for sketching, as Kerikan once mentioned you enjoy, but also for chronicling the journey. That carries value for a sense of progress and in anchoring oneself, not to mention for reflection following a return," Tanzan recommended before handing her a quill, a squat vial of ink, and narrow sticks of wax-coated charcoal.

Araina tucked them away and thanked him in a faint, stilted tone.

The ancient warlock then went on to offer, "Forgive me for not being able to see you off, my dear, but my time is nearing. Is there anything more we can give you? Anything more you'll need?"

"Is…*is* there anything more I'll need?" she responded with a dense pleading in her eyes. It defied the resolve over the rest of her face and her stiffened shoulders. Tanzan placed his trembling hands on them.

"Forgive me again. It was a silly thing to ask. Only a habit. I ask it of all who part from this place. Clearly, you are ready and able as you are. There is no question of that."

"Perhaps there is one thing."

"Anything."

"Please push me out that door. Or tell me I'm already late. Or that you haven't time for this. Any of those will do. Otherwise, I fear I'm rather stuck."

Tanzan smiled.

"I will only say you mustn't miss the light of dawn over the Noxprimma step. It's a sight to see it caught in the trees as you rise to meet them. I needn't tell you daylight will not wait for farewells."

"Thank you."

"You are most welcome, Araina. Off you go then."

She turned and let herself into the hallway. The green and amber light fell faint in the blue haze of dawn. Trinera stepped into it from the stairwell.

"The southern yard," she informed with their passing.

Araina's pace slowed at the end of the hall as she perceived the giggle of an infant when the study doors were briefly parted. She then resumed her passage down flights, across landings, and finally out into the new day's air.

Sol waited at the solitary tree, his sword and quiver of bolts fastened on his belt and crossbow strapped between his shoulders. A pack like the one Araina wore at her hip was slung below it.

"Good morning," she whispered.

"Morning."

"I haven't seen Den. Perhaps we should just get on without—" The witch was interrupted by flapping from the gapped wall. Pidgie landed at her feet. The elf on his back yawned loudly.

"This hour ain't fit for anythin' but sleepin'. What's the use in usin' it for leavin'?"

"Cover," Sol answered and began walking.

"Cover from what?" Den asked.

"Cover 'til we reach the wooded step and cover when we leave it."

"Does that mean it will be dark by the time we reach Dekvhors?" Araina inquired, trying to meet Sol's stride across the grass.

"Likely."

"I wonder if that will make the first one harder to find."

"Dark shouldn't matter for you though, right?"

"I suppose that's the idea, isn't it?"

Tanzan's foretelling of dawn and its coating of the treetops was not untrue, though the canopy was more stark than lush. The witch had almost forgotten to expect it. And while it lessened her mettle, it served as an easy indicator of distance from the abundant grounds at their backs. The stiff and unfamiliar wrappings of sandals functioned as a further reminder of every step.

"I'm sorry, I just need a moment." Araina knelt and began to unravel them.

"Sure you want to do that?" Sol asked.

"I know, I know. I'm going to need them more than I realize." She grimaced as she removed the ties from where they dented her skin. "Or so I've been told. I'll take the risk for now. This ground looks smoother than the shore."

"Gets rockier in a few miles."

Despite the warning, Araina slung the sandals around the strap of her pack.

"I'll put them back on if needed. Other than rocky ground, what should we expect over the course of this trail?"

"A slow slope. Land's like a broken bowl. We're heading up the low, broken side. The Noxprimma make up the high unbroken side. Dekvhors Lake is the bottom."

"Rocky or otherwise, it's nice to be traveling with someone who knows the land."

"Ya sayin' I didn't back at Barrier's?" Den challenged Araina's remark from overhead. He and Pidgie kept pace hopping and fluttering between the low boughs.

"I didn't say that. But it's nice to know whether or not there's something like a massive, sucking swamp in your path. By the way, is there one, Sol?"

"No."

"Feh, path's change, alright? Expect one thing an' you're only ready for one thing."

"He's not wrong about that," Sol conceded. "You're talking about Barrier's End?"

"Yes," Araina confirmed. "Have you traveled through it?"

"Not me, but it's infamous among some Hagen. Not an easy passage, I hear."

"Ain't so bad if ya got someone who knows where they're goin', eh, Rainy?"

The witch rolled her eyes.

"That's how you two came to meet?" Sol asked.

"How 'bout we tell that story over breakfast?" Den promptly proposed and directed Pidgie to a low branch in their path.

"We stop when we have more cover." Sol veered to pass them.

"Cover again. This ain't enough? Feh, he supposed'a be in charge'a mealtimes 'part from everything else?" the elf asked Araina as she too sidestepped the branch bobbing under his and Pidgie's weight.

"We'll stop when we have more cover," she echoed.

"I see how it is." Den drove Pidgie to resume his fluttering.

"*It* isn't anything. We've just all our roles to play. And if I remember correctly, yours is one of reconnaissance. Why not fly ahead and tell me when the soil gets rockier?"

"Good thinkin', Rainy. Best way to get'a look at soil is from the sky. If I didn't know any better, sounds like ya just wanna get us picked off by fleshfalca."

"By what?"

"Fleshfalca," Den repeated.

"What are fleshfalca?"

"Birds. Like harpies and vultures in one," Sol answered.

"That sounds made-up," Araina contended.

"In a way they are. They scout enemies, kill them, and bring back bits of uniform, weapons…and whatever else."

"They're trained to do that?"

"They're bred to do that."

With Sol's explanation, a dark curiosity tightened Araina's brow. "By whom?"

"Probably that baron guy," Den said.

"Machalka," Sol added.

"Machalka?" the witch asked.

Both Sol and Den looked at her, then one another. Their collective paces slowed.

"Tanzan didn't get into all that, did he?" Sol raised an eyebrow as Araina's further pointed inward. She shook her head. "Let's get over this slope and find a clearing." The soldier resumed his stride. "Might as well get that sorted."

* * *

Up and over the incline, they set down their packs and unwrapped the first of their provisions. Through the chewing of her apple, Araina kept her eyes on Sol, as though her staring would coax details Tanzan had purportedly missed. The soldier idly ate his seed cake while Pidgie pecked at the crumbs on the ground nearby. To Araina's frustration, it was Den who finally broke the silence.

"Guess this ain't bad for pack grub," he stated through a mouthful. "Not gonna get any fresher than this, huh?"

"This is just for when we aren't in a place to resupply or forage. All the same, now's a good time to forget sumptuousness in favor of sustenance," Araina advised.

"Still an improvement over pemmican and rusk," Sol observed. After the final bite of his cake, he brushed away the remnants for Pidgie, then stood up, stretched, and looked as though he was ready to continue on their path. Instead, he surveyed the trees bordering the clearing and asked, "So you haven't heard the name Machalka before today?"

"You say that as though I should've," Araina replied.

Sol shrugged. "But you know about Vexhi?"

"I know of them." She looked at Pidgie as he approached and set her apple core on the ground for his eager sampling.

"How much?" Sol asked.

"That they fight Svet Hagen, about land, I think. People in Drudgenwood were very uneasy about them. The town was evacuating because they had advanced further west about a week ago."

"You've never seen any?"

"I don't think so. Would I know it if I had?"

"The lower ranks wear grey. Their officers, dark yellow. Machalka's their high commander, among other things. Though, more often than not, he's just called the baron. And if Tanzan didn't mention anything, then you probably don't need to know much. A little surprising though."

"Why is it surprising?"

Sol shrugged again. "Word is he uses alchemy and other things that seem closer to what your folk do. I thought you'd know more than I would."

Araina squinted into the treetops. "Only a detail. An obstacle in a long path."

"What?"

"I would guess that's who Machalka is then. Tanzan mentioned armies and alchemy." The witch sighed. "So he's the reason we're here."

"Did Tanzan say anything more than that?"

"No. It was almost like an afterthought."

"No reason to change that. Just be mindful of Vexhi if you see them. Shouldn't even matter since they don't know who we are and we'll keep it that way."

"Wait, what other animals is he breeding? Is that something we need to worry about out here?"

"I've never seen anything beyond the field."

"It true that guy's fortress is ten miles around? Heard they drained half a' ocean to fill the moat," Den remarked.

"Lot's been said about it," Sol responded then looked at Araina, who was lost somewhere in a contemplation behind her eyes. "Not our concern either way. The miles uphill are though. Ready?"

The witch nodded, rose, and met his steps upland.

The light of their day curved over their passage, which had also shifted from a maze of gapped broadleaves and branching trunks to a narrow trek through rough-barked, bristle-limbed giants. They crowded and then thinned just before the land abruptly dropped and a great lake filled its depths.

"So that's the bottom of the broken bowl." Araina craned her neck to observe the lulling surface and the stretching inlets where it spilled. The moon, full and rising, lit the Noxprimma's quartzite cliffs and deepened the shadows over its foothills. She kept the scene with half a mind to sketch it later.

"Stay closer to this side," Sol advised from a few steps ahead.

"Are we that easy to spot?" Araina sped to narrow his lead.

"Always move as though you're easy to spot and strike."

"I'll keep that in mind. To where are we moving?"

"Down. There're thicker woods along the western shore. Then we work a route east and get closer to your end of things." Sol briefly turned. The placid expectation in his dark eyes nearly stole Araina's footing on the stony trail. She fast looked away, sturdied her grip on her pack, and kept her view to the prongs of Pidgie's tail feathers overhead.

The descent leveled into a thicket. A boggy field of grass and rocks stretched beyond and ringed the vast, dark lake. Sol stopped just short of it. He looked at the elf and pigeon as they landed in one of the bordering trees and informed, "Den's going to take it from here."

"Gonna take what where?" Den impatiently inquired.

Sol reached into his pack and recovered a spyglass. He took a few steps toward the edge of the trees and set his view east. Araina squinted in the same direction. In the moonlight, it was difficult to distinguish the rocky banks from the water's glowing reaches, except for one lined with little specks of sharp cold light.

"You see those lights there?" Sol gestured with the end of the spyglass.

The elf tipped his chin to affirm.

"Do a wide sweep but take it slow. Don't let it look like a loop. See if you can find out what's happening there."

"So ya just tell us what to do and we go do it? Just like that, huh?"

"That's generally how this works."

With Sol's toneless confirmation, a sour little tightness held to Den's jaw. He looked to Araina, who offered nothing through the acute disquiet on her face.

"You two'er lucky I ain't got nothing else goin' on for more money or better food. C'mon, Pidgie."

They departed across the lake. Sol watched their flight through his spyglass.

"Any regrets on offering him a job yet?" Araina asked.

"We'll see what he comes back with."

"What are you expecting or hoping that will be?"

"Remember why we're here three days earlier than planned?" Sol moved his view from the eyepiece and briefly to the witch. Her sigh almost turned into a whimper as she stared at the scant lights across the way.

"This is bad, isn't it?"

"Probably not after a closer look. They've got the right shore but they're too far south, provided Tanzan's map is right. They're still in our way though. North side's too steep to cross on foot. That means we move through whatever's lit up. And that means going through town."

"Will that be difficult? Or detrimental to staying unknown?"

"Depends on what we learn from Den." Sol moved to the very last of the trees and gestured for her to follow. He pointed south and handed her the spyglass. "That's our likely route. Difficult, doubt it. Detrimental, not if we can help it."

Through the glass, Araina observed another series of lights. These were warmer, larger, and layered in such a way that they told of structures and torch-lined streets.

"Going across the lake is out of the question?" She returned the spyglass to Sol.

"You're that strong and silent a swimmer?"

"Strong at least. But I didn't mean swim the full distance. That's a lake town, right? So rather than pass through it, why not *borrow* the first boat we come across, unnoticed, row out to the correct inlet, also unnoticed, swim to the shore, and avoid whatever those lights are altogether?"

"Not a bad plan but for all of that unnoticed. Unnoticed is up to someone else. Never leave part of a plan up to someone else. 'Specially with the moon as it is."

"To ever be disappointed by such a beautiful moon."

Araina looked up at its continued rise. It caught Pidgie's wings as he and Den descended from over the treetops and dropped from branch to branch overhead, tailed by quite a bit of creaking and snapping.

"Full'a Vexhi," the elf reported. "Just lackeys in grey though."

"At the ready?"

"Nah. Passin' in and outta a cave. Regular dressed folk're there too. Mostly haulin' dirt and rock. Ain't armed or nothin'."

"You saw townsfolk in the mix? You're certain?" Sol inquired.

"'Bout half and half. Guys with shovels wearin' grey uniforms or normal clothes," Den explained with a shrug.

"That works." Sol collapsed the spyglass.

"What works? How are we going to slip past all that?" Araina looked to him. He reopened his spyglass and set it on the torchlight in the distance, holding it for a long moment before quickly snapping it shut again.

"No need to slip past. We're going to blend in."

"Blend in? That sounds rather risky," the witch slowly speculated.

"It's all risky, but this isn't going to be as hard as you're thinking."

"Well, that still leaves a wide berth as far as difficulty. Though I'd like to believe you."

"Good, because this won't work otherwise."

"You still haven't explained what that is."

"First we look like them, move among them, and then past them. If we do it right, we can take our time. That means you can take your time when and where it counts."

"I'd prefer that. So how do we look like them?"

"Need to swap indistinguishable for unremarkable. That's why Den's going to find us some laundry."

"Laundry? Feh! Thought I was done."

"Not yet. Find us a clothesline in town and meet us on the outskirts. Then you're on lookout."

"Ya know me and Pidgie're faster when we're kept fed," Den grumbled.

"Perhaps there's a cheese shop in town. May still be open," Araina wondered aloud, looking at the elf.

Without a word, he nudged Pidgie with his foot. They took to the sky.

"Thanks for that," said the soldier.

"You're welcome."

Chapter Fifteen

Uniforms and Guises

A raina left her pack hidden in the brush with Sol's, along with, to her surprise, all of their weaponry. After bitterly returning the sandals to her feet, she followed him to the edge of the trees and south along the shore grass, until they crouched a stone's-throw from the lake's edge.

"I see a lot of perfectly suitable little rowboats," she whispered, staring at a line of vessels moored a short swim away.

"We've got our plan. No rowboats required." Sol eyes were fixed on the town's rooftops.

Araina crinkled her nose at his assertion. After spotting Den and Pidgie, the soldier led her up a short typha-lined slope, away from the lake, and into the outskirts of Dekvhors town.

They came to clotheslines strung between windows. A fair selection of garments, forgotten after sundown, waited overhead. Sol silently directed Den to a faded blue work tunic, which the elf shifted until it came away and into Sol's grasp. A white blouse and red skirt then tumbled down into Araina's narrow catch. Sol lastly gestured to a flaxen shawl, intercepted it as it was freed, and steered them away from the torchlight.

"Try to shadow your face." He handed the shawl to Araina before dropping the blue tunic over his head. The dark sleeves of his bandit's shirt were unfastened and rolled beneath the pale fabric.

"Why?" Araina hoped to gain equally simple cover from the blouse but found the straps and laced center of the bodice were awkwardly exposed beyond the rather-open neckline. With a sigh, she retreated behind a rain barrel, where she unlaced and removed the bodice from underneath. The skirt was thankfully enough to cover the hem of the trousers at her calves.

After the witch returned from the rain barrel's cover, Sol began to assess, "It's just…"

"Just what?" Araina couldn't be sure if he was scrutinizing the overall effect of her provincial disguise or how very low its blouse fell around her shoulders. She veiled her hair with the shawl and tossed the end across her front.

"...Still easy to tell you're a witch."

"To bad there ain't nothin' to be done 'bout that nose," Den remarked with a smirk. Araina narrowed her eyes and thrust the folded bodice at him and Pidgie.

"Here! Do not lose that! I'll need it back the instant I can be out of this."

"Looks like part'a ya's already on their way, Rainy," the elf added with a laugh. Pidgie gripped the fabric in his little claws. Araina huffed another growl and tightened the shawl closer to her neck.

"So now we begin walking to the eastern side?" she asked Sol.

"We'll head in that direction but could do with more information on what we're walking into." He brushed the trail's dirt from the lower portion of his trousers. "Tavern or pub'll do. You familiar with them?"

"I've been in a Landers' pub. Once."

"And she wrecked the place," Den interjected with a grin.

"*You* did that!" Araina corrected and returned her attention to a slightly curious Sol. "I was mostly just there for accommodation...and some information."

"This should be easy for you then. Likely to be a lot of soldiers. When one strikes up a conversation, see what you can learn about what's happening on the eastern shore. You're asking because your brothers are looking for work."

"How will that enable us to pass?"

"I'll cover that end. Just learn what you can." He motioned for them to proceed down the alleyway. "Keep mannered and unmemorable. Don't give anything back unless it's false. Den, you stay close enough to keep watch but far enough to remain unseen."

"...That makes sense. Gonna 'least lemme get'a drink?"

"You're keeping watch outside," Sol clarified.

"I ain't even goin' in? Feh! No promises I'll stick around if ya take too long with your little make-pretend game."

"I'm afraid that option is no longer on offer," Araina reminded him. "But you're not alone in wanting this over with quickly."

"Heh, don't speak so soon, Rainy. Might be plenty'a fellas eager to show ya a good time. 'Specially if ya keep that nose outta view."

She kept her glower on the elf and hurried to close on Sol's lead.

When their steps aligned, he silently directed her down one way and another, crossing over alleys until they stopped behind an empty cart—a modest shield before a well-lit square. Sol nodded at a corner building with arching windows. Its overhung, upper exterior was gripped by dead vines.

"Wait a few minutes after we're inside, then keep on that roof until I signal," he instructed Den before turning to Araina. "Ready?"

She further tightened the shawl and nodded. They stepped out from behind the cart and walked across the square.

The tavern's door opened and spilt out chatter, laughter, and hollers over a scratchy fiddle, along with two young men in grey uniforms. They guffawed and sauntered along the cobblestone, paying no notice to Araina and Sol on passing. At finally encountering Vexhi and the waft of their drunken joy, she thought back to Sol's urging to be mindful of them and dared to find ease in the contradiction. It prompted a small smile, which flattened away after Sol drew back the door for her passage.

The loud smokey tavern was full of grey uniforms, all belonging to men— human men, with not a single woman, dwove, dwarf, or other being among their ranks. Every one of the very few women among the tables and horseshoe-shaped bar appeared to be working. Were they not carrying drinks, slicing bread, or shifting stews in pots, they were turning cards. The motion of their hands appeared all the more dynamic under the locked attention of the Vexhi who sat very near. The coins upon the table were too few to be wagers on chance, but enough to barter for fate.

With Sol a half step behind, Araina eagerly gave way for him to take the lead. She bumped the back of a chair in the process, quashing any hope of remaining unnoticed. Somewhere in the raucous muddle, she could have sworn Sol sighed. He pressed a hand to the center of her back and guided her toward two recently abandoned places at the bar. Araina kept her eyes to the dark, liquor-stained wood and steadied herself upon a wobbly stool.

"Give questions, take answers, stay forgettable," Sol muttered beside the shawl. He smoothly leaned away and propped his elbows on the counter. A barmaid approached from the other side.

"Evening, sir," she warmly greeted. "For you…and miss?"

"Ale and cider'll do."

As the barmaid stepped away to fill the order, Sol quickly and quietly stated, "Take whichever but don't indulge. Remember, brothers looking for work. Shawl."

Before Araina could seek clarity or express comprehension, or lack thereof, Sol shifted toward the man on his right. She then realized the shawl had slipped down her hair and below the blouse's neckline, revealing attributes memorable and notable. She worked to secure the covering and nearly overturned the tankard set in front of her. On steadying the vessel and exhaling every bit of air in her body, the distance between her and the left stool suddenly shrank.

A gruff voice announced, "Break's over."

A landing of tankards on the bar, the scraping of stool legs, and boots shuffling to the floor preceded a dense shadow. It continued to eat the comforting gap beside her. With her vision forward and her shoulders tight, Araina carefully raised her arm and tucked a loose wave of hair fallen over her left eye. It revealed a large hand extending beyond the stiff, bronze buttoned cuff of an ocher yellow sleeve. Dense fingers lifted and then rapped down on the counter.

The thick voice demanded, "O'Barbs."

Araina's eyes swung to the right, but Sol was nowhere in her periphery. Whether he was simply leaning too far out of view was not clear. His voice was no easier to detect in the swelling cluster of sound. The witch was momentarily stirred from an acute unmoored sensation as the barmaid placed an oblong black bottle and pewter cup upon the bar.

"That cider alright for you, miss?" she flatly asked.

Araina found she could only nod. The barmaid turned away. With unsteady fingers, she reached for the tankard's handle.

"Interesting ring," the gruff-voiced man commented.

"Th-thank you."

"Must've been quite a trade." He uncorked the black bottle and poured a dark liquor into the cup. "For a reading?"

Araina's hands hovered near the cider. She took hold of it to hide their quivering and looked over, following the row of bright buttons and ocher sleeve to square shoulders, a stiff bronze-clasped collar, and a stony face below an officer's cap.

"Pardon?" she asked in an elevated pitch she did not recognize.

"That ring's for sealing messages and proving a name. No small thing to give up. 'Less your customer stole it. Have your cards with you now, sweetheart? I pay well if my fortune is favorable and the reading attentive."

"Begging your pardon, sir. I don't do readings."

"No?" The officer lifted the drink and emptied it in a single swallow. "Other services then?"

After pouring more liquor to the very brim of the cup, he shifted on the stool, revealing the breadth of his form and a series of emblems in silver and brass.

"No. I-I'm simply passing through town. My-my brothers, they've been looking for work." With Araina's every stumbled word, the officer's smile broadened, which was then obscured through another greedy gulp at the cup.

"Diggers, eh?" he asked before swallowing the remaining quantity.

"Diggers, sir?"

"Only work they'll find here. Lake's fished clean. Mills all but stopped. But our Baron, he brings work to the people."

"Oh? That's awfully fortu—"

"Takes care of folk wherever he unfurls a flag. His men, us, we take care of them. Steady work. Good meals. Safe roads. Anything they'd ever need. Anything you'd ever need."

The officer reached and pushed the edge of the shawl just near Araina's cheek. She pulled her shoulders in and lifted the tankard to her lips, sending his hand away. She scarcely took a sip, using the vinegary liquid as cover and for far too long. Again, the officer refilled his cup and proceeded to gulp away. Araina placed the tankard on the bar and leaned back, sensing a thick wall of bodies behind her. Somehow the officer's stool seemed closer.

"Could…could you tell me more about it? The work? To ensure they're suited to it?"

"Oh, digging'll suit any sort, but what a sweet sister they have to ask it. Does she have as sweet a name to fit the rest'a her?"

"Ara- Ah- Aradia,"

"Sounds like a seer's name."

"Only a family name. So they would be tunneling? Or mining for something, perhaps?"

"Could call it that. Pay's better though. Better than anyone'll offer these days. And to the digger who'll find the prize, that man'll never have need of work for all his days."

As he returned the liquor to his lips, he finally looked away from Araina, who could not tell if the drawling statement was the effect of the drink or simply some longing for the outcome he described.

"That must be quite a prize. A treasure of some sort? A type of jewel?"

"No jewel. But a treasure greater'an any other," he explained and reached to a purse hung from his belt. His movements were notably strained as he revealed a square of paper with a broken wax seal. Below brief script was an approximation of Ecivy. Araina stifled her gasp at the all-to-close depiction of that which she conjured from a blank page.

Struggling to return the slipped shawl over her shoulder, she again turned for Sol, this time without much discretion. He was gone—his seat taken by a grey-uniformed body. Forms like it seemed to multiply as Araina's eyes darted for some sign of the faded blue work tunic in the dim smoky air. There was none, nor any trustworthy or sympathetic faces to catch her wordless pleads. She could no longer suppress the quickening of her breath. Then she felt large fingers on her chin. They pulled her face back.

"Knew there was something to you. Look as though you seen it before. Not often seers play coy as this. I like it," the officer slurred.

"Is…is that's why your men are so interested in readings and cards? To help them…find whatever that is?"

"An' other services, sweetheart. Know yourself, not many jobs left. But those that hold, they pay. Don't hav'ta be a digger that finds it. Seer, reader, company, all'll do just the same."

"I-I assure you, sir, I'm not a seer or reader or anything. I just felt a bit of faint. The cider is…stronger than I'm-I'm used to. I'm afraid I must… I-I think it best if I—"

"Oohh," The officer flatted his hand over half her lips and cheek. He brought the other to her bare shoulder—the shawl having fallen to the floor behind her stool. "Then we must get ya to a place to rest a'time." He pressed upon her skin with his urging. "I'm no position now myself t'let my men see. Have some time 'fore I make my rounds. We rest together 'til then, eh? Then we see the beautiful moon. The tunnels."

"I cannot. I—"

"Oh, I like a coy sort. Very much. Can't trust 'em, come on too strong. Not you. Just right."

He curled his heavy hand along her chin. His thumb slumped along her right nostril, almost pressing it. Araina made no sound through its confines. Even as she weighed the futility of doing so, her focus fell fast to her burning palm and the light screaming below. For every impulse rising within her, its bubbling held below Sol's words from that day, when he first witnessed her casting, and what the Vexhi would do on learning of it. Lost in it, she was hooked around the arm, pulled from the stool, and away, into the shadows of a narrow hall before a stairway.

The dragged ascent was rapid and fluid, made all the easier as Araina desperately pressed her palms together, tight and guarded against the blouse. She stumbled, the tip of her sandal caught the next step, and her knees hit before she could catch herself. Though her left palm opened flat to the wall, the light yielded. It burned and raged, and yet, was at her will to be summoned. She allowed her body to be pulled up, submitting herself to the passage where she might finally put it to use.

The officer had little more than heavy breathing to share as he shoved open the nearest door and hauled her through its threshold. Araina frantically took stock of all objects within the small room—a clouded glass window opened into the night air, a lantern upon the table below it, sack mattresses on two slouching beds—nothing to serve as a reachable and unremarkable means of defense. The click of a lock behind her tolled through her every cell and left her a cold mass, all at once quivering and frozen but for a metallic heat in her throat and her raging left hand.

She dared to turn, and, on comprehending the distance between the officer, the closest bed, and herself in the narrowing space between, cried out, "Wait!"

To her surprise, he stopped—silent but for the gruff, eager huffing through his slack lips—and looked at her.

"Could we not light the lantern?" she asked.

Her request was met with the drag of his hand over her shoulder and a stumble toward the lantern below the window. Araina spun, backed herself to the door, and lifted her quaking palm. She stretched her fingers and permitted a trace of light, then allowed it to grow. She raised it higher, steadying it to align with the back of the officer's capped head, but suddenly, he dropped with a grunt.

The light, still holding over her extended hand, was now faintly cast upon Sol. Araina jerked her arm and tried to fold it away, but the small burst went free. Barely clear of the window, Sol sidled away from its charge. It toppled the lantern with a crash.

She let herself droop down the door. The cold skin of her legs trembled against the floor planks. Tears ran, hot and silent, blurring Sol's silhouette. He crouched down at the officer's body for a long moment, then stood and crossed the room. Araina shoved away the wet trails over her cheeks as he knelt and extended his hand.

"You alright?"

She remained rigid and guarded, breathing hushed notes. Sol retreated and sat upon the bed.

"Was ahead of you for a while. Can always count on officers to go to the first door. Anyone's in there, they just order 'em out."

Araina stifled a sob behind her hand. On recalling the feeling of the thick fingers in the same place, the cry escaped, hoarse and short. The bed creaked, though Sol remained.

They both sat in the dark—all silent but for the witch's suppressed and steadying breath—until he informed, "You gained us some time. Take what you need of it. When you're ready, I could use your help. Lantern's in a state and I got nothing to light it. Be easier to get ahold of that uniform if I can see it."

"Uniform?" she asked through a sniffle. "That's how you're going to get past—"

"Not much use if it's just me. 'Course that depends if you can stand to be on the arm of someone wearing it, even as a guise. Couldn't blame you. But then, you've come this far."

Araina's eyes narrowed in the darkness, then dropped with another sniffle. She shook her head and let her hair fall before her face, then tossed it away.

"They know what they're looking for. There's a drawing of it in his pouch. Just an outline but it's close. They're so much further than thought. There's no time to be taken at all."

"Still got what we need to stay ahead."

Sol rose, neared, and offered his hand again. Araina exhaled languorously and accepted his hoist. She summoned a small sphere of light and followed him across the room. Under its glow, he went to work unfastening and finagling the ocher jacket from the officer's debilitated form. He found the cap where it had fallen from the blow and tucked back a torn seam.

"We left everything behind. What'd you use to strike him?" Araina asked.

"Broken shutter frame. Just enough to get 'em down. Wager it's the liquor keeping him there." Sol pinched the cap's fabric back into shape. He placed it on the nearest bed and fastened the jacket over his bandit's shirt. The witch drew up more light as he fixed the officer's belt and saber in place. Lastly, he donned the cap. "Convincing?"

"Enough that I'm having trouble keeping hold of this light."

"Good. We can use it for target practice later."

In the side pocket, Sol discovered a key separate from a ring of others. He checked its fit in the door and parted it a hair's width from the frame.

"Can't we leave just as you came in?" Araina whispered.

"So you're a good climber too?"

"No. Terrible at it. But I'd gladly fall out of that window than go down there again."

"A Vexhi lieutenant climbing out a window with a peasant girl isn't ideal for avoiding attention. Better that they just walk out the door. Now seems a good time to do it. Won't be long before some of that crowd heads up here and the one behind us starts to wake up." Sol moved his focus from the crack in the door to the witch beside him.

She stared back through tousled waves. Her arms gripped tight across her center. He looked away and asked, "Lost the shawl?"

"On the floor. Downstairs."

"Getting it will look worse than leaving it."

"No one noticed me when it fell off, if that's your concern. Doubt they'll remember who was underneath it, if I ever occurred to them in the first place."

Sol turned toward her and lifted his hand from the door handle, then hesitated. Araina kept still. Whether he was reaching to correct something about her appearance or do otherwise, she could not tell. He returned his view and hand to the door.

"Doubt I need to tell you this uniform has effect on what people do or don't do. When they notice things or look away. Thanks to you, we can take advantage of that. If you're still…"

She nodded limply and followed him into the hall.

After a twist to lock the door behind them, Sol tossed the key into the shadows and lifted his elbow to her. Araina tensed her jaw and placed her fingers over his arm. They descended the stairs.

Distracted by the rumble in his stomach and rhythmic rise and fall of Pidgie's breast below his back, Den missed the first whistle sent to him from across the square. The second was disregarded based on its origin from a Vexhi officer. On the third, he finally recognized Araina's uncovered mop of hair, bouncing in step with a figure in dark yellow.

"Huh. Well ain't that interestin'."

He woke Pidgie with a nudge and settled over his back. They flew from their dent in the awning, eastbound, just behind and above the soldier and witch. His amused chuckle swelled as he and Pidgie briefly perched beside the path.

"Nice kit, General! Right down to the toothpick on the belt. How'd ya get ahold'a all that?"

Sol only answered with a curt tip of his capped head. The elf grumbled at the prompt and followed in flight.

Araina's eyes kept to the wheel-streaked and boot-trod soil that formed the northeastern trail around the lake. All the while, she tried to push away the feel of the fabric below her hand and smell of it at her side. She was eager to clear them for countless reasons—the greatest were in favor of sensations she did not quite know how to anticipate.

Kerikan's lines crawled through her brain: the description of scent, motion, and weight of air to know a loosened Meridian point. All that came was the scented memory of the black liquid and aged parchment, lacing a speeding arrhythmia of her pulse. She wondered whether that was the start of it or simply a heated dread, foretelling that no sense would actually occur.

A press of her hand between Sol's elbow and his side tore her back. It alerted her to the approach of two men. Their frayed, dusty shirts told of long days of toil.

"Evening, sir. Miss," they muttered, depleted and in unison with their heads held low—whether out of exhaustion or in response to the uniform, Araina's stolen glimpse was not enough to decipher which.

Sol replied with a gravelly utterance.

When the men's southwestern footfalls were far behind, he whispered, "We'll be upon more of them soon. I'll get you a head-start. When I stop, keep going."

"I haven't gotten anything to follow yet," she confessed.

"Just keep moving until you do. Stay out of sight and find it."

"If I do and you're not caught up, what do I—"

"I'll find you. In the meantime, try not to look as though you've got a secret...or a death sentence. We're fine. You're just keeping a Vexhi officer company for an evening."

"An evening down in the mines," Araina acidly voiced.

"Just a backdrop to power. Holds potency for some."

After seething forth a disgusted little note, she mutedly pondered, "There may be more to it than that. At the tavern, he wanted to bring me here because he thought I was a seer. Seems these men will take any help they can get, regardless of efficacy. If they use alchemy like you said, wouldn't they know better?"

"Doubt there's much alchemy this far down. All the more reason to look like you're where you should be."

"For our purposes, I hope I am," she muttered, trying to suppress what appeared so apparent on her face. She thought back to the shawl on the tavern floor, the risk of recovering it, and its lost use for obscuring her unease, then returned to her search for sensation. It remained mostly unanswered—though Pidgie's flapping seemed fuller and the rolling of the lake more rhythmic in the air. She could examine the measure of them for only so long; they fast came upon the entrance to the tunnel.

The dirt path led to an inclining walk of split logs. It connected to a deck of planks, built over the shore's rocks. The structure provided easy passage for men, tools, and carts passing in and out of a carved opening into the wall of the inlet. Lighting it all was a series of rope-strung lanterns. They held a strange cold-toned light that clung and wavered within the thick glass, like liquid set aflame. Araina squinted into it as they embarked. The emergence of men from the tunnel stole her opportunity to ask Sol about the odd shining vessels. She instead silently surveyed the scattered mining equipment with an artificial detachment. It was difficult to maintain as the lantern light sharpened.

A pointed gleam rose, not only from the suspended vessels, but the moon's glare on the rocks and slick emersed weeds beyond the landing. With it, a scent of copper, blood, and soil rode upon Araina's inhale. It lingered, caught in her nostrils, then behind her tongue, and up into her sinuses. She could not be sure whether she was detecting it in the air or secreting it within her body. Then, the smell of black liquid seemed to dribble from behind her eyes and join the visceral, vaporous mix in her throat. It drew her. Her hand slipped from Sol's arm.

A vocal exchange stirred up behind her, then it frayed and broke away like salt-eaten rope. A deepened, authoritative version of Sol's voice traded with subordinate utterances. Araina went on drifting. She stumbled over the edge of the deck, fell onto her side, and then resumed her lured steps through the rocks and weeds. The voices slowed in some notice, then flattened below a crash of metal tools—toppled and scattered about the mucky shore. Sol's growled exclaim and the thudding of boots upon the planks came after. They were little more than distant thuds and clamors from where Araina trekked—deeper into the inlet and along an interlacing pull of scent, warmth, and the frequency embracing her skin.

It all converged into a singular sense when she stepped into a shallow stream. Lake water traded into a hollow formed by fallen rocks. They appeared as a bubbled mass, fused by sediment, weather, wind, and eons. A low parting was just enough to permit the witch's form after some finagling for her hips.

She called forth her light and revealed a cavern touched with pale moss and fucus weed. The thick and cold air traveled through her lungs like windswept rain and sharpened the heat below her skin. Its clash rose with her pace into the stream, which widened and deepened to her ankles, calves, knees, and waist. Soon, she was in a small pool. Her light rode its surface in buzzing ripples. Araina stared below, down toward her feet, and let everything go dark as she sank.

Her hands smoothed through the water, across flat rocks with no clear borders or edges, until one seemed to rise to meet her. She touched the stony center, then spread her fingers—so much so, that it felt as though they would stretch beyond the flesh of her hand. Her pinky and thumb dragged until pain crawled to her wrist. With the motion, the markings of Ecivy presented themselves in relief. Araina read them by touch, then drew up light to see them.

Sol stood with the officer's sword drawn and held in his right hand. His left remained on the wall of the cavern—having felt through the darkness to a dim luminance. He watched it shift across the rocks, cast from a glowing pool. Its intensity wavered and grew when a dark form broke the surface.

Araina emerged, her face scantly visible through soaked waves of hair. A flat mass, barely larger than the spread of her hand, was clutched to her chest. She trudged through the shallows, her light broadening at the sight of Sol. As he realized the shifting darkness was disjointed and separate from her movements, he swiftly reached and curled her fingers to snuff her cast.

Overhead, a cold glare of lanterns and hurried voices leaked from a narrow cut into the rock. The witch and soldier froze, listening to tools scrape at the opening above. The exclaims hastened and more sharp light was thrust into the cavern, shrinking their cover. Sol pulled Araina from the darting beams and back through the cavern.

They came to the narrow opening before the inlet and waited. Searching shouts echoed behind them. Ahead of them, the lull of the water and their own breath fed back from the curves in the rock. Araina felt Sol's fingers blindly brush her arm and climb to her shoulder. He moved his jaw against her ear.

"Keep below the weeds. Get in the water. Move west. Give me a head start." In between his whispered instruction, he tugged at the officer's jacket and tossed it away. He then slipped out of his bandit's shirt and fumbled it around Araina's shoulders. "Stay in the dark. I'll slow them down. Stop for nothing."

"No, wait, Sol—"

"See you in the woods."

Before she could whisper further protest, Sol crouched, turned, and twisted his way out through the opening. His hand suddenly reappeared, pulled the officer's saber after, and withdrew without a trace. Araina looked between the rocks and out to the shore to find he left neither track nor clue of his plan or direction.

She set Ecivy on her knee, pulled her arms through his shirt's sleeves and her head through its collar. With a quick pull of the red skirt's tie, she let it drop away from her waist and kicked it free. Araina waited a breath, swallowed back her trembling, and shimmied through the opening. She dropped the moment her hips cleared and crept upon her stomach, following the stream to the lake as silently as she could manage.

Submerged to her chin, she listened to a rush of voices and shuffle of boots sound from behind. Half a dozen Vexhi strove to traverse the rocks leading to the cavern. She sank to her cheekbones and looked back to the shore, where she spied a pale form among the tunnel's deck poles. Whether Sol was waiting to execute an improvised ambush or was simply trapped and hiding, it was no clearer to her than any of his other maneuvers. That he was aware of just how many sword-carrying Vexhi were emerging from the tunnel above, she held doubt.

Araina gripped Ecivy and wedged as much of it as she could into the stiff fabric of her tulitiere. She gathered the end of Sol's shirt into the waist of her trousers and fully disappeared below the lake, swimming with all her strength toward the closest mooring.

Sol was given precious moments to creep between the deck poles. The quantity of overhead footfalls and slick maze of surrounding rocks made him abandon any immediate offensive. Even as the muck clung and hid his bare back and chest from the moonlight, opportunities to proceed in any direction were obscure and shrinking. There was little sound or movement from the lake—not a sign that Araina had cleared the eastern shore. When he came to the underside of the ramp, he heard men drop down into the weeds. He readied the officer's saber.

Through the drag of Sol's sleeve, Araina reached up to a mooring. Her legs pushed to keep her afloat as she kept Ecivy pressed to her skin. A tethered length of rope led her to a small rowboat. She fought to drag herself within, dreading the cacophony she made in the process. On centering herself in the little hull, she realized the commotion on shore was far greater than her roaring breath. It was also an urgent call to gain footing.

Araina rose to her knees, then her feet, extended her left arm, and with more urging than she had ever put to it, summoned light. Briefly she wondered if the amassing shine would have been enough to distract the Vexhi. As the voices onshore heightened by the instant, her wondering ceased. She swiftly dropped her hand and sent the sphere across the water.

Sol spotted the luminous swell when the first Vexhi spied him in the weeds. He watched the glow leave its floating place in the distance. It streaked overhead, above the deck planks, and into the tunneled rock wall. A great crashing followed. Though he staggered at the sudden force right along with his pursuers, Sol fast regained his focus and footing. He sped from the aghast Vexhi before they too dashed from weeds—gone to help their comrades in the rolling cave-in.

Araina watched the dots of light move, stop, and then frantically turn to whence they came. She resecured Ecivy, filled her lungs, and dropped out of the rowboat. From mooring to mooring, she swam until her exhausted legs touched lake bottom. In a dark overgrown pocket of half-dead cattails, she recouped her breath and listened to a rising clang from Dekvhors town. She again tightened her fingers around Ecivy and pushed through the broken typha stems. A familiar flapping followed her upland through the brush, though it was no longer rhythmic or defined.

Sol too moved from weeds, into the lake, along moorings and lines, and reached a shadowy slope. From mud, to rock, to gritty soil, his tracks met Araina's. A small light grew at his approach of their former vantage point in the brush, then faded once the soldier's visage became clear to the witch. She rose from her place beside the elf and pigeon and silently presented his wrung-out bandit's shirt.

After slipping within the damp fabric, he belted his sword and quiver at his waist and strapped his crossbow and pack across his center. Before Araina could bend to take it, Sol stooped and gripped her pack. It, along with the officer's saber, remained in his carry as they left the thicket's edge and sped into the trees. At the first well-covered clearing, they all nearly fell into sleep.

Chapter Sixteen

Summonings by Fire

Excepting Pidgie, who hunted pokeweed in the underbrush, Araina was alone in her wakefulness. It allowed her to change back into her bodice without fear of prying eyes. She decided that simply discarding the blouse, now stained and frayed, would have been greater insult to the woman who would find it missing along with a red skirt and flaxen shawl. The witch instead folded it into her pack. The sandals followed, though she was more tempted to toss them into the brambles, particularly as she examined her pitted and chafed ankle skin. She brought her knees closer to her chest, felt the bruising from the tavern's stairway, and dropped her face to the dark fabric of her trousers.

The steady snoring at her back lulled her to the previous night. It evoked echoes of the officer's grunted breathing, her and Sol's hurried air across the cavern, her panting against the rowboat's hull, and how very loud it seemed then—how she feared it would somehow alert the men so far away on shore—and how that worry was thrust behind the singular impulse to steer them from the pale form in the weeds.

Araina lifted her face and stared, unseeing, into the cluster of trees and brush. She recalled Sol's assurance, that there would be no need for rowboats, and all that followed the moments she dispelled it. With ample room to wonder if she had taken lives and how many, the witch moved through the question of how she could have cared so very little, and then how easily the dappled light of morning stole that tidy indifference.

With a slow glare over her shoulder, she looked at the soldier asleep across the clearing. His dense chest rose and fell. Just beyond it, the officer's saber rested. That it was still there for her to observe birthed more stinging questions and notions that simultaneously made her eyes feel heavy and her teeth clench. Araina exhaled sharply and removed Ecivy from her pack.

It appeared to be such an ordinary thing, almost aggressively so. The markings conjured by her fingertips were hardly ripples in its earthy surface. Though the duet of snores remained unbroken, she again checked over her shoulder to confirm that neither Sol nor Den had stirred. She repeated the summoning motion across the face of it. The markings rose up, then faded.

Araina unfolded the blouse and slipped Ecivy within. She overlapped and knotted the fabric in a tight bundle, then tucked it in the very bottom of her pack. As she stood and turned, she found Sol looking at her from the ground.

"If anyone deserved a late sleep, it's you," he remarked on the end of a yawn.

"Sleep came easy but didn't stay." She walked back toward the center of the clearing and sat down as he sat up. "I was about to gather kindling. I thought perhaps I'd make tea."

"Best to hold off for now. This was enough distance for the dark but not breakfast." He stretched and tipped his chin toward Den. "Will he be a problem?"

The elf was still snoring on a mound of leaves.

"You mean more so?" Araina asked, stirring half a smile from the soldier. "Based on experience, I expect he'll make a fuss about being woken, then he'll complain when he learns breakfast won't be a grand or leisurely one. He's also not had a chance to point out that he's gone without supper, cheese, and ale, and that we haven't yet profusely thanked him for his assistance. But you're more than welcome to wake him and find out for yourself."

"May be better to just head out and see if he catches up."

"Provided we eventually cook something, it's not a question of if but when."

"We are overdue for a meal," Sol admitted and climbed to his feet. An audible growl rolled from his center but was fast muted by an irate snort from the elf's nose.

"Oh? Overdue for a meal? Ya think?" Den, having ceased his snoring somewhere in the witch and soldier's exchange, sat up and went on to assert, "Any idiot they stick under one'a those caps knows, if ya do nothin' else for an army, ya feed 'em! That didn't rub off on ya from that smelly uniform, General? Got me flyin' cross this way and that all night! Ain't even woken by bacon sizzlin', not one pancake fryin', just humans jabberin'!"

"You weren't far off," Sol said to Araina. "Sure you're not a seer?"

She did not match his smile, nor did she do much to stay the narrowing of her eyes. Araina then looked at Den and the snarl turning his right nostril.

"How far to Radomezen?" she asked Sol.

"Four days."

"I suppose I could manage pancakes," she proposed. Den's tightly folded arms loosened as she reckoned, "Flour, milk, an egg...or rather two for a proper batch. Perhaps even jam. There should be a decent market, considering it's a port town. For now, toast, honey, and tea are easily done. Could even bake an apple or two…"

"With decent distance and cover," Sol advised. "Wager there's some just over that slope."

"I'm not going further than that without a cup of tea," Araina quietly insisted in Den's direction and slung her pack over her shoulder. Before moving to follow Sol, she turned to the elf and tendered, "Thank you for yesterday. Couldn't've so much as gotten started if not for you and Pidgie. And thank you for keeping my bodice safe."

"Only did all'a that 'cause I was expectin' cheese. Still am!"

"Four days to the next market," Araina reminded and proceeded after Sol.

Den finally let his arms unfold. He whistled for Pidgie and they followed upland.

Fueled by a sweet and warm breakfast, they covered substantial ground up into the Noxprimma foothills and out-trekked Sol's wariness of any pursuit. A stream met them at midday and gave welcome opportunity to refill canteens and make an attempt for fish. The soldier took to its edge with his crossbow readied.

"I don't think I've ever seen anyone fish like that. Don't you need a line to pull them in after you…shoot them?" Araina asked.

"Should be fine. Bolt weighs them down and the stream's shallow and slow enough to pull them out."

"That doesn't leave you with a quiver full of rust? I've some fishing line and hooks," she offered.

"Not with these. Coated. And not necessary," Sol declined with his eyes set on the water's edge.

"Feh, hope you like your fish in pieces. Guppies here ain't big enough to handle that," Den said.

"On a short draw. Just enough to pin 'em." Sol ended his explanation with a shot. He rolled his sleeve, crouched, and reached into the water. The bolt, pierced through the body of a yellow perch, was pulled free. He tossed the fish aside and reloaded.

Araina moved upstream. She tightened the strap of her pack around her center and waded into the water.

"Den, do you think Pidgie would be willing to part with a worm if he finds one? I wouldn't mind making a more traditional attempt at a catch."

"Ain't gonna catch nothin' if ya go trompin' through the water like that," Den called from a rock's edge.

"Just soothing my ankles for a moment."

Araina looked at the minnows swimming about the hems of her trousers. She stooped and attempted to roll a few in the ample fabric for use as bait. As she teetered to keep her balance and pressed the pack to her hip, her hand flatted to the hard shape of Ecivy. The water surrounding her suddenly began to stir in tight concentric rings. The flow of the stream shifted, creating a tiny maelstrom that dragged her feet from the river bottom and sent her toppling. With her hand knocked free from the touchpoint, the stream resumed its slow pace downland. Araina reemerged, sputtering, amidst uproarious laughter from Den and the splash of Sol's boots as he trudged toward her.

"What was that?" he asked and offered his aid.

Araina flipped her dripping hair out of her face before accepting and answering, "I touched it."

"Touched what? It? You mean—"

"Yes. While in the water. Oh no! Sage's sprigs!" she gasped and rummaged for the canvas fold in her pack.

"Nothing like that happened yesterday," Sol observed.

"Oh good." Araina exhaled on examining the line of still-dried herbs and refolded the canvas. "Beeswax. He thought of everything." She smiled, then turned back to the soldier. "Remind me to go over these sprigs with you."

"Why'd that happen now and not yesterday?"

"Perhaps because I drew it up again."

"Drew it up?"

"Earlier today. I drew up the markings. I think I may've…woken it up a bit more. So to speak."

"And that changed the flow of a river?" Sol stared back. Den looked on curiously.

"Well, this is only just a stream," Araina asserted and splashed back to its edge. "But that is a possibility…among others."

"What are the other possibilities?" Sol inquired.

After a thoughtful exhale, she turned. "It does not matter. Only uncovering and carrying them. No exceptions for changing the flow of streams or rivers, or anything else." She looked away and wrung out her hair.

"Wait, Rainy, *you* made that happen?"

"It might be fairer to say I enabled it. Partly. And very much accidentally." A tightness fell across her brow. "And it seems I've scared away the fish in the process. Shall we look for more upstream?"

She swiftly pressed forward, furthering a buffer between the intrigued and bemused looks of her companions and the waves of fear and fascination creeping through her brain.

The half-dozen perch were meager fare, especially after gutting and frying, but when seasoned and laid on toast, they anchored the meal. Hunger and exhaustion made the modest supper far exceed the sum of its parts. Den had so gorged himself, he barely managed to finish his last bite before falling asleep—belt undone, kerchief askew, boots kicked off—and far too close to the fire. Araina dragged him by the ankles near a nestled Pidgie. She rolled the cloth from the bread to serve as his pillow. He did not stir as she lifted his shoulders and slipped it underneath.

"You're very kind to him," Sol observed.

"More than I should be?"

He shrugged. "You didn't seem eager for his company before."

She brushed the dirt from her knees and blinked at the sleeping elf.

"I suppose I don't mind it as much. At least not more than anything else. I admit, he reminds me of a time before. By a fire, around the trees…before I knew anything. It's nice to pretend I'm still there." She watched the firelight reach across the conifers and tall rocks circling their camp, then its cast on the soldier's face. "I do see why you thought it a good idea to include him." She looked away, and lower than she thought could be heard over the snap of the kindling, added, "Among your better ones."

"Take it you would have done some things differently," Sol confronted.

Araina looked back at him, unable to tell if the fix of his scarred face was inviting conversation or tempting conflict. She returned her view to the fire and prepared to settle on the ground near Den and Pidgie, until the soldier prodded, "Might be difficult to hear you over there."

"Apparently not difficult enough," Araina murmured and rose.

Sol shifted his pack, quiver, and crossbow for her to take their place, followed by the officer's saber, which spurred her to inquire, "May I ask why you've kept that?" with poorly hidden sharpness.

"Leaving it would've been a loud invitation to our direction. Then I thought it might be useful for practice." He lifted it again and tilted its blade in the firelight. "More substantial than your misericorde. Might be a bit too weighty though. Clumsy thing."

"I don't want to look at it let alone use it."

"Not even against men who carry the like?" Sol asked with an eyebrow raised.

Araina shifted her glaring and looked back at the embers beyond her scabbing feet. She slumped forward.

"Have I not done enough to them?" Her query was blunted by the burrow of her chin into her forearms.

"Not sure who's got your concern, but if it's the men in that mine, keep it. They were out searching for us. Well, me. Bit easy for me to favor sides in that case. But even then, they're not worth the consideration." He moved the saber back behind his pack and went on, "Speaking from experience, they wouldn't have given us much if things'd gone another way. Had you not done what you did." His assurance gained a scant glance from the witch. "That why that thing bothers you?"

"No. That's not why."

"Something to do with one of my less than good ideas then?"

"Seeing it calls to mind how you acquired it. How easily I ended up there. How fast... Then I see the lantern on the floor. And I think, had I not thought to ask...had you not been..." She let her dread-laced pondering fade into a slow exhale.

"We'll get rid of it in the morning," he declared.

Araina looked away as a short rush of wind pushed the smoke in their direction. Sol lowered himself on his elbows. The snapping, shrinking wood in the fire peppered their silence until he added, "For someone who seems to think so much, you miss some obvious things."

"Such as?"

"A few about yourself. Might call it an underestimation."

"How so?"

"Had I not been there, that saber would've been of no more use to him than it is now. Wouldn't've gotten a chance to draw it."

"What makes you so certain?"

"Because you were ready. Was almost on the other end of it." Half a smile crossed his face as he recalled, "You were more than ready."

"Why do I get the sense that you were waiting for that? Is that why you let me get backed into a corner as you did? Was it to gain an estimation of what I would do? Or just a uniform?"

With her interrogation, Sol sat up.

"No. No, Araina. *That* was unintended. I climbed through the window, remember? I wasn't biding my time on the other side of the door. Couldn't very well pull you off that bar stool either. Not without a worse mess to follow. You were ready just the same. In addition to your swimming and the range of that light, not to mention how well you gut a fish, that's impressive."

"That's just from living on the shore."

"Not all of it. Don't let the rest get lost, even if it was no small misstep that you ended up there." Sol settled back down and looked away before adding, "But no small learning experience either."

"One I could've done without. Unless you're speaking to your own?"

He only shrugged.

Araina glared. "So you let someone else live a mistake and still gain the lesson? That's awfully convenient. Have I provided you with enough of one or should I anticipate more?"

"You misunderstand. And despite being very clear that you're not a soldier, now you know a little more of what it's like to be one."

"What do you mean?"

"A decision is made and you follow. Means you might get hurt or worse. Doesn't matter how you got there, whether you want to be, or if it's over your head. All that matters is your response. There's a lesson in it. Maybe for you, but it mostly belongs to the decision-maker. The command. He finds out what you can and can't do, whether you live, die, or end up somewhere in the middle, and then uses that. One outcome decides others. Now, imagine if you never had the choice to be part of it in the first place."

"But I—"

"Yes, I remember what you told Tanzan," Sol said.

Araina looked at the cast of the firelight across his skin and the little dents and ripples from slices healed over—some tidier than others.

"Were you not given the choice?" she asked.

"Given the same as you. Not long before."

"I mean before that."

"Before what?"

"Tanzan introduced you with a title, didn't he? A Svet Hagen one. Sergeant, was it? But you were in Crest troops barracks…and yet, not in either uniform at the banquet. When Den asked you what side you were on, you said mine…for now. Whatever you are, were you given the choice to be it?"

"You've got some memory."

"It was just days ago. And they've been of the more memorable sort, at least for me."

"Why does what I am matter?"

"I don't know if it does." She fiddled with the star below her throat and curled her body back to her knees. "I would love it if none of this mattered. Then I could go back to not caring about uniforms or officers, or if there were any men left in that tunnel, or the feel of that…"

"If there was a way around all that, we'd've gone it."

"Even if it meant losing a learning experience?"

"Means I'd lose a few of 'em. And yes, even then. Same goes as far as moving forward. From here on out, we have to steer clear of uniforms and officers, disguises or not. Let's hope no Vexhi have as good a memory as you, 'least not for faces."

"I won't miss drinking with them," she wearily remarked, drawing the start of a laugh from Sol. It faded when she asked, "So you're not Svet Hagen, then?"

"No."

"I know you're not Crest." Araina searched his face then nearly gasped, "Wait! Vexhi… Are you a—"

"What sense would that make?" Sol's brow furrowed.

"Maybe a turned or exiled one? You know so much about them."

"Know your enemy."

"Which should make you Svet Hagen."

"I'm not a Hagen. They just utilize me sometimes. The title, as you put it, or rank, as they would put it, is shorthand for when I do get mixed in. Saves some confusion. I don't have a side the way you're thinking of it."

"How do you know what I'm thinking?"

"Alright, what are you thinking?"

"A mercenary?"

"Not quite right either. Doubt you've heard of what I am. But to answer your question about whether I had a choice in being it, no. That didn't start with a decision. Not mine, at least. Expectations were placed on me and I got very good at meeting them, then exceeding them. Regardless of how I felt about it."

"Part of that sounds familiar."

"Because of yesterday?"

"Because of my Crest, only not exceeding or meeting much of anything." Araina shook her head with a trace of a smile. "Never mind. Was it your family who placed these expectations on you?"

"Just part of where I was born. All firstborn sons go through it. Not all get through it. I did. Every time." Sol exhaled roughly. "Made me useful."

"For what? And to whom?"

"A few things. And, your folk, for now. And the Hagens, fairly often. And me. I'd like to get those things off the battlefield as much as you'd like to have your plants growing."

"So it wasn't just about being asked or ordered?"

"My answer wasn't that different from yours. The asking was my answer. I see why we each make sense for this. And when there's a mission, and the terms and strategy are sound, and I'm part of it, I don't have many questions past that."

"No?"

"Soldiers do not question. They do what they can because they can. And if I can, I do."

"No more complicated than that?" Araina squinted, slightly mystified.

"It's a kind of life that removes complication. For some, that's a draw. If they've any say in it."

"I suppose I could see some appeal. I'd love your certainty at least."

"Already got it. You're just fighting it. Don't know why. Maybe because you haven't seen the reason you're out here and I have."

"Should we be wary of them here?" Araina's voice fell as she asked. "I know you said they appear at fronts…but how will we know if and when we see one?"

"Don't think they've been encountered this far west. Except at Shoda."

"Why do I know that name?" The witch peered into the fading fire, as if the embers would reveal the answer, then finally gasped, "Margret! Her brother was there…"

"A Hagen?"

She nodded.

"Rough one. Some made it through."

"I hope he was among them. She asked me to tell her anything about it. Now that I'd be able to, I'm glad I'm not there to do it." Araina sighed. "Landers and their seers."

She moved to her knees, picked up two thick branches, and dropped them on the embers. With a drag of her hands, she pulled them into flame. Sol admitted a short, amused note.

"With all that's happened, fire-raising is still impressive? And you've seen me do it twice already. No wonder you think I underestimate myself. Maybe you're just easily impressed," the witch suggested.

"It's...something. And you do. And no, not in the slightest."

Araina's smile faded as she looked at the darkness behind him. "Does firelight have much effect on them?"

"It's telling. By the shadows."

"That light we saw, in the glass strung around the tunnel. Do you suppose it's to do with them?"

"Could be. Only recently seen Vexhi carrying whatever that is."

"Fiwrn," Araina breathed.

"Huh?"

"That would enable the manipulation of light. Or it could be Yurkci. But then, what if it's not just the one by now?"

Sol shrugged again. "They're still at one less. One they were close to. But not close enough, because of what you did, backed into a corner or otherwise."

"I still can't help but think you're hoping there'll be more of those."

"More of what?"

"Corners. Learning experiences."

Sol looked at her and the resilient pondering behind her eyes. "Learning experiences tend to happen whether or not I hope for them. And like I said, if there was a way around, we'd have gone it. Couldn't go past so we went through. And we got through."

He opened his pack, pulled out his cloak, and spread it on the ground. After rolling the hood to a cushion, he settled upon it.

Araina retrieved hers, and before unfolding it, said, "If you see suitable reason to keep that sword, don't get rid of it just because of me."

"We're fine without it. Rest up."

"Goodnight, Sol."

"Night."

Chapter Seventeen

A Proposal Amid Warnings

Araina's pace was caught, like the sun on the first glimpse of the sea in the distance. After four days through the steepening and monotonous passes of the outer Noxprimma—and the longest stretch of time spent away from her own shore—morning light on saltwater was captivating.

"Alright back there?" Sol called over his shoulder.

"Sorry," Araina answered and hastened to close their distance.

"Still won't give those sandals another chance?"

"That's not why I slowed down. And they've been given another and then some."

"Better than nothing over that last rock field though?"

"It was a choice between bloody soles or the usual toes and ankles, so I stuck with what I knew, but I'll not wear them again, rock fields or whatever else lies ahead."

"Your friends will confirm whatever that is, right? We're asking for a Cecily? A Cecilia?"

"Ceedly. And yes, they've our next points."

"Wait, wait, wait," Den interjected from overhead. "We ain't gonna rush there, are we? We got a shoppin' list."

"I've not forgotten, but we are on our way to Crest grounds. They'll likely have the sort of food we left behind."

"Ain't just pancakes, Rainy. Don't forget 'bout cheese and ale. And beef. Need plenty'a that if we're goin' wanderin' back into witch lands."

"That amounts to a rather scattered market trip. Probably not wise if we're trying to keep from notice," Araina speculated before turning to Sol. "Would word of what happened at the lake have gotten here before us?"

"Depends on Vexhi presence. Unlikely we'll see as many as at Dekvhors."

"That sounds favorable. That means there're Svet Hagen?"

"Not in Radomezen. It's built on commerce, not conquest. Merchants there'd never let any one force get too comfortable if it'll cost trade. Might be one of the few towns Machalka hasn't bought yet."

"So we're clear then?"

"Well, we're leaning on that and whatever cover we had from darkness. Still not ideal for a leisurely shop. Might be better to split up. My right boot needs a patch. So's the seam on the cauldron. Due for a new novaculite. More short bolts never hurt. If your folk have us on an eastern route, I don't want to rely on any smiths that way."

"I guess that leaves us to cover the vittles…the growing list of them," she sighed.

"Must say, ale would be something to have," Sol remarked across an almost rapt exhale before adding, "And double whatever beef you get for Den."

"Please don't make me go to a Landers' butcher shop. I wouldn't know how or what to order."

"By the pound and salted so it keeps. Not that there'll be many options."

"Bet it'll all just be labeled *meat* now. Or just *grub*. May even be grubs. And if they got those, get 'em for Pidgie."

"Why don't you do the ordering and I'll just carry it?" Araina suggested to the elf.

"Nah-ah, ain't dealin' with humans out here."

"Why not?"

"Ya think they're curious 'bout witches, when's the last time ya think any seen'a elf? Ain't in the mood for questions and stares."

"I doubt they're very curious about witches if they're so near Crest grounds. Besides, if you're tagging along with me, you'll be seen either way."

"Could always give me back my old hidin' spot, Rainy."

"Absolutely not." Araina's revulsion rolled from her upper throat. Upon spotting Sol's raised eyebrow and dimpled scar, she insisted, "Don't ask."

Past a stone wall and below the reaching gables and woven awnings of shops, a continuous red brick thoroughfare told of Radomezen's prosperity. It bustled with shuffling trade and chatter. A salt-edged breeze carried baking bread, pipe smoke, animal feed, and frying fish. Sol squinted through the crowd.

"If I remember, this town has a large fountain in its center. We'll meet there in an hour. Have enough slates?"

"I should," Araina reached for the coin purse in her pack and slipped its draw around her wrist. "Provided the list remains unamended, finally."

"Can't be sure'a that 'til I see what's on offer," Den cautioned with his and Pidgie's landing on her pack.

"Are you certain you don't want company, Sol? The compact and opinionated sort?"

"Feh, forget it, Rainy," he quashed. "Ain't spendin' my day lookin' at a buncha soldiers' toys or huntin' for clotheslines neither. C'mon, 'fore we're left with the crumbs."

"See you in an hour," Sol bade and swiftly proceeded across the brick, leaving Araina quite stuck with her shopping companions.

Starting along the stands bordering the shopfronts, the witch's steps were eased by the lack of uniforms—grey or ocher yellow. But on surveying the wares and their sellers and buyers, she felt comparably observed, and not just for the elf seated on the pigeon perched on her pack. Eyes crossed her face and clothing. Some townsfolk slyly turned from their browsing and exchanged low words. Keepers behind their booths held cordial smiles as she approached, but only to unnerving effect.

She thought to retreat until a voice at her side said, "Oh don't mind them, love." An old woman smiled from behind a cart of tea crocks and crates.

Araina slowly drew near. "I was just noticing their...notice of me."

"They're confused. Been so long since Crestfolk've been here, they've mixed you up with a seer. They're nervous about that sort."

"Why would they be nervous about seers?"

"Trouble over the mountains. Man was robbed and pummeled by one at the lake town not yet a week ago, but what's to expect when you invite them by the dozens? Don't let it irk ya, love. Most'a us still know the difference. Now, what can I get you? Finest teas you'll find for miles, if there's any left to be found."

"I don't suppose you'd have any raspberry leaf? You say a man was hurt by a seer?"

"I'm sure whatever he got, he had coming. One of the Baron's vandals. Folk're all in a flap about how a seer girl could do it. Thick mix of trouble whichever way it's stirred."

"I gather you're not fond of Vexhi."

"Don't make any more secret of that than they make it easy to be un-fond. We'll have none of it. Still trying to bully their way in. Wherever they put their boots down, they tear up land, drain lakes, seize crops, cellars, and stores faster than blight, locus, slugs, and weevils put together. Not in our town! What was it you asked for, love?"

"Raspberry leaf."

"I may've some left." The old woman tapped at the canisters with her fingertips. "Bear with me, love."

"Please take your time. Do you suppose that's why you don't see many Crestfolk anymore? Because they're being mistaken for seers?"

"Oh, no. Been a time since we've seen them. The warning about the seers's just gone 'round," the old woman clarified as she picked up a small crate and raised the lid. She frowned. "Must have your pardons, love. Haven't much left and it's not the freshest. Air must've got to it."

"That's alright. Perhaps you'll ease the price then? I only need a small amount."

"Suppose I could. I've about half an ewe's ear. How much would you like?

"A quarter of that should do."

"Four slates then."

"I'm sorry, four? Four full? For raspberry leaf? And after the discount?" Araina asked.

"That's with the discount, love."

"Well, I'll do with an eighth then. Must be fine tea to fetch such a price." The witch tried to smile as she freed two slates from the purse. The old woman shook out the tea leaves on a square of cloth.

"Fine it is. But you understand, love. Had to raise my prices 'less I go hungry myself."

"Has food been scarce here?"

"We've been lucky though not spared. We hold on as we can, no matter what that grey plague promises. At least most of us do. Don't listen to those chipped-crock-skulls who say otherwise. You'll hear 'em shouting up and down the road before long."

"I see. Well, thank you, ma'am."

"You fare well, love."

As Araina turned from the tea cart, Den muttered, "You just pay two full slates for a handful'a dead leaves?"

"I never expected it'd cost so much. I wanted to keep her talking."

"Ain't even a good sort. Feh, raspberry leaf. That's women's tea."

"Tea that eases women doesn't amount to harm for men. Does look dreadful though. Imagine what your and Sol's meat will cost. And then the ale? You may have to choose between that and pancakes."

"Not'a chance. Sell somethin'a yours if we gotta. Like that little star 'round your neck, or all that metal dangling from your ears, or those damn shoes ya keep moanin' about."

"Doubt they gain much with all the blood on them."

"Betcha that ring'a yours is worth plenty'a meat, ale, an' cheese."

"I could just sell you. Then I wouldn't need half the meat or ale, or any cheese at all." She raised an eyebrow. "I could just spend whatever amount you fetch on better tea. Maybe even some chocolate—"

"G'head and try it. Not one'a these hoi polloi could open a bid for what I cost."

"For your sake, better hope no one makes an offer."

With the occasional stare and curious murmur at her back, Araina procured a meager quantity of eggs, what was said to be salt beef, but no flour. She instead decided on hardtack that could be ground. Her slates were depleted halfway through the planned quantity of coffee, leaving nothing for ale. As the shopkeeper bundled her order, he told of a trader near the town's center buying anything made of silver, copper, or gold. Following her thanks and exit back onto the brick, Araina brought a hand to her earlobe. She weighed a filigree-trimmed hoop against the thought of vocally disappointed but thoroughly sober companions until her thoughts fell below a swinging bell and a roared chant.

"Out with the Vexhi! Baron'll take us not! Gone be the blight! Keep our town un-bought!" Through responding jeers and applause, a large wooden spoon crashed against a dented kettle.

Another shout countered, "He'll feed us for he needs us! Open the city! Earn more than pity! He needs us! He will feed us!"

Another round of shouts followed, and yet another voice called, "No Vexhi! They bring curses! Demons! No Vexhi!"

Araina craned her neck to see through the thickened crowd. Among the whispers stirred by the latest warning, she focused on an exchange at her shoulder.

"What now? Did he say a demon?"

"Yes! You didn't hear? Vexhi digging released a lake demon. Destroyed half of Dekvhors with a lightning storm!"

"That can't be true."

"My husband heard it earlier."

"I'll not believe such a thing."

As her eavesdropping became apparent, Araina quickly diverged from the swelling clamor. The ringing bell, crashing pot, and accompanying discord proceeded onward along the brick. With it, the crowd thinned and uncovered the central fountain. The trader's cart waited just beyond.

"Foot caught in somethin', Rainy?"

"I'm just recalling what little good has come of ale when it's near you."

"Lookin' at it all wrong. Ale brings folk together. Shortens miles. Stretches laughs. Sure makes me more agreeable."

"And quieter?"

"After enough'a it." The elf grinned. Araina sighed, removed the topmost hoop from her right ear, and approached the cart.

"Good morning, sir."

"Miss," the trader greeted.

"How much would you give me for this?"

The trader took the earring, fiddled it between his fingers, and appraised, "Fine craft. Thin though. Few things I'd trade."

"I'm afraid I'd only be interested in whatever slates you could offer, unless you have ale."

"Bit early, isn't it, miss?"

Araina blushed. "It's not for now and it's not for me."

"I can do five slates."

"Oh dear, is that all?"

"'Fraid so, miss. 'Less it fuels bodies, fire, or armies, prices've slipped."

"I see. And for a second one? With a stone in it?"

"What sort?"

"Turquoise. A very fine sea green."

"Same size?"

"Nearly."

"Let's have a look."

Araina removed a smaller hoop from her left ear. The trader examined it and counted twelve slates from the purse on his belt.

"If you don't mind a bit of advice, miss. You'll get more for that if you spend it on rum. Shipment just arrived at the pier. Ale's no easy gain with wheat gone the way it has. Don't know if your friend'll mind the difference."

"The pier? Perhaps it's worth finding out. Which way would—"

"Off past the fountain there, where brick turns to plank."

"Thank you kindly, sir."

"Luck to you, miss."

Araina checked the length of shadow cast by a shop's signpost. "Still enough time to make it there and back."

"Sure ya wanna do that? Sailors're almost bad as soldiers," Den warned.

"My father was a sailor," she informed him and turned north, off the thoroughfare.

"That so? How's he feel 'bout havin' such a hoity-toity daughter?"

"I never met him. But he was a captain and also Crest, so he probably wouldn't have been terribly surprised."

"Ain't gonna find that sort down there."

"Well, I've already sold two earrings. I'll go see if I can buy them back. Then we can just wait by the fountain for Sol."

"Ya know that guy ain't gonna sell 'em back at the same price. How ya think that stuff works? Might as well see if the cheese shop's opened up. Or hunt down ale just for me. Ya can tell the General they sold out. He ain't gotta know otherwise."

Araina faced the rising waft of salt and the persistent sparkle on the water. She adjusted the strap of her pack and stiffened her shoulders.

After disrupting Pidgie and Den into the air, she extended, "Sorry, gentlemen," then observed the signpost on which they perched. It indicated the downhill path to the pier. "If getting the rum is a hassle, I'll just turn around. We don't have any Vexhi to worry about, after all."

"I ain't one to turn down a swig on someone else's slate, but ain't this a bit outta the way? 'Specially for someone who's scared'a taverns?"

"Well, if…" Araina moved her eyes from the glitter and submitted herself to the elf's curiosity. "I just want to stand by the ocean for a few minutes. Just a moment would be enough to keep me…" The witch swallowed her drifting voice. "And if I can get something to make miles shorter and laughs longer, or however you put it, so be it. I get the feeling if I keep you and Sol in good spirits, it keeps me out of taverns. We have the time. Keep lookout overhead if it makes you feel better."

"Eh, tide reek makes me wanna retch. But g'head. The more ya say rum, the more I want it."

"I won't be long." She passed the sign post and her companions, and followed the brick down to a walk of weathered planks.

Through a survey of stands and blankets with all manner of wares spread over their surfaces, Araina spotted a stack of standing barrels. Dark bottles of varying sizes were aligned across a supported board. She approached and inquired on the amount of rum she could get for her slates. The merchant said nothing, selected a bottle, and slid it before her. Her payment was surrendered with a muted thanks. Purchase in hand, she hurried between the crowd and stands to face the gently tossing wind and waves.

The witch closed her eyes, wanting only to hear, smell, feel, and imagine it her own. She tried to envision it with gulls and harbor seals and without the massive ships, the racket of loading and unloading, the wafts of tobacco, and the grumbling, chuckling, and griping throughout the air. The sheen from the water, breaking the darkness behind her eyelids, almost led her there, until a bold voice proclaimed, "That's a smile I know."

A wiry man with tangled twists of hair crossed behind her and leaned over the rail. "I wear the same when on my ship, at the helm, when you can nary see the land but for a speck. Then you know, steady on and it'll be sea, only open sea. I know it on a face that aches for it. Though I don't know that I've seen it on the face of a witch…one so sun-kissed. And with a taste for rum, no less. Ah, where're my manners? Captain Barzillai Boon." He bowed at the waist.

"Oh. Beg pardon. The rum isn't for me. Someone is waiting for it and I'm past due getting it to them. Good afternoon, sir." Before Araina could fully turn away, he intercepted.

"Strange times that witches are delivery girls."

"Indeed."

"Whatever your pay, I can offer better. And that's in addition to the wage of the waves and freedom."

"I must decline. Thank you. Good afternoon," she bade and again attempted to depart. He blocked her path in turn.

"But you've not yet heard the full terms of my proposal," he informed her, low and close enough for Araina to smell a melding of smoke, meat, and citrus from his unshaven jaw. Even as her left palm buzzed, she shifted her grip on the bottle's neck and judged its weight against the time needed to open her pack, retrieve the dagger, and free it from its scabbard.

"Once I've heard them, will you let me on my way?"

"But of course. And I'll do you the courtesy of keeping it brief. Don't think I've missed the way you're holding that bottle, sweet witch. I promise I've been hit with bigger and better without a blink." His whiskered smile buoyed with his boast. "But it tells me you're all the more suited to my needs. The witch I need is not an ordinary one. And not a crystal-keeper or card girl either. I'm looking for some very special artifacts. It's said witches, the genuine, savvy, sturdy sort, are what it takes to find them."

"I've never heard of such things."

"Then why do you wear such a look on that sturdy, sun-kissed face?"

"…Because I've been asked similar…and recently. What's so special about whatever it is you seek?"

"Honestly, couldn't care even if I could say. I just need the price one'd fetch."

"If you need money, how are you offering me a job? How are you able to sail as a captain? Or so you've introduced yourself…"

"Oh, a captain I am, just not one currently able to sail. My ship waits, but I cannot reunite with her without a very large sum. Just one of those artifacts is worth it over, and over, and over. The witch who helps me with its regain will be rewarded over, and over, and over."

"Regrettably, I am not she. And if that's all there is to your proposal, I'll say good luck, and once more, good afternoon, sir."

"And to you, witch." He finally let her step away.

After enough distance upland, Araina dared to peer back and confirm she had not been followed. She reached the sign post and discovered Den and Pidgie were comparably absent from her forward path. They were instead spied between gathered crowds, sitting upon the stone rim of the fountain. Sol was at their opposite, looking out past the rabble. Araina exhaled thickly before her approach, trying to clear the hurried apprehension that drove her steps.

She handed Sol the bottle. "Ale wasn't easy to come by, so I thought this might do."

"Rum? …And no small amount of it. Where'd you get this?"

"The pier. Did Den not inform you of where I'd gone?" Araina took out her canteen and drank. She tipped it into the fountain and refilled it, trying to hide the quiver in her hands.

"Just landed here a second ago after I got sick'a waitin'. And last I checked, lookout ain't mean messenger," Den retorted over his shoulder.

"If ale was hard to come by, we'd've just done without," Sol stated.

"But before, you made it seem as though…" Araina sighed and looked across the passing cluster of faces. "Well, the option was there and I thought it better than nothing."

Sol uncorked the rum and brought it to his nose. The inhale sent his eyebrows upward. "Can't speak to better, but it's not nothing. Little of this'll go a long way."

"Let's see 'bout that," Den eagerly turned and reached for a taste.

"We'll sample it when we've cleared town." Sol quickly corked the bottle and turned to Araina. "Get everything otherwise?"

"What I could with the slates I had. And you?"

"Everything but the novaculite. Might find something on the way."

"Which would be this way?" Araina tipped her head eastward.

Sol affirmed with a nod and they proceeded.

Chapter Eighteen

Intentions and Inclusions

Not long after the last of Radomezen's red brick disappeared into rocky soil, Sol veered and cut a path across sprawling grass and thick trunked trees.

Den was quick to assess the new route. "Alright, I'd call that plenty clear'a town."

The soldier shortened his stride and asked Araina, "You got a thimble to fill for him?"

"Real clever, General. I can handle a bottle. Ya just better hope I don't handle the whole thing."

With the elf's bluster, he and Pidgie flapped down to a protruding root. Sol skeptically handed him the rum. Den set it down, propped a leg on the bottle's shoulder, and uncorked it. He lifted the neck with a smooth raise of his stocky arms and took a swig, losing only a few drops down his chin.

After a hearty inhale, he declared, "Think they sold ya barnacle burner, Rainy. Ain't bad," and took a second swig.

Sol looked at Araina while he wrestled back the bottle and offered, "What about you? Looks like you could do with some…for some reason." He watched her eyes shift along their tracks. "Araina?"

"Wha— Beg your pardon?"

"Got that same look you had at the lake."

"Oh? How far've we to go now?"

"Few more miles." He corked the bottle and they resumed their path.

"If we're sent east, are there many more towns along the way?" she asked after yet another survey over her shoulder.

"Here and there."

"Will it be necessary to rely on them?"

"Depends on how well we're supplied and how far we're sent."

"I wonder if it might be better to avoid them. Even if Vexhi aren't present, Landers could be a problem."

"What makes you say that?"

"One approached me at the pier. Claimed he was a ship's captain. He wanted a witch to help him find an artifact, or so he called it, to sell."

Sol looked at the bottle, then her. "How much this rum cost?"

"Twelve slates."

"Wasn't even worth a trip down to the pier. Why go to the trouble of avoiding Vexhi if you're going to engage with vessel vagrants?"

"I warned 'er," Den added, the spirit still warming his throat.

"Warned me? You couldn't wait for me to get that rum. I did it for both of you and your ridiculous shopping list. And I didn't engage. I told him nothing."

"Nothing?" Sol asked.

"Of course. Absolutely nothing. He did the talking. Just like at the... I-I at least learned that Landers may be doing a better job at distinguishing Crestfolk from card readers than Vexhi."

Sol sighed through his nose. "Not sure that information was worth the risk, rum or not."

"Have a taste 'fore ya say so," Den said with a grin.

The soldier sighed again and, without a break in his stride, took a swig from the bottle. He let the sting settle and welcomed the heady flush that followed.

"Not worth it," he confirmed and looked over at the witch, whose apprehension had given way to frustration and chagrin. He watched her carry it around her tired, warm eyes. "But not bad. And you can come off sentry duty. No one's on our trail."

They came to a hedgerow reaching well above all of their heads—the lushest stretch of vegetation encountered in all their steps. Its vines were so thick and tangled, it scarcely permitted a view of the structure beyond but for scant glimpses of shining blue glass and pale stone. Sol looked through the thorny tangles, then at the map, then back to the barrier. "It's just past...this."

He went on incredulously observing the seeming endlessness of it. Araina approached but stopped as she examined the leaves—resembling corner-notched arrowheads—and the talon-like curve of the thorns. She raised her hand toward the tendrils. They slithered in response. She withdrew her reach and turned to her company a short distance away, just as Sol unsheathed his sword.

"No! Don't!" she gasped, too late, as the plant wriggled forward and around the blade, guard, and grip, then began working its way around Sol's wrist and forearm.

"Let go!" Araina cried out

"Me or this thing?!" he growled.

The briars burrowed into his knuckles and flesh. He dug his boots into the grass and against the formidable drag of the twists. Pidgie startled away into the trees with Den. Araina called forth her light and threw it into the plant. A portion of its reach frayed and shrank back. Sol fell with a grunt. More vines slithered along the ground, sending him retreating on his elbows and heels while Araina struck it again and prompted their withdrawal. Sol stared, dumbfounded at the sight of his sword held deep within the plant's lush core.

"Are you alright?" The witch knelt and examined his arm.

"I'm fine." He blinked back into the tendrils. "Hit it again."

"I'm afraid that's not going to work." Araina unwrapped the now-wilted vine clinging to his wrist.

"You're telling me that's stuck in there?"

"For now."

"Let me see your misericorde," the soldier insisted.

"What makes you think that will yield a different outcome? Keep still." She proceeded to remove the briars from his skin.

"What then?" His nose crinkled nose with each pluck.

"In case it wasn't made clear, those vines will pull in anything that gets close enough, even something attempting to sever them. And, even if I hit them clear from your sword, there's no reaching in after it. I'm almost certain these are vineguards," she explained, wonder peppering her voice.

"Just blast the thing to a pile'a leaves, Rainy," Den encouraged, still on Pidgie and safely perched in the nearest tree.

She wearily looked back to the elf and summoned more light. She thrust it beside Sol's sword and swiftly repeated the action several times. While bits of tendrils fell away, the plant writhed and thickened in response. The gaps filled in almost as fast as Araina created them.

"See? Vineguards. And a rather prosperous sort. I suppose I could try to hit the sword directly, though I don't know what that would do to it." She stood and offered her aid to a clearly thwarted Sol.

"Then don't." He took her hand and reclaimed his feet.

"I won't. Besides, even if I could manage to force it to the other side, we can't very well go collect it. No. Getting through this sort of barrier requires a more passive approach. We'll need some help for that."

"And how do we get it?" Sol asked, his dark eyes fixed on the few bits of steel not enveloped in green.

Araina again approached the barrier, stopped as she heard it wriggle, and squinted through to the blue glass beyond.

"We ask for it. Or one of us will. The one who can get over." She turned to Den, who looked back warily as she continued, "You two could clear that height."

"And then what?"

"Knock on the door on the other side."

"I ain't interested in flyin' a mile over this thing. Or knockin' on doors when and where I ain't expected."

"Since when? And you might be expected, at least Sol and I should be. Just mention our names. Or Trinera or Tanzan."

"What makes ya so sure this bastard bush ain't gonna reach up and grab us outta the air?"

"Just go quick and high. I'm ready behind you just in case." Araina flattened and presented her left palm. "I'll not let anything happen to Pidgie," she vowed.

After a conceding grumble, Den drove Pidgie up into the branches and they took off, far above the vineguards.

She squinted through the leaves but could gain little view beyond the slithering tangles. Sol, staring into the foliage with his chin planted on the curl of his slightly bleeding forefinger, could not be stirred from his captive sword. His stubble-framed scar was deeply dented with irritation. The one crossing his cheekbone was stretched by the same force.

"Don't worry," Araina said. "This isn't going to be as difficult as you're thinking."

"No? If there's no getting through from this side, how does someone do it from the other?"

She tapped at her chin, alerting him to a lingering streak of blood, and explained, "If someone's using vineguards this aggressive, they need something that calms them for passage. That something is called a zeadase."

Sol shoved his punctured sleeve across his skin. "What's that?"

"Usually a liquid or dust."

"What's it do?"

"Well, as loss of light brings leaves to change and drop with the season, a zeadase also triggers that process. It will send a plant into a quiet stage on contact. It's ordinary witchery, though I've never seen it on this scale."

Araina looked away to marvel at the abundant tangles and how very far they stretched. While not rivaling the heartening beauty of the conservatory or the herb plots back at the tower, the quiet danger in its lushness sparked the witch's smile. Before she could further indulge in imaginings of ocher-jacketed Vexhi or particularly bothersome Landers attempting to barge through it, Den and Pidgie swooped down from above.

"No good, Rainy. Bunch'a kids running the place! Told 'em what ya said. Almost shut my damn head in the door!"

"Hmm. Perhaps you should've asked for Ceedly…"

"Well ya didn't say that! I told 'em moon snake and they laughed in my face. '*Prove it*,' they said. Little snots!"

"Try again. This time ask to see Ceedly. Show them this. Be very careful with it, please." Araina slipped the seal ring off her finger and handed it to Den.

"Better be gettin' both'a your shares'a rum for this!" The elf and pigeon took to the air again.

Araina reset her view on Sol, who remained fixed on his sword as if he could draw it out with his eyes. He rubbed his wrist all the while. She neared and examined his sleeve, the skin below its tears, and the little lines of blood that surfaced.

"The itching will subside. Remind me to stitch it up for you." She dared to touch the fabric.

"Not too concerned about it at the moment. How long does that zee… zee dice…"

"Zeadase."

"How long does it take to work?"

"With a plant this large and…active? A few minutes? Hopefully not more."

Sol resumed his staring. The silence between them revealed the sound of fabric dragging over the grass.

As it drew near, a women's robust voice called out past the vineguards, "Araina of the Moonserpents and Sergeant Solairous Ekwidou?"

"Yes. Hello?" Araina answered.

A cloud of fine blue dust floated through the gaps in the tendrils. It landed upon the leaves, vines, and briars, causing them to shrink back. Sol's sword tilted.

Another cloud sent it drooping toward the ground. A slender hand then appeared from the other side and pushed away the limp tangles.

"Come along then. You'll want to collect that now. We've only moments."

Araina reached into the plant and gripped the hilt. After puffing away the clinging blue particles, she returned the sword to Sol with a knowing smile. It was promptly sheathed while he watched the witch maneuver through the barrier.

"Don't dawdle now," the robust voice warned as the surrounding un-dusted foliage rustled. Sol pushed through, clearing the vineguards to meet with Araina and a woman nearly his height. A hefty cloth bag and large feather with its edges tinted blue waited in her hold. In addition to being clad very much like Trinera, her form was no less poised or statuesque.

"Welcome to our library and home. I am Ceedly of the Drakheirs. Pardon our precautions and our slightly delayed preparation for your arrival."

"This is some fortification you've created," Sol remarked. The dormant gap at their backs was already starting to revive.

"Cultivated is more accurate to say," Ceedly declared.

"Never seen anything like it."

"Indeed. We foster this particular strain because of its naturally aggressive carnivory and the ease of sporing a compatible zeadase. They're not found this way in the wild. Unfortunately, such barriers have only become more necessary."

"I think I already know the answer, but why is that?" Araina asked.

"I'm certain you know the answer. It's not only Vexhi now but Landers made desperate enough. We can discuss that more in my study, along with some very pressing news."

Ceedly led them across a stretching field of wild flowers with weathered statues erupting throughout. Though their deftly chiseled features were stolen by time and weather, the stone beasts were arresting. Both Sol and Araina were taken by their powerful forms and the radiant blue glimmer of the glass dome atop a grand stone temple.

They reunited with Den and Pidgie, awaiting on the rails of a large veranda where more ancient statues sprung from white and grey stone. The very same stone was stacked and rounded to form grand steps to the arched entrance. Hung from the center of its doors was a massive, verdigris-dulled emblem portraying a winged creature. Its tail looped round to serve as a knocker, though it appeared too heavy and antique to function. Windows of more blue glass crawled the lower level and obscured short silhouettes. Retreating giggles and chatter sounded from the doors as Ceedly parted them.

"Pay no mind to the students," she said and permitted entrance into a long, paneled hall striped blue with tinted sunlight.

Before Araina and Sol were whisked upstairs to a study, their provisions were taken to the larder. Den made no complaint of his exclusion when a large lunch in the kitchen was suggested as an alternative. Tray-carried versions of oil-coated beans with a soft crumbled cheese, seeded and peppered bread, amaranth leaf pastries, and tea were served to Araina and Sol on a low table among bookcases and an intricately carved desk.

The instant their plates were cleared, Ceedly announced, "There've been some changes. And not in our favor." Her voice was thick and collected—and quite the contrast to Araina's full-eyed apprehension.

"We're too late?" she asked.

"Since you are here, I trust you've recovered the touchpoint from Dekvhors?"

"Yes, of course. It's in my pack."

"Then we cannot be. We are, however, further behind than planned."

"We've been moving as fast as possible."

"This is not a failing of your movement," Ceedly clarified. "It is an underestimation of resources. Or simply a stroke of fortune not ours. In short, it means there are fewer to be uncovered and more to be recovered." Ceedly's eyes pressed upon Sol as she spotted the stiffening of his shoulders. "But as Tanzan has doubtlessly made clear to you, recovery is not your work. Only to uncover and carry," she added.

"How many remain?" Araina asked.

"We suspect three. We've the reflections for two. Plotting is underway for the third. But it will be a few days more."

Araina's eyes fell to a wounded contemplation until Sol asked, "Isn't it better this way?" Both she and Ceedly looked up.

"If Vexhi have done the work of collecting more, doesn't that save us time?" the soldier elaborated. "They're in one place to be captured. And if Hagen and Crest have started to marshal in full alliance, we could actually breach that stronghold."

Ceedly leaned against her desk and set her equable eyes on Sol.

"I'm not surprised to hear you see it in that light, young man. You're thinking as your role would have you. What's possible when our and your forces march upon that stronghold is… Well, I'll only say that plotting is underway as well, but it is not happening here."

Something waited behind Sol's tensed jaw.

Ceedly went on, "If the Vexhi have two more in their possession, found recently and not by chance as with the first, that means their alchemists have been particularly busy. It means they've been successful in uncovering resources we trusted as only ours. If we rely on them to shorten our steps, they may race past us entirely."

"Should we not start after the two that are mapped in the meantime?" Araina suggested.

"It's been made very clear you aren't to move until you move for all of them. Reflection specifics cannot be risked in a message, even in cypher, and there is too much danger in twice-trodden footprints." Ceedly turned and sat at the desk. "And there are still matters for you here." From a drawer, she removed a folded paper. "Araina, Tanzan wrote that you'd be carrying something Kerikan of the Moonserpents included with the book and key, and with it, you'd have questions."

"Yes. For quite some time now."

"May I see it?"

Araina took the rosewood box from her pack, opened it, and presented it to Ceedly, who took it between her long fingers, turned it in the light, then cautiously replaced it in the box.

"What do you know about it?"

"Almost nothing. Aunt Kerikan told me to carry it and not speak of, play, or do much of anything else with it. Tanzan said it's been in my family for some time but little else. The Coven asked of it as well, with some debate over whether I should have it...or something or other."

"But no one's spoken of its purpose?"

"Tanzan came the closest. He told me it was associated with a ritual, though not one related to the laws."

"Accurate but vague," Ceedly remarked.

"Indeed. He mentioned that you'd be better able to offer answers."

"Provided you want them."

Araina kept her view to the crystalline cylinder in the box and slowly contended, "Every time I've said yes to something like that, I found myself looking fondly upon the days before I had given that answer. But, that Aunt Kerikan asked me to carry it, despite it being unrelated to the laws, I admit I wonder why. How many uses could a flute have? And what could they be to merit such...regard?"

"Well, it's not a flute, not truly. It's simply been modified to produce sound. It's not meant for anything that might be called music. And your great aunt's inclusion of it with the book and the key was telling," Ceedly explained.

"Sound but not music… For some sort of ritual…" Araina considered its texture, fragility, and the delicate reverence of Tanzan's hold and then Ceedly's. She thought back to its hidden place at the cottage and for how long it may have rested. A small, slithering gasp trailed her view over to Ceedly, then back to the object in the box.

"It's not…"

"Not what?" Ceedly encouraged.

Though rendered to little more than a bystander, Sol's eyes shuffled between the two women. He was comparably eager to hear whatever caused Araina's voice to falter so.

"Ceedly… Is this a throat?" she dared.

"A what?" Sol asked, thoroughly perplexed and slightly revulsed.

"A petrified larynx, to be precise. Later crafted to produce notes in imitation of air over vocal cords. Araina, your guess tells me you might be more familiar with this little tool than you initially realized."

Araina stared across the shadowy rows of books, then recalled sitting on the floor of the cottage below its bookshelves. A chair waited at her side. She had used it to reach the top shelf—just as she had in retrieving the book and key. That time it was harder; her arms were shorter. She was shorter—so short, she could not see what she had freed. It did not matter. Anything would do for a peek in the time Kerikan was away. Surely anything in those special books would amount to being a bit smarter, a bit better of a witch. It would only make her great aunt happier—or at least be enough to make Kerikan leave her alone to paint and play. It did not work. It made it worse. Upon the braided rug, with her eyes fixed on something called therianthropic bargaining, Araina didn't hear the old witch return or approach. The book was forcefully pulled from her hands. Then some toil-heaped punishment followed. As it was endured, her thoughts kept to the woodcut beside the words—the one of a witch, a great otherworldly bird, and the fallen form of its kin in some engagement of dire importance—one she could only partly grasp before the book was ripped away and slammed just shy of her nose.

"Therianthropic bargaining," Araina breathed.

"Truly an incredibly valuable and rare opportunity." For the first time since their introduction, Ceedly's dignified face carried something hesitant and protected. Araina went on staring, dually daunted and compelled.

The thick silence prompted Sol to break from his confused spectating and ask, "Opportunity for what?"

A sympathetic sigh preceded Ceedly's response. "How can I best explain it to one who…" She sighed again. "There were opportunities arranged by ancestors from times before Crests were so defined. Back when lines drawn between us and the sort we call Landers were not through name and grounds, but decision. Our choices to bond with the experiences of beasts, rather than modify or fortify against them, amounted to certain understandings. Some of these, as Araina named, have been called therianthropic bargains. They almost always involve great beasts, the sort that Landers sought to fell. Our folk instead kept them safe and hidden, and their hunting and nesting grounds untouched. And to better maintain this preservation, Crestfolk were granted certain rights over the bodies of beasts slain out of fear and conquest by Landers. They could be harvested for pieces like this…let's call it a pipe. This pipe is a method of connection. It's essential in a rite that bonds bones, and sinew, and strength. The abilities gained through this are, well, significant. Truly altering. And are reserved for only very important purposes and circumstances."

Sol, appearing no better informed by the answer, looked at the witch across from him. "So what does that mean for Araina?"

"That, young man, is ultimately up to her."

Araina closed her eyes and swayed her head in short sweeps. "H-how did this come to just sit in a chest at the foot of her bed? And why would she…"

"How it came to her, I don't know. Your Crest is old, Araina. Your family line within stretches to its origins. It's not all that perplexing to know that if one of these still existed, it would be kept by a Moonserpent."

"She treated this as though it were a third piece to the two. To the books…or rather, the book and the key. She had me find this first and made it seem as if it were the more important among them. Would she've intended that it be used by anyone who had been charged with—"

"Which would be you," Ceedly reminded.

"But if she ever thought that would've been… She would *never*. She didn't even trust me to…" Araina's eyes darted about the surface of the table. "Would she…" For a brief moment, her view crossed up to Sol, who only stared back. Ceedly had a little more to offer.

"I cannot speak for her. I only know her through renown. I expect she could have excluded it, had she not intended that whomever relied upon the book and the key should also have this at their advantage. Whether she knew or intended for that to be you, and at that time, I know no better. But it could not have been lost on Kerikan the world she was leaving behind. Perhaps she wanted to give whatever she had to whatever was left of it. All those things your Crest had kept for so long. Which reminds me." Ceedly reached into the pocket of her skirt and placed the seal ring upon the table. "Intentions and inclusions aside, there is still great risk for which to account. It is not a simple rite. Though, perhaps she knew if you'd reached someone able to explain it, and if you'd correctly interpreted the rite, she trusted you'd survive it. But, as I said, I cannot speak for her."

"What do you mean survive?" Sol promptly asked.

Ceedly looked at him for a moment and slid the folded paper toward Araina. "This is the oldest description I could find in the time since Tanzan wrote to me on the subject. It will read more as riddle than instruction, as these things do. It is yours to carry out. If and as you choose."

Araina unfolded the paper and examined the thin script and accompanying diagrams. Their geometric forms were interwoven by primitive symbols and the complex spiraling motifs that adorned the oldest of things in her world.

As she studied the work, Sol reiterated, "What do you mean survive? There's a chance this is lethal? But, Araina—"

"There is some risk of that with these matters. There is also the risk of nothing coming of it and simply spoiling an immensely rare artifact," Ceedly asserted.

"Spoiling it?" Araina asked, hardly lifting her eyes from the paper.

"The heat and moisture from your breath will affect its intricacies. Unfortunately, there's only slight separation between petrified and putrefied with such delicate pieces. Your chance is limited and there's little room for error."

The right side of Araina's mouth curled wearily. "That seems most fitting of Aunt Kerikan."

"Is it worth it…whatever this is?" Sol continued to watch the tethered dash of her eyes.

Without hearing him, Araina muttered, "Aceridon? Ceedly, am I reading this correctly?"

"You are."

"And there's a place to perform this here?"

"You are on the grounds of a temple. This has only been made a library in recent generations. The altar remains."

"Will you show me?" Araina took the seal ring from the table and slipped it back on her finger.

"Of course."

"Araina, wait," Sol cautioned.

The witch turned to him with her eyes full and kindled.

"Are you sure you know what you're doing?" he asked.

"Compared to almost everything else as of late? Perhaps a little." Her smile and his wariness did little to counter one another. "You're not underestimating me, are you?"

"No, but I am going with you."

"I'm afraid you'll only be able to do so for so far, Solairous," Ceedly informed. "You can travel the path to the altar, but Araina must approach it alone. Araina, you will need time to interpret and decide whether you can answer the demands. And then, if you will."

"If one, then so follows the other."

Ceedly nodded. "I'll arrange for your supper to be brought here."

Below lantern light and with most of her meal untouched, Araina hunched over the description of the rite. A blue-stained cloth rested on the table between her and Sol, who sat, running a semi-translucent stone along the edge of his blade. A raspy chime followed the movement of his hand. With every third or fourth sounding, he looked at the witch, but she took no notice. She was near motionless until she suddenly lifted her head, stared at nothing, then brought one foot to the cushioned bench. She bent forward and ran her fingers over the scabs on her ankle and above her toes. Some notion widened her eyes and briefly parted her lips. Araina returned her foot to the floor and reentered her absorption without a word.

"You alright?" Sol asked.

She affirmed with a melodic murmur.

"This isn't bothering you?"

"What isn't?" She finally looked over.

"The sound. The sharpening. I can do this outside."

"I hadn't noticed. I thought you couldn't get one of those."

"Saw it on one of the shelves. Not a novaculite but it's close. Ceedly said she uses it to weigh down pages. Some type of quartz. Told me to take it. It's doing the job."

"It's not bothering me, though I couldn't blame you if you went outside. So much cooler than the last few nights."

A Moonserpent Tale

"Den's out there now. Found a deck of cards downstairs and tried to get a game going."

"Awfully sporting of him." Araina's eyebrows tightened skeptically. "Even with our lack of slates?"

"He wanted to stake the rum."

"Personally, I'm wary of that combination…elf, cards, and drink. But I don't think you need to be."

"Told him it wasn't fair since you'd not gotten a taste yet."

"I appreciate that. Tonight's not the night for it though. Ceedly was right to compare this to a riddle. And throat or flute, this is rhythmic. No room for mistakes."

"You sure you want to do it?"

"You think I shouldn't?"

He shrugged and observed, "It's surprising. The same people encouraging you to take a mortal risk are also relying on you for quite a lot. Bit contradictory, as I see it."

"Even bearing in mind what you said as far as decisions, and lessons, and soldiers?" she contested through a smile.

"But your folk are not… It's just not something I would've expected."

"Crestfolk must seem so strange from the outside. But risk and reliance don't counter one another. Not with this. And besides, to have this in my carry and *not* make the attempt would be…" Her caught breath eventually gave way with a short, pained tone. "I *must* try this, Sol."

"Even if you've done fine without bone and sinew, and… I'm not going to pretend I know what any of that means."

"It's easier shown than said. And I've only done fine because I can cast and because *you* can do everything else. And as far as casting goes, this isn't…*unsimilar*."

Sol looked at her with no loss of bewilderment.

"Witches and soldiers," she mused. "If I explained it, *really* explained it, I'm not sure you'd believe me. But, if it goes as I think it could, we wouldn't have to rely on Den to get over any vineguards."

Though Sol's dubiety was unchanged, he acquiesced and moved to resume his sharpening, until, at guarded volume, Araina said, "If I'm being honest, Ceedly, Tanzan, the Coven…they've acted like my great aunt always intended for me to get this far. I don't think she did. I don't think she'd so much as imagine me here, let alone ever attempting this."

166

"But that's what you're doing."

"I am."

"Why?"

Araina looked down at the crowded paper. Something bitter twitched in the bulb of her nose before she confessed, "Because lately, I can't remember…I can't be sure which Kerikan is real or right, mine or theirs. I want mine to be wrong, the one who saw me as a courier more than a witch. But at the same time, I want to be wrong about that. Maybe mine was never real."

"Will this answer any of that?"

"I don't know. It feels like another corner, one that she's created. This time I want to see what I'll do. I'm already rather backed into it."

After a long moment, Sol nodded, brought the stone back to his blade, and offered, "Let me know if this interferes with your study."

"I will, but it won't."

Chapter Nineteen

More Riddle Than Instruction

C eedly escorted Araina and Sol across the morning sunlight, streaked through the gapped trees and stretched long over the rear veranda. They trekked to the end of the field, where a patchwork of dried weeds and bowed wildflowers gave way to a path of rhyolite.

"Follow this until it seems you've entered into the earth, then it will descend again. That is the passage to the altar. Solairous, you must not continue beyond that drop. Araina, I wish that nothing comes between you and your strength as you proceed. Come what may, I will be eager to learn of it on your return."

"Thank you. My apologies in advance for whatever trouble Den gives," Araina offered.

"Not at all. I understand he's been amusing company in the kitchen."

With Ceedly's assurance, Araina and Sol looked to one another before giving gracious nods. They turned and continued down the stony slope.

In the long quiet between them, Araina's gait became hobbled and her pained breath audible. Sol looked down at her feet, the sandals tightened over them, and the tracks of blood from their wrappings. Streaks of it collected and spilt over her forefoot.

He grimaced and remarked, "Thought you were through with those …As you should be."

"I am," she informed through gritted teeth.

"Then why are you wearing them?"

"They've still a purpose to serve."

"You have to keep them on? You're leaving a trail behind us."

"Yes. Just a bit longer. It'd be pointless otherwise."

Noting the firm fix of the witch's eyes, Sol said nothing more.

* * *

The afternoon sky clouded and gave way to a sparse rain. Only noticeable in small, dark circles left upon the stone, it provided no real remedy from the heat and dust that rose with the land. The rhyolite walls stretched to steep and imposing cliffs. They narrowed, then widened, on and on, as though forming a pulse, which ceased with an abrupt drop. A slow, shadowy descent waited after.

"This must be it," Araina observed and knelt to remove her sandals. Even when unknotted, they clung in place, stuck with thickened blood. She dragged them free, joined their ties, and slung them over her shoulder. After a slow drink from her canteen, she left it and her pack with Sol.

"What about your blade?" he asked.

"Weapons cannot cross an altar unless they're part of the— Oh! How stupid would that've been!" A low laugh trailed her exclamation. She reached for her pack and removed the rosewood box. After wiping her hands on her trousers, she gingerly lifted the pipe.

"Should I bother to ask how long this will take?"

"I wish I could answer properly. This will work or it won't. I imagine it won't take long before either outcome is apparent."

"There's no way I can—"

"No. Not for this. I'll be back as soon as I can."

"Well, if you need me to…"

The witch nodded—only to relieve him of his attempt.

He watched her crouch at the edge of the path, lower her legs down one after the other, and drop out of sight.

The tapering, narrow crack in the land caused Araina to feel as though she had slipped into a hard and sudden dusk. While her steps landed easier without the cutting binds of the sandals, her pace was labored and cautious for the pipe—kept between her fingers like a wounded butterfly.

The rock overhead, always closing but never merged, finally yielded. The ground lifted and led up to a flat, round stone. It exceeded the size of the cottage and perhaps rivaled the reaches of the tower's great hall. Araina, not yet upon its edge, pushed away the thought of stepping upon a giant serving platter.

Her eyes traveled the looped trees that framed it. They had arched so completely, their limbs tangled into their roots. A few tiny rippled leaves clung to the jagged branches, while a mass of them had darkened, crumpled, and collected in the stone's center. Araina fought to keep her lower lip up and steady as she connected the sight to one of the intricate diagrams that accompanied the rite's murky description.

Beyond the bent border of trees was open land. Despite her and Sol's descent into earth and rock—and that she, alone, had gone deeper still—the furthest edge of the altar lay to a canyon, one seemingly limitless and primeval. The witch scanned it, exhaled starkly, and found little else to do but begin. She lifted one blood and dust-covered foot and placed it down upon the stone with an inhale.

Steps to breath.

She held it, counted, then let her air seep free, silently. The next sequence sang through her mind.

Air to wind. Wind will cease. Live again. Take all within. Sound from breath. Heat and flesh.

She waited, kept her eyes to the leaves in the center, and watched them curl among one another. With their stilted revolution, she took another step and inhaled in pace with the touch of her sole to the stone. A breeze mounted. It slipped through the looped trees, sighing and furthering the desiccated leaves in their scratching, hesitant waltz. This time, she laced her exhale with a touch of her voice.

Air ridden on flesh made thin. Heat caught. Held to carry. Steps to breath. Air to wind.

Araina proceeded toward the center under the same pattern of steps, counted waits, and respiration. Her red and grey tracks cut over weathered engravings. Their lines converged, and with their narrowing, the slithering breeze stilted into a pulse.

"Of flesh the same. Of heat. Of air," she whispered between it.

The wind, siphoning through the trees, grew quick, tight, and powerful. The sweep encompassed all and drove the leaves—repelled from one another, and then collected, spread and then collected—racing past her ankles, over her feet, and back again. At the last engraved line before the center, she aligned her soles and stood. With her pause, the leaves ripped away to the frame of tangled roots and limbs and left her as the only organic thing upon the stone. On and on, the air siphoned and slipped like great wingbeats.

Araina lowered the ties of the sandals from her shoulder and called out, full voiced, "Of flesh of the same. To feed and carry pain. Of heat. Of air." She let the blood-coated leather drop before exhaling, "Of flesh the same."

The wind halted. She raised her trembling hands and brought the pipe to her lips. In some startled tangle of concentration and instinct, she nearly took a step back. Though she fought the retreat, the small breach in rhythm hindered the filling of her lungs. It tainted the length and purity of her call. The glassy, hollow sound echoed far, but was met with utter stillness and heart-sinking silence.

The witch waited and put the entirety of her senses into her fingertips. They strained to feel for any indication that the pipe had changed. All she could gain was the sense of how her hold quivered around it. After a swallow and inhale for her life, she tried again, ringing a new flittering call to the trees.

This time, a reply roared back—a great rush of air that ripped and pushed at her from all sides. It sent her locks wild over her face, blinding her to the source of a horrifying scraping that landed upon and charged across the stone. Araina kept her fingers tight to the pipe, shook her hair away, and faced the aceridon.

With its narrow muzzle inches from the witch's toes, it snatched up the sandals with thick rows of incisors. A spade-shaped tongue maneuvered the leather past pairings of severe canines. For all the awkwardness of its chewing, the aceridon was large enough to simply swallow the offering. With every shift of its muscular body, its chatoyant eyes gleamed resinous, then fell opaque as jet. The raptorial power in its two legs and clawed feet, the lushness of a silken mane over its chest and at the base of its fanning ears, and all else comprising its form, were dominated by a pair of wings. The immense things were like jointed sails. Even semi-folded and cast down from the creature's sinewy shoulders, they were shattering. Each of their points ended with a curved claw of bone. They flared slightly and further tussled the frozen witch's tresses.

As terror, awe, beauty, and apex might stared into her, poised for something, Araina could barely close her lips around the end of the pipe. She sent forth another measured sequence of sound and took a slow step back.

The aceridon called in kind—its voice concurrently thunderous and shrieking—and at such volume that an ache rang through Araina's skull and the vessels of her neck. She swallowed thickly and pushed to answer, but the surface of the pipe upon her lower lip revealed a tiny malleability. When she called through it again, the slick tone permitted no illusions, nor did the aceridon, who responded not with a call, but a growl.

Its eyes glistened and dulled, rolling over her with a climbing rumble in its throat. Then it fixed its stare upon the pipe. Araina, hardly able to keep her fingers upon it, tried to create a call once more. She could only conjure a hollow, aqueous whine. She lowered the instrument from her lips and hot tears followed down her face. The aceridon drew a breath and parted its jaws. This time, they released flame.

The witch fell to her knees and reached out to part the blaze. It was scarcely cleared from her sides, but not without a grazing singe over her arms, shoulders, and face. The pipe crashed to the stone and limply cracked like a clam dropped by a gull. She squinted at it through her choking. The aceridon watched her sputter, then it moved its gaze to the pipe. Its narrow snout twitched. The gleam in its eyes flashed and then held in a seeming meditation. Araina reclaimed her footing and struggled to hear the clicks in the creature's throat. The aceridon's eyes set back on her.

She braced herself for another wave of flame and the test of whether it could be parted in enough time to dash and reach the passage—its imposing narrowness now a clear and limited means of survival. But then, there was her light and the question of what it would gain. Above that, there was the utterly profane audacity of it—for a Crest witch to attempt a strike on such a creature after rousing it.

The clicking and rolling in its throat crescendoed. Araina readied herself, whether to move fire or summon light, she did not know beyond the spreading of her fingers, nor did she have the opportunity to discover, as, in place of flame, the aceridon released a cacophony of bellows, shrieks, and rolling chirps. It surrounded her in a sourceless wave, crumbling her to the stone.

Swept by a paralyzing flood of sound, she could not so much as shift her clenched fists to her ears. The din seemed to congeal her blood and simmer the marrow of her bones. The skin over her scapulas began to stretch and then tear. The fabric of the bodice followed in two vertical rips—sliced open by symmetrically emerging claws. Flesh-gripped appendages rose after. With a shallow scream of blood, wings grew from Araina's back.

Before unfurling its own wings, the aceridon regarded the motionless witch with one last shift of its eyes and twitch of its snout. Its claws across the stone broke the pure clutch of silence and ceased Araina's wondering of whether she had been deafened. It departed—gone to the sky over the canyon—far beyond her view, which still held tight to the stone.

Araina could not move her upper back without a bold retort of pain. Blood continued to collect in the fabric of her bodice and tulitiere. The wounds throbbed as the wings slowly warmed and fused their connection. They stubbornly shifted, permitting a shuddering control, which gave way to a flex—first on the right and then the left. Finally, and still upon her knees and forearms, she spread them.

Araina rolled her wings out and down. When held to the light, the grey flesh changed to a steely, pale indigo. She dared to stretch them further and observed the shadow cast at her sides. It spanned nearly triple the reach of her arms. She straightened her back with a wounded cry. With another, she brought one leg forward, then the other, and rose up.

The ends came below her knees. The tops extended to a full reach above her head. They obeyed her as she folded and let them hang like an unworldly cloak. She opened them again and they asserted their force, enough that her soles flattened and then drove against the stone.

Araina began to laugh. Then she cackled, delirious and unabashed, to the looped trees and blood-speckled stone. It was broken by a wince and cough at the painful toll of it. On catching her breath and senses, she tightened her wings and left the altar.

The clawed tips nearly touched the arching walls of the passage. The perilous thought of grazing the thin flesh sent her wondering how easily it could be torn. Even with the incline of the land, and her singed skin and ripped back, such wonderings shortened the distance between her, Sol, and open sky.

The sight of two clawed wings appearing from the shadows nearly caused Sol to drop Araina's canteen and draw his sword. He stared as the witch rose to the upper trail, confirming the appendages were indeed attached to her. He did not speak or move as she approached, or when she took the canteen from his hand and hoarsely thanked him before a long drink.

"Was I gone for very long? It took ages and then it seemed to be over so fast," she uttered.

"You...you've... This was supposed to happen?"

"It was among the better outcomes."

"You've got..." Sol went on stammering and gaping. When his view crossed from the claws and over the dim flesh to the darkened spots at Araina's sides, her singed face and arms, and the blood trailed across her shoulders and dampening her curls, he picked up his jaw and asked, "Araina, are you alright?"

She rigidly nodded. "Will you tell me how long the wounds are?"

"Wounds?"

With a twinge, she gestured toward her shoulder blades. "From where they extend. I don't know how well you can see."

Sol cautiously shifted one of the tears in the bodice and glimpsed a raw, gleaming split in her flesh. He grimaced.

"Maybe about the size of my hand."

"They feel like they're running down the whole of my back."

He picked up her pack and took her canteen.

"I can carry those," she protested.

"So can I. Let's get back."

"Thank you. I expect it will be quicker without the sandals," Araina remarked as they proceeded.

"They served their purpose then?"

"My vulantemp. The aceridon gobbled them right up."

"Should I ask what either of those are?"

"A vulantemp is an old concept. Translates to a submission of scars. It's a bond built through trial or something shown on arrival as evidence of pain in getting there. For a rite like this, it helps if it's edible."

"Bison leather," Sol concluded.

"With a coating of human blood. And the aceridon is the creature that accepted them."

"What would you've done if you didn't have the sandals?"

"I'm not sure." Araina thoughtfully lifted her eyes before adding, "But I probably wouldn't've."

"Now that you have, are you always... I mean, are those always going to be..."

"No. They shouldn't... No, no, they can be called back. I think..."

Sol surveyed the wings again. "Not that they aren't impressive, but you might be a little more conspicuous as a witch. Unless you're just going to be flying everywhere from now on?"

"I'd argue that would also be conspicuous. But no, they bond with bone, and sinew, and strength. The nature of these things is that they can also be concealed. I simply have to learn how to fold them away, so to speak. They're just a bit stiff for now. And then I'll have to learn how to..." Apprehension tensed the witch's inflamed face.

"How to what?"

"I just remembered that I'm not very good with heights."

"You don't like heights but you've gotten yourself a pair of wings. Last night you made it seem like you thought this through."

"Well, if nothing else, you did say they look impressive."

Den and Pidgie took flight from the back veranda when Araina and Sol came into view. On approach, the elf's jaw went slack. He drove Pidgie to the grass, slid off the bird's back, and tried to circle the witch.

"Rainy— What? How?!"

"Please stop before you trip me or I squash you, or both." Araina's voice dwindled. Before she could ask Den to fly back and report her and Sol's return, Ceedly appeared and stared for a long moment, then proceeded across the field.

"So you've done it. Are you in much pain?"

"It's subsiding."

"She needs help," Sol interjected. "The wounds on her back are sizable."

"Well, naturally," Ceedly assured before turning to Araina. "Have they gained full feeling?"

"Yes. Other than some stiffness at the larger joints."

"We shall get you cleaned up."

"There's one thing I'd really like to take care of first. I was hoping you could help with it."

"And what is that, Araina?"

"How do I put them away?"

"You wish to hide them when you've only just gained them?"

"I don't know how else I'm going to get this bodice off and I hate the thought of cutting it. More so than it's been already."

Ceedly laughed. "Yes, we can take care of that."

She and Araina proceeded along to the veranda, leaving Sol, Den, and Pidgie.

"Now that Rainy's got those, am I done with this lookout business?"

"Leave reconnaissance up to her instead of you? Even if that made any sense, afraid you're still stuck," Sol reminded the elf.

"Pfft, gotta be more choosy with job offers. But eh, looks like Miss moon snake lived through somethin' else. If that don't call for'a drink to celebrate, hate to see what else it's gonna take, General." Den eyed the packs Sol carried, theorizing which held the rum.

"Wouldn't it be better to wait until she gets off the ground first?"

"Why not raise'a glass to both? Heh, gotta say I'm lookin' forward to watchin' that part."

"Will you give her a few pointers at least?"

"She'd hav'ta ask him."

Both he and Sol looked at Pidgie in the grass and his strutting hunt for seeds. Sol then turned toward the pained sounds carrying across the field and watched as Araina awkwardly maneuvered her wings through the door.

"May be in for a wait before she gets in the air," the soldier surmised. "Still have those cards?"

"Hah! You're on, General! Winner takes the bottle!"

Chapter Twenty

Marked on the Map

Medicinal scents wafted across the small chamber while the sound of a filling basin echoed across the brass of the waiting tub. Araina, kneeling beside it, kept her shoulders hoisted and tense.

"Another deep breath. Now bring them higher, past your shoulders, toward your ears," Ceedly guided. The wings shuttered forward. "Good. Now, do you feel where they end?"

Araina nodded between shallow lung pushes and leaned into her knees. Ceedly approached and lowered the basin to the floor.

"Relax your shoulders slightly. This spot, bring them here." She grazed her fingertip to the space below the wound that parted for Araina's right wing. The trace of a touch summoned a cringe and quick gasp. Tears rolled from the witch's clenched eyes.

"Once they reenter your body, they will bond. You'll have ample room if you breathe with their progress. Slowly. No need to rush."

Araina tightened the wings as slim as they would fold and curved them as high and far as they would reach. When the bottom claws touched the wounds' ends, she gasped and grit her teeth. Her eyes went on watering through their reclaim, left and right in tandem. She fed the flesh, bones, and joints, pulling the bulk of each wing so they smoothed and withdrew into her body. Finally, the top claws sank away, and with them, any indication of the wings but for splits in her skin and bodice. Araina released another seething exhale.

"Well done," Ceedly praised.

"If it's this painful withdrawing them, I don't know if I'll ever take them out again." Araina cleared the tears gathered below her chin.

"Provided they emerge with some frequency, the required muscles will strengthen. Calling them free, and then away, will go faster and come easier, and with far less pain. Now, we'll see what can be said for these wounds. Keep still as you can, please." Ceedly wrung a cloth from the basin. "I see your skin is singed as well."

"It—" Araina breathed through her clenched teeth and the sting of the liquid. "It-it came upon me with its fire. I wasn't expecting that."

"One method for confirming a Crest child."

"I dropped the pipe to alter the flame. It took notice. I can't help but wonder if that was the point. It almost looked relieved. ...Pleased to see it destroyed. It obliged right after. I'm starting to feel, perhaps, as though...as though I've exploited something."

"It accepted your vulantemp. That means it is a bargain. It only becomes an exploitation if you do not live up to your end of it, of which it expects you are capable, clearly."

"I suppose I'll have to trust that." Araina sighed in concession and discomfort.

"You can trust that ancient creature knows its world has been altered. That fact is plain to it as it is to us. It was bound to expect someone, submitting herself to its strength, for its strength. It chose to answer. That's all the more reason you must use those wings rather than question your means to and now owning of them."

"I hope I'm the last human it ever meets, Crest or otherwise."

"It's within your ability to ensure no human has reason to meet it."

Araina listened to liquid slosh in the basin and trickle away as the cloth was wrung again. She hissed at another touch to her wounds.

"These need to scar properly to ensure they stay open. A long herbal soak will aid that, along with your burns."

"Forgive me for depleting your medicinal stores with all this."

"We'll manage. You can take a meal after your bath. I'll leave you to undress and soak. You can be out of that bodice through its lacings alone."

"Thank you, Ceedly."

Araina's traverse of the lower corridor was slowed by the settling of her supper, blood-loss, and the sway of the chemise. She was grateful to be lent it, though the gratitude fell to guilt when the fine linen and overlaid lace was cut to keep the fabric clear from the wounds—an alteration upon which Ceedly insisted. Her hair was swept and braided over her shoulder for the same reason.

Before reaching the stairs to the upper quarters, she heard laughter through the blue glass windows. It was not the curious children's giggles that met them on arrival, but deep and loose laughter—the sort that filled taverns. Den's contribution was quite recognizable. On assuming the other chuckling voice belonged to Sol, Araina tried to recall if she had ever heard his laugh beyond a blithe timbre or amused though stifled tone. She looked down at the chemise, gauged the call for sleep from her body, and decided propriety and exhaustion could yield to curiosity—at least for a moment or several. She turned and found the nearest door to the back veranda.

Neither Den seated upon the railing, nor Sol with his back resting against it, noticed Araina's approach. The last of the day's light caught on a red crystal tumbler, held askew by the soldier.

On observing its glitter, she confronted, "I thought the rest of that rum was to wait until I'd gotten to sample it."

Sol and Den turned.

"Look who decides to show up!" the elf said just below a shout.

"And wingless," the soldier added, wearing a smile as slick and unencumbered as the witch had ever seen.

"An' empty-handed. Coulda 'least've brought out s'more'a that cake. Could live off that stuff." Den leaned back and lifted a crystal stopper to his lips. Its overturned hollow served as his glass. The decanter to which it belonged appeared from the other side of Sol's knee and was eagerly tilted to refill the tumbler.

"So you've gone through the rum and now you've raided Ceedly's stores?"

"You hear 'er? Shows up cake-less then goes on callin' us drunks an' thieves. She ever let up?" Den slurred and shook his head.

"Oh but we are men and elves of honor. 'Specially in the midst of witches. The rum awaits. *This* is a liquor we've been gifted. Consolation for our idleness," Sol explained and extended the tumbler. "Made with some berry I never heard've but am glad to know as a liquor."

"Rosaberry," Araina identified on bringing it to her nose. "They grow in the centers of flowers that look like dog roses. Mind how easy it goes down."

She lowered the glass to Sol. He did not take it.

"Fascinating, Araina, but I gave it to you to drink." He then slid along the step, creating a place for her to sit.

She sighed through her nose, held the chemise to her calves, and took it while Den chuckled, "Wish someone would tell 'er she oughta do less thinkin', more drinkin'. Feh. Witches."

"You could do it," Sol suggested through a smirk.

"Listen, Rainy, an' this is importan', ya oughta do less thinkin' an' more drinkin'."

"How's to argue with that?" the soldier asked and watched Araina raise the tumbler to her lips.

"She'll find a way." With the glassy echo of Den's voice through the stopper, both he and Sol burst with a laugh. Araina lost the fight in joining. After a sputtered swallow, she wiped the sweet, heady spirit from her mouth.

"While it is a sight to see the two of you getting along so splendidly, albeit with *strong* lubrication, and at my expense, I'm just taking a long route to bed. I will say goodnight to you both before I hear the name *Rainy* from two drunken mouths." She returned the tumbler to Sol.

After a thick swallow, he protested, "C'mon, Arainya. You can't go. This is a celebration, for you. An' 'cause Den lost the cards. Now we got nothing to wager on or with. So we called it a draw an' split the bottle. Square and fair."

"Celebration for me?"

"For those monster wings ya got now! Then them goin' back in. It's a celebration of ya fittin' through doors 'gain!"

Araina crinkled her smile at Den's guffaw and turned to Sol, expecting the same. Instead, she found a clement simper and soft awe settled over his dark eyes. He reached for the braid over her shoulder, held it a moment, then smoothed his hand down its length.

He leaned to spy her wounds through the chemise cuts and mumbled, "No small feat. Though, maybe not be the worst thing. Early night. If learnin' to fly in the morning."

"Exactly my thinking."

"Wha'did I jus' say?" Den grumbled into his nearly empty stopper.

Araina gripped the chemise, shakily rose, and warned, "Finish the rest of that decanter and I wager you'll miss my attempt. Not that I wish to have an audience."

"Wager? Hey! Forget cards. We'll stake on a race 'tween Rainy and Pidgie!" Den proposed.

Sol unsuccessfully stifled his laughter.

"Goodnight, gentlemen," Araina bade and left them to their slurring amusement.

Sol found the corner of the pillow a poor shield for sunlight. It awoke a cutting pain across his brow. Immediately after, a weight over his body became apparent, particularly at his feet. He wiggled his toes and squinted down the length of his form, confirming he had indeed fallen asleep in his boots, as well as his trousers, and a single cuff of his sleeve—still fastened around his wrist. The rest of his shirt was inside-out, twisted, and dangling off the edge of the bed. He groaned, pushed a bitter, syrupy version of his own saliva across his tongue, and sat up. A small though dense mass rolled into his side. Sol sharply leaned away as a tussled and similarly afflicted elf snorted awake.

"Waspscum," the soldier grumbled. "You're here?"

"Wasp scum? Huh. Gonna use that." Den rubbed his forehead and pulled his fingers across his bristled chin. "Guess Rainy's door was locked. That, or I was bangin' at the wrong one. 'Sume Pidgie's with 'er. Had I seen 'im, I'd'a gone through the window."

"You stay in her room?" Sol asked with hoarse distaste. "Does she know about it?" He untwisted and reversed the sleeve up his arm then backtracked into the rest of his shirt.

"On the windowsill with Pidgie," Den clarified. "Whadda ya worried 'bout, competition 'er somethin'?"

Sol squinted at the elf, then returned his throbbing forehead to his hand.

"Damn sweet spirits," he muttered into the basin near the window. After pouring water from the pitcher, he all but dropped his face into it.

"Hey, seein' as we're surrounded by nothin' but witches, ya figure they got some hair-of-the-dog tricks or potions, right?" Den proposed, searching for his lost kerchief in the rumpled linens.

"Ask at your own peril. Might come with a told-ya-so."

Sol let the water roll off his face and lifted his view to the window. As he blinked through the parted curtains, his tightened eyes widened at the sight on the back veranda. Araina stood on the rail of the landing, balanced upon her toes. Her wings, again revealed, swept at the air. They dragged her up and then forward in a slow gliding fall. They stretched then held, pushing her back and upright. With the touch of one foot, then the other, she returned to the ground.

Sol grabbed the cloth on the dresser, hastily dried his face, and turned away from the window. He scanned for, spotted, and swept his belt from the floor.

"What's goin' on?" Den asked.

"See for yourself." Sol fastened his sword, then exited the room.

Den located his kerchief, gave it a shake, and tied it over his hair. He slid off the bed, scurried up to the dresser, and after a quick view through the window, exclaimed, "Ah, waspscum! Missin' the show!"

* * *

"What do you think? Look like I have the basics?" a breathless though smiling Araina asked the passenger pigeon perched upon the upper landing. "Seems to be a matter of just fighting a fall at the right moments."

Pidgie blinked his little orange eyes and responded with a scratchy quarter-coo, one the witch chose to take as approval. A creaking of the nearest door on the landing tore her attention.

"Oh dear, my good sir, seems the quiet part of our morning has just come to an end," she mutedly assessed before calling, "Good morning," to Sol as he appeared. He shielded his eyes and gave a sluggish wave before lowering himself to the stairs.

"Sleep well?" Araina softly inquired.

"Can only guess. Know that waking was worse." He rubbed his brow.

"Let me fetch Ceedly. There are remedies for this sort of thing, although I did warn—"

"Do they work?"

"I can't say from experience."

"That a witch thing or just discipline?" He peered at her through the spread of his fingers.

"Bit of both?" She shrugged with a smile.

"I'm fine. Don't let me disrupt your practice."

"You're not the one I'm worried about—"

"Rainy! What ya doin' on the ground? Up ya go!" Den called along his march to the stairs.

"I'm afraid you missed the more entertaining portion," Araina informed him, causing Sol to take stock of the dirt streaked across her ankles, knees, and elbows.

"Early lessons hard learned?" he asked.

"A few missteps. Not as awful as I was fearing. It's hard work though. Ceedly informs me the most I can expect from them are short speed and modest height. I lack the form of an aceridon and the hollow bones of a bird. Humans are not meant for flight after all, let alone one as pear-shaped as I."

"And your regard for heights?" Sol asked.

"That railing is no small drop if you're standing on it."

"And ya ain't got wings," Den countered.

"Better to learn to swim from the shore rather than cast overboard. I've still some time to practice. That said, Sol, we should expect to meet with Zunera this afternoon." The smile faded from the witch's dirt-smudged face as she added, "We're close."

"Glad the two'a ya got more'a your little secret meetings lined up. Any plan for breakfast 'fore that?"

"You'll be pleased I didn't bring out that leftover cake last night. It's been given new life, which looks as though it could benefit you both. Follow me."

"What's the use in followin' ya if you're just gonna get stuck in the door?" Den mocked.

Araina provided no response but for a single step retreat. She stiffed her shoulders, tightly folded and raised her wings with an inhale, then drew them into the wounds of her back.

"Was wondering how they just disappeared yesterday," Sol said.

"We can remain inconspicuous after all."

"'Least as close to it as ya were before," the elf remarked as he trailed them indoors.

Poached eggs over potatoes, coffee, and the previous day's cake—toasted and buttered—waited for them in the kitchen. More practice on Araina's part and spectating on that of her companions followed after, until she and Sol were directed to the highest floor of the temple.

At the end of a curving staircase, they crossed into a circle of light stained blue by the overhead dome. Its saturation reminded Araina of those passages to and from Tanzan's study and the green and amber tint that served as the afterglow of curiosity satisfied for better or worse. The recollection kept her a step short of the door, giving Sol clearance to knock upon it instead.

"Please come in," a young woman's voice responded.

They entered a circular room below another dome of glass, this one clear and set in a complex spiraling framework. The iron curves and cutting angles looked more like a chart than any decorative or architecturally driven arrangement. Below it were spyglasses on tripods, open books on lecterns, and a round table covered in scrolls, abacuses, compasses, and a series of tools driven by pendulums and cranks. Their crowding obscured the face of a young woman, seated with a baby swaddled and sleeping within her arms.

"Araina and Solairous? I'm Zunera of the Sanabrights, the stellidentin put to work on the last of the Meridian Reflections. Pleased to finally meet you both."

"It's an—"

"No need to whisper," Zunera assured Araina. "She's just had her lunch. Believe me, you'll not wake her with anything short of a shout."

"Sounds fortunate," Araina remarked, her voice still at a whisper.

"Quite the change from my first. Please take a seat." The witch and the soldier, both wary of the complex spread of instruments, cautiously accepted while Zunera went on, "For a time, I thought to apologize for the delay in confirming your next steps. But now, on matching the Reflections to the maps and reports of the terrain, I almost want to apologize for where they'll send you."

"Why is that?" Araina dared.

"Which one of you navigates?"

Sol nodded to confirm.

Zunera stood up, approached Araina, and asked, "Would you mind for just a moment?"

Before Araina could answer, the sleeping baby was lowered into her arms. Zunera then slid out a map from below a pile and placed it before Sol.

"I'm pleased to say the nearest point is not far. It's not quite a two-day trek from here, through a small stretch of woodland, and in the heart of these grasslands." She pointed to an inked circle upon the map.

"Doesn't sound like anything meriting an apology so far," Sol stated as he observed the portrayed landscape.

Araina lifted her view from the deeply sleeping baby. "And the next two?"

"They may merit it. They will not be easy passage. Not anymore. You'll be far from Landers' territory. That's favorable considering the trouble they've given us. But, you won't have many opportunities to resupply either. That carries its own difficulties."

"Has the land slipped that much?"

"The traces carried back by the birds and reports from similar grounds claim such. From what I've heard, supplying our scouts without the usual support of the season and land has been challenging, even more than expected. You'll be sent with provisions that will keep you sustained for a long while despite all that. Just the same, if you see an opportunity to hunt, fish, or forage, take it. The next point lies at the lowlands here." Zunera pointed to the next marking.

"And the third?" Araina braced herself.

"After the longest stretch between any. You'll have forest to traverse, then willow swamps, but it may be the most barren you'll have seen in all your steps. I don't know if you'll have to worry about Vexhi, but that land was once home to dwovflin, the largest remaining population this far south. It's been said they haven't fared well. They may be hostile to anything that doesn't look as they, and more so since Vexhi have pushed their borders north and west."

"Dwovflin?" Sol asked.

"They're smaller folk. Shorter than dwoves, taller than trolls, though closer to their features. Myself, I only know them by descriptions. But hopefully, you won't get a chance to see any."

With Zunera's warning, Sol's eyes met Araina's. The baby stirred slightly, prompting a break of their shared curiosity.

Araina swayed in her chair. "Is the third within their borders?"

"Beyond, though they may be on the move for more fertile ground. In reaching the edge of the third's location, your race against Vexhi will have tightened. Solairous, I'm sure you already know what lies within miles of this spot on the map."

The soldier smoothly nodded. A series of questions flooded Araina's throat. None could gain lead before Sol asked, "And from there?"

"You turn due west," Ceedly informed and approached the table. In their envisioning of the foretold route, no one noticed her entry. She smiled down at the baby in Araina's arms and lifted her into her own.

"So Aunt Ceedly is late for nap time," she cooed before her voice returned to its usual fortitude. "Small companies of our scouts have been making slow progress from the southwestern passes of the Noxprimma and through the Gour Morken Flats. Behind them, Svet Hagen troops will rally to push back Vexhi. And behind them, Crest forces, ready to receive you and the four points you'll have in your possession. Then, your part is done, Araina, or rather held, until all are recovered. They'll then be yours to seal. Since any patch of soil permits it, whether they'll be brought to you or you to them will depend on what comes before."

"Have you gotten word from the Coven specifying my position following the rendezvous?" The soldier's face, stalwart as his tone, held a waiting ardency. Though Araina recalled traces of it when Sol suggested reclaiming touchpoints in Ceedly's study, it pitted a troubling density in her stomach at that moment—the first with a foreseeable and mapped end.

"In Trinera's most recent letter, she mentioned it was under discussion. No decision has been made that I know. By the time our troops reach you, I imagine it will be."

"Is there anything else we should know?" Araina's voice quivered more than she anticipated.

"Nothing more but for any answers you require. You'll be fully supplied to leave in the morning. Though our borders have been clear, it will be best if you get started before the light. If you've any word for Tanzan or Trinera, I'll have it sent with one of my red-tails."

"Could I trouble you for a quill and well? I'd like to make some notes on the map. And from the look of the route, some rope would be useful, if available," Sol requested.

"No trouble at all, Solairous. I'll amend the provisions. And as far as your map marking, I will make a place for you in my study," Ceedly offered then asked, "Araina, is there anything…"

"If you've any silk thread or something of comparable strength." Her voice remained quick and fractured.

"Any particular color?"

"Black would be ideal."

"Of course."

"I'll go tell Den we're due to leave early," Araina tendered with a low sigh. "Is there anything he might require?"

"Perhaps just a hardy supper. Enough to fill him up for another month, if that's possible."

Sol smiled at Araina's plea and tried to catch her eye. She stood and exited the room.

His work at the map complete and his things gathered for a quick depart at dawn, Sol found Araina seated on the front steps. Clad in an unfamiliar red dress, she worked a needle and black thread along the tears in her bodice.

"Have you raided a clothesline without me?" he interrogated.

"This dress has been properly borrowed and stolen shawls didn't seem necessary. Just something while I reinforce these openings in the fresh air." Her stitching slowed little as he sat beside her and watched her fingers dexterously loop then smoothly knot the thread.

"You sew as fast as you swim."

"Just don't check the tidiness of my stitches if you wish to remain impressed." Araina ran the tail back up into the fabric, clipped the end, and rethreaded the needle. "I'll mend your sleeve if you'd like."

"Only a few small tears. Hardly thought about it since. Not worth the bother."

"It isn't one. And let a tiny tear remain and the whole of it's as good as unraveled. I'll wait if you'd like to change into something else so I can—" Sol extended his arm and let her rest it across her lap, prompting her to state, "I'm glad you trust me with a needle."

"I'll take my chances. I know how much coaxing it takes you to properly swing a dagger. So why'd you vanish so soon after we'd gotten our route?" he asked as she went to work.

"Perhaps I was just excited to do some sewing." Her voice was flat as her eyes were focused, following her fingers and the needle through the fabric over Sol's skin.

"Hmm. The look of a woman eager to do some sewing. Crossed your face right as Zunera mentioned we'd be within miles of something."

"The stronghold of which you and Ceedly spoke, isn't it? The one Den mentioned as well."

"Is that what has you looking so concerned? That last point is as close as you'll ever get to it. Easily avoided."

"And for you?"

"What do you mean?"

"You look as though you intend to get closer to it. Not just intend. It's as though you can't get there fast enough."

"That would be the final front," Sol said, his voice breezy as he looked at the weathered statues in the distance. "A place for soldiers but not witches, as pledged."

"I've not forgotten."

"Well, if the miles before it have you looking as you do, you've forgotten other things."

"Such as?"

"Why you needed that thread. Why there are rumors of a lake demon and vengeful lightning rolling through Radomezen. Enjoyed that when I heard it at the smith."

"It's not… It's just… I-I think I forgot, after we turn west, that means…" Araina looked at him and found little clarity or courage to choose her next words and say them aloud. She only resumed her stitching.

It ceased again when Sol stated, "My mission and yours is marked on the map. No question needed past it. Well within our abilities. After is after. Whatever that is, it's also well within them."

"I'd love your certainty."

"It's there for the taking." Though Sol's sleeve was thoroughly mended, his arm remained on her lap. She slipped her hold from his wrist, only then aware she kept it. He leaned in to observe her work. "Tidiest stitches I've ever seen."

"You just lack a critical eye."

"I wonder what you'd make of how most soldiers keep their socks together."

"I can only imagine. Though I'd rather not." Araina wove in the tail and clipped the thread. Sol unhurriedly reclaimed his arm.

"Don't blame you."

Chapter Twenty-One

Elevated to an Impasse

Whispered thanks were exchanged for wishes of well faring and Araina, Sol, Den, and Pidgie set out with the light of dawn. When they came to the eastern edge of the vineguard border, Den and Pidgie quickly cleared its reaches and waited beyond. Araina took a tightly rolled paper tucked into the strap of her bodice and blew the fine blue powder kept within. The zeadase settled upon the leaves, giving her and Sol safe passage through the tendrils and away from Crest grounds.

With so many imaginings born from Zunera's descriptions, the immediate trek seemed all the duller. The heat over-rendered the hours and spoiled any sense of ease to be gained from flat land. The monotony was only broken by the last truly fresh meal they could expect for a time—rice bread, walnut butter, and pepper-barley cakes—and the spectacle of a single grasshopper that sparked from the grass ahead of their steps.

When they lost the sun, Sol suggested they keep their path by torch and continue for a few further miles into wooded cover. He proceeded to assemble one aided by the light at Araina's palm and beeswax provided by Sage specifically for the purpose. The carried flame guided them into a border of thin trees and along stretching shadows. Den rode on Pidgie, who rode upon Araina's shoulder. Her pace kept with Sol's while swift and roaring winds rose with their passage.

Not far along their leaf-whirled trail, Sol stopped suddenly, catching something that seemed separate from the straining of branches and the howl of wind. Araina looked to him and grew the light at her hand. After a silent tip of his head, she closed it away and they resumed their steps, until, moments later, something mounted in the cover of a great gust and struck the torch from Sol's grip. It was whisked from the brush before it could extinguish or set the leaves aflame. A weight clamped over Araina's mouth and a zealous squeeze closed around her arms. Den and Pidgie were ripped from her shoulder with half a cursed exclaim and trill of distress, which silenced abruptly. Sol's call was muffled and pulled down with the rest of him. A clamor of metal followed.

Forced against a restraining body, Araina's balance was claimed. The push of a jaw knocked her head to her shoulder. A scratch of whiskers along her ear and cheek carried a scent of smoke, meat, and citrus.

"Oh, could I ever imagine my patience reaping such reward? How I've been waiting for a witch to come out of that thorn garden. Can I tell you how much it delights me to see it's the delivery girl?" Boon almost sang, gleeful and low against her skin.

Newly lit lanterns joined the torchlight at her back. One was carried before her, giving her a short glimpse of Sol in shadow-thickened underbrush. A boot pressed his face to the leaves. Another figure knelt over his back and bound wrists. His sheath was empty at his side. His crossbow, quiver, and pack were gone as well. Araina's breath quickened into Boon's hand.

"Ooh, oh, I see," he said with relish. "Worry not. This is all in your hands. But I want nothing from your mouth, legs, or those little fingernails. No tricks. We're going to keep things simple and relaxed, because whatever you try, falls on him." Boon forced more of his weight upon her, pressing until she was reduced to the ground.

"Bind her. Do it as they said," he commanded. After Araina's pack was unbuckled from her center, her arms and legs were forced forward and her right wrist and left ankle were bound. So followed her left wrist to her right ankle. With her limbs crossed, her body folded, and Boon's hand still suppressing her mouth and nose, a panic for air muddled any clarity in her brain. A lantern was then placed on the ground between her and Sol.

The man kneeling on the soldier's back leaned to his ear and snarled, "Not a sound."

The boot at Sol's skull was lifted and he was yanked upright by his hair. Chunks of dirt sputtered from his lips with a choke. Reflected lantern light flashed across the darkness as Sol's sword was spun and its point was brought to his neck.

"You can watch him die by his own blade," Boon submitted to Araina. "After, by the point of it, you can do some digging. Wager it'd go quick, stout as you are. Needn't be wide or deep, not for a box this tight. No treasure in it. Just an extra thick sack with a fat pigeon and what I think is an elf. Must feel as though they're underground already. Can't be easy to breathe. Even harder than it is for you, so I'm going to remove my hand. Besides, seems a requirement to resume our little conversation. Don't you agree?"

His hold yielded just enough for her to nod.

"Let's start with your name. You neglected to mention it on gaining my acquaintance. Curious if your manners've improved since."

After Boon removed his hand, a desperate gasp of air preceded, "Araina."

"Oh how suitable!" He grinned and let her slump to the dirt. "My little thorny salt flower, indeed. So perfect I'd think it a lie, but not with those eyes slick as they are. Pleasure to finally exchange a proper introduction, Araina. Now remind me where we left off."

"Will you please let them out?" she pleaded.

"Beg pardon? I'm afraid that doesn't sound familiar."

"Den and Pidgie. Please… If they can't breathe…"

"Well, if it's going to distract you."

Boon tipped his chin. After a creak of hinges, muffled flapping and shouting became audible again, then briefly distinct, until the hinges creaked once more and a latch clicked. Boon tossed an empty sack on the ground before Araina. She said nothing. Her widened eyes strained to catch Sol's.

"More distractions? I assure you he's breathing just fine. For now, you can limit his troubles to a neck ache and a mouthful of dirt. Again, Araina, remind me where we left off," Boon prompted.

"You…you asked for my help."

"That's not quite right. Seems you've a poor memory. That would explain why you've forgotten to properly address a captain. Permit me to aid your recollection." Boon crouched and fixed his stare on her. "I asked for nothing. I *gave* a very generous offer."

"You offered me a job. Aiding…" Araina breathed each word. "Searching… for some type of artifact, Captain."

"And you declined, despite the rewards. If I recall correctly, you held a bottle of rum at the time, one near-poised to strike a blow. I do admire a woman who's ready for anything. You can tell a lot about one like that, which is useful when you have to be ready for her."

Araina rolled her thumbs over her fists and tensed through the strain of her bent body. "Is that's why you've bound me this way, Captain?"

"You're surprised by that? Mustn't take anything for granted with witches. Their dangers. Their uses. Confront the former, gain the latter. And I am still seeking a witch, but I'm no longer offering rewards. Not even terribly interested in those artifacts. The ones you pretend to know nothing of."

"Then what use do I serve, Captain?"

"Have you not heard? Witches themselves now fetch a fine price."

Araina lifted her eyes to Boon's and fought the metallic rush of panic in her throat. She felt the scars at her back budge.

"A price offered by whom, Captain?"

"There are many buyers in many ports. And as with so many things, prices rise by the day."

Despite her fear giving way to ire, she kept her voice supple and low. "Do they still compare with those offered for an artifact?"

"Beg pardon, witch? Are you suddenly familiar with those artifacts? That's a change."

"Per your previous offer, Captain, a witch like me is just a means to them. And means, valuable as they are, seldom cost as much as the end. Would that be accurate to say?"

"Not inaccurate." Boon crossed his arms.

Araina kept his gaze but strained to hear Sol's breath as it seemed to shift.

"...Then why settle for a lesser gain?" she slowly asked and leaned upright as she could manage. "I've noticed you've at least...seven men helping subdue us? A lucky number. Clearly, you and they understand the risk you've undertaken, Captain."

"Indeed, witch. And *clearly* you can see that risk has been averted."

"Has it, Captain?" She widened her eyes at him.

Though he did not answer, his fallen smile begged an elaboration.

Araina obliged. "Not to flatter myself, but you *are* dealing with a witch. If my employer...pardon me, if my *captain* sent me on such a venture, and he had the opportunity to reap greater benefits for about the same amount of trouble, perhaps even less, I'd expect him to take the higher reward. Surely that would mean my share would grow as well. That is how these matters do tend to work, do they not, Captain?"

In the midst of her melodic summation, Araina noticed the sword at Sol's throat go slack. Though she could ascertain little from the dim lantern light, some of the men appeared to turn to one another. Low and sharp exchanges stirred up at her back. She then reset her focus on Sol, his blade, and the light held in its perfect edges. It awoke workings in her brain and lifted her right eyebrow. She flattened it as Boon's hardening view moved from his whispering men back to her.

"I see cross-binds don't dampen your confidence as they do your powers."

"Regarding this particular arrangement of binds, Captain, I feel I should inform you of something. But I don't dare…" she warned, her voice descending into a whisper, causing Boon to lean in as she added, "…out of fear of humiliating you."

"Humiliating me?"

Araina nodded, her eyes wide.

Boon snickered. "So you think me a man of fragile esteem? You're mistaken. Go on. Share your little secret, witch. Loud and clear as you like."

Araina's voice remained discreet. "You haven't actually cross-bound me, Captain." Boon's brow furrowed below a weighty mix of curiosity and wariness as she went on to offer, "I could tell you how to remedy that, but it would amount to considerable disadvantage for me. I'd also need to take care of something else first."

"And what's that?"

"Sparing my other companion the trouble of that neck ache."

"A less patient man would point out your lack of leverage."

"Well, Captain, as I said, I don't like to flatter myself, but frankly, you know you can't say for certain which of us lacks leverage. As mentioned, you haven't actually cross-bound me. If you'd have that sword lowered, I'll not only tell you how to correct your mistake, I'll permit you to do so."

"He's worth such a submission?"

Araina's voice dropped again. "I know you already know the answer to that, Captain."

Boon picked up the lantern between her and Sol. In its glow, he contemplated her face, then turned and took Sol's sword in his own hand. In a rapid sweep, Boon circled it to Araina's chin and steered her eyes to his.

"Well then, witch? Let's correct that pressing little mistake."

She swallowed against the precisely honed edge. "Cross-binding requires thumbs crossed to toes. Not wrist to ankles. I could've been out of these sorry little constrictors at any moment."

Boon's eyes narrowed in an agitated recollection.

He looked sharply at his men and growled, "That's what they said at the docks! Bind her properly!"

Araina kept still as the lantern was placed beside her, Boon shifted the sword and the ropes were briefly removed and reattached—awkwardly tethering her thumbs to her halluxes.

"Yes, you see, you've cross-bound me correctly now, Captain."

"Thought that secret lost to history, didn't you, witch? Only hidden."

"Indeed, Captain." Her eyes shifted to the sagging angle of the sword in his grip and her smile dropped as she amended, "But it doesn't matter because it doesn't do anything."

In a sudden jerk of her hands, the witch ripped her thumbs from the loops around her toes. She kicked the lantern and swept her hand over its broken cavity, pulling a wave of spilt flames into the air. With a rope-stumbled push to her feet, she revealed her wings and broadened them to their limit. Boon and his men were sent back with a start. Araina pulled the blaze higher and fanned her wings, furthering the recoil. Sol maneuvered to his feet and moved to dash through the fray, but as Boon's bearings were regained, the soldier once again met with the point of his sword. The witch's wings held taut and the flame steadied below her stretched fingers. Sol's eyes moved to Araina's left hand. It was spread and poised for light.

"Araina, don't st—" Silence was forced upon him as Boon nicked his neck in reprimand.

"I needn't elevate this beyond an impasse. But I will," Araina vowed, low and hexing.

"At what cost, witch?"

"I'd be satisfied knowing you'd want to be rid of me as much as I do you, Captain."

"Araina, don't—" Sol bit his statement, the skin of his neck was scored once more.

"Oh, I never deny a woman satisfaction," Boon remarked.

"Resubmit your offer then. With some changes to the terms."

"And they are?"

"I get you an artifact. I know one nearby. We'll not have to spend a full day in one another's company. We are left unbound, unharmed, our provisions intact, and above all, you never speak of us to anyone."

"The height of our manners and silence for an artifact. Those are your terms then, witch?"

"Yes."

"Done."

Their agreement did not relieve any stances until Araina dragged the flame down—more out of shrinking tolerance for its heat than true concession. Boon gradually lowered the sword as the fire dwindled to smoke. Sol was only permitted to pass when Araina's wings folded away. His face and form were iron while she went to work unknotting his binds. The chest containing Den and Pidgie was then tossed down at their feet. More muffled curses and flapping rose with its landing.

On freeing Sol's wrists, she dropped to the chest, and at its latch, whispered, "Den, are you alright? Is Pidgie hurt?"

"Open this box so I can rip that leach-saddle's eyes out!"

"In good time. For now, stay quiet, please?"

Another muted roar erupted through the chest's joints. It simmered into an exasperated, incoherent growling.

Araina flipped the latch and raised the lid. Pidgie immediately flew into a tree overhead. A cluster of feathers drifted down upon a battered Den. She let him seethe and tie his kerchief back on his head, then rose and looked at Sol. His face further sharpened with silent fury as he watched Boon manipulate his crossbow.

"I said our provisions were to remain intact!" Araina demanded.

"And so they shall stay, witch. Accounted and held, if necessary, but intact." Boon removed a loaded bolt and tossed the crossbow on the ground. Sol's quiver was untied, examined, and given to one of the men.

"That said, my thorny sand flower, since you've revealed yourself to be a weapon, some balance must be retained," he added and passed Sol's sword to another man, who kept it at the ready. He then went on to search Araina's pack. Her field book, canteen, canvas-wrapped herbs, her portion of their vittles, their cookware, tools, and all other essentials were emptied to the ground. The pile was crossed over with lantern light. Her dagger was taken and tossed to a third man. Araina's blood went icy when Boon came to the cloth-wrapped Ecivy.

"What witches' nonsense is this?" He dug at the knot with his fingers.

"A compress to ease the pain of woman's moon humours." Araina tried to keep her breath out of her voice. Boon dropped the still-knotted bundle to the ground.

He moved to Sol's pack. Though the soldier looked on, rigidly fuming, he took pause at the teetering dread over Araina's face and tried to recall anything he carried for which she so feared—she appeared no less perturbed than when Boon held the touchpoint. The search was fast halted by the bottle of rum.

"Well, hello again," Boon greeted it. "Hardly missing three swigs. Good to know our little delivery girl can be mostly trusted." He let Sol's pack and the rest of its contents fall to the ground. With the rum in hand, he turned to Araina and looked at the broken lantern, still smoking at her feet.

"Again, witch, some balance must be retained. Consider this restitution for that *very* exquisite lantern. Such destruction for the sake of proving your little point." Boon shook his head, uncorked the bottle, and took a greedy swig.

At their feet, Den grumbled, "Son of'a…"

Through a rum-moistened smile, Boon ordered, "Tidy up and bed down. We rise with the sun."

Araina and Sol both dropped to their scattered belongings.

Through a whisper at Sol's ear, she implored, "Please, I need your sharpening stone."

He silently picked up the bundle of salt beef from the ground and pushed it to the bottom of his pack. Drawing his hand back out, he held the quartz stone hidden in his fist and pressed it to her hand. She shoved it in the front of her bodice and proceeded to gather the rest of her things.

Sol parted his lips, but could loose not an utterance as Boon turned and called, "Look spry now! Seems your decline to board my ship is a blessing if this is how idly you move." He slumped against a tree, and after another swing of rum, thrust his chin toward the nearest of the men to assign, "First watch."

The subordinate fixed his eyes to Araina and Sol as they knelt to the ground with their packs. The others drank from their own stores of bottles and flasks and paid little notice to much else.

At Araina's ear, Sol snapped, "What is this?"

"Barzillai Boon," she sighed.

"No! What are you doing?"

"Sorting it out. Is your neck alright?" She gingerly touched her finger to the splits in his skin and wiped away the blood.

"I can't answer for anyone's neck at the moment."

Before she could respond, Pidgie flapped from the trees and landed upon Araina's knee. She cupped her palms and let him nestle in their hold. Den made no acknowledgment and went on grumbling about rum, wasps, and vessel vagrants. Unable to find adequate and discreet consolation, the witch said nothing and continued smoothing Pidgie's feathers. She then looked up at the dirt streaks and dour pall over Sol's face.

"I'll keep watch first?" she delicately offered.

"No, Araina. Rest up for whatever witchery you've apparently got planned."

"This won't require much witchery. Only ignorance of it."

Chapter Twenty-Two

A Wide Berth

Hours before dawn emerged pale between the trees, Boon and all of his subordinates—including the one most recently ordered watch—were asleep on the ground. Sol had also given out. His shoulders slipped from the tree trunk and Araina woke to find him slumped against her arm. She tried to keep it still and him undisturbed as she etched the quartz stone.

With only a pointed rock to scratch such a dense surface, the process was taxing—and worsened by the rope burns across her thumbs. Her work was only just visible with the aid of charcoal dust and whatever zeadase residue could be streaked away from the paper. She examined the vivid specks of blue within the crowded and cryptic nonsense, then slipped the stone back into her bodice.

"Razor's still in my pack," a half-awake Sol muttered below her shoulder.

"Your face looks more in need of a wash than a shave. Perhaps a bit of salve." Araina faintly observed.

"Could get three. Similar heights."

"Three what? Men? Sol—"

"Get the bolts. Take the other five. Easier with your light. Could use it, 'long as it's the last thing they see."

"It's not necessary. Nor is the need to fight three men with a razor."

"You had the upper hand," he sighed. "Why'd you give it up?"

"You had a sword at your throat. And I haven't given up anything."

"Looks that way."

"That's the beauty of it. Just follow my lead as you navigate." She extended a solicitous smile, though he could not see it where he remained slouched.

"Makes as much sense as anything else you've said," he remarked, sounding as though he would fall back into slumber. He was given little chance; Boon woke moments later and began calling his men to their feet. Sol released a dry, rocky groan and stood up, bumping the corner of the chest near his feet. Within, Den snorted and blinked in confusion.

"Oh, right. Damn near forgot where I was. Smack in the middle'a this mess ya got us in."

The elf glared at Araina, who softly disclosed, "I'm moving us to the end of it."

"Think ya could pick up the pace? Maybe try blastin' 'em to bits. Ain't we all got our *roles to play*?"

"You're not the first to suggest that. Too much room for error."

"Still plenty 'a room for it."

Araina had no space for assurance or retort as Boon approached.

She lifted her pack and greeted, "Good morning, Captain," in as bright a voice as she could manage.

"We've yet to know the sort it'll be, witch. I want you leading and your boy flanked by us." With Boon's instruction, his and Sol's eyes met. The soldier gave nothing but a rigid glare. Araina wondered how much of it she was owed as he only maintained his stance and let her respond.

"I'm afraid that's less than ideal. He navigates."

"Oh? Then what makes you so valuable in our little arrangement?"

"That becomes apparent as we reach a set territory, the path to which he directs. It's good of you to call such to attention, Captain. Better you know now that I'll need a wide berth as we near it."

"A wide berth for what, witch? To fly?"

"No, Captain. We've agreed to terms. I'm entirely capable of fulfilling my end without deception."

"Do understand that your assurances hold little water," Boon chuckled through a sneer.

"I fail to see why. As long as my companions lack wings, excepting Pidgie of course, I am as grounded as they. And even less of a runner. As I thought I made clear, I'm bound to them regardless of actual binds. The space and silence I'll insist upon will be for *your* safety, Captain."

"*My* safety?"

"Yes, yours and that of your men. Unearthing this artifact is going to be dangerous." A grave look crossed Araina's face. "You will need to keep your distance and you mustn't distract me."

"And if I prefer to take my chances with it rather than you?" Boon countered.

"I suppose that's your decision, Captain. But at least know what lies with each choice. Little more than a glimpse of its raw form can blind a man in an instant. I could see that being a hindrance at the helm. That aside, stay too close when it's unearthed and it's said to cook the skin. It is a powerful thing you seek. Why else would it fetch such a price? Surely you knew you'd need a witch to do more than just dowse it out for you? Did your prospective buyer fail to explain that?"

Boon's pressing glower began to fracture with each question. "How long will all this take, witch?"

"The purification process? It depends upon a number of things. Of course, I know you'd prefer it done properly rather than quickly. But rest assured, I've no intention of prolonging our time together. I wish I could say the same for your crew. Are they always this slow to collect themselves?"

Boon pushed a gruff exhale through his nose and called back to his men, "Smartly now!" before returning a fierce eye to Araina. "How far out then?"

"Sol?" she cued him with all sweetness.

"North, after the last of the trees. 'Til you pick up the trail." His tone was as stark as his posture.

"Did you miss any of that, Captain?"

"Let's get on with it then, witch."

Boon kept barely a full stride behind Araina and Sol. Without opportunity to confirm signals or signs, Sol had nothing to rely upon but the witch's eyes. His fixed observation was fruitless as her view swept through the brush and moved clear of his. More than once, and despite the reduced weight across his back and lack of at his hip, he lowered his hand at the empty sheath. With each futile drop away, a grinding exhale followed.

Araina tried to ignore it, though there was little comfort in their wooded surroundings. At every edible tuber, mushroom, and usable bit of moss she could only march past, the witch felt as though her teeth would crack. They clenched from the thought of the wastefulness and kept locked tight with the sense of Sol's rising frustration. Every motion of his sinewy form carried a surging proclivity to swing, slash, strike, and threaten everything she had gained. Then there was Den, upon Pidgie, upon her shoulder. The elf's curse-rich muttering—almost swinging the remaining hoops in right ear—sent Araina's fingers up into fists. The potent stewing at her sides blended too easily with the impatience chasing her heels, along with wafts of tobacco and malodorous brawn.

The impetuses remained as they turned north to grassland. Soon after, a throbbing pain in her brow joined the fray. It filled her ears and played with her sense of the horizon. Then came an arrhythmia through her veins, the taste of copper, blood, and soil, and the sharpening of the shadows and sunlight over layers of dead grass. She stopped in her tracks and locked on a spindly growth in the distance.

Araina barely heard the grunted exclaims that all but collided into her back. The sweep of the air was too full and euphonic. It echoed the rolling waters of Dekvhors and fused with her pulse. Boon demanded something from over her shoulder. Sol closed in at her side and voiced some hastened and hushed inquiry. Den punctuated it with a snipe. All of it was dampened below the churning of the dry breeze around her and the hot blood within. She brought her hand to her shoulder, let Pidgie climb upon it, and lowered him and Den to the ground.

The witch cleared her throat, trying to soften the passages in her lungs, and insisted, "I'll need that berth now." Sol followed as she took a step, prompting her to turn and flatly add, "From all of you."

In spite if his discernible scrutiny, the soldier remained and she resumed her path.

"That stays here!" Boon thrust a finger at her pack.

"You already know I've no arms in it," she protested.

"You've days of supply if you've waited 'til now to flee. Blame only yourself, witch."

Araina pulled the strap off her shoulder and handed it to Sol with brief whispered thanks, then rushed away.

The pull across the field was startlingly strong. She met it graciously; anything less would have kept her turning to confirm the places and safety of her companions, but its draw kept her facade steady as her steps. The pain lessened in her skull, her fingers eased away from her palms, and her breath passed freely once again. It sharpened her vision and defined the dark spindly mass, first as a large dead tree, then as an imitation of one.

The tall, black form revealed itself not as a single growth, but a twisted tangle of many thinner trees. Their joining formed a hollow cone, topped by a crooked eruption of branches and fed from a hairy spread of roots. Araina slowly traversed their reach over the cracked soil and desiccated weeds, scouting for a suitable entry point in its base. After half a revolution, the witch found one and crawled within the convergence of trunks.

The hollow was hot, dark, and gave scant space for her to turn and trace her fingers. She summoned light and reached across its interior, far as her fingers would stretch, until they landed upon a pocket of bark. It buzzed faintly, as though she discovered a nest of exhausted hornets. Araina loosened the papery layers with her fingernails. Her rope-burned toes stung through her balancing. Finally, the crumbing edges of Mtolin rose from the black wood. She curled back her light, drew up its markings in the darkness, and the touchpoint came loose in her hand. For just a moment, she allowed herself to bask in its density. The witch then sighed across the stifling confines and crawled out to return to everything that waited beyond.

Keeping to the roots, she swapped Mtolin for the quartz stone. The trade was coarse and awkward. Though she could little tell of its frontward appearance, she swept portions of her hair forward to obscure the shape below the bodice. After a final survey of the quartz stone and its etchings, she summoned a sphere of light and sent it into the sky overhead. Distant exclaims followed. She rose with the mock artifact nesting sacredly in her palms and left her cover, hoping her plodding, reverent steps would bolster her solemn mien, which felt rather fragile once Boon charged forth.

"Careful, Captain!" she warned and stifled his reach. "You must not jostle it!"

Boon fought a fervid twitch. He flattened his hands for Araina to delicately surrender his bounty.

"It's…it's warm," he observed.

"Yes, some heat will remain even after it's been purified. Though that will soon fade," she said with feigned dejection.

Boon stared into the engraved forms and the specks of blue and black crossing the stone's clouded layers. "These markings… What do they mean?"

"Powerful things, Captain. I would advise you to cover it until you reach your buyer. But, I urge you to carefully reconsider that. In the wrong hands, this artifact could—"

"That's no longer your concern, witch."

"Very well. Then our end has been fulfilled. Now yours."

With his eyes still set on the stone, Boon grumbled to the nearest of his men. The others gathered and craned their necks to observe their gain. Not an instant after Sol's sword and quiver and Araina's dagger were tossed down, Sol grabbed them, passed the quiver and dagger to Araina, and readied his blade.

"Has your boy forgotten you're still outnumbered?" Boon said.

Sol sheathed the sword and snapped the crossbow off his back. In an astonishingly fluid motion, he freed three bolts from the quiver in Araina's arms. With two laced and ready in his grip, he loaded one, cocked, and shot through a twist of hair topping Boon's bowed head, which promptly snapped upright.

"But armed," Sol retorted. Boon's men readied their weapons as the soldier had already reloaded and drawn. The third bolt still waited between his fingers. "Keep that quiver close," he muttered to Araina.

"Again, our terms, Captain," the witch asserted. "It'll be easier to forget where you've gotten that if you turn your back first."

"Hole through the skull might help."

"Thank you, Sol. I'm sure the captain can do without the extra persuasion. Not while his ship awaits."

"Indeed, witch," Boon sneered.

"Again, I'd cover that and be on your way. Not only for the power it holds, but for all others who seek it. What I said at the pier was true. You're not the first who approached me." With her warning, Boon pulled a handkerchief from his collar and wrapped the stone.

He smoothed through the frayed lock atop his head. "The lower that bow gets, the more we show of our backs."

Araina looked at Sol, who was poised to do anything but, and all but inaudibly exhaled, "Sol, please."

His eyes shifted to her for half an instant, then to her open left hand. His finger uncurled from the trigger and he eased the crossbow downward.

"Smartly now, boys," Boon ordered, and with his men, marched back along their tracks beyond the reaches of the grassland.

Araina, Sol, Den, and Pidgie remained in silence and stillness until nothing could be heard but a slow sweeping wind. It carried rolling grey clouds. Sol then urgently lifted the quiver from Araina's hold, fastened it at his side, and slung the crossbow on his back. He returned her pack through a heavy toss, startling her as she barely caught it.

"Have you picked up on it yet?"

The witch stared back at Sol, perplexed.

"We've lost too much time!" he further prodded.

Araina slung her pack over her shoulder. "Not as much as you're fearing." She reached in her bodice and revealed Mtolin with a smile. "I thought you were with me as far as that. You led us to the correct spot after all."

"Huh?" Den asked, stretching his view from the ground. "Ya actually got that thing?"

"You both thought that was all a show only so we could look for this after? That would've been a waste of time."

Sol stared, his brow furrowed and his jaw tight.

Araina went on to offer, "My apologies for the loss of your sharpening stone. I'll make it up to you. I'm sure we'll find something similar. Which way now?"

"Don't know."

"What do you mean?"

"Need a new route."

"What? Why?"

"To keep clear of them."

"Of whom? Boon?" She blinked at Sol, baffled that the tight vexation in his eyes and the strain in his scars had not yet fallen away. "He is clear."

"That's not a certainty."

"But I just—"

"When he tries to sell that thing and learns it's worthless, what do you think he'll do? Don't think he'll be open to any more of your terms."

"Or, just as likely, whoever buys it from him is another mindless Lander. One who's no better at identifying what it is, or rather, what it isn't. He gets his bounty and we're fully and safely rid of him just the same. That was the point of everything I did!"

"Anyone offering a sum that amounts to a ship probably isn't just a Lander. They're Vexhi. And they'll know exactly what that stone isn't."

"What makes you so sure? You said yourself how clueless lower Vexhi were at the lake. I doubt Boon's bargaining with alchemists."

"What makes you sure about that? I'd call it a gamble. Because now he knows what we look like and where we've been seen. And the moment your end of that bargain falls apart, so will his. I'll point out again, the rum wasn't worth it."

"Ain't even get much of it," Den groused.

Araina stared back at them, mouth agape until her faltering deflated. She turned and knelt in the grass. From her pack, she retrieved Ecivy and undid the wrapping with which Boon's fingers had so struggled. She folded Mtolin in kind. On tightening a new knot, the sight and feel of her scratched thumbs ignited a wave of wrath.

"Alright then." She spun back toward Sol and Den. "You've both made it *very* clear how my going to the pier, for rum, which was meant as a kindness to both of you, was such a grave mistake. One I spent the last night and day correcting, as best I could under the circumstance. But since my approach has fallen so short, why don't you tell me how either of you would have handled all that?" Both of them looked back at her. Sol drew in a breath to answer but Araina sharply continued, "Because, as Boon just pointed out, we were clearly outnumbered and out-armed. That left nothing to do but outwit. The clearest, cleanest response. It's not as though he knew what he was doing."

"Did you?" Sol challenged. He knelt down, opened his pack, and took out the map.

"How can you ask such a thing? He cross-bound me! Or at least made the attempt. That's a very old sort of Lander nonsense I didn't think *any* of them still believed. Lost to history, *if only!*" Araina nearly spat. "The more misguided they are, the more set they are to exploit. When you see that for what it is, you can overpower it without a drop of blood spilt."

"An outcome carries that carries risk." Sol's low and loaded assessment further narrowed Araina's eyes.

"Oh, but it's all risky. I remember what happened after you told me that. After you had me in the midst of—"

"That was different."

"Yes, it was." The witch's voice darkened. "Boon was nowhere near *that* threat."

"That was different because some risks are unavoidable," Sol rejoined. "And I'd argue the opposite."

"How so?" she snapped.

The soldier rose to his feet. "That officer wasn't looking for who you actually are, no matter what was on that slip of paper. He wanted an amenable, card reading peasant girl. Boon knew he needed a witch and he found the one witch he needed. You don't just leave him to—"

"Boon doesn't know what I am any more than that officer!"

"What officer do ya keep talkin' 'bout?" Den asked before an amused little smirk crossed his face. "Oh ho ho! So *that's* how ya got that uniform!"

Sol's view swung from the elf and back to Araina. Her shoulders teemed with waiting force. Her left hand fell and stiffened at her side, but her eyes went glassy. She turned to the twist of trees in the distance and the darkening sky overhead.

"Araina…" Sol exhaled.

A ruffle of her voice rode her breath. "I did not approach or invite Boon any more than I did that officer. I didn't know going to the pier would be such a mistake. I wanted to see the ocean and…forget everything for a moment." She looked back to Sol. "But it's interesting how you doubt my ability to come through a mistake of my own making. And yet, you expect me to come through one of yours as though it were an inevitability. Not just that, but a *learning experience*. Was there nothing for you to gain from this one?"

"No doubt," Sol answered. He crouched and unfolded the map over the grass. "What?"

"No doubt to be had. None whatsoever. That was clever. And more gainful than I was expecting. And yes, bloodless, for the most part." He rubbed the pair of cuts on his neck. "But keeping things bloodless in a situation like that, it carries consequences. It means we have to prepare for them." The soldier traced his finger in a bending, cresting, then jagged line across the map—one running mostly parallel to a smoother option drawn in ink.

"To obscure our tracks, our route needs to get more complicated. Boon may not be good with what witches can and can't do, but he knows how to track, or has men who do. He knows how to ambush, or has men who do. That's how he knew to use the wind as cover. We have to make our steps tougher to follow, for anyone. It'll toll our supplies, our time, and our strength." On lifting his view from the map, he found wounded comprehension had replaced Araina's ire. He added, "For us to get through that, I can't have any doubt. And I don't. None whatsoever."

"I still don't see how it would've been better to…" her voice slipped into the dense breeze. She returned to her pack, retrieved her jar of borage butter, and handed it to Sol. "For your neck. It's for hair but it should soothe skin."

The soldier nodded his thanks.

"Eh, trackin', ambushin' or not, if we're hardly gonna live through this, what makes ya think that vessel vagrant would?" Den challenged.

"That's the point," Sol answered.

"The way his men reacted, when I mentioned the greater price he'd get for the artifact, rather than…me. If he doesn't get anything for it, how is he going to afford the same men or others to come after us?" she wondered aloud and watched a raindrop fall upon the map.

"Always someone desperate enough. Men follow promises easily as actual payment. Maybe more so. How persuasive a shipless captain will be in trying to round up a winged witch, who deceived him with a scratched-up stone…hard to say. Wonder how that'll overlap with rumors of a lake demon."

Araina focused on the two remaining circles waiting for them on the map, then on Sol's scarred hands keeping it taut. More raindrops plunked between them.

"And if he manages that, and somehow catches up on either path, what's our approach?" she asked.

"Same as mine from yesterday," the soldier answered.

"I trust you would have taken it beyond an impasse."

Sol looked up at her—the bark dust clinging to her brow and the smokey depth of her lids sharpened the warmth of her eyes. He folded the map and stood up. After streaking a dab of the borage butter on his nicked neck, he returned the jar.

"Was with you until you didn't. I told you those wings are impressive. Downright intimidating from a certain vantage. And that fire. You *had* them. Other than the rum, stopping all that to set terms might've been your only major mistake."

"Well, from my vantage, that sword only came away from your neck for so long. And I'd love it if I never heard mention of that rum again."

"Likewise that officer," Sol softly retaliated.

"Done," Araina accepted.

"Well, I'm gonna mention it to say rum or not, I'm still waitin' on pancakes," Den reminded. The witch opened her pack and dug out a small twine-tied box.

She opened it, and on discovering eggshells and yoke-soaked paper within, tallied, "One survivor. I'm sorry, Den. It'll have to be a small batch."

Through a scowl, the elf muttered, "Just let that vessel vagrant catch up to us."

Chapter Twenty-Three

Sidesteps

Araina spat away the rainwater before calling down to Sol, "Ready?"

He tugged back his gloves, gripped and layered the rope over his boot, then shouted up to the plateau's edge, "On your call."

She folded a wing and turned back to Den and Pidgie, perched on the bowline that secured the rope to a jut of rock.

"Yell if you feel that move," she requested.

At the elf's nod, she stretched her wings, cupped them forward, and, with a layer of cloth to buffer her palms, took up the slack. She sent down another call and Sol started up the rope.

The witch's feet slid across the wet stone. She swept her wings to counter the pull. Her arms strained, her calves and ankles ached, but the rope followed back, speeding and easing Sol's climb. When a gloved hand appeared, a rush of relief pushed away the pain of her stance. She increased the sweep of her wings and Sol pulled himself onto the ledge.

"That made a big difference," he remarked through the regain of his breath.

Den and Pidgie cleared the bowline as Araina pulled it and began coiling the rope.

"I'll take your word for it. I'm thankful to've been saved the climb entirely."

Sol stood up and surveyed the ascending slope of rock before them. It limited their immediate path to a narrow though not impassable ridge. He removed his gloves and shook away the rain before tucking them into his belt.

"Don't think you'll need to do any more flying too soon," he tonelessly assessed. "Could put your cloak on."

"I'd rather keep it dry for sleep. Besides, what better way to rinse clean the stench of Boon. If it goes on like this, I can wash my hair as I walk."

"Eh, witches and their preenin'. Gimme dirty if it means dry." Den shielded himself from the misting of rainwater puffed from Pidgie's feathers. "How we supposed'a get a fire goin' for pancakes?"

"We follow this down into a valley. Might find dry cover there. And don't curse the rain, Den. It covers tracks. Covered tracks mean time to cook," the soldier answered.

"So Rainy's got the rain on 'er side."

"And you two were worried." Araina handed the rope to Sol. He didn't return her smile.

"That's today. Going to take another five to get us back on our original trail. Whether we can keep it, we'll see." He draped the rope around the bulk of his pack and warned, "Watch your step this way. Slippery."

Araina let him pass. She tightened her wings, her face falling as they slipped below the scars, and followed along his tracks.

The promise of pancakes was only just fulfilled, but after so many hours in soaking rain, across and then back down the plateau, Den could not find complaint when hot food entered his mouth and belly. Sol and Araina did with lesser fare of the remaining rice bread, coated in the last of the milk, paired with crumbles of hard cheese to ease its souring, and cooked until it joined into a savory porridge. Though thoroughly sated, Den insisted on licking whatever had clung to the cauldron. His slurping and ranting—on the insult of temple cheese being kept secret—echoed through the copper vessel. Araina heard little of it. She was lost in the rhythmic combing of her hair, the scent of the borage-butter, and the sound of rainwater that sped a thin stream near their camp. Her daze broke when Sol unloaded a modest yield of firewood.

"Driest I could find." He tossed a few branches into their clinging fire.

"I'll look for more near the stream. I have to rinse my hair."

"Will that take long?"

"No and I'll not be hard to see. Here." Araina unfolded her hand and revealed light. "If it goes out for a moment, it's only because I need to wring out. Otherwise, I'll keep it lit."

Sol accepted her assurance and settled among Den and Pidgie.

Through a traverse of rocks and old branches too soaked to hold a flame, the witch came to the stream and bowed into it. Her light shrank and then disappeared while she smoothed clean her tresses. With her view to the clouds, she wrung out her hair, then looked to the darkness over the rest of the valley. It was broken by two, small round flames. They drew near, keeping low and together, and revealed themselves as eyes—familiar ones. Araina slowly rose to see their owner. It stopped and looked into her but did not approach.

Across the distance, she heard Sol call, "Alright?"

Araina peered over her shoulder and answered with a new sphere of light. She turned back to the open valley and found only night.

"Yes, on my way."

She lingered and strained to catch a sheen of burgundy fur among the vacant shadows before crossing back over the rocks.

"No luck?" Sol asked on her return.

"Nothing dry or substantial."

"See something out there?" He studied her face in the fire's cast.

"No. Did you?"

"Only your light."

She nodded. "Just moving slow because I'm tired. Shame about the firewood. Of course it's the first chilly night in weeks."

"Your cloak stay dry?"

"I'll have to check. Some tea would be perfect on a night like this, though washing that cauldron feels like too much of a bother."

"Might do alright if you don't mind elf spit. Been licked to a polish." At Sol's account, Araina wrinkled her nose and looked to Den, waiting to hear a defense. He was asleep on his back with his hands framing his rounded stomach.

"I'll clean it in the morning," she decided and crept to her pack to retrieve her cloak. "Oh no," she breathed and looked skyward to the meager revelation of stars. "I almost lost track. It's the equinox."

"Crest holiday?"

"Always was my favorite. It's the first one without..." Araina sighed. "Maybe it's better to be away for it this year."

She pulled her cloak free and squeezed the fabric, finding it well-touched by the rain. The blackness of it held her. She was unable to look away, unable to drape it and settle back near the shrinking fire. The thought of the night below a damp cloak gripped her in a draining paralysis. Her body went rigid but for tears wanting to flow free. Quenching as they would have been, she held them, feeling they were not worth explaining to Sol—nor were they the sort that would stay easily hidden. They nearly slipped when she was startled by the weight of warm fabric across her back. She turned. Sol pulled the cloak down over her shoulders and fastened it at her neck.

"What are you doing? This is yours," she protested.

"Laid it out while you were cooking so it had a chance to dry." He took her damp cloak and tucked it under his arm. "This one'll get its chance while you're asleep."

"I'm not sleeping."

"You're sleeping while I have dry kindling to keep watch. If it runs out before morning I'll wake you for light."

"You've barely had any sleep since we left the—"

"That's why I have little energy to debate." He reached back, pulled the hood over her head, and lowered it well-past her eyes. "Rest up."

Scents of soil, leather, dried leaves, and something abstract—yet just as richly organic—became acute. Araina adjusted the hood and cleared her view of Sol spreading her cloak over a rock near the fire. He settled at its side.

"Goodnight," she bade and curled into herself.

She listened to the weak snaps of bark caught by flame, waited for it to soothe and then fade, and for her thoughts to follow in turn and give way to sleep. She waited, then pleaded, then grasped. It would not come. She sat up.

"Please let me take first watch. I'm not able to sleep whether or not you insist I do."

"Today's trek should've knocked anyone out. Look at him." Sol gestured to a deeply snoring Den. "He wasn't even walking."

"The necessity of it is having the opposite effect," Araina confessed.

He sighed. "Listen—"

"How do you hurt people?"

"What?" He stared back, his brow creased.

"How do you know when…or rather, how do you decide… If there are other options, how do you let yourself…" Araina stammered, her breath dropped away for a moment. "I understand when it's a choice that's not really a choice. As it was when it was between you and the men in that mine. And when I didn't know you were just beyond the window—sorry, I know I said I wouldn't mention that again. I could do it those times. And faster than I realized. But, how…how do you harm someone when there are other…when you're not quite backed into a corner?"

Sol exhaled. He leaned toward the fire, looked through it, and found the witch's eyes, sunken and waiting behind damp twists of hair. His view dropped away.

"Just have to see the corner as a little wider. Maybe you're not as backed into as you could be. You might have a few steps behind you. But you know not to let it get any further."

"Even when you could sidestep, so to speak, and prevent it altogether?"

"Not with the same certainty. You fight what's in front of you, when it's in front of you."

"You never get stuck in the thought of what that carries? What cannot be undone?"

"Not after enough times. Then it's just forward or back. You or them. Corners get wider. The steps behind you shrink. You take your chances before it takes them from you."

"Should I have known to look at Boon that way? Should I have known that trying to keep my advantage rooted in something other than force, would've led to such...failing?"

Her question impelled a gravelly sound from Sol's chest.

He looked skyward, closed his eyes for a moment, and muttered, "You're..."

He opened and set them back on her, trying to reconcile the young woman shadowed below his cloak with the one he first saw in the cavernous hall, and the one he saw there again, gowned, lips painted, cheeks flush in the prism-cast light among the crowds, and then the one who met him, morning after morning, with an antique misericorde in her grip. He ran through it all and then saw that swelling sphere of light above a rowboat and the clawed tips of blood-streaked wings as they emerged from a descent.

"I don't need to tell you what you are and what you aren't. I just need to remember it." Sol looked into the fire. "You make it easy to forget." A small, amused recollection crossed his face. "He called you a weapon, didn't he?" The soldier's smile ebbed. "I don't need to tell you what you are and aren't, but you're not that."

"I sense that's disappointing."

"No."

"I thought, if I'd just kept him talking, if I kept feeding that nonsense...that was the means I had for keeping us alive. And it did. But now that choice is keeping you from sleep. And that's keeping me awake. It might mean everything is—"

"So we're both awake. We're alive. Boon's behind us. How far?" Sol shrugged. "Doesn't matter until it matters. And if it does, won't be any need for you to keep him talking."

"I'd feel more assured by something else."

"What's that?" Sol asked, struggling to suppress a yawn.

Araina rose, unfastened the cloak, and walked over to him. She draped it around his shoulders.

"If you'd sleep." She lifted the hood and folded the edge just clear of his forehead, then returned to the other side of the fire.

He yawned again, full-throated. "Seems you've backed me into a corner on that."

"Sorry it's not one comfortable enough for decent rest."

"Afraid it doesn't compare to beds at the temple, drunk on…what was that liquor again?"

"Rosaberry."

"I hear they grow in the centers of flowers. Fine stuff until the day after." He rested on his pack and observed, "'Least this hood smells nice now. Bit damp again but not a bad tradeoff."

"The least I could do."

"No, the least you can do is wake me if you hear or see anything. Got it?"

"Of course. Goodnight." She watched him settle again, only to sit back upright.

"Your blade. Keep it close."

"My pack's right here."

"Useless in there. Wear it. No Landers to give you any looks out here."

At his prompting, Araina rummaged the dagger and scabbard from her pack. She belted it around her waist.

"It is now on my person. Anything else?"

"Wake me if you—"

"You'll know if I see so much as a moth, and I would so love to see a moth…"

"If you get tired. When you get tired."

"If I do, I will, but I won't. Goodnight, S—"

"Enough!" Den hoarsely roared. "Shut your faces up, both'a ya!"

"Night, Araina."

"Sleep well, gentlemen."

The wax-coated charcoal slipped from her fingers. Its precise little snap against a rock sent her face up from the bindings of her field book. She looked at her sketch—confident from the degree of smudging that she had not drifted off for more than a moment. Her view moved up and found the red wolf standing over

Sol. Its muzzle drew near his hood, breathing steam and baring teeth across the sleeping soldier. Araina sprang and thrust out her palm to summon and send forth light. None appeared.

"Steadfast drain fast," it snarled. Its voice, nowhere in the air, was fed to her in a watery, tight sound, as though pushed through some siphon in her skull.

"Get away from him!" The witch's voice was comparably dark and rough.

"Bleed smooth, empty quick."

Araina reached to unsheathe her dagger. Though the scabbard waited at her hip, the blade was gone. She caught its glint below her fallen field book and rushed to grab it. She rose, poised to dash and strike, but there was no wolf to receive it.

Though her light answered her latest push, it revealed nothing beyond the reaches of the camp. The cold traces of morning showed only rocks and weeds over to the stream. Araina sheathed the dagger and returned to her place upon the ground. She furthered her light and eased it over a soundly slumbering Den, Pidgie, and Sol, then let it dwindle below the curl of her fingers. She reclaimed her field book, tucked the broken charcoal in its bindings, and watched the slow bleed of dawn.

They crossed beyond the valley and back into forested foothills, where they took shade and rest. Sol urged Araina to regain sleep while he marked the map and prepared the salt beef for him and Den. She took the opportunity in the grass and broken sunlight. Sol then went to work tallying their provisions.

The damp trek across the plateau, coupled with the expected length of their altered route, tainted and placed new limits on their vittles. As he shaved off edges gone fuzzy and discolored, cut away pitted spots, and set softened but salvageable pieces out to re-dry, Sol gauged what could be gained through hunting or foraging and its cost against miles and hours. He then pondered how he would rely on Araina's lead in identifying edible options along their path, but without fully alerting her to the urgency for them.

On returning her share of the supplies to her pack, her field book dropped free and opened. Sol found his likeness looking up at him from the grass. He blinked down at it, then raised it. His eyebrows lifted on observing the brushy charcoal streaks that amounted to his portrait—one perhaps a little too refined, yet honest and attentive.

"Find anythin' interestin' in there? Got 'er nose in that thing every time we stop," Den asked over the splintered bit of twig clearing beef from his teeth.

Sol closed the book and replaced it in Araina's pack. He walked over and touched her shoulder. "Hate to do this, but we're packed up."

Araina shifted onto her back, sighed away the lingering density of her sleep, and smiled. "That was almost too nice."

"...You can pick up where you left off before long. I'll take first watch tonight. Den can take the second."

"Feh! Better be some'a that coffee left."

"We'll have enough firewood for that?" Araina sat up.

"Plenty. But if you see anything that might stretch our food, it's worth picking up."

"Is it that bad?"

"Just could be better. Probably not worth mentioning apart from you knowing how to spot things I never would."

"We passed so much when Boon marched us through those woods. It's still driving me mad."

"No gain from that. We'll find more ahead."

Chapter Twenty-Four

Harsh, Dark Things

Though lacking in hardiness, paltry bits of mallow, lamb's quarters, and late-ripening mayapple broke the monotony of the chestnut biscuits and sweet potato rusk that became their staples. By the fourth day of departure from their original route, Sol and Den had learned to spot viable edibles almost half as keenly as Araina. The benefits of their new proficiency were fast limited by the land, which went flat and dry, then starkly barren. The witch's share of their silent, steady pace through it was broken by something large and metal. Sol halted with her stumble and turned back to examine the dented, partially buried shield that caught her foot.

"That'll've left a mark. You alright?"

"Nothing that won't blend in with the rest." She pressed on the thin slice above her toes. Sol dropped the shield and looked at the field before them.

"Try to watch your step without looking too closely at the ground."

"How? And why?"

Before he could answer, Pidgie landed on Araina's head, with Den, who remarked on their delay, "Food or money? Ain't no other reason for stoppin'."

"Mind flying ahead to see how long this goes on? Circle back if you see anything notable toward those trees?" Sol requested.

The elf nodded. He and Pidgie took off above the weeds.

"How long what goes on?" Araina rubbed her scalp where the pigeon's feet had clung. Sol pinched a lingering feather from her hair and puffed it away.

"The battlefield we're going to cross."

His answer induced a dire scan from Araina.

"A former one," he elaborated and adjusted the straps across his chest. "No reason to meander just the same. Not while the sun's moving." He resumed his steps. Araina followed, into a sugary-sour haze.

Despite the soldier's advice, her view continuously slipped to the rumpled ground. There seemed no other method for avoiding the bits of metal, splintered wood, scraps of fabric, an occasional glove, a split shoulder plate, then a boot with flies crawling across its thickly stained cuff. The buzzing rose with her passage.

Araina hastened her steps to shorten the growing gap between her and Sol. She skittered around a gauntlet, then a black-curdled helmet, and almost put her foot in a decaying face and better portion of a skull. Her balance slipped away. A fleshy, oblong mound of yellow, brown, and grey met her on landing.

Its layers were dry and stretched, then slick and spilling. The center had given way to a maroon slurry of stringy tissues and mucousy movement. The sight of it—the many textures that comprised the shriveled yet bloated mass—stole Araina's means and focus to flee from the stench, even when she finally understood its source as a human torso. Her gaze remained until she was gripped by her shoulders and her vision went to black—not imposed by her eyelids or any sensory loss, but by the fabric of Sol's shirt. As he looked into what she had nearly fallen, the length of her silence and stillness set off an odd little disquiet.

He eased her back to confirm, "Alright?"

She only blinked.

"Araina?"

She eventually affirmed in a lolling nod. They returned to their feet.

"Keep your eyes up. I've got our path." Sol pressed her to his side and guided her forward. They pushed on straight, then to one side and soon another, as though keeping in step with a quick, disjointed dance—one driven not by music, but metal shards and swollen, leaking viscera at their feet.

"Never see one like that before?" Sol inquired before concluding, "No, why would you've?"

"How far along is that?" Araina responded, her air slipping away from her words.

"The first one? Maybe just over a week. The one we just passed, a fortnight at least, and the one we're approaching, I'd say ten days. Eyes up. You can trust me if the smell's not enough."

"You said this was a battlefield." She choked slightly and pressed her nose to her wrist.

"Any doubts about that?"

"For just one battle?"

"Yes. Don't tend to reuse them too quickly for obvious reasons."

"Do they last for so long? Like sieges?"

"No. Not in the open. They're all about numbers. You're striking and defending bodies, not structures."

"Then why are some so much further along than others?" Araina asked through another gag.

Without an immediate answer, Sol shifted their steps slightly to the left and instructed, "Foot up, nice and high. Now back down."

She blindly cleared whatever hurdle lay before them. Whether it was a broken blade or body, the fetid air had gotten so thick and the buzzing of flies so droning, the ground may as well have been one collective, rotting mass. Sol felt the tightened rise and fall of her shoulders below his arm.

"Just a little further. We've passed the front. On the winning side now. It'll get easier to breathe soon. And I had that same question for Tanzan. Men felled in the same battle, same day, even by the same swing. Some go putrid after they hit the ground, others keep like kings in repose."

"So you omitted some details that day you described them. He had no answers?"

"That detail didn't seem necessary at the time. He thought it was related to them, but had no answers on how or why."

"That's why you wanted to cross this before dark." Though her breathing had eased, the witch's voice was low and cautious. She could not help but let her eyes drop once more, if only to view their lengthening shadows.

"Just want to set up camp far and clear of this. Early rest gets us an early start tomorrow, which gets us to our old path all the sooner."

"We'll be in the thick of them now, won't we? I'll need to keep watch through the night…"

Though Sol no longer swept her along, he kept his arm across her shoulders while he amended, "Not alone. And they're through with this front. They've other ones to thicken." He slipped his hold free and turned toward a scattered stretch of trees where Den and Pidgie waited.

As Araina shifted to look back over their recent steps, Sol caught her cheek and prompted, "This way."

The witch tossed another branch into the fire and placed their cauldron on a stone at its side. She removed a parcel of tea leaves from her pack.

"How long did it take you to get used to it?" she asked.

"The sight or the smell?" Sol responded.

"All of it."

"Depends what state they're in. And how you look at them." He slowly rose out of a crouch and scanned the trees before briefly stopping to examine a charred caggis root. He tore off an end and handed it to Den, who thanked him with a wordless tip of his chin and began chewing.

"Sure you don't want any?" Sol offered and sat down.

"Thank you, no. I associate the taste with being ill."

With her decline, he placed the root between his teeth and squeezed out a smokey, slightly bitter liquid that went hot, then sweet on his tongue. He let the heat clear his sinus.

"Apart from the smell, I used to think the ones we saw today were easier. So far gone from what they were, you just tell yourself they have nothing to do with what you are. Just old meat or rubbish. The newly fallen were harder. They look like you, only split open, broken, or spilt out. They *were* you, only with one bad block or weak strike to set you apart. But you get used to them too." Sol leaned away, spat the shredded root over his shoulder, and swallowed the last of its residue. "Think I was seven when I had to do my first clearing. Took some time for that to…sort itself. But it serves its purposes."

"Clearing?" Araina asked.

"Before you're handed a sword or a stick, or even shown how to hold a fist, you haul bodies. You and as many other kids as it takes to lift and clear them from the circle. You learn what a sword, or stick, or fist can do. The sight and the smell of what's left over. And the weight of it. Weight without anything left to move it. Just slack muscle with no use. Think that strikes more than sight or smell when it's on you. Then you learn to make more of it. Or become it."

Araina's eyes, wide and glassy, searched his. "Sol. Why were you…"

Den's own curiosity stifled his chewing and buoyed his back from Pidgie's breast. Sol's brow creased then smoothed.

"What use is it?" He pushed his tongue along his teeth, loosening a bit of fiber, and swallowed. "Knowing any of that… It's not going to make today easier. Likely to do the opposite."

Araina's silent, reaching gaze locked on Sol's until it broke with a sudden sputtering. The boiling in the cauldron spattered her ankle.

"Hex-bile!" she hissed and moved it to the dirt.

The water rolled to a simmer and stilled. She dipped a bowl within and dropped tea leaves on the steaming surface, then did the same twice more. One was handed to Sol and the other placed before Den. The back of the seal ring on hers sent a small chime through the air.

With its fade, she explained, "I don't doubt you. But I do know that within the harshest, darkest things, some fortitude to face what they are is kept. Those things will strike whether or not you know them, but knowing them gives some chance to steel against them. Or at least lessen the blow." Araina sighed away the steam from the bowl and touched the rim to her lips. "But it's not that alone," she added through the repel of the heat. "I don't ask out of any hope to make today easier. I want to know because out of those things, you've come to be here."

Sol put his bowl on the ground and surveyed the trees again.

"You don't need fortification from any harshness I've lived. As I'm here, you're here. Why do you think that is? Apart from just the reason they neglected to give us a lantern." His lips gave way to a smile.

"So optimistic of them," Araina conceded with a laugh. His smile broadened.

"Well, torch wax makes better sense. Lanterns are finicky and noisy. And I wouldn't call it optimis—" Sol shot to his feet, his sword drawn before he was fully upright. Pidgie trilled and fluttered away in alarm, leaving Den fallen on his back. Araina's tea spilt to the ground. All else about her froze but for the pulsing at her back and palm.

"Sol…" her voice slithered.

"On your feet. Slowly." His braced, precise tone sent the witch's blood roaring. She stretched herself from the ground, her eyes never leaving the shadows that so held the soldier's gaze. "Just beyond the fire. Between those trees."

She could see, hear, feel nothing beyond the snapping of the fire and the air gone cold across her skin. Her fingernails dug into her palms, reminding her to uncurl her left fist.

"Boon?" Den rushed to confirm in a shaken hiss.

Araina remained fixed on the firelight flickering across the trees.

"I-I don't see any—" Her voice swallowed away as the darkness between the middle distance and beyond the reach of their fire rapidly shifted and engorged. It sucked and flattened away any visibility—as though devouring a hole in the night itself. It twisted, bled, then shrank as some living, moving form of the dark past utter, consuming blackness. It floated overhead, blotting stars and night sky alike in a hemorrhaging arch.

"Araina…" Sol urged in an odd oscillation.

The witch's left hand sprang with light. The swelling thing descended between them and entirely shrouded their view of one another. The tip of Sol's blade breached from the center. For an instant, a weak split appeared in the void before it coagulated back into a singular form.

"Araina!" Sol prompted again.

With a gasp, she shook free of her terror. Her sphere of light surged, and with a swipe of her arm, she loosed it into the twisting mass. A clash of pressure stole the air and pulled the firelight. The umbra crumpled and dissolved along with the glow. The flames from their little pit steadied—seeming to synchronize with their stiltedly returning breaths.

"What…" Den wheezed, then, on fully regaining a lungful, roared, "What?!"

Araina was locked in her stance. Sol too was unmoving but for his eyes, first stuck in the place where her light claimed it, then they swept to her. His fallen jaw lifted and fostered a slow, elated awe. A low, rolling laugh eased from his throat. He sheathed his sword, closed the distance between himself and the witch, and cupped her hand away from its taught, frozen reach. The soldier marveled at it, then curled her fingers over the pale slash in its center. He drew it into a cherished hold and dropped his brow to her scalp.

Warm and astonished laughter pulsed across Araina's temples. She began to tremble. Sol raised his head and watched her face shift, as though a veil had fallen away and revealed some skewed version of a long-anticipated discovery. He let her hand slide free and she slipped to the ground. His smile sank in kind.

"Araina, now do you…"

She gripped her knees into her center and buried her face against them. The soldier only blinked at her recoiled form in the firelight.

Den further demanded, "One'a ya wanna tell me what—what that… What just—"

"You explain it to him," Araina muttered.

Sol looked over at the elf, dragged an exhale from his core, and sat down.

"That was an umbra."

"A what?"

"That's what Tanzan and the Coven called it. They started showing up after food went scarce and battles spread out and sped up."

"*What?*" Den persisted.

Sol turned to Araina again. She remained buried below a mass of tangled waves and strained ringlets.

"Imagine if death got a little ahead of itself. Think that's more or less what that is," the soldier attempted to explain.

"But what *is* it? It's *death*?"

"It...it *makes* you dead. Or, it's what deals with you after you're dead..."

"Huh?" the elf huffed.

Sol sighed and rubbed his forehead. "It takes what you are...and passes it...on. Listen, it's been a while since it was explained to me. Apparently, they're doing what they do sooner than they should. Tanzan said something like, they're death summoned—"

"The essence of death risen too early," Araina recalled. She dropped her hair from her face and set a wet cheek against her arm. "But what if that's not what they are?"

"What do you think they are?" Sol asked.

"What if it's not just life they take, but suffering?" she proposed, wafting and depleted.

"Huh?" Den added, yet again.

"What do you mean?" Sol urged.

"Suffering has to go somewhere. With time, it transforms. Into hatred, resolve, wisdom. ...It becomes something else. What of that carried and unused? The sort that's held and festers? It must go somewhere when a body cannot live to hold it or use it. If they're simply death, they'd be everywhere. But they're here. Death has already done its workings here..."

Sol blinked into the fire and breathed an icy note. "That's why they rise at fronts? Soldiers go limp or they writhe. Some rot fast, others slow. It's suffering that determines it?"

"Battles where few have choice in the fighting. They're hungry. Their land barren. The lives for which they fight cannot be regained. And they stand to face foes carrying the same anguish. Perhaps that's what umbras rise to meet. Not lives run out, but anguish held...or clashed and mixed. Not death alone, but all that comes with facing you'll be claimed by it if you do not cause it. That breeds suffering. It is the very stuff of it. Suffering must go somewhere."

"To them?" Sol mulled.

"Mine got stuck and lit up. And it claims them. And you..." She lifted her tear-streaked face to the soldier. "You've lived through every one you've encountered, close and often enough to know how they move...to know how to separate them from simple darkness. You *struck* it. You and that blade. Fortified by things you would not tell. Harsh, dark things."

Both Sol and Den stared as they considered Araina's quivering musings. Their pondering abruptly broke when Pidgie flapped from his overhead refuge. A smirk crossed the elf's face.

"Feh!" he spat. "Who cares what they are? Ya took care of that thing like it was nothin', Rainy! 'Long as we got you, let 'em come!" With his exclamation, Araina returned to the burrow of her arms. "Whatcha sulkin' 'bout over there?"

"I hate it. They were right. It worked and I *hate* it. They'll never let me... I'll never be able to—" Her words slipped into a poorly concealed sob.

Sol pulled the cloak from her pack and knelt before her.

"You got first rest. However long you need it to be," he whispered and unfolded it.

"Wait, wait, wait. Ain't we need Rainy to keep watch? What if another one'a those *things* show up?" Den rushed.

"You saw what we're dealing with now. You're just as capable as keeping watch," he answered the elf and rolled the cloak over the witch's shoulders.

"Not a chance! How'm I suppose'a tell the difference between that thing and that...*thing*."

"Cloaks don't rejoin after being sliced in half. Between the two of us, we'll know whether or not we need to wake Araina."

"Is that likely to happen?" With her meek inquiry, she revealed her eyes above her forearms. "Are more likely to follow now that we've—"

"No," Sol affirmed.

"How can you be sure?"

"Because that's the answer I give to someone who needs to sleep."

"Take it if ya can get it, Rainy. One'a those urka things show up again, and he won't wake ya, ya can bet I'm gonna," Den grimly assured her then looked up to Sol. "Hmm...we got anything to bet on it?"

Sol shook his head and turned back to Araina—curled on her side, hood over her head, and away from the fire. Something moved across his chest and fell at his hands, urging him to steady the tight shaking below the cloak and steal her from the stubborn sentry post she would doubtlessly hold. He instead lowered himself to feed the fire and kept stock of the shadows.

Chapter Twenty-Five

Poised to Strike

W hen chestnut biscuit crumbs, carried by a hot misting sigh from Den's mouth, hit Araina's cheek, she nearly knocked the elf off her shoulder. Her hand was only stayed by the presence of Pidgie below him. The passenger pigeon was startled away just the same by the brisk wiping of her face.

"What is wrong with you! It's bad enough to constantly hear your chomping!"

"Alright, alright." Den clung to the biscuit as Pidgie steadied in the air. "Just sick a' these damn things."

"We're all sick of them," Sol interjected, low and sharp.

"And if you're going to moan about them, do it far from my face, you loathsome little wart belch!" Araina snapped.

"Ain't easy to chew while flyin', and the General's got too much junk clangin' from his shoulder. And whaddya expect, ya hoity-toit? Ain't my fault we're stuck with dry crumbs, zig-zaggin' extra days through wasteland, all 'cause *you* needed to go inhale flotsam and clam piss!"

"Before you spew another word from the cracked chamber pot that is your mouth, remember I can fly after you. Don't rely on Pidgie to shield you. I'll pluck you right off that sweet bird's back!"

"G'head and try. Ya been livin' off nothin' but leaves and nut dust too. Doubt ya could catch up even if ya get off the ground, big hips."

"Sol, may I see your crossbow for a moment?"

"Much as I'd like to see your attempt, it's not worth the bolts or your energy. Another few miles and you take it into the lowlands."

"That means downhill." Araina's voice softened. "That's something."

"Until we have to turn back up it."

"To alter our path again?"

"No. Resume it. We bend north and keep that for a time. Then we head down into the willow swamps."

"Do you think we're truly clear of him?"

"Not a certainty and therefore a possibility. A slim one though."

"I am sorry, Sol." Araina dropped her eyes to the dirt. "I know what a toll it's taken."

"We're not as poor off as we could be. Got a long stretch between this and the next one. Might find decent hunting." He shrugged. "Maybe something hardier growing?"

"If there's anything edible below this half of the sky, I will find it for you...and him. If only to shut him up."

"Something to strive for. Don't let it distract you."

The dry shrub-land thinned to a sloping field of bunchgrass so wispy and clumped it scarcely allowed passage. Araina's view of it swept with her traverse, rolling, slowly downward, then slipping steep. When it became a trial to stay upright, she stopped in her labored sliding steps and dropped between tussock mounds.

"Anything yet?" Sol asked, having lost track of their distance since they entered and then cleared the area circled on the map.

"Possibly," she answered more tenuous than he liked.

He too dropped back and watched her gaze slide about their surroundings. The witch squinted, swallowed, and stiffened her back, then remained poised and unblinking for many long moments. She briefly focused on Pidgie as he and Den landed ahead of her. Her view moved to Sol, who idly drank from his canteen and appeared ready to reach for the map again.

"I'm guessing neither of you smell that?" she asked.

Sol eased his lips from the spout and shook his head.

"Don't look at me," Den said.

"Didn't think so," she whispered and swallowed the telling traces lining her throat.

With her rise, a buzzing gravity caught her knees and ankles. A breeze of cedar, broken pokeweed, and mildew drew her further downland where the bunchgrass mounds soon rivaled her height. The air and her movement past the wisps hastened from a crumbing rustle to a smooth rush. When she came to a crushed circular mound, the sense sharpened like cicadas of a relentless summer. Araina knelt before it, parted the blades, and revealed a narrow, tunneling cavity. Sol crouched and observed it from over her shoulder.

With the scratching chirp still ringing in her ears, the witch barely heard him say, "You're not expecting me to follow you into that, are you?"

"I'm not expecting most of myself to follow me into it," Araina flattened herself to the curved walls of earth. She pushed her head and shoulders within. "Though maybe living off chestnut meal and wilted mallow for days now will've made a dif—"

Her voice, along with her hips, caught against the opening. A growled sigh, thick with chagrin, briefly interrupted her struggle. Den laughed boisterously enough to be heard from beyond the confines.

"Need'a push? Maybe some grease?"

Araina grit her teeth, dug in her fists and elbows, and with a persistent wiggle, her lower half cleared the threshold of soil.

Sol watched her feet descend beyond sight and informed the elf, "You know which of us is going in next if she takes too long, right?"

Den's tireless chuckle slipped into a frown. "Make it quick, Rainy!"

Through unnerving grazes of dangling roots, Araina inched along the hollow. After a modest distance, the beats of her breath began to echo. She sturdied herself on her forearms and drew up light to reveal a significant drop just a reach away. A slow sloshing of liquid called from below. She wriggled to the edge of the descent and warmth rose to meet her skin. The dark earth gave way to a water-carried reflection and pale veins of what looked to be travertine.

Araina stretched her right arm across the hole and gauged the density of its edge. With her grip, the soil fell away in clods. Their dense plunges thickened an exasperated, claustrophobic urgency to follow them downward. She half-considered the risk of snaking below headfirst. The foolish notion was interrupted when a large chunk broke into bits and uncovered a broad root. She nearly thanked it aloud as she grasped it, dragged her legs forward, and leveraged herself into the drop.

Her feet, knees, and then her elbows splashed into the water and met with smooth stone. A brief crescendo of pain buzzed across her limbs. Then came the sense of heat. It carried away the cold, gritty soil—pleasantly at first. Far less soothing was a faint swell of iron and formic acid that seemed separate from the Meridian-leaked scents already lacing her airways. Araina stood up in the shallow flow and summoned light again.

Great twisted roots birthed eerie shadows as she proceeded. Others lay in the water and threatened to pull her down. The soothing warmth at her ankles heightened to a steaming tingle—holding just below a singe. When she thought she could stand it no longer, she came to a hairy vegetative cluster blocking the upper portion of her path.

The fibers had all but fused into an oblong, cocoon-like heap. Araina dared to touch it, then slipped the edge of her fingernails between its layers. After some urging, her hand eased into the chilled wet thickness. It nearly swallowed her to her elbow before a familiar density seemed to find her fingertips just as they sought it. A texture rose to meet her blind touch. After Fiwrn was pulled from its tuberous home, its markings smoothed flat below the witch's light and the drawing scents faded from her throat. The formic vapor fully stole their place. Its acrid haze and the rising heat at her ankles spurred a new urgency—one for clear and cool air.

Pleading for another fortunate root to reveal itself and grant a means above ground, she swayed her light ahead and then back. In her frantic searching, she almost missed a glare separate from her own—small but sharp and waiting some unclear distance away. Araina splashed toward it. Her left hand illuminated her scattered advance through root pillars while her right clutched Fiwrn close.

The distant glow swelled. The water, growing hotter, rose and sped with it. Past her knees, thighs, then waist, it swept. She was pulled down with a yelp and could do little but endure as it towed her on. Just as she thought she would be scalded, then boiled alive, a rush of cold air found her face and sky met her squinted view. She tumbled into an open spring among a sloping thicket.

Between gasping lungfuls, she stumbled and splashed to its edge. Araina caught more breath and released a hoarse shout up the hill. Her call soon convoked Den on Pidgie.

"Oh nice!" the elf exclaimed at the steaming water. He and Pidgie flew downland to Araina, where she sat and continued to push for air. Den dismounted, disrobed entirely, and splashed into the water.

"Ah! Hot!" he huffed.

"I could've told you that." She rolled her eyes—trying to keep them clear of the stripped and splashing elf. She placed Fiwrn in her lap and wrung out her hair.

"Was that one easier without Vexhi knocking overhead or Boon waiting across the way?" Sol inquired on his approach. He crouched to dip his hand in the spring.

"Not sure I'd say easier." Araina tipped her reddened nose to the flow from the hillside. "That feels cold compared to what's inside there."

"You alright?"

"Just need air. Now that I'm out of it, it almost feels nice to've had a hot bath, even one excessively so." She squeezed the water from the hems of her trousers.

"Gotta say, but for discard of braies, I think Den may have the right idea." Sol lowered his crossbow and quiver to the ground. He removed his belt, sword, socks, and boots, and stacked it all atop his pack. Araina opened hers and tied away Fiwrn as the third in the cloth bundle.

"I'll leave you both to take avail of it, however…freely you choose. Think I'll follow this a few steps. I'd like to see if I can find any mimnous or lepflora."

"Those food?" Den immodestly lifted himself onto a rock to ask.

"The lepflora's root is," she answered and swung her view to the brush opposite him. "And mimnous tea will help the stomach cramps it can cause."

"I take it it's not worth one finding one without the other?" Sol gathered over the shed of his shirt. He tossed it on the stack and entered the steaming water.

"A gamble at the very least. Fortunately, they both grow near hot springs. I'll see if any still exist."

"Need to go far to find out?"

She shook her head and, well within Sol's view, tightened her scabbard and dagger around her waist.

He nodded, dropped to his shoulders, then submerged.

Den leapt from the rock like a toad as Araina passed and offered her forearm to Pidgie.

"Care to keep me company, my good sir? Perhaps there's some pokeweed berries on the way."

The passenger pigeon fluttered up to accept and hopped from her wrist to her shoulder. They left the elf and soldier to their soak.

A bounty of burst thistles awaited Pidgie near the spring's edge. Araina had less luck. She squinted past the brambles and into the vines and spindly trees of the hillside. With Sol and Den's splashing still audible, and Pidgie calm near her feet, she approached a patch of yellow blooms some dozen paces into the thicket. Their weak petals fell away with her touch. It did not bode well for their tubers. She went on to shift the soil from their stems, and before she could fully loosen their grip, Pidgie suddenly trilled away in alarm.

Araina rose and slid her dagger from the scabbard. Somewhere uphill, a tangle of vines snapped. She caught nothing in her immediate surroundings, nor anything in the distance beyond the wooded slope. A rustle of leaves told of another, lower approach. A gravely, whispered exclaim hastened ahead of her.

Him? she almost hissed aloud.

Between the rising panic of the thought and her pulse, she became acutely aware of the abrupt silence at her back—not a hint of Den or Sol. Her grip on the dagger was tightened by the memory of how silently and swiftly the torch was knocked from Sol's. A branch snapped, a new whisper followed—closer still and somewhere to her right. She spread her left hand and readied a faint spark. At a sudden dashing just beyond her view, her wings burst forth and her light swelled beyond her hold—blindly startling away into the vines and shadows. An arrow immediately answered and sank beside the joint of her left shoulder.

Araina staggered back with a gasp. Another arrow ripped from the shadows, through and out the top of her right wing. A third shot cleared the center of her left while a fourth sailed and completed a trio of bleeding splits in the indigo-grey flesh. A scurrying further stirred up the slope. More clamoring followed from downhill. She shuttered her wings into tight arches and, in spite of her pierced shoulder, moved to draw up light. Her arm screamed with crushing pain and ignited a primal cry. Out of panicked haste to be rid of its source, she touched the arrow's blood and resin-slicked shaft, then discovered the terrible, rupturing cost. The bone-scraping sting tossed the horizon askew and sent her to her knees.

Through her shaking, grey-bordered vision, she caught a glimpse of what appeared to be dark tussock dashing through the brush. It became fleetingly apparent as hair—a thick, seemingly living mass of it. Its movement was separate from a barefooted sprinting behind her. A crossbow bolt flew over her head, another sang through the air over her right wing, followed by another at her left.

Sol skirted ahead of the witch seemingly without lifting his feet from the ground. A counter of two arrows ripped from the vines, one he dodged, the other sank just short of his toes. He loaded, drew, and sent two bolts in response. Quick shouts rose after, then retreated. All went silent but for another readying draw and Araina's wounded breathing. Sol turned and knelt before her, his crossbow still poised on the perimeter.

"I-I'm so sorry, Sol. I'm so sorry. I thought—" she uttered through a pang and tried to shake the clouding of her sight.

"We have to get to cover or move where they'll be an easier spot. Can you fold your wings back?"

After jittering the dagger into her scabbard, she cringed through their withdrawal. The short, blood-trimmed rips descended away with a hot sting. The gripping pain from her shoulder remained and reasserted itself with any movement of her upper body. Sol slipped an arm along her side and across her back. Through his attempt to aid her upright, another sharp cry broke from her lips—spurred by a brush of the crossbow's lath against the arrow's fetching. The soldier sucked back his alarm and rapidly slung the weapon away. He sturdied his hold and guided her out of the thicket to the stream's edge.

"Den!" he shouted upstream. "Den!"

The elf appeared, breathless, and like Sol, wearing only trousers. His little eyes widened at the sight of the witch and the arrow protruding from her shoulder.

"Wha—"

"Where's Pidgie?" Sol demanded while giving Araina anchorage to kneel.

"With her," Den stammered.

"Find him and circle. See if anything's closing in," he instructed without breaking his examination of Araina's shoulder and the slick hafting resting at its puncture. The primitive though precise knife-shaved shaft and unfamiliar fetching gave no answers on the arrow's tip or barbs. He tried to suppress the apprehension birthed by its mystery.

"I-I gotta get my boots."

"Go!" Sol barked.

Den bolted back upstream, fast as his bare feet would permit, whistling for the pigeon all the way.

Sol felt a brush against his arm. He caught Araina out of a slow droop.

"Araina?" He closed his grip on her right shoulder and locked on her eyes. Her pupils had flooded her irises, leaving only slim maple rings around black wells. Her lips were reddened and swollen—the lower gone slack and glossed with saliva. "Araina?"

She answered with a heaved gust of breath, as though ripped out of a dream.

"What do we have for pain?"

"Oh…" she slurred with more air than voice. "Was supposed to…show you…" She slid away from his hold.

"Easy. We'll get that arrow out."

"Mm hmm." She went limp and fell forward.

"No, no, no, no…" He caught and eased her to the ground. On pushing scattered tresses from her face, a feverish blaze met his touch. "Don't move. I-I just need to get something for the— I'll be right back."

"Mm sorry, Sol. Ni' thou…"

Sol raced upstream to their packs, where he nearly crashed into Den on Pidgie.

"Ain't nobody out there—hey!" the elf shouted with their narrowly avoided collision.

"Grab the rest."

Before Den could voice any confusion or objection to the command, Sol dashed back downstream with Araina's pack. He dropped at her side, lifted her face, and found the evening sky reflected in her yawning pupils.

"Araina?"

She only responded with a sudsy gasp.

Sol's eyes darted between her and across the dozen narrow pockets and dried sprigs revealed from rolled canvas.

"You know what any of these are?" he shouted to Den.

"Huh?" The elf blinked back, fully dressed again and dragging one of Sol's boots behind him.

Sol rolled his dripping brow into his palm and swallowed hard. He lowered his face near Araina's and felt her cheek burn beside his own flushed skin.

"I'm going to make this quick as I can," he vowed and unlaced the join of her left bodice strap. He lowered the front portion clear of the wound. From her pack, he took cloths from some part of their long-ago-eaten fare and placed them beside her shoulder. Sol then laid his forearm across her chest and framed her wound within the crook of his left hand, evoking another strained gasp.

"First part. Nice and quick." With the shaft of the arrow in his right hand, he sharply snapped away the bulk of it.

The witch's cry rang through his ear.

"Next part." He swallowed a thick sigh. "I'm sorry, Araina."

Sol pinched the remaining portion of the arrow above the hafting. He tightened his jaw and began to shift the barbs. The wound answered with more blood. Araina gnashed her teeth, seethed, and fought to wriggle away. Sol's eyes strove to keep clear of hers and their flow to her ears. She weakly gripped to claw him free. With a press of his forearm, he flattened her back to the ground.

Through his urging, one barb emerged from the widening puncture, and despite the steady surge of blood, he confirmed the notch's curve. He braced himself for the coming force and pushed the arrow's point back. Araina ran through the apex of her voice and strength as the tip was angled and both notches appeared beyond her flesh, slick and red. Sol slid the point free and tossed it to the dirt. He held a cloth to the running wound, dropped his head, and listened to the subsiding race between her gasps and his own roaring pulse.

The first cloth soaked through. He swiftly exchanged it with the next. Araina's eyes held shut and pained, then slowly softened. Though her skin remained ablaze with something coursing and raw, her voice rallied somewhat as she again told him, "Sol, I'm so sorry. I thought it was—"

"Just keep still."

After the latest saturated cloth was swapped for a clean one, the soldier moved to rinse his arms in the spring. Red-tinted drips rolled across the crescent dents from the witch's fingernails. He shook the water away and pulled his shirt over his head. His socks and boots followed over his feet. Only then did he notice the joint stares of Den and Pidgie—both fixed on Araina.

Sol informed the elf, "We need to make camp here. You get everything from upstream?"

Den nodded.

"See what you can do for firewood. Kindling at least."

Den nodded again and turned away.

The bloodied cloths were collected, rinsed, wrung, and laid over a rock. Sol returned to Araina's side.

"When you're able, I need you to tell me which of those plants help with pain. Might be a long night otherwise."

"Doesn't hurt much now," she said weakly.

"No?" He furrowed his brow.

"No." Araina opened her eyes and revealed unrelenting, glassy black. Despite the rosy flush across her skin, she began to shiver. Sol retrieved her cloak and blanketed her up to the wound. With one of the spring-dampened cloths, he proceeded to clear the blood from her jaw and neck.

"I'd wonder what you'd make of the arrow. Something strange on the hafting."

"Tipped, isn't it?" she exhaled.

"Looks like it. *You* look like it. What are you feeling?"

"A wave that will not ebb. The ground is upright and I will not stop sliding." She reached and curled her hand around his wrist. "You're steady though. Not sliding at all."

"You don't feel any pain in your shoulder?"

"I haven't one."

"It's still there. In a bit of a state. But still have both."

"No. Gone where the wings go. Unless that wolf has it. May've the whole side now. Light and all. Rest's just cold."

"That's some fever you're brewing. ...And fast." Sol mopped her forehead. "Try to keep still. We'll get a fire going."

"I raise fire."

"I know. I've seen." He smiled. "Den and I'll manage it tonight. Just bear with us if it takes a bit longer to get going." He took her hand from his arm and held it a moment before rising to find their flint and steel.

"Sol," Araina breathed, summoning him from his search. "The one on the end. Nearest the ties. That one's hunger."

"What about fever? Or pain? What do they look like?"

"Fever? All useless on Moonserpents. Useless Moonserpents. Just anchors and ships. Ships and harbors. Harbors without their seals. They've all gone. It's such a mess, Sol."

He could only stare as the witch fell away from her words. He left her to find sleep somewhere beyond.

Chapter Twenty-Six

What Heals, What Harms

Squinting through the halos that burned from every light-touched surface, Araina focused on Sol's thickening stubble and the dense bags below his eyes. She fought to keep still while he wrapped her shoulder and imagined the sunken, smokey skin below hers was no better—telling of a night stolen by visions too murky and chaotic to be proper nightmares.

"I'm terribly sorry about your arm," she exhaled.

"My arm? From where you…" Sol almost laughed. "No comparison. Though I wonder where the strength of that grip was that first day on the south lawn." He cautiously knotted the ends of the improvised bandage and caught her from another droop. Araina looked at his scarred hand around her right shoulder, then the cloth wrapped around her left.

"Perhaps it'd be better to stitch it?" she suggested.

"It's mean but it's narrow. I've seen worse close up on their own. Reckon you're in enough pain without my needlework."

"Pain's gone. Just feels heavy."

"For now." He squinted into her pupils. "Whatever's poisoning you above it may be on its way out."

"That or it's just weak."

"Here." He passed over her canteen. "Couple boils got most of the sharp taste out of it. Den barely complained."

"Where's he gone?"

"Foraging. Told him to do another perimeter check while he was at it. I don't think they'll be back though."

"Dwovlins," Araina presumed with a rasp and pushed through a swallow of water. "I thought I saw one run. Looked like Lem."

"Lem?"

"In Barriers' End. Didn't know what he was back then."

"He shoot at you with tipped arrows?" the soldier inquired as he relieved her of the canteen.

"No. ...Ferried me across a swamp. Cost me a lock of hair."

"Sounds preferable to the lot out here."

Araina's eyes welled. "I'm so sorry, Sol. I... I didn't want to take the chance that it was—" Her voice weakened further then broke.

"No. Mistake's mine this time. I shouldn't have—" He swallowed away a gruff sigh. "No more apologies, got it? Last one'll be from me for that job I did yesterday. I'm no surgeon as it is, but I couldn't stand the sight of..." He turned and grabbed the rolled canvas of sprigs. "We've got more important things to focus on. First, getting you in a better state. Good a time as any to finally go over these." He presented the line of herbs. "You said this was for sustenance, right?"

Araina shook her head. "Hunger pangs."

"Right," Sol added, confused by her correction as they looked at the very same pocket.

"Only quells the feeling. It doesn't feed."

"I see. Still, no small thing. What about for fever?"

The witch looked at the encouragement across his exhausted face, then stared at the line of green, brown, and silvery sprigs. After many probing, ponderous moments, she found them to be nothing more than tidy clusters of dried leaves on woody stems—no names, no properties, no purposes beyond their desiccated shapes.

"I... I..." The hollow wheeze of her voice slipped into rapid gasps.

Sol searched the small but growing squall of panic behind her eyes. It evoked baffled unease in his, which only hastened her fight for air.

"It's alright. You'll try again after more rest. If you're not in pain, that's enough. We'll get you moving again. Things will come clearer with some steps."

After her lungs steadied, Araina's calm wandered into something shadowy and bitter. "May not even matter. Who's to say they're any stronger than this poison?"

Sol let her question hang amidst the flow of the spring and the sound of Pidgie's approach at the edge of the thicket. He stiffened his shoulders and folded up the canvas.

"May not matter," he conceded. "Only matters that you're stronger. There's little wondering about that."

Even as the selection of herbs was taken away, Araina's view remained at the blank space across the cloak over her legs. Sol stood up and proceeded to collect their things.

Beyond a rigid rise and slow return up the tussock covered slope, they found their trail, north and days on to willow swamps. The cover of trees was kinder to Araina's eyes, but the shadows spurred their own trouble in her periphery. They separated from the shapes that cast them and stalked her pace. Quick tips of red glimmered at their edges. They dashed and flanked the spaces between her footfalls. But with Sol taking no notice and Pidgie not trilling away from any of it, she said nothing, even when the light went low between the trees and the predation worsened. It subsided little when they made camp just ahead of a new descent in the land.

"Feeling up to this?" Sol placed a final piece of firewood on the stack.

Araina stirred from a faraway vigilance not fully based in their surroundings. Her widened eyes completed a stark climb of his form and locked on the empty space over his shoulder.

"If not, I'll—"

"No, I...I'll get it," she finally answered. "I just don't know if I can strike the flint."

"Got that covered. When you're ready."

She moved to stand in a labored push. Sol left the flint and steel on the ground and went to her aid. Despite her weakness, she tensed below his touch.

"Has it started to hurt?"

"No. Not much."

"What is it then?" he implored, unnerved by her limply guarded posture.

"Nothing," Araina closed her eyes only to quickly open them, as though some terror waited just beyond. "It's nothing."

He took his hand from her arm and touched her forehead. Its heat rose to meet his fingertips. "Help me with the fire. We'll check on your shoulder after."

She nodded and frailly lowered herself to their pile of kindling.

When her right hand flattened and hovered, Sol struck the flint. She motioned, single-handed, in rhythm with her lungs. But unlike so many other dusks, the sparks darkened away to thin smoke.

"I-I'm sorry. It's difficult with one hand."

"It's alright, I'll just—"

"No, I can get it. I'm ready."

Sol struck the flint and again sent sparks into the leaves. Araina narrowed her eyes, lowered her right hand, and with a wretched yelp, brought her left hand forward to join it.

"Araina!"

Discarding Sol's exclaim, she inhaled, exhaled, and pull the flames up with a loosely symmetrical drag of her hands. The dismayed soldier stared at her in the spreading circle of light. She gripped her shaking left arm with a steely rage, releasing it only to shove away her tears.

"Why would you do that?!" he demanded.

"Because you're losing the light and you need it. Where're Den and Pidgie? How would they find their way?"

"Do not do that again! So you are in pain. Let me take a look—"

"There's nothing to be done."

"Neither of us know that until I check. Hold still." Sol dragged her hair off her shoulder and began to untie the bandage. "Den and Pidgie are fine. They're right back there. Pidgie got caught up in some seed. Den found more caggis root. He's digging it up. I mentioned it after we stopped. Remember?"

On uncovering the raw, crescent-shaped parting in her flesh, Sol's bafflement at her lapse sank into a sympathetic aversion. The wound's edges were dark and gripping. He swallowed hard and briskly opened his pack.

"...Plenty to be done about this. Can already tell it would've been worse without the spring water. No need to stitch it either. Just have to keep that fever on the retreat." He soaked a cloth from his canteen. "Wager the hardest part of this will be getting you to—" The soldier bit his words.

Araina only stared into the fire wearing pallid disquiet.

He went on to warn, "I'm going to clean around it. I'm barely going to touch it but it may sting."

With the lightest graze of her skin, Sol conjured a hiss.

She breathed it away and muttered, "It drags on and on. And then it goes. Fast. You just don't know it yet."

"What does? What don't I know?"

"Why those lifeless leaves won't matter. Another cluttered, useless thing to carry in the face of another fever."

Araina glowered at her pack. Sol ceased his cleaning and reached within, revealing the canvas. He untied it and ran his eyes over the row of sprigs once again.

"What if it were me?" he posed.

"What if what were you?"

"What if it were me, or Den, or Pidgie? Worth a try then?"

At his suggestion, the creasing detestation around Araina's eyes slanted into a sorrowful pondering. "I…"

"Imagine the worst thing is they wouldn't work, right? But if anything's left to them, might be just enough. Might be more than enough." Sol laid out the canvas before her and began rewrapping her shoulder. "The only one you remember is the one that would help me and Den. Maybe Pidgie. I don't know as far as birds. He's had no trouble finding food besides. You told me about that one, the one that would help us as we are," he tallied low at her ear as he knotted a new bandage in place. "But which one helps you?"

He slipped his hand around hers, brushing her palm. She did not move but for the almost reflexive curling of her fingertips. As though seeking to draw up something, they found raised slashes over his fingers.

"That's the one I need. Please, Araina?"

"Nice fire!" Den called at their backs. "Got somethin' for roastin'."

Sol's hand tightened, then fell away. He stood to see the elf approach with a root slung over his shoulder and Pidgie following after.

"This'll make that nut dust go down easier." Den plunked the root on a stone near the fire and shoved it into the gathering embers with the push of a twig.

"One that size'll take a while. You'll keep an eye on it?" Sol asked.

"Ain't like there's nothin' else to do," the elf grumbled and settled upon the ground. "So we got one more'a these things 'fore we head back?"

Sol nodded. "Another five days. Then west." He took out a biscuit and snapped it in two.

"Can't tell ya how much steak I'm gonna get when this job's done." Den poked at his roasting harvest.

"Might have to go far to find a seller," Sol muttered and put a biscuit-half in his mouth. He chewed slowly and looked back at Araina as she squinted at the sprigs in her lap. "Clear your mind, then try again. Maybe sketch something?"

Araina finally lifted her face and nodded.

Sol brought forth her charcoal and field book.

"Could you find my ink and quill, please?" she requested. "I need to try something else."

Sol obliged. Araina folded away the herbs and began scrawling in silence.

* * *

The weather went grey and misty when an eerie swamp of willow trees and boggy pits claimed their further descending path. With most of the leaves gone from the drooping branches, they created strange sounds and ripples across the opaque water at their roots. Three days through it, no one had grown accustomed to it— only exhausted by the spindly shifting that fed constant wariness.

Even as Araina found short focus to forage, the land gave little to stretch their provisions. The need to boil every sip of water from the surrounding pools strained and scattered their steps, which were now driven by the search for dry firewood as well as progress along the map. Sol's eyes fell to it with the same vigilance kept over the witch's wound and the waves of her senses, which were first fractured, then restored, then, locked in a stillness.

Araina missed Sol's call as she shuddered below her cloak and kept guarded from the damp evening breeze. Her muttering recitation of odd, almost ominous and ancient-sounding words further voided the soldier's summons. The sequence went on rushing from her lips, growing stranger as it sped. It stopped at the mounting approach of boots over soil. The witch also halted. Her wandering had taken her to the edge of a root-framed puddle. The sparse raindrops on its surface kept her eyes as Sol neared.

"You didn't hear me? We got enough kindling for the night. Come and rest."

"I thought walking might help me remember."

He circled and peered below her hood, observing the flush across her nose and cheeks—the latest of a cycle. "Even if you can't, they're all medicinals, aren't they? Is there much harm in just trying one and being wrong?"

"They harm as well as they heal," she replied through a dark snag of her voice. "*That* is important to remember. And one must never confuse anything for what it isn't. She told me that. She would tell me how it would matter so, very, much. But what then, when they neither heal nor harm? I do not know, for I know them no longer. And I've stopped trying to remember."

"You just said—"

"I'm trying to remember something else. Something much greater than those dead leaves, but on which all leaves shall rely. He made me burn all that. And so I must get it back. You'll need it. You'll need it so a front remains. For you. You can take them on your way to it. I am sorry to have delayed you from it. Another mistake."

"What are you talking about?"

"I don't know whose it was. May've been hers. If she saw it all and it only being a delivery was only a lie. Wings haven't made that clearer. Maybe it was Tanzan's. He conjured it from me that first night. Gleefully...with those questions. Or was it the Coven's, Trinera's. What the blind notions of this miserable Crest does to them. Or maybe it was yours, Sergeant Solairous Ekwidou. That day, when I heard that name and you saw it. My mind holds nothing, but I remember your face." She moved to touch his cheek. Her hand stayed and she only breathed—grasping for something in her memory and from his dark, searching eyes. "It fell together then. With another strike at a fireplace. Behind your eyes. Like winter soil. So much hidden. So much held."

"Araina..."

"I've lost all of it, Sol. I cannot recall the workings. How they come together. Their very names. Without that, there's no... Though I think it may not matter. Tanzan and his tests. The first steps into this. I will keep trying, nevertheless. Once again, trying in spite. And, I'll write them before this claims me. But even then, it's the touchpoints that matter most. You'll take them."

"Take them?"

"I cannot be the—"

"Araina, no."

"Sol, please. You—"

"Araina. I won't hear this."

"Sol, do you not see—"

"I will carry *you* the rest of the way," he informed her in equal parts vow and threat. "I will slice through umbras and Vexhi and run you past them. You're not... We are *days*—"

"Days are too much. That's what fevers do to witches now. I remain on my feet but I burn. He made me burn it. Just a test. Just torment. Fuel. It's as she would've done. No. Not this time. I can give you the pieces. It's enough, Sol. Enough to get started, enough to keep going, and enough without—"

"Stop," he rushed, almost gripping her shoulders until he caught himself. "Araina, listen to me. I will not touch them. That wound is closing. You are still here. You've held on for days and miles. The mission remains and so will you. You...you know its necessity better than any of us. The strategy is sound. Still. That is it. There are no more decisions. We only see this through."

"But it is not sound. Sol, please." She gripped his forearm. He felt her tremble as she pleaded, "If you take them now, it will be enough to get them somewhere.

While you've strength and sustenance. Before they amass. Before too much is lost and they're drawn by me. You can get far enough and—"

"No. I will not hear it. Now come rest up." He slipped from her hold and turned back to their camp.

Still sat up before the fire, Sol was bested by exhaustion. Once his breath plunged into a steady telltale density, Araina rose from her feigned sleep and began scratching at the field book. The quill barely obeyed her hand as it shook, clutched, and ached from every attempt, every word, every symbol, every line that was only wrong. Her furious rasped breathing, a close companion to the scrawling, was made all the more scattered against Den and Sol's deep, rhythmic snores.

"Grief," a familiar growl interrupted at her ear. "Is that what you've named me?"

The quill went slack in her ink-stained fingers. "What does it matter, your name?"

"What does it yours?" the red wolf snarled.

"Moonserpent," she hissed.

"My Araina."

Kerikan's voice ripped through the hood of the cloak. It gripped upon her heart and up the length of her throat, where it squeezed like a talon and awoke a foul sting of metallic rage and agony. The inkwell fell over. The field book and quill dropped from her knees into a slowly spreading puddle of black. Araina turned. Though it was the old witch's voice and summoning, the red wolf waited with threads of steam escaping its jaws.

"Follow. Find what remains."

It dashed between the trees.

Araina wobbled to her feet and stumbled in its wake, barely tracking its fiery tail past dark pools and through the bare sweeping branches. She was fast out of breath, dragged by her feverous body and the drape of the cloak. She unfastened and let it fall from her shoulders.

The wolf became nothing but a streak of red in the distance. Araina began to flail and slip, and then stumbled into the dirt. Down she slid into a pit at the edge of a stretching puddle. She let herself lay, and her shoulder sting and bleed, and waited for her tears to give way. They would not come.

"Arainas." At the low echo of Kerikan's voice, the young witch's view crept up to meet with the old, her form centered and sending slow ripples across the dark water. "Flowers of the Nymphrain rosoidea. Seems an impossibly chilled time for them to bloom. Even the latest sort in the warmest autumn. Did that young, old man claim you were named for an impossible thing? Not simply the thorns that draw blood? You drew so much that day. It would not stop, my Araina. And you are mine. For I thought it my own life draining with hers. Your name. The thorns. I could think of nothing else."

Araina struggled to rise. A thick rush of red surfaced over the bandage and down her arm.

"And so goes what remains. This is why one must never confuse anything for what it is not. For if it does not heal, it can only harm. But know this effort was a noble one. We surely cannot say that for many. Can we, my Araina?"

A great heaviness oozed behind the young witch's eyes. She watched the old fade into the swing of the stripped branches before her vision went grey, then dark.

"Hey. Wake up." Den slugged Sol's wrist.

"Wha—" the soldier gasped awake.

"Rainy's gone."

Sol shook out of his slump to see only her pack, canteen, field book, and quill lying next to the overturned inkwell. He shot to his feet. "You hear anything?"

"If you didn't, what makes ya think I woulda?"

"Search overhead."

Sol sped along the barefoot tracks in the soil. When he came to her cloak, a sharp, cold pang seized across his body. He swept it up, tossed it over his shoulder, and grabbed the hilt of his sword. But when he saw no footprints continuing among hers, he slid the blade back in its sheath. The stumbling prints led on for a few further yards, then slipped into a pit where she still lay.

Sol lifted her. Through her loll into the crook of his neck, he contended with the sapped sharpness across her once soft, sturdy form. Her dirt streaked face was icy. He dared not breath until he heard a limp gurgle from her lips.

"Araina?"

She stirred, and through a seethe at the reawakened pain in her shoulder, uttered, "Sol?"

He could only stare ahead at the dark puddle and the sickly sky and bare branches reflected sharply in its opaque surface. Their invert dissolved his sense of the earth below his knees. The race of his thoughts faded into his pulse and dulled into dazed sensations. It all converged into a sense of damp warmth—

Araina's blood, flowing through the bandage and over his shirt. He eased her upright.

"…How? How are you here?"

"I followed it," she weakly confessed.

"What did you follow?"

"I thought it was grief. It's something else."

"A dream."

"I wasn't asleep."

"Doesn't mean it wasn't one."

"It's getting worse. Please, Sol. Take them."

"You need a new bandage." He lifted her to her feet, wrapped the cloak around her shoulders, and guided her out of the pit.

The elf furrowed his brow at the witch and her blind gaze. Her sunken eyes remained unmoving even as Sol peeled the bandage from her shoulder and a blackened wound was revealed.

"How much longer we doin' this?" Den asked through a grimace.

Sol only moved to his pack.

"Rainy?" the elf urged.

Araina slowly eased air to and from her mouth until a hoarse, flat sound crawled forth and formed, "Yes, Den?"

"You gonna just…" He looked back to Sol, then to her, and exhaled, "Never mind."

"We're going to get a fire going. Just need more dry wood. That just needs to breathe." Sol pointed to her wound. "We still have tea. You'll drink some. You'll sleep a while. Then it's just two days. Even if we start hours from now, it's just two more days, Araina." Sol smoothed limp, tangled curls from her unblinking face, finally finding heat. He then gestured to Den. "Make sure she stays…that she rests," he instructed and quickly turned off through the trees.

Den stared back at Araina and the black-crusted crescent claiming her skin. "Rainy, is he…"

"Always a test. Never not a trial to see whether I'll fail. How poorly," she muttered.

"Huh. Well, I'd call this one done."

At the elf's remark, Araina broke her lost contemplation and blinked at him.

"Don't know how ya haven't yet. Look at ya. Tea? That's his plan? Gettin' hard to watch this."

"He's…"

"Uh huh. Soldiers. Ain't the worst I come across…maybe. Still all the same though. Only orders. Follow the mission. Look at what that's doin' to ya."

"Maybe he's right… Maybe I'll—" Her voice broke.

"Maybe nothin'. Keep goin' on like this and, hate to say it, Rainy, but it ain't lookin' good. One'a those urka things comes, and you're in some pit or somethin'…and forget it. Not the way I wanna go. Feh. You'd think he's trying to lure one of 'em here."

"I…I tried to—"

"Time to change somethin' up 'fore it's too late."

"He won't… I-I asked him."

"Maybe askin' ain't enough."

"I can't go. I'd never be able to—"

"Go? You? Ain't what I meant. I'm wonderin' how you're gonna make those two days he's goin' on about."

"Talk to him, Den." Araina slowly shut her eyes. Tears slipped after. "Please."

"He ain't listenin' to you, ya think I'm gonna get anywhere? I say it's time we work 'round 'im."

"…How?"

"Ain't wanna say it before, not when he's 'round, but why don't ya just let Pidgie and me go get ya help? Enough'a this lookout business. 'Bout time we got bumped up to rescue."

"Not me. The touchpoints. They're all that matter."

"Why's it gotta be you or them? We can just take 'em with us."

"You? You'll take them?"

"How big'er they?"

"The size of my hand. Three of them."

"How far they goin'?"

"Crest grounds. I-I don't know who's at the rendezvous or where it is. But…Ceedly. The temple. They'd have to go there."

"Blue glass place with the bastard shrubs and good cake? Eh, day's flight for us. If they're heavy, day-an'-a-half. Should be fine though. Pidgie ain't had trouble eatin' or gettin' exercise. Think he's fatter an' stronger than when we started."

Araina's breath quickened. "You must…you must get them there. Den, please, you—" Her shoulder began to bleed with the heaving of her lungs.

"Take it easy, Rainy. When we doin' this? From the looks'a ya, sooner the better."

"It would have to wait until... Soon as Pidgie has enough light to fly. I-I'll leave them at the opening of my pack. The white bundle of cloth. You'll have to take them before..." A new stream of tears slipped from the witch's eyes. "...Before he wakes."

"With the way he's sleepin' lately, leaves us plenty'a time. Had to pound 'em in the arm to get 'em up before."

"It's all that's left to be—"

"Don't sweat it. We got it from here."

Chapter Twenty-Seven

Trust

A raina exhaled across the steaming water as it soaked the biscuit and formed a runny porridge.

"Little rest made all the difference. Lot of ground covered today. You look a lot clearer too," Sol declared with a fragile smile and flicked the map taut.

She could not lift her eyes from the rim, nor could she manage a full swallow. Her bowl was gently placed before the elf. "Den, you can finish this if you want."

"If ya say so," he accepted with a shrug.

"You need to keep your strength up," Sol advised.

"I haven't much of an appetite tonight." Araina turned away and rummaged through her pack. Small pained noises escaped her lips with her rifling, alerting the soldier.

"Need a hand—"

"I'm fine. Just looking for a bit of charcoal. Must've slipped from the bindings." The cloth-wrapped touchpoints shook in her hidden grip. She pulled them forward and tucked them just beyond the pack's opening. Her hands came away with the field book, a sliver of charcoal, and the folded canvas of herbs.

"Going to try again?" A small glint rode on Sol's question.

"I thought if I sketched the leaves, perhaps it'd kindle something."

She untied the field book's cover and turned to the pages hardened with spilled ink. She tore them away and dropped them into the fire, creating a tattered gap between those that remained useable and her past sketches—flora, fauna, horizons, then Pidgie in a fine ruff collar, Den holding and drinking from a bottle twice his size, and Sol, his face softened by liquor held in red crystal. Her quaking fingers could barely keep the charcoal.

"On second thought, I may be too tired to—Sol!" she shouted and burst to her feet.

An umbra snaked from the willow nearest the soldier's back. The witch summoned and sent a flutter of light into its core, withering though not dissolving it. Araina cried out again and shot another flickering sphere. It crumbled the void away. Sol stared, only just off the ground, his sword not fully freed from its sheath. His breath fanned the hair overgrown and shadowing his brow. Araina shrank to her knees and gripped her left arm.

"Just what we needed," Den grumbled.

"How did I not…"

"Because you're exhausted," Araina answered the soldier through a wheeze.

"I…" His bewildered gaze was only broken by the witch's seething. "You…your shoulder. Did that reopen—"

"Leave it," she exhaled through her teeth. "I'll not bleed out before it clots. You *need* to sleep!"

"So do you!"

Araina looked away from him to Den and Pidgie. On observing the steadiness over the elf's face, the tremor in her hands smoothed. She took her cloak and awkwardly pulled it over her shoulders, flinching as the fabric fell over her left side.

She turned back to Sol and hissed, "Only until second watch. Then you until dawn."

He conceded with a nod.

Araina lowered herself and burrowed into the cloak. She waited, listened, and feigned sleep.

Hours on, when she could no longer bear another moment staring against the night, she righted herself and looked at Sol.

"Go on. Yours until morning."

He heard something in her mention of morning—something dreaded yet fortified. Though he searched to define what was halted in it and her warm eyes, coated slick, he could not focus or fight for it. His body dropped into a dense sleep.

A muted tapping filled the last sensations of the soldier's dream. It did not cease when he woke to the feel of cold air beyond his hood or the clouded daylight across the pit of their former fire. A soft rain dented the ash, and yet he was dry. He rolled back and found himself shielded by indigo-grey flesh. Two pale lines told of closed splits. He listened to the drops hit Araina's wing for another breath and tilted his view to find her holding it aloft as his cover. Her cloak had been shed and the rain roll over her skin. She sat, staring.

"You'll freeze like that," he said.

"Skin's too hot. Dirty," the witch droned.

He again looked up at the mended tears—so much cleaner and smoother than the black crescent of her shoulder—and faintly appraised, "Your wing's healed." He came out from its cover.

Araina did not respond. Her left wing was kept tight at her back. Before it and between her dripping waves of hair, the bandage was soaked red. Her form held stony but for her grasp and push of air as she shuttered her right wing. She withdrew them both into her back, bracing herself throughout. A thin mix of blood and rainwater crawled down her arm.

"Shouldn't have let that go last night. Let me rewrap it." Sol moved to his knees and picked up his pack. After slipping his cloak from his shoulders, he looked across the pit of ash, and on seeing no sign of Den or Pidgie, asked, "They off foraging?"

Araina still did not look at him, nor did she answer. Her back stretched and her breath quickened into a tight heaving. Tears sped from her cheeks, too rapidly to be mistaken for rain.

"What happened?" Sol asked in a muted recoil.

Her face pulled to the sky, her lips parted and pleaded for air, and finally uttered, "I had to."

"What?" The bandage in Sol's fingers slipped away. He rose to his feet.

"You would not." She dropped her face then finally met his eyes. "I had to."

"What've you done?" He shook his head in heavy sweeps. "You didn't…"

"I made a choice. You would not. For soldiers do not make them."

"You…you made a choice that day. A decision—"

"No. No, Sol. There've been only tests. Tests presented as decisions. But I've finally made one. While I can. While it may still matter."

"But you—"

"Have we neared another battlefield?" She stumbled to her feet and met the clasp of his eyes. "Would one lie here?"

"What?"

"Not likely in swampland like this, is it?" she pressed.

"What are you saying?"

"It's us! *We* were enough to bring it last night! I could barely strike it! You did not see it or sense it! And you don't see me! You'll bandage this wound without end but you don't see!" She crumbled to her knees and worked to stifle her weeping. "Oh, Sol. I-I wanted yours to be right. All that you... There was no doubt. No blind faith. Now, there's so much of both. You won't see how far...how close it comes. How fast it claims. Light and wings won't matter. I've less to fight it now than I did hers. This...this time, I...*I* needed a courier. And now they're moving. As long as they are moving, there will still be a chance. Still a fight. A front. A chance for those who remain. For you. There's nothing left of—"

Sol dropped to the witch on the ground and gripped her from the bottom of her skull. She did not move. She half-expected him to lower his hands and, out of risen rage or resigned mercy, squeeze any lingering bit of life from her body. She would have let him gratify either, but he only held her there, waiting in a near-threatening tightness. His jaw stiffened. His lips battled with something then moved to her ear.

"Keep her," he hissed. "Keep her moving. Keep her alive. That's what I was told. That's what I decided. Nothing at any front. Only here. With you, *as* I see you. No doubt. No faith. Just trust. My decision holds because you've given me *everything* to trust that you can do this. Still."

His hands slipped and he wilted in a resigned bow.

"I don't care what choice you've made. I don't care if it was a mistake or foresight. But I see you. As you are. All that you are. I know what you have in you because of what I've seen. And I know there's one more. That's what's left. To uncover and carry. To keep you moving and alive. It's on the way home, Araina."

The rain went on darkening the thin fabric across his shoulders until he was lifted from the surrender by a shaking touch along his jaw. Sol raised his head, held Araina's eyes, and slipped his hand to her cheek. He drew in. When his lips found hers, she let them stay, then seized on them, until she could no longer stand the endlessly rising ache he summoned. It sent her into his shoulder. Sol wrapped her into him, feeling her tense and then ease through the shuddering of her wound, and kept her there.

"That elf doesn't want to buy a ship, does he?" he whispered across her hair. "Just steak, right?"

"Thank goodness he likes the cake at the temple," she muttered into his neck.

"That's where they've taken them?"

"Yes."

"When?"

"Before you woke. Before the rain."

"We'll hope they keep ahead of it."

Sol reluctantly tasted the water cupped in his hand, then immediately spat it away. He wiped his mouth on his sleeve and spat again. "Can fungus go rancid?"

"Why not?" Araina sighed. She waited behind him with the caldron.

"Things moving in it too."

"There's nothing dry left to get a boil?"

"Not enough."

"I remember a deeper pool across that way. Maybe the rain will've thinned it. Want me to go and—"

"No." He turned and ran his hand over her slowly drying hair. "I'll go check. Stay and rest more."

"I'm alright. I can at least try for kindling here while you do. Might be enough."

Sol nodded.

She handed him the caldron and watched his trek around the murky shallow and off between willows.

At the trunk nearest their camp, she felt for loose shards of bark. Without yield, she went to the next, then another, and another before uncovering a pry-able strip. With whatever strength remained in her right arm, she pulled. Fast depleted, she stopped and regained her breath, then took the dagger from her hip.

Through the chipping of the blade, she heard, "Hey Rainy."

The hilt almost slipped from her hand as she spun. "Den. W-what are...did you—"

"What's that?" The elf raised his eyebrows from the other side of the willow's roots.

"You're... Where's Pidgie? Where're the—"

"Back this way. Could use your help with somethin'."

"What—"

"Be faster if I show ya. C'mon."

"Tell me you didn't just leave them somewhere," she implored, sheathed her dagger, and pushed the sweeping branches from her rushed path.

"Nah, they're safe." Den scurried on, keeping well-ahead of her weak stumbling.

"Where?"

Araina struggled to hold her bearings through the maze of drooping willows. She lost them when gloved hands reached after her and closed over her mouth and throat.

"Hey! Easy!" Den snapped but only watched as she was ripped her from her footing and her neck was squeezed.

She kicked and reached for her dagger but another form pulled the hilt from her panicking hand. Her clawing sent blood running from her wound and did nothing to stay the thick grasp over her airways. The desperate emergence of her wings broke it and briefly knocked back the grey-uniformed ambush.

With everything in her lungs, she roared, "Sol! Run!" before she was pounced upon again. Her wings were crumpled forward. A third and new grip closed over her throat from the front. Her shoulder went on burning and bleeding while she strained her fingers but could not form so much as a glint.

"Watch her hand!" warned an ocher yellow-clad officer on horseback. He and another trotted through puddles and between trees while a fourth grey-uniformed Vexhi followed on foot. They watched Araina's kicking and thrashing weaken as she was lifted from the ground.

"Hey!" Den again protested to no effect.

With the relentless compressing of her larynx and her weight pulling from her neck, she slipped from her senses. Her clawing dwindled, her wings tightened and curled into her scars, and she went limp.

"Like that?! Ya had to do it like that?! Where's the guy with that green stuff?" the elf demanded of the first officer.

"None to spare. Those were the orders. Take it upstairs if you want. They're out of patience with this. You included." Following a gestured command, Araina's body was bound and slung across the back of the second officer's saddle, then ridden away.

"Where's the soldier?"

"Who cares? Ain't got nothing. All her."

"Where?"

"Probably back that way." Den shrugged.

The officer turned to the four grey-uniformed Vexhi and ordered, "Get to it."

They proceeded through the willows.

Pressed to a trunk, Sol readied his crossbow. It and its single loaded bolt were all he could salvage after Araina's cry ripped through him, he raced back, and the approach began. All else he could claim was cover. His quiver, among the packs and beside the pit of ash, was ill-placed with the pace and distance of the strides—four of them, in pairs, away from southeastern hoofbeats. A dense layer of chimes told that each pursuer wore a short saber and held a single-grip bow, like his, and that their armor was light to none—for speed or out of impatience. A second bolt would have opened an easy path through them and before the horses had gotten far. As the first pair came into range, there was little time to lament the quantity and locations of his arsenal.

Sol swung around the trunk and shot below the eye of the rightmost Vexhi. The bolt chipped into the socket and sank. Saliva spritzed across his comrade's nasal guard and his body fell, twitching. His helmet rolled between the packs and the quiver. The strike scattered the next pair and what remained of the first. Two dashed back, one behind his nearest tree and the other low among its lifted roots. The remains of the first pair held ground near his convulsing comrade, at the ready and fixed on Sol's cover.

"You're outnumbered. Surrender now and it'll go easier," he demanded.

All that answered was a delicate ting of copper. Half an instant after, the caldron was ejected from beyond the trunk in an abrupt thrust. An onslaught of bolts dented and pierced its surface before it crashed to the ground.

Advanced by the startle and led by his sword, Sol dashed from the opposite side. He whisked the blade's tip over the neck of the nearest Vexhi, then charged past the sputtering, spilling body and stooped to sweep up his quiver. A bolt sang past his ear. Another caught him in the side and forced him back to his cover with his grip just short of the strap.

He sturdied himself against the trunk and hissed away the wrath of the protruding bolt—skewed and stayed by a rib. With a grimace, he sheathed his sword and plucked the bolt from his flesh. After a quick wipe on his trouser leg, he examined the size and state of it. "Close enough," he exhaled and loaded it into his crossbow.

Sol gauged his injured range of motion through a stifled stretch and listened to the sharp whispers of the final pair. Having complicated their situation past silent and certain signals, his mettle was fed. When he heard only one static, loading click from across the camp, he decided not to bother with the quiver and again sprang from his cover.

A bolt sailed toward his shoulder. In his dodge, Sol shot and hit the spine of the retreating Vexhi, who stumbled, fell flat, and proceeded to roar in agony. The one remaining reloaded. Though he shot for Sol's chest, his flagging aim only cleared through the exterior of the soldier's left bicep. It gained the Vexhi no time to reload or draw his saber before Sol's blade was upon, through, then out of him.

Sol turned back to the one still staring from a blood-filled eye and twitching from a punctured brain. "Imagine you're not going to tell me much."

The Vexhi confirmed it with an empty moan.

Sol snapped his blade to loosen blood from its edges and sheathed it. He then reunited with his quiver and slipped out two bolts. Wincing through the clutching sting in his arm and side, he loaded the crossbow and drew. The latest bolt joined the other in the Vexhi's skull, this time through the back. The low moan and twitching ceased. A distant wailing remained. Sol reloaded and held his side as he sped to it along the retreating tracks.

Though the last Vexhi's legs had gone dead amidst the maze of willows, his upper-half roared and gripped at the dirt. The tip of the bolt still extended from his lower spine. Sol crouched and rested his finger upon it. The already tremendous screaming somehow crescendoed. It curbed into slick, depleted wheezing when Sol withdrew his touch.

"The stronghold or somewhere closer?" he asked, waited, then returned his finger and impelled more screams. After a moment, he withdrew.

"S-st-strong—"

"Thought so." Sol removed the helmet from the last Vexhi's head. After discharging a bolt into it, he jogged back along his tracks.

From Araina's pack, he took the remaining chestnut biscuits, the canvas of herbs, her canteen, cloak, and field book, and tucked them into his own. He slung it around his punctured body with a groan and headed west.

Part Three

Chapter Twenty-Eight

Alive and Awake

An ether-like scent, simultaneously smooth and sharp, coating and cutting, asserted itself within her airways. Then came a sense of warm submersion up to her collarbones. Though light thinned the cover of her eyelids, they would not yet part; little of her body would move but for her lungs. Through a push, they gave not but a scratch of a sound.

Finally, Araina's eyes opened to a rippling chartreuse fog striped with dark twists. For a moment, she thought it was seaweed stretched by an afternoon tide. It swayed and revealed tanned then sickly flesh. It was hers below her tresses and within a filled metal tub. Her arms were limply folded over her breasts. Her legs were an inert pile bent across the bottom.

Utterly deadened and untethered from her body, all the discomforts—the blisters, scrapes, and cuts—and all the great dire pains—the wound at her shoulder and the crushing bruising at her larynx—were more memory than sensation. Somewhere past the throb of her pulse and the edge of the tub, a slow dripping became apparent. Then came footfalls and a quietly startled voice.

"Oh... Y-you're not supposed to be awake yet," it tensely observed in an accent like Den's, only throatier and gentler in cadence.

Araina could not lift her head to view the source. She could only shift her eyes, but still she saw nothing beyond a soaking veil of hair and a haze of steam. The footfalls fell away, then returned, then fell away again and left only the dripping. Alone with it, she realized she was able to swallow, move her tongue, and twitch a finger. The footfalls came back, then neared, and a shadow fell over the tub.

"So, listen, I-I imagine you... Look, just bear with me. It'll be better for both of us if we...we'll just pretend you haven't woken up yet. Not that you can do much about it, but...seems only fair to mention it."

Still unable to respond, Araina found she could faintly shift her wrists and ankles—though to little effect. The shadow moved and a young man came vaguely into view. He was imposingly tall, even when he stooped alongside the tub. A creak sounded after, then a draining grumble. The liquid surrounding Araina's body began to drain away, leaving a cold sting across her skin. The impulse to tighten her limbs over her bare form was only meekly obeyed by her sluggishly recouping muscles.

A hand shifted her upright and a circle of fabric was dropped over her head. A long, primitively seamed shift unrolled low over her shoulders and gathered at her hips. The young man pulled her limp arms through one side then the other. His motions were smooth though utterly impassive, as though he were saddling a horse or collecting eggs from a roost. She was leaned back against the tub's edge and he departed yet again.

The settle of steam revealed walls of white stone, a workbench, and rows upon rows of vials, bottles, and jars. Basins, scales, and tools were set before the array, along with an outlying stack of black fabric, her belted scabbard, and the hilt of her dagger. A smaller pile of pale garments lay beside that, which were lifted by the young man.

Araina could still do nothing but follow with her eyes. She went on gauging little twitches of returning mobility. Finally, she was able to loll her head back and see the face of the young man as he balanced the pale fabric on the tub's rim. His eyes were glacial. They would have been eerie had they not worn such a mix of apprehension and diffidence. An odd little sheen of fascination joined it when he caught Araina's struggling focus.

"How're they going to make this work if you can't stand or speak? Anything yet?"

The witch only heaved a small rasp.

"Hmm. Be back in a bit. These are your...other things." He touched a finger to the stack of fabric and quickly withdrew it. Araina recognized them as her tuliterie and knee-knickers. "No harm in you having those, I don't think. Your arms should be back soon. We'll see if you can...take care of that before I get back."

He moved from the tub and passed the work table, but quickly backtracked and declared, "Oh, that wouldn't've been good." He then gathered her bodice, trousers, scabbard, and dagger, along with a handful of small things that chimed on collection. Araina guessed they were her seal ring, copper star, and remaining earrings—all gone from her body.

On observing his exit, she realized her neck was responding. Moments later, her shoulders and arms obeyed in a dragging tremor. She knocked her undergarments down with a flaccid nudge, then engaged in a laborious, disjointed struggle to clumsily secure them over her hips and breasts and below the cover of the thin shift. Firings in her brain continued to coalesce, then began to race, but did not get far in their spiral before the young man reappeared with an older one, who marched to the tub.

Araina had little strength to recoil from the charge. Her weak legs twisted in the fabric of the shift. She still had no voice to protest beyond gasps when a glowing green spark appeared and clung to the tip of the old man's forefinger. He pushed Araina's forehead back, then brought the glow to her throat. It disappeared and sent her into an immediately unconscious slump.

Sol swatted his head against his fading focus and the drumming stings from his ribs and bicep. He squinted down at the crumbling biscuit in his hand and weighed his canteen before tossing his head alert again. A gruff, vocal breath slipped from his throat and he emptied the canteen into his mouth. The biscuit was dropped into the parcel with the remaining dozen and returned to his pack. The canvas of herbs was recovered in their stead.

Sol grabbed the end of a sprig—the one tucked closest to the ties—and pinched the woody stem between his teeth. It's brittle, fibrous texture fell behind a slow tingling over his tongue. An increasingly unbearable taste told him he was supposed to either swallow it quickly or had interacted with it in too raw of a form. He removed it from his teeth, put it back in its place, and folded it away. While working the sharp liquid numbness through his mouth, something hit his stomach, dense, warm, and filling—and yet of no aid of that constant, deep-drilling pang throughout his center. He rose out of his huddled place in the brush and proceeded, almost blind, through the woods and below the forest's gapped canopy—guided west by a scattered revelation of stars.

When dawn began to steal them away, so an umbra did of his flagging push forward. Sol's blade was drawn, flew free, and slashed again and again, until the void was torn to a fluid shredding. Entreating all that was left in his legs, he sprinted to gain ample distance while the umbra congealed back into a singular form. Its state and position were difficult to confirm through a shuddering glance over his shoulder, but he saw his blade had been entirely cleaned of Vexhi blood. Too exhausted to fully consider or comprehend it, he sheathed his sword and rattled his head awake once again.

Not another mile on, he lost his pace and his path to a fallen tree limb. The crash of his chest against the ground spurred a ringing pain that immediately rolled him over. His body slid down a leaf-littered slope, causing the puncture in his side and arm to resume their bleeding and raging. He let the twinge sail through him and lay in the underbrush. All sense of gravity and time fell away.

"Ekwidou?" a woman's voice incredulously uttered above his splayed form.

The soldier fought to part his eyelids. His vision eventually cleared to reveal a distantly memorable face below the hood of a Crest scout's short cloak.

He blinked back and eventually rasped, "Imari?"

"You're alone? Where's…" She looked out among the wider woods.

Sol closed his eyes again and swallowed hard before answering, "Vexhi."

Imari breathed in a rapid shudder before kneeling to help him upright. He groaned hoarsely.

"Wounded?" she whispered.

The soldier faintly bobbed his head.

Imari let him lie. "I'll be back."

As she sped through the trees, Sol let his head drop and his senses slip away again.

A faded brown oil-cloth met his returning vision. A chill fell over his bare shoulders and briar-grazed face. His body was blanketed, bandaged, and cradled by a cot. The interior of a scouts' tent merged across his eyes and memory. He tried to rise.

"Don't!" Imari scolded. "Don't you dare. Unless you need it to answer my questions, you do not move it, understand?"

Sol swallowed bitterly and nodded with his skull to the pillow.

"Now, how long ago and where?" Imari demanded.

He sighed and furrowed his scratched brow before recounting, "Yesterday. Afternoon. No, morning? Eastern edge of the willow swamps."

"What did you see?"

"Only heard. Had to take cover to take them. They already had her."

"And the laws?"

Sol narrowed his eyes into the lightly luffing fabric above him. "No word from your end?"

"No." Imari's brow creased.

Sol pushed a stony seethe from his throat. "Then, with them. Or on their way."

"What of the elf?"

He shook his head. "Gone."

"Got all that?" Imari quietly asked over her shoulder.

Sol then became aware of a quill scratching and paper folding. He heard boots across the ground and saw a brief breach of sunlight as the tent's flap was lifted.

"You're lucky you were found this far. We and other scouts've been pushing forward to catch you up. So this is why there hasn't been any sign of you for so long."

"Had to change our route. Then...she was wounded. We lost days... Four, five. Lost track. Lost them in the swamp just trying to keep her—" The soldier swallowed his words.

"Wounded how?"

"Arrow in the shoulder. Tipped with something. She went feverish fast."

"Hmm. Dwovlins?"

"She thought so. I couldn't see much. Got her wings too but they healed."

"So she does have them." Imari loosened her crossed arms. "Wasn't sure I believed it. You've seen them?"

Sol faintly nodded, opened his eyes for an instant, and tensed them shut again.

G reen light glinted along the periphery of her slowly returning vision. It clung to a man's finger until he curled it away across his thumb. When he moved out of his crouch, the witch's view was opened to a small, scattered group of onlookers, including the startlingly tall young man. She and they were all on a massive slab of stone. Empty glass lanterns lined its octagonal edge. Beyond it, a expanse of dry earth and limp grass rolled to a towering wall.

The witch shuddered as a crisp charging wind fell across her upper arms and rumpled the shift at her feet. Her hands and forearms were linked behind her back—each palm pressed near the opposite elbow with her fingers spread wide by straps. The binding simultaneously suppressed her ability to cast and free her wings from their scars.

"Stand her up, please," the centermost of the onlookers instructed.

The witch was hooked by her arms, hoisted, and briefly held until her feet flatted to the stone. She was then left to wobble and shiver.

"Welcome, Araina of the Moonserpents," the same man greeted through a smile. "That is the proper method of address, isn't it? Please correct it if otherwise. And pardon the binds. They'll be necessary until they're not. I thought we'd get on with getting there. Hence where you stand. It's equal parts altar and workspace. For your folk, I know there's little divide between the two. The same can be said here. Come." He gestured. "I'll show you."

Paralyzed by confusion, futility, and the sense that an attempted step would mean falling to the stone, the witch only stared and shivered until a presence gripped and walked her forward. The onlookers spread as she was relayed to the centered man, who led her to a beveled cut in the platform. After daring to lower her view within, Araina fought to remain upright at the sight of Yurkci, Weraln, Celuf, and then the familiar Ecivy, Mtolin, and Fiwrn. They were laid out upon an iron grate above a mound of soil. Narrow steps framed and provided a means to the touchpoints—all but Aqzim. The witch almost fell to them. The centered man caught her arm. "Thrilling, I know. Our efforts and yours finally come together. Equal parts, for now. The final has been found and arrives in a matter of hours. I'd call that impressive timing. Although, I am far from impartial. But then, we needn't be in envy of the other's resources. Nor do I see reason why our combined contributions should cease. That's why we're sharing this with you. By the way, I welcome your thoughts as they come, Araina."

Her quivering wheeze eventually formed words. "Where is he?"

"He? Beg pardon?" His eyes shifted to one of his cohorts. "Oh…the soldier. In good time. Plenty of it for inquiry and answers and whatever else you require soon enough. For now, let's steady our attention. Then we can get you out of the cold and those pieces back where they'll also be safe. And I know what you're thinking. What safer place for them but in the ground? Properly tucked in by your hands, arranged precisely, and locked away by touch and sound. That's what's led you to us, after all. Has it not?"

Araina did not answer.

She was walked by the arm to the far edge of the slab while he went on, "Now, to do as you've been charged, that would mean many things that your sort finds favorable. But that gives me pause, Araina. I have to wonder, are they really all that favorable? I question your people on *so* much. I needn't point out the state of you on arrival. A state and then some, to say the least. Though it's not my end of things, I can say for a fact, our forces would never be left with so few devices with the world as it is. The result was, well…as I said, a state and then some. I'm glad that's all been corrected. My alchemists really do fantastic work."

He let his grip come away and stood beside her with his view fixed on the stretching wall.

"Just of think of what else is possible through such skill. Not merely preservation, but creation, enhancement, a world shaped and perfected. Molded to one's expectations and precise visions, rather than the other way around. The other way around creates so much mess, doesn't it? Just think of the alternative. *Really* think of it, Araina. Because it is obtainable. Now that you're here."

He caught her eye and the shivering in her neck and shoulders. His smooth smile broadened, then fell.

"I see we should quicken our pace and get back where it's warm. I'll get to the most important part then. You see, to keep or change them, it all requires the same unlocking. When something is locked, it stands that it contains something potentially useful or perhaps sacred and highly valued. You can't truly decide what it is to you and how it would best serve you until the lock is confronted. The only constant is the necessity of a key. Soon, that's all we'll need."

"To do what?" the witch droned.

"Keep the contents accessible, malleable, useful. Held as tools rather than coveted, static relics. And take chaos and refine it to precision. Untethered to those restrictions your people do so love to capture and archive at any cost."

"And then?"

The centered man looked thrown by her question. "Have you no desire to correct imperfection? To shape a world as you see fit? To shatter the limits and weaknesses that have brought you here?"

"But you've brought me here," Araina weakly observed before pushing her voice to assert, "Your attempts to shape what you call chaos. That's what has brought me here...sped by my own failings... But it was your fraying of it. The result of that has me here. And the state that I was in was—"

"Minor setbacks. Not a true outcome of our work. Simply the cost of seeking out the tools, not accessing them. Once that's done, there's no complaint you could have that won't be remedied and improved. Nothing that can't be done to surpass very flawed originals. Failings, yours or otherwise, need not exist."

Araina blinked at the clouds rolling beyond the wall and breathed, "It's nonsense."

"Oh?"

"If you knew. If you knew what it was before you touched any of it. If you *knew* it, and how impossible it is to truly know all of it, you would see that your ends are only senseless, groundless notions. It's nonsense. You cannot account for all it is, let alone bend it. Nor would you seek to do so." Her eyes fell to the hem of the shift rippling in the wind. "It is its imperfection. That is its malleability. Beautiful as it is harsh. Consisting of as many fragile yet fortunate things as forceful ones. Beyond desires or terms of any one life it permits and sustains." The witch's voice slipped like gossamer in the wind. "But even that has ceased. It's gone and going now."

"Oh, but it remains. It's with you. I hear it as you describe it so," the centered man observed in a gliding, curious tone, before proposing, "Why, you could simply recreate it. Only just as you wanted. And I mean *you,* Araina. For we need you."

"For what?" she hoarsely snapped.

"For the key."

"Still. You've dragged them out, now the last of them, as you say, but you still lack that. Well, you're no closer now that I've been brought—" Araina choked on her words as it flooded back, all of it, free from the cloudy cork of her fever and poison-slicked wound.

"Why, you look as though something just occurred to you. I do hope it's the merit of our offer. I don't think I need to explain just how generous an offer it is. What a privileged position it affords. Do I, Araina?"

She hardly heard him as the intricacies, the arrangement, the words, and the workings to seal it all, seized upon her as a terrifying epiphany—one she would have to guard with every part of her being. The witch was torn from her revelation as the centered man swiftly grabbed her jaw.

"Listen well," he ordered through a low, blistering snarl. "Since you'll be with us for a time, you should know how things are done here. When I ask, when I offer, when I instruct, I never do it twice. And I do not wait. It's now and now only. In case it's not clear to that bane-addled little brain of yours, I am telling you to give it to us. The names that call them, their positions, the hand work. Your submission of that is very, very much in your favor."

The embed of his fingers in her skin sent Araina's eyes to his with an acrid, primal strike. Her voice rallied behind it. "No."

He lightly loosened his grip on her face, then pushed it down her neck and up again. His fingertips dragged away in an ominous, indulgent evaluation. It restored his smile.

"Such a shame you don't see the value in the pliable and the unrestricted. That's the only way to truly bend something without breaking it, even when it will beg, and plead, and scream to be broken. But I digress."

He grasped Araina's arm and spun her to face a massive structure erupting from the ground many dozens of yards beyond the octagonal slab. He watched the witch scan its density and loosed a thin sigh. "Phase one, gentlemen."

With the proclamation's fading, a green spark again awoke in Araina's periphery. She was gripped at the scalp and her throat elongated. The glow sank through her skin and everything fell away.

Chapter Twenty-Nine

Captive

A raina woke within an iron-barred cell kept in a narrow stone room. A rectangular slit in the door and a squat gap of a window, high on the wall, were her only means of light. They were enough to give some sense that she was many floors up and facing an eastern wind, which surged shortly after nightfall. Fierce screeches and wingbeats sounded between the gusts—calls fed to and from others at shifting portions of the sky. She worked to crane her neck to see anything of it. With her arms still folded into the leather binds, her balance was a muddle. All she could find after she teetered up the wall was night—until a small, stacked silhouette appeared on the window's ledge. It flapped down, carrying a sharply whispered protest. "No! Stop!"

The passenger pigeon landed before Araina's cell with the elf clinging to the straps of his little pack. The witch could do naught but match Den's wide-eyed stare and breath through her roaring impulses. Pidgie strut along the floor. Just before he slipped between and below the cell bars, Den dismounted in a scramble. While the pigeon came to nestle beside Araina's feet, her eyes were clasped to the elf.

"The whole of it?" she asked through a tone she did not know was waiting within her body. "From the tavern? The ale, my dress, Barrier's End? All of it?"

Dually taken by the hexing voice from the darkness, Den recoiled slightly. "Just'a job, Rainy. Pidgie! C'mon! So ya seen 'er. Let's go!"

Despite a sharp whistled prompt, Pidgie did not come away from Araina's ankle.

"Why the urgency?" She lowered herself beside the pigeon.

"Ain't none."

"So you've nowhere else to be? No steaks to eat? Riches to spend?"

"Dunno what ya gettin' at, but I ain't got any ships to buy at the moment. Heh. Ever think ya just shoulda taken that offer? Those things woulda ended up here at some point. 'Least you coulda sailed off 'fore the trail really wrecked ya."

Araina blindly glared at him and tugged at the leather straps for yet another futile attempt to open her left palm. The witch's rage, briefly risen over her depleted anguish, returned below it.

She closed her eyes and disdainfully mused, "Sailed until the seas the dried up." Her lungs labored. "From the start… Sailed from all of it. Everything but…" Tears spilt down her face then ceased as she gasped, "*You…*" Her view snapped back to the elf.

"Me?"

"You were there then…when it happened! After you watched on! What happened? What happened to—"

"Hey, listen. No way I knew it was gonna happen like that. I told 'em to do it the other way. With that green stuff—"

"What happened to Sol? Where is he? Is he here?! Is he alive?! Is he—"

"Alright, I'll tell ya. But ya gotta promise ya ain't gonna kill me if ya ever get outta those things."

"I don't need to kill you," the witch assured him. Den could hear her teeth join as she elaborated, "And I have *everything* in me to do it. It's almost beautiful how pure it is. The very thought of it. How something could be *so* without question. And yet, it's useless. Loathsomely, stupidly useless, because you've done it for me. You've killed all of us. Now, where is Sol?"

The elf, almost entirely retreated to the far wall, obliged. "Alright. Just don't let on that ya know. Got it?"

He gained no response beyond a sheen of her eyes, cutting into him through the darkness.

"…Ain't here. After they got ya, they sent four guys back to deal with 'im. Didn't stick 'round to see it, but none of 'em came back."

"How long ago?"

"Two days tomorrow?" Den shrugged.

"Four," Araina hoarsely contemplated.

"I said two. Two days."

"Four Vexhi. He had his sword. His bow. Was it on his back? But his quiver was with… Near the fire? He would've…" she breathlessly attempted to recall. "He was still so exhausted. I did that to him. Oh, Sol. Please be alive. Sol…" She let her face drop and began to weep.

"Eh, this is why ya don't go lettin' yourself get attached on a job, Rainy."

She swallowed her sob and locked back on the faint traces of him. "Have you trouble taking your own advice? Or were you lurking at that window for other reasons?"

"Huh? Your noggin go all shaky again? Ain't ya hear me yellin' at 'im? *Pidgie* brought me here. And I'm 'bout ready leave 'em right where he's sittin'…"

"Strange how an incredibly obedient passenger pigeon suddenly flies you to places you wish to avoid. Are you certain someone hasn't hired him?"

"Alright, so *I* was curious. And so what, I did a job. Done lots of 'em. Just 'cause I did this one ain't mean I liked it. Was just supposed'a be about gettin' to some beach cottage, then followin' whatever witch comes outta it. Then I was supposed'a report where she ended up. I listen in here an' there, and be done. But you kept bein' useful. Meant I was too. Don't mean I was happy 'bout it. Ain't like you were. Ya forget how ya fell to damn pieces after ya got that urka? Don't change the fact you were good for it."

"The umbra… Your reaction was genuine? You haven't seen them before? Not here?"

"Huh? No. They don't go puttin' me on the battlefield. Ain't my line'a skill."

"Well, you'll have other opportunities to deal with them, thanks to the results of your *skills*."

"Eh, that ain't how they see it goin' up in this wing. Word is they're gonna blast those things away just like you can. Maybe even control 'em."

"What are you talking about?"

"Plan to do it with that light'a yours. Think they're gonna use 'em out there when push comes to shove, like those sky monsters 'a theirs…after they get it outta ya."

"For how utterly stupid that is, how do you know all that? Did they tell you?"

"No one tells me nothin' I ain't need to know. Sometimes even less than that. Heard somethin' like it from Sprout."

"Sprout?"

"Glyn."

"Glyn?"

"Uh huh. Old buddy a' mine. Though one'a the younger ones 'round here. Ya already met 'em. He's to thank for your shoulder and your nice clear head, or *clearer* head at least. Even fixed up your neck. That was nasty business. Like I said, Rainy. Just 'cause I'm good at a job don't mean I like it. Not always."

"Then why?! Why do this?"

"Why you doin' it?"

"You already know why! Because otherwise everything goes on dying!"

"Heh, that ain't why. Lotsa folks're worried 'bout that, but they ain't go raisin' their hand to fix it. Ya did it 'cause someone asked or someone told. And they asked or told ya 'cause they saw ya were good at somethin'. Or there's somethin' you're good for. Same as me. Ain't no more complicated than that."

"You keep saying you're so good at whatever you are. Good at what? Deception? Or does this simply grant you some sort of satisfa—"

"You're overthinkin' it, Rainy. Figure ya'd be done with that by now. And no, ain't deception. Though I ain't bad at that. I mean, look where ya are. But nah. Simple as size."

"Size?"

"Yeah, size. Ya think the General's the only one who saw use havin' someone small 'round? I'm easy to miss. No one notices what I notice, when I slip away, or when I show back up. You humans think you're so over my head. Just gotta find a way to get a higher view. Ya think these are just for show?" He pointed at the tips of his ears under his kerchief. "Just 'cause I ain't interested don't mean I ain't listenin'. Loud snorin' don't make me a heavy sleeper."

"Why use all that to advance this? Do you truly believe what they say? That nonsense Machalka spoke of…about a malleable, perfect world, or whatever it all was?"

"Machalka?" The elf chuckled. "You weren't talkin' to Machalka. That was Bladgen. Head'a the alchemists. And I dunno 'bout what they say any more than what you're tryin' to do."

"Then why do *this*?"

"Already told ya. Reward didn't hurt either."

"What reward was that?"

"Nothin' ya can counter from where ya sit, so don't worry 'bout it."

"Then help me get somewhere else."

"Nice try, Rainy, but don't forget, I seen how ya go about fulfillin' your end of a bargain. Heh, witches. I'll give marks for tricky 'til it actually counts."

"You've seen a lot in your time spent with witches. Drank a lot. Ate a lot. Was your enjoyment of all that a deception as well?"

"Good at my job, but ain't that good. Either way, 'fraid soft cake, sweet booze, and comfy curtains ain't gonna tip any scales, if that's what you're gettin' at. Alright, 'nough chatter. Pidgie! C'mon!"

Araina felt the cushioned weight and warmth leave her side. After Pidgie strutted clear of the cell, Den climbed his back.

"Wait! What else do you know? What happens next? What's phase one?" she rushed.

"Already told ya, they ain't tell me much 'round here."

"Then use those little pointed ears and everything else humans miss to find out. Please, Den?"

"Ain't that a change from how ya sounded when I got here? You're funny, Rainy. Funny an' forgetful. I'm done takin' instruction from your side. Never really was."

Den nudged his knee along Pidgie's girth, sending them up and out the window. Araina was again left alone with only an empty view of the night sky.

S ol shuddered with each stroke of the novaculite. He stayed lost in the sweep and the slowly subsiding stings at his arm and side until Imari entered the tent.

"What are you doing? I'll thank you for staying out of my things. And those poultices are useless if you keep moving. Put that sword away and get back on the cot."

Sol dropped the novaculite into her extended hand and returned his blade to its sheath. He lowered it to the ground with a muted grunt and superficially settled over the cot's coverings.

"What's the hold up?"

"There isn't one." Imari returned the novaculite to her case. "Unless you're referring to your transport. That's on its way, though there's a lot ahead of it for now. Not that you've any reason to be in a rush. We're properly secluded and supplied. You'll be on your way before we need to break down."

"My way?" Sol sat up. "Transport? Transport where?"

"West."

"Stronghold's east."

"I'm well-aware. You're due back west. Questions and your compensation are waiting, as are messages from the Hagens. Likely they want you back. You can argue with them about where you are in which offensive."

"Offensive? What's the rescue plan?"

"Haven't gotten word on anything."

"What? What are they waiting for? We're right here! A day, day and a half march away? Why aren't we—"

"I know you've been away for a while and through a lot, Ekwidou, but this is a scouting post, not an armory. All I know is they're proceeding with the current approach."

"Which is?"

"The breach." Imari plucked a burr from her collar, avoiding Sol's caustic disbelief and thoroughly tensed scars.

"That doesn't make any sense. They can't move to breach if—"

"Svet Hagen are pushing for it. I imagine there's too much moving and too little to supply it at a slower rate—"

"What about her? She...she's still—"

"What I told you is all I know." Imari finally looked back at the glaring soldier, wearing a resigned blankness against his fierce visage, which was made slightly less-so by the glisten of salve smeared over his scratched brow and cheeks.

She sighed. "I don't like it either, Ekwidou, but I don't know what to tell you. Obviously, things have gone a little...askew. We simply have to trust that the Coven will get it sorted. They may have already. Lack of assertion doesn't always mean lack of action. Don't forgot, you're not dealing with Svet Hagen. For now."

Sol ground a breath through his nose. "I need to send a message."

"All the birds are out currently. And when I said supplied, I didn't mean we have ink to spare. That's our blood out here. You know that."

"Won't take much."

Imari sighed again and tossed her head at the trunk serving as a writing desk on the other side of the tent. "Mind your manners and keep it to one sheet. And finish your breakfast. Won't just be ink and parchment that's limited if you let your meals go to waste."

Sol looked at the oat loaf, berries, and mug of tea gone tepid, all awaiting him upon a small crate. He barely thought about the spread after noticing it. Not a trace of hunger had occurred to him, even as a sense of atrophy began to whisper across his body. He grabbed and took an ample bite of the dense seeded loaf in full view of Imari.

She raised her hood and exited the tent, calling, "Stay out of my case!" just beyond.

Sol chewed for another moment, then rigidly rose. On lifting a quill, inkwell, and a sheet of parchment from the trunk, he spied Araina's field book resting below a strand of cypher beads. He slipped a finger through the book's tie and sat back upon the cot. With it steadied on his thigh, he laid the parchment across it, and between bites of oat loaf, scratched a few lines. The message was folded and placed on the trunk with the quill and inkwell. The field book stayed on the cot. After snapping a handful of berries between his teeth, he untied the cover.

First he looked through the sketches and left the words; it seemed less of a trespass and as though it might be enough—a link and a means to confirm the lines were not made so long ago and the hand that made them was real and reachable. Least of all, it was something beyond the brown cloth surrounding him and begging a slice long enough to leak his form.

He turned through pages and the horizons beyond trails, the high vantage of Dekvhors, the twisting stream that had its flow briefly altered, and the view from Radomezen's port. Then he found things he did not recognize—a ferocious, long-snouted bat with wings like hers, insects he could not recall ever seeing or noticing, spiraling silk webs, precise depictions of seals, gulls, and seashells among dune grass. There were the portrayals of him, the elf, and pigeon—caught in moments he could remember and others from angles and imaginings that belonged only to her.

He returned to the one page he had seen before. On viewing his portrait across his knee, it evoked the moment after he closed the cover, touched her shoulder, and her hair spilt over the grass. He saw that bit of sleep regained after the night she asked how to do useful harm. A waft of borage and rainwater seeped up into his brain and the book nearly slipped from his hold. Sol let it droop and closed his eyes. They could only open to meet with the brown fabric overhead. He seethed, dropped his view, and passed his image to wander into tight lines of ink.

What that red crystal did to him. Winter soil just before spring. It warmed them awake. He's paying the cost now. Shamefully curious to see it, if he lets himself have it. Or does he keep it behind that stubborn prowess? Cannot linger to discover. Must instead be getting off the ground. From the railing first. Seems enough. A balcony or window is still too much. And the roof? The thought alone! Though I'd like to see Ceedly's aviary. Must get on with the worst of my falling before they've much chance to see.

He turned the page. The sketches and script became quick, scattered, then sparse—more seashells, songbirds, a sailboat, a view of a rocky shoreline from a partially shuttered window, and another portrayal of him, asleep in his hood and upon his pack. The lines were smudged, then sharply whisked across neighboring script.

He's made it such a tangle. Hurts worse than anything. Worse than wanting it all back. Worse than wanting it renewed. I can no longer see it as it was, nor can I see it with him. But I cannot see me without either. What impossible little world and eon would permit it? What could ever make it enough? Why soldiers and witches and not simply he and I? To be as that, before the shore, tea at sunset and again at sunrise. Never a need to learn another bit of witchery beyond the preservation of that. Impossible though. Such a mess.

A thick gap across the bindings separated the remaining pages. All that was kept before the back cover were ink-stained edges and faint, shaking outlines of crumpled leaves. Sol closed them away and looked at the line of sunlight cutting past the tent flap. He shoved the last of the oat loaf and berries into his mouth and opened his pack. With the field book slipped in and the map out, he went to work.

A rectangle of sunlight took shape across the stone. Araina watched it slither from her bound slump within the cell until the door's bolt slid and in stepped the very tall young man. He crouched down before the bars.

"Good morning."

The witch found no greeting to return.

"Would you mind coming closer and turning around?" he requested.

"For what?"

"Need to check something. It'll be quick."

"Check what?"

"Your scars. On your back."

"Why?" Araina's weakened voice sharpened slightly.

"Just need to compare them to yesterday. Won't hurt or anything. But if you could come closer, that'd help."

"Why should I?"

He shrugged. "I just need to see." He then rose out of his crouch. "Guess I'll just do it downstairs."

"What's downstairs?" the witch's eyes stretched to meet the frosted resignation in his.

"Main laboratory."

"What happens there?"

"Depends what needs to get done."

"Something to do with my wing scars?"

"No. 'Least I don't think so. That's just for my own observation. Was hoping to take care of it before anything got started."

"What's going to get started?" Araina further lifted her body from the stone.

"Heh. I heard ya ask a lotta questions, given the chance. Maybe we could trade? Lemme take'a look while you're awake and upright. Then I'll see if I can't give an answer…or two."

She shifted onto her knees, hobbled to the bars, and turned. The young man pushed her hair aside and lowered the shift, stretching it just below the start of her shoulder blades and upper portion of her wing scars.

"Hmm. Not even a bit. Amazing…" He tossed the fabric back up to her neck. "That was all. Thank you."

Araina swung her hair from her shoulder, faced the bars, and asserted, "Now my questions."

"Which one?"

Her eyes darted about the floor, then set back on him. "What are they going to do with me?"

He puffed a vocal stream of air from the side of his mouth and gripped the back of his neck before divulging, "Don't know the details. But they're gonna try to get some'a…the information they mentioned yesterday."

"How?"

"Not my specialty."

"What is your specialty?"

"Ya know that's more than two questions?"

"I was hoping you weren't keeping tally, Glyn."

"How do you know my name?"

"I presumed it. Based on talk from a friend of yours."

"Hmm." Glyn's lips curled and dimpled his smooth cheek. "He's been in here?"

"He has."

"Bit surprising."

"Is it? I know he almost always likes a conversation no matter the circumstance."

"That's true."

"I sense you have that in common. Is that why you're friends?"

"Den's just seen and done a lot…and I like to learn things." Glyn shrugged, then smiled. "*That's* my specialty."

"Is that how you're able to heal wounds and fevers overnight?"

"Wasn't just overnight. And that's more my job than my specialty."

"So what did my wing scars have to teach you with regard to either?"

"That they're different from the other wounds," he answered with a flicker. "And…you've got *wings* under there? And then you can cast? I only ever read about that and I had to go through *a lot* to get those books. Gotta say, I wanna see it. Doubt the bosses are gonna let you show it off though." He almost laughed.

"I'll see what I can do for you. Though it would be much easier to satisfy your curiosity without these binds."

He again rubbed the back of his neck. "I should go."

Araina watched his exit before the dense slip of the door's bolt dropped her eyes to the stone.

Left lost to the afternoon and the maddening cramping from her elbows, back, and shoulders, Araina only found escape in the moments caught behind her eyes, which called forth their own ebb and flow of reverie and agony. She could define all of it—where the sun or moon sat in the sky, the tones of their exchanges below the snap of firewood or above the clangs of buckles shifting in step—but she could not relive his touch, no matter how persistently and precisely she recalled and longed for it. It swelled a pitting anguish that made her tug at the binds and drum up the pattern from its start, until it was broken by the slide of the door's bolt.

Bladgen, dressed in a long smock along with two other men, passed the narrow threshold. He stared into the witch through the cell bars. Her defiant hold of his gaze was betrayed by the rise and fall of her throat—the capacity of her lungs cluttered with the dread of where she would wake after that green glow appeared. Bladgen experienced similar complications trying to obscure his own anticipation as he disengaged the cell's lock.

"Just the key now," he said.

Araina tried to rise but was fast gripped and dragged to the gate. A spark of green grew and stole all resistance.

Chapter Thirty

Tapped and Forged

Imari pushed open the tent flap and attempted to inform, "Alright, Ekwidou, the kestrel's back. There's just enough light. Where's your—" Her question fell away at the sight of the cot. Nothing lay upon it but the pillow and blankets—tightly rolled by the hand of a soldier. His pack, boots, quiver, crossbow, belt, and sword were no longer piled at its side. The neighboring crate held an empty mug and a cloth with only crumbs and dots of berry skin on its surface. Fresh rolls of bandages, once waiting beside a jar of goldenseal salve, were gone. Imari sighed at the stretched lower portion of the tent's fabric and moved to the trunk. Araina's field book rested there no longer. She lifted the unsealed message that waited in its stead.

Urgent. Hold the breach.
Requesting immediate assignment as lead for rescue and recovery.
No amendments to original terms.
Solairous IX
Son Ekwidou and Soldier of Airaharin

Imari huffed another sigh, knelt, and pulled her gloves from her hands. She took up the quill.

Araina's binds had changed with her location. Strapped supine to a grated surface, her wings still could not emerge from their scars. Her ability to cast remained comparably suppressed, this time by a tightly wound swathe of leather that forced her left hand into a dormant fist. Above her own fright-filled breath and a hastened shuffle of boots, a long squeaking moved along the stone floor. She dared to look toward the sound.

A squat old man was being wheeled upon a gilded chair. Rows of smocked alchemists framed his path across the massive room while Bladgen followed the whining roll to the witch. The old man gripped the ornate bronze arms and wobbled forward. A throaty bleat arose with his squinting. Araina fought to keep from his doddering perusal, but the odd black veins that gripped his eyes roused her own curiosity. Another disapproving snort echoed through the laboratory. "*This* is what's taken so long?"

"I can assure you it won't take much longer, Sire," Bladgen promptly answered. "As I explained, we start with one path. That may be where it resides. The words will simply rise in the process of forging it."

"What of your men? They still search?" The old man teetered and glared beyond the cap of his doublet sleeve and the chair's bolster to the rows of silently waiting alchemists. "Seems they only stand around."

"But for your glorious presence now, they toil without end, Sire. Night and day. They could uncover it at any moment. The whole of our resources is devoted to it. One method or another is bound to give. I'm confident it will be she. And even so, you needn't question any investments. If it is found of our own accord, she remains a resource. A vessel to be tapped."

"My serum?" the old man grumbled.

"As good as in your goblet, Sire."

"Hmm. On with it then."

The old man slumped back and was wheeled away—his departure no quieter than his arrival. Bladgen's eyes kept to the chair's progress. When the doors were shut behind it, his gaze dropped to the witch.

"The man really is something. The last grandson of a once great emperor and the thickest of a sterling line of blood. The pittance of his inheritance didn't stop him from amassing all that you've seen here, all that's brought you to it, and all that will follow. So much to be admired, asserting a destiny. Bending a path inspite of a set route. Now he's eager to move from forging roads to realities, and you get to join us in that facilitation. Some would call that an honor, Araina. At its most essential, it's an opportunity."

He stepped away, loftily surveyed the surface of one of the many surrounding tables, and went on to declare, "You really should see them. You know yourself how dull just one or two, or even three appear. I could almost understand how one would be tempted to simply shove them back into the dirt. But when you see them in their cohesive potential, waiting to be fused and serve as a means, an immeasurable mechanism for all others…it elevates them. They're inviting utilization. It's plain to see it, Araina. And maybe we could give you a peek, but let us get a few things out of the way first."

A short chime of metal preceded Bladgen's footfalls, which were joined by others. Four alchemists closed in, two of whom carried wide metal basins. The other pair held small bowls. The broad stretch of their hands told of contents weighty, valuable, or volatile. Araina could smell nothing, nor could she bring herself to seek further details. Her body could only hold to a paralysis, set by some feeble notion that anything she could not see simply did not exist to harm her. It had limited protection as Bladgen touched two fingers upon her throat and tapped them in contemplation.

"No. Not yet. I still need you to speak. Though, something's there, isn't it?"

Her breath froze when Bladgen traced his forefinger down to her collarbone and drummed just below it.

"Better," he decided, withdrew his hand, and explained, "In a moment, you're going to feel a bit of pressure. Then you're going to feel nothing but. Keep in mind, however, this is going to be reserved. Downright frugal. I thought since I was so generous on our first meeting, you should be given a chance to reciprocate. You just say the word, so long as many other words follow. This is the sort of process that can go on and on, or it can be made to end quite quickly. I hope that's all clear, Araina. But if it's not, give it a moment."

Bladgen returned his fingers to the same spot of skin and brought his other hand forward. The edge of a short razor was revealed beyond his sleeve and created a quick deep opening across her skin and the vein below. Araina gasped as hot blood spilled down her side and rained through the metal grating. She could scarcely gain any comprehension through its plunks to the stone or Bladgen's movement to her side. He rolled her arm within the limits of the straps and sliced the inner portion of her elbow. Another vein opened, its flow teemed over her skin and trickled to the stone. Araina's panicked gasps echoed through the laboratory as her vessels moaned in a crushing, throbbing harmony.

"While it's flowing, gentlemen," Bladgen prompted.

The men with small bowls dipped their fingers and pinched a tight quantity of gritty black sediment. It was spread over and kneaded into the witch's opened veins.

The substance tore through her like parasites with bodies of broken glass. The alchemists took their hands from the siphoning openings and simply watched and waited. Though the incessant command to stay silent chanted through every passage of her brain, she could do nothing but scream and writhe. The blood spilling through the grates fast darkened and thickened to syrupy black. The two empty metal basins were slid to catch the newly tainted flow. Above them, the agony went on and on, and beyond Araina's capacity to roar.

Bladgen took a small glass cup from the table and returned to collect a modest quantity of the dark liquid. He held it before the wall sconces and the sun fading beyond the long windows, then he lowered it to look upon the witch. Her movements were reduced to trembling drags. Her voice gone to a scratch.

"You've gone awfully quiet, Araina. That was only a pinch. Although, maybe it's sufficient. …Is it? Our quills are at the ready. *We're* at the ready to rise to your every word. What are the names? What are their positions?"

After gaining only a reply of wounded air and tight convulsing below the slick fabric of the shift, he prodded, "Again, this is an opportunity. Something to be cherished." With a sigh, he idly scratched his eyebrow and called, "Glyn." The summon unheeded, he again demanded, "Glyn!" and scanned the room.

Hesitant footfalls preceded the appearance of a tall, smocked figure with eyes so glacially lustrous, they defied the shadow of his hood.

"Yes, sir?"

"Are you unwell today?"

"No, sir."

"No head-colds? Wax buildup? Sudden name changes?"

"No, sir. My apologies, I—"

"Tell me where she is. Can I get a second round and start really asking questions?"

"I…I can't say this early on. I won't know until she's been…" Glyn looked at Araina then down to the floor in quick calculation. "I only have enough for one more soak before I'd have to brew a new vat."

"Remind me how long that takes."

"Still a day, sir."

"Thought you had it down to half."

"Not for an adult human."

"Even for her? She's short enough."

"It's based on the last time, from her arrival. But this is somewhat more—"

"A top-notch job on that, once again." Bladgen reached up and pounded on Glyn's upper back. "Suppose that's all the more reason I should trust your prudence. But can't we spare a shade of optimism from our recent stroke of luck? If we try for another half-basin today, are we deluding or depriving ourselves?"

"It would be a risk. That's a fair amount of blood to recoup. The more often and heavily you…tap, the longer she'd need to soak."

"Twelve of one, half-dozen of the other." Bladgen's grin gave way to a hearty laugh.

He raised the glass of tainted blood to the light again while Glyn slowly cautioned, "Sir, it's possible to push this too…that is to say, there's a point of no going back."

"How about we see what she's made of first? Then we'll go back for more. You can prepare accordingly. We'll get a nice early start. That sound prudent enough to you?" Bladgen punctuated his proposal with another slap on the young man's back, then turned and called, "Clotted yet?"

"Nearly," the alchemist closest to the faintly breathing witch answered. "Shall we green her?"

"Doesn't look like she has much left to complicate things. Save it. Snuff her wounds and get her in the tub."

Sol ran through the last of the daylight, gripping his side and keeping steady-on across a tight northeastern curve. His view swung along the stretching shadows, over the trees, and to the field they bordered. When he spotted the first trace of a flame in the distance, then another, and another—popping up as pinpricks along the dark horizon—he stopped and moved to the woods' edge.

After a drink from his canteen, he slipped a hand into his shirt and freed the map from the outer-most layer of bandages. The descending night stole the definition of a new line of ink—made along the southern-most edge of the woodland. He looked out at the distant fires, grown from dots to thin dashes of light.

"'Course you're on time and track for once. Beat you in the morning then," he pledged and folded away the map.

With a flinch, he shifted his crossbow and pack to rest at his side, then lowered himself against a tree and settled below his cloak. He retrieved Araina's and gathered it into his center. His chin rested across the fabric. The watery, floral scent of borage still held between traces of soil and blood. It anchored him for a few hours.

The scream startled Araina awake as though it were not her own. She threw herself off her stomach, certain some mass was moving to crush or restrain her from across her back. It was nothing more than the same palms-to-elbow binding and the aching weight of her own arms. She lay across them, depleted from her bleeding and contamination, and yet in no bodily pain from either—she wondered if that somehow made it worse.

Beyond the small window, her eyes met fading stars. She tilted away, back onto her side, and let her sobs pour forth. They kept her from the scratch of claws on the window ledge, which briefly ceased while a prehensile tail ensured adequate bearings. The scrape continued down the wall, to the floor, and just beyond the iron bars.

Araina caught her breath only to again gasp it away when a small opossum met her view. It did not retreat, hiss, or so much as twitch its wiry whiskers at her stark upright push. She waited for some cryptic string of words. Instead, it buried its face into its little pink forefeet, looped in its tail, and curled itself into its underside. Its grey coat smoothed and flattened from fur to felt, then fabric. It grew, wider at first, then longer and taller—reaching well-past Araina's head where she sat, then her standing height, and higher still. The form had become a slender figure in a stained charcoal robe. Glyn pushed back its hood, and with a nod, greeted, "Rainy."

"Y-you," Araina stammered past her quivering lower lip, then weakly added, "I suppose you would call me that."

"You mind it?"

She closed her eyes. "No."

"I could go by the fancier one. The one they use—"

"No." She wiped her cheek on her shoulder. "What's brought you here this time?"

"You already answered it."

"If I mind being called Rainy?"

"That you're awake and talking." He crouched down and leaned in to spy the space below her collarbone, where a thick though thoroughly healed-over slash remained. "And closed up. Wasn't sure about that last batch for such a short time. Not bad."

She recoiled at his examination. "Is that all then?"

He shrugged.

She found nothing across his youthful face that told of any understanding or appreciation for how his satisfaction fell upon her. His small surprise at his success was entirely disconnected from its origins and ends. Araina wondered if he had simply acknowledged and discarded it, or had perhaps never considered it. Still, he remained before the cell, looking upon her with a fascination fixed somewhere beyond her bound form. With little else to do but feel for hamartia or at least leverage within, she gently said, "You've mastered therianthropy. That's impressive, particularly for someone so young."

"Wouldn't say mastered and I'm not that young," he bashfully retorted.

"If not for your height, I'd think you were twelve."

"I'm eighteen."

"Only a year younger than I. Or perhaps two now…"

"You don't know how old you are?"

"I'm not sure how many days've passed. I'll be twenty in…twenty-two days from the equinox. It hasn't been that long, has it?"

"Still a few days to go. I thought you'd be *a lot* older than that."

"I imagine I look it now."

Glyn shrugged at her weary presumption and settled upon the stone. "I mean, I thought that before you showed up. For all your powers, I thought you'd be an old witch, or 'least an older one."

"I'd call what I have abilities. And even then, I don't have many. How powerful they are…" She sighed. "Clearly, you've abilities as well."

"Not as many as I'd like."

"So you're after more than therianthropy? And unheard-of medicinal mixing?"

"Want whatever I can get. Gotta keep most of 'em quiet though."

"Why is that?"

"They only let you get ahold'a so many around here."

"That hasn't stopped you though. Is that why you've entered through the window instead of the door, as you had…yesterday? Or the day before that?" Araina asked with a squinted reckoning.

"Yesterday," he clarified.

"Thank you. So that's why you would need to keep your passage here quiet. Or was it simply that you wanted me to see what you can do?"

Glyn smiled. A thin sigh slipped from the corner of his mouth. "Since you closed up really quick the last time, I wanted to check back. Sometimes the mind rebuilds later than the body. That, and I just needed…a bit of a break from work."

"Are you not fond of your…" Araina tried to blunt the contempt rising in her throat. "Your work?"

He shrugged. "Work's work. Lets me do what I really want, for the most part, 'long as I don't let one interfere with the other. And 'long as I watch what I show off. Not much time for it recently though."

"I see. Were you not so busy, what would you rather be doing?"

A short note of radiance escaped his lips and settled in his eyes. They moved across the air with visionary relish. "I'd be back in those books. Get more. Then get to work. The type of stuff your folk do."

"My folk?"

"Yes."

"You realize Crest workings and witchery are almost entirely antithetical to alchemy, don't you?"

Glyn only shrugged.

She went on, "One is rooted in a purest exploration and embrace of natural laws. What they permit, what they limit, and everything that results. The other only seeks to understand as much as is required to bend all of that."

"I guess. But why not take what can be gained from both? I think there're ways."

His zeal birthed a dark amusement in the witch as she wondered aloud, "The thought of what you'd do to any bookshelf that I've been sat in front of... Is that why you're here now? To see what you can learn from a Crest witch?"

Glyn looked down, his narrow nose twitched as though repelled by the essence of some imagined consequence. "Could get in a lot of trouble being here. But...dunno if matters. I kinda wonder what they'd even..." The creases over his brow smoothed with his snicker. "Sometimes a bit of chaos 'round here is...interesting. That's why I wanted to start on this whole project. And how I helped it get started."

Araina's eyes slowly widened at his smirk. Her lower lip dropped away. The notion that he had not only contributed to her predicament, but could have spurred the whole of it, drove like a blade through her brain. She unconsciously tugged at the binds. Their restriction was just enough to reclaim her focus and steady her to reply, "...I-I imagine Crest books in the hands of an alchemist...helped with this...this whole project?"

"Uh huh," he answered. His smile held.

"Now that you've done...this, what then? What's next for someone so adept and curious?" The witch tried to steady her breath.

"Haven't had much time to think'a that. Not lately. Things're busy again, though not interesting. But this is nice. Just talking. Den's no good for it anymore. Haven't see him much since he got back. Almost never in this wing."

"No? Why is that?"

"Said it's too loud and stuffy or something. Gone to play cards with his ogre buddies. Weird for him. Never picky about noise. Usually he's the loud one."

"So he is."

"So, I was thinking…I know why ya wouldn't, but you've been…nice 'bout talking to me. Guess I just wanted to see if maybe, I dunno, you'd tell me about what you can do and how."

"To inform your cohorts?"

"I'd call them bosses more than that. And nah. They aren't expectin' me to do that part. Not my specialty, remember? It's like your wing scars. I'm only asking for me."

"You can understand why I might not believe that?"

"I guess so. But, I'm not askin' you to tell me any of that…the part they're going to keep trying for." Glyn's face finally revealed something other than curiosity, diffidence, or keen fascination, but only a glimpse of it. It quickly slipped away as he almost breathlessly stated, "It's just…I've read about *all* this stuff and I don't have *anyone* to ask about it. I got more questions than I can count."

"As do I."

"Heh. And it's gettin' late." He looked at the light of dawn filling the window. "Need to get ready soon."

The witch briskly raised her head. "Then we'll be quick."

"Quick with what?"

"Your questions, my answers. And so goes mine for yours."

"I dunno. I—"

"You're already here, Glyn. I don't know what kind of amazing mix of alchemist and warlock you are, but I've some idea that therianthropy, even as a small marsupial, it requires an immense amount of energy to be done just once. And then a second time, presumably, for your departure. And it's still not completely eliminated the risk from being here, speaking to me. Why waste all that on little more than you could've gained by simply entering through the door?"

"Well, they don't give me the keys much. And…I dunno how much I can give back."

"I credit you for fairness." Araina almost smiled. "Under other circumstances, perhaps, it'd be nice to share a game of tafl or throni furta. That said, it's really up to you what you give back, isn't it? As it's up to me what I will answer and how. Why don't you take the first turn and see what it yields?"

Without another word of prompting, he asked, "How does casting work?"

Araina's brow tensed. "Think of it as struggle that…holds and amasses over years. It turns to force if allowed to flow. It's sometimes referred to as the lamp of pain because it tends to be luminous."

At the explanation, Glyn's expression migrated across a terrain of confusion, then disappointment, then disquiet. "Is that something you can *learn*? Or do on purpose?"

"To the best of my knowledge, it's only something you access if it's there. Any learning is in the use of it, not its creation."

"Hmm. They're not going to be happy about that." Glyn's eyebrows tightened, then twitched with amusement.

"Who? Your bosses?"

He chuckled. "Down there right now trying to figure out the component elements so they can reproduce it."

"Reproduce it? They're trying to figure out casting from my blood?"

"Parts of it."

"My…" Araina thought back to the landing of Bladgen's fingers at her throat. "Is that why…why they ran that *glass* through me?"

"It's not glass. It's a distilling catalyst. It makes it easy to modify and then break down thicker liquid substances for analysis. It's sediment so it can…crawl. Usually we'd use it on someone under green glow. But they want you to be awake for it."

"They're not going to find the ability to cast in my blood." The witch's eyes drooped to the thickened dash of skin above her breast. "I don't think."

"Then the Baron's not gonna get much from that serum. Eh, don't matter anyway. 'Long as it looks and tastes like it will."

"So that was Machalka," Araina almost whispered. "He wants to cast?"

"He wants everything. Lately, serums and things, 'least far as I know."

"Is he ill? Is that why his eyes are so strange?"

"Can't say." Glyn's focus fell to the gaps between the iron bars.

"You can't say or you don't know?" Araina pulled it back.

"Don't know. The black over his sclera started showing up after some treatment. I dunno what, only that they sometimes pilfer chemicals from my workbench for it. Other times, they have me mix them. They don't tell me much. Next question's mine, right?"

"I've lost track. You go ahead."

"How do Crestfolk live so long?"

"We don't. Landers' lives are just oddly short."

"Same thing." Glyn smiled.

"I can assure you, Crestfolk do not live forever. Most don't have exceptionally long lives. We've the same bodies as Landers and any other humans. We've had others come to us and live as long as we. It's all in the knowing of what to do in the face of sickness and injury. Although, that's changed—"

"Wait. I thought Crestfolk had to be born in."

"You're born into a Crest, but to become Crestfolk is possible. There are places and ways besides birth, I've heard. I just don't know that it's all that pursued. Landers tend to stay where they are and as they are. That's why they're called such." Her telling made Glyn's gaze flare until she asserted, "My turn then?"

"G'head."

"Did the four Vexhi ever return?" She shrank back with the release of the question.

"Four Vexhi?"

"Yes."

"What four? You mean the company sent after you?"

"Yes. Sent with two officers. After me and the soldier."

"I don't get much downstairs news, 'less my brother mentions it. Military movement isn't all that important in this wing, 'specially now. But, come to think of it, Giles was complaining... Waiting on a spare squad to go back and see if they could find anyone in some swamp..."

"Did they?"

"Don't know. No one's said anything that I've heard."

"Will you tell me if they do? If you hear anything? If you tell me *nothing* else, will you tell me that?" Araina implored.

"Alright." Glyn shrugged "Why not?"

"Thank you."

"It's gettin' light out, Rainy. They'll notice if I'm not down there soon. But real quick, tell me how you got wings. How do they work?"

"That's not a real quick thing I can do."

The young man groaned and rose from the floor. "Ahh, alright. Wait, the vorousvoids, are they... Is it like Den said? And your light can just..." He flared his chemical-stained fingers.

"Vorousvoids? You mean umbras? I don't know what Den told you. You've seen them yourself?"

"Only heard. From Giles and then Den. He said you can shoot them outta the air!"

"Casting seemed to be enough to dissolve them. But they dissolve the light as well."

"Better than the riumm glare, I hear."

"Riumm glare? Is that what they have in that glass? The lanterns…the captured light?"

"Good way to put it. Wasn't on that assignment but I hear it's effective for pushing 'em back."

"I see. I hope at least you remain unacquainted with them. Though I don't see that holding so long as your bosses continue."

"They're pretty sure they'll only have to deal with that part for so long."

"Do you share their certainty?"

Glyn only shrugged. "Well, been nice, Rainy. 'Til next time."

Araina fell back into a gelid dread and Glyn's smile dropped. His hood followed, over his head and down to his upper lip. He pulled his sleeves past his fingers and curled his chin into his chest. His form below the robe shortened and thickened. The fabric frayed and bristled, then became grey fur as he shrank down to a rounded hunch. The resulting opossum raised his little white face to the witch before scurrying across the floor, up the wall, and out the window.

Chapter Thirty-One

A Bit of Chaos

Glyn's distinctive height and verglas eyes were all Araina could bring herself to focus on while she again tested the straps that held her body to the grating and rendered her left hand inert. His aloof slouching made the shuffling preparations of the other alchemists more kinetic. Their scattered forms aligned when Bladgen entered the laboratory.

"Tell us, Araina, has anything come clearer with the dawn of a new day? Any reconsiderations? Names or positions to share?" he immediately inquired on approach.

The witch held to silence like a hilt.

"Your blood had much to tell. Won't be long before we can do without the bother of wicks and wax. So much less glass to shape. Light comes at a high price in a place as this, vast as it is, working all hours of the night, as we do. If I could begin to tell you the cost of making that sediment, it'd send your mind reeling, not unlike the rest of your insides."

Bladgen's head tilted to his shoulder, as though an askew angle of the witch would reveal something. He righted it and took one of the small bowls from the nearest table.

"I mention it because I really do hope that would be enough. Sometimes just a thought is sufficient," he mused and let the sediment spill between his fingers. "That is everything in life, after all. The thought of pain. Has that ever occurred to you, Araina?"

But for another challenge of the binds, she kept still and silent.

"It's all that makes us move or stay. Lesser examination might lead one to think extraordinary feats are born out of desire for standing, infiniteness, power, even love. But look deeper. It is only an aversion to pain. Simply guards against and responses to the agony of meaninglessness, futility, betrayal, grief. What a powerful, useful thing it is. The way it drives us to meaning and consequence. The very fuel for every monumental achievement, every great triumph."

He returned the bowl beside the others. It rested there for an instant before an alchemist claimed it. Another followed suit and two more neared with empty basins while Bladgen moved to Araina's side with the short razor. "So much greatness to be found when you let it nip at your ankles a bit. And when you let it swim the channels of your body—well, you would be one to determine what gain is to be had of that."

He rolled his fingers and spread the skin below her collarbone as he proposed, "Do you know how much greatness we stand to achieve, you and I? And through naught but words. Tell me their names. The first sequence. The arrangement that bonds. We only need that. It will take just moments. Painless moments. Just speak them. Or you could write them. Draw them? Tell me however you prefer to do it. It's a choice that opens up endless others."

Araina gave nothing but a flinch against the force of his fingertips, still holding her flesh taut.

"No?"

Bladgen then sliced her skin but not yet the vein below it. "This reminds me. I was thinking I would proceed in this matter with the soldier. Shallow but plentiful. You can really get lost in that process. Idle away a day or several. Of course, it would have to be after we deal with that tongue of his. That's no small or thin cut. But well worth it for the bother he's become. Asking so many questions. Making so many pleas. I've told him, not until he quiets down and you speak up."

Araina's eyes eased out of their waiting wince. She rolled her head toward Bladgen and stared, boldly.

"Thought I'd mention it, since you asked after him only just recently. Forgive me for neglecting to do so. Perhaps this is as good a time as any? Perhaps it will bring that sequence to mind? I know he'd find your cooperation favorable."

The witch thought back to his claim of all the telltale qualities of her blood and briefly wondered what other words he would offer for the sake of saving sediment. She let her head loll away—defiantly clearing her view of his building irritation. The force of it could not be ignored as he dragged over the slash again and cut the vein below.

A crushing throb flooded her senses while her chest, shoulder, and side rapidly went hot and wet. The drips upon the stone came after. Bladgen then moved to the same place at her opposite collarbone and held the skin below it. "Now then, Arain—"

"Sir," a subordinate alchemist interjected.

"What?"

"The next opening needs to be lower than the heart. And opposite the first."

"Vigilant as always," Bladgen droned. "We're opening two paths today."

"At the same time, sir?"

"Yes. Have the quills at the ready. She'll give." Bladgen split another opening above Araina's breast. She rang back with a shriek.

"We may lose her too quickly, sir," the same alchemist warned.

"Did you not hear what I said?" Bladgen proceeded down to her right arm, split the vein above her elbow, then did the same with the left. "Can you not also hear that dripping? She's spilling as you quibble."

He walked back to a table, and from it, lifted Aqzim. "You underestimate the work of our Glyn. Or perhaps you're just annoyed he's robbed you of a late start. We've him to thank that she's ready so soon." Bladgen looked up from his examination of the touchpoint. "Drip, drip, drip is all I hear! Get to it!"

The alchemists pressed their pinches of black sediment to the witch's wounds. Again, it forged scraping, caustic passages through her insides. Her blood went black and fell loud across the basins. All the while her roars carried, then withered, and soon subsided into exhausted rasps. Bladgen nodded to two more alchemists waiting with folded cloths. They pressed them to Araina's wounds—just enough the stifle the flow while she weakly writhed.

He held Aqzim before the witch's agonized face and stated, "I was about to ask if this one looked familiar. I'd momentarily forgotten it stayed just out of your reach. What is its name? Where does it fit? It's the center is it not? Perhaps the north-most? Tell me its place and evocation. That will earn you a nice bath. Hours to sleep after. Doesn't that sound much better than the sticky, tired state you're in? Where does this little piece fit? What word calls it to life?"

Araina shook, seethed, and fought to spill nothing but air between her gritted teeth.

"This is becoming rather inefficient, Araina. One might even call it wasteful," Bladgen declared. He gestured to the alchemists holding her wounds. They raised their stained cloths and her blood began to roll free again. Araina squeaked as the alchemists dipped their hands within the bowls and awaited the next signal.

"Yes? Out with it," Bladgen hummed.

Bracing for the surge again, her grip began to flail. She weighed the submission of a lie—vaguely rearrange the words that screamed through her brain and gathered at the end of lips—or simply deny that cataclysmic cognizance Bladgen caught cross her face. She could dare neither. Any slip of any word might be enough. The seven, gathered and resting together—only steps from her bleeding body—seemed to drag it with the same pull of the man who kept her hovering above death.

Araina only hissed through her teeth.

Bladgen signaled and the sediment ripped through her again. He placed Aqzim back on the table and called above the witch's fractured screams to instruct, "Prepare a third path."

"Sir, we've only so much more to gain from the two," the nearest subordinate cautioned.

"Glyn?" Bladgen beckoned.

"Yes, sir?"

"Anything to that?"

"I-I… Sir, I wouldn't—"

"But you said yourself, the response earlier was exceptional."

"I-I…"

"Open a third," Bladgen insisted.

"Where, sir?" the subordinate asked.

"Doesn't matter. Just need her voice intact."

"Sir…"

"What?!" Bladgen's growl echoed across the room as Araina's cries had faded into silence.

"She's out."

Bladgen turned and frowned at the limp body of the witch. Her face had fallen to her shoulder. Her limbs, coated with a gritty syrup of black and crimson, had gone slack but for where the binds held them.

"I haven't time for histrionics! She just needs a wakeup call." He marched over, razor in hand, and grabbed Araina's ankle. He drew a quick slice across the arch of her right sole. She did not twitch. He cut her again at the left and also gained nothing. Bladgen's frown deepened. He sighed and turned away. "Get her in the tub. I want her back in a few hours."

Araina's slowly clotting wounds were wrapped and her restraints unwoven from the grating. The nearly full basins of her blackened blood were slid and lifted from the ground. A moment later, they sloshed and all but spilt to the stone as a great clanging rang beyond the laboratory.

Bladgen and the others thrust their attention to the alarm pulsing from the western windows. They vied for views of the lines of motion just visible beyond the height of the curtain wall, except for Glyn—who could see over their heads even from his distanced slump. His attention shifted when, on the edge of an echoing crash, he thought he heard a damp thud on the floor.

He froze on witnessing the witch, barely revived and crawling across puddles of her own blood. She grasped toward the table with the touchpoints. Glyn could only stare as white claws ripped the fabric of the slicked shift and great grey-indigo wings began to unfurl. Araina pulled at the leg of the table with her right hand and wobbled forward on the support of her balled-up left—fighting to stay upright against her own depletion, the slices in her flesh, and the viscid sanguinary grip below her.

With the subside of the final toll, the scrape of table legs on stone cut to Bladgen's ear. He turned, gawked, then shoved between the huddle of his cohorts. Through his sprint, he grabbed the razor and pounced upon the witch. He began to slice at her wings. It sent her onto her back. The blade fumbled between his fingers, haphazardly cutting beside Araina's left eye, earlobe, and cheek. She scratched at him with her right hand and thrashed with the tethered stump that was her left. The lower curve of her wings stretched and ripped at his back with their claws. Growling and gasping, she tried to keep her grip on consciousness and vie for the razor. It all began to slip after Bladgen tossed the blade away and squeezed upon her neck.

"Sir, you—you needn't! Sir, we're ready!" one of the onlooking alchemists called. He and two others waited with their forefingers glowing green. All were otherwise frozen in stupefaction. Bladgen squeezed. The witch choked. Her torn and bleeding wings flattened, folded into themselves, and retreated below their scars.

"Sir, please!" another urged. "She can't be brought back if—"

Bladgen spat in resignation and dropped his grip, letting Araina fall limp to the stone.

"Get her out of my sight!" he ordered and fiercely wiped her blood from his face and hands. Through a noisy swallow, he felt the fingernail-dug trails along his neck, then reached to the slashes at his back. The claws of her wings had torn through the layers of his smock, his jerkin and shirt, and skin below. As he felt the split fabric, an occurrence gradually quelled the wrath in his face.

"Bind her from the front next time. Let her show the wings again. She'll speak or I take them."

Two of his subordinates nodded and left.

One of the few who was not frantically clearing blood from the floor asked, "And the approach?"

"But for a bit of noise to work under and more nagging from downstairs, that's not our concern, Lealon. If they try to make it so, just give them more birds," he answered before barking, "Glyn!"

The young man moved from his place along the wall, still trying to lift his jaw. "Yes, sir?"

"You saw what's marching?"

"Yes, sir."

"She needs to be up and speaking *long* before that gets in range. Understood?"

"I-I don't know if—"

"Understood?" Bladgen repeated.

"Yes, sir."

The witch's body was carried out of the laboratory while Bladgen marched out the opposite door. A sharp slam and prompt snap of a lock followed. With it, Glyn's view fell across the western windows. A small, familiar face stared back from one of the low sills. After catching Glyn's eye, Den sidled to the outer ledge and out of sight.

Chapter Thirty-Two

Before the Front

Sol's wooded cover began to thin away. Beyond the last of it, sandy soil and yellow weeds stretched to a massive moat—faintly detectable by a thin and strange miasma. It circled the infamous stronghold's stark, reaching curtain wall. The structure was sharply uniform but for lines upon lines of arrow loops and spikes of sentry towers along the uppermost ramparts. The highest floors of scarce turrets were only just taller than the gatehouse, which appeared impossibly dense for its thrust into the sky. The sight of its portcullis through his spyglass drove Sol to wonder whether there was any ore left in the ground. As though prompted by his observation, a distant clanging rang from the stronghold's summit. He lowered the eyepiece and watched the drawbridge rise.

The tolling and the creaking hoist brought nothing of that familiar fueling squall. Any gain to be had from thunderous lines of troops—just behind and south of him, and the impetus for the order to rise—was nowhere. That whetted icy edge, salvaged from fallen comrades and held to be thrust into foes to further salvage quenching, fluid heat, was not only stolen, but eliminated. It was taken with her. Something else had formed in its stead, something sapping and scattered—and yet no less honed.

Too much behind that wall, Sol thought. Too much distance between it and him, too little between him and the two armies moving to breach, and then too much that could be sent crashing. All that saved him from the spiral was the notion of a keyhole, crack, or gap. It was almost enough to stir some gainful tempest—the thought that one only needed to be spotted. That it needed to be before the first stone was cast, quashed it all.

The soldier again raised his spyglass and scanned the base of the stronghold, its moat, and the thin strip of land between. Insurmountably precise and heavy as it appeared, he held that it would need tenfold its land to feed and supply the numbers required to defend it, let alone justify it. More stone than structure, Sol almost muttered aloud, even as he could not help but marvel at that portcullis once again.

While he went on to compare the stretch between finding a gap and one being gashed, he shifted his spyglass southwest and looked at the lines, amassing and holding just out of range. Through the lenses, the blurry rows defined to carts, horses, oxen, and siege engines—the greatest with which the Svet Hagen had to bargain and barter for food, medicine, and fuel. They were guided and flanked by glinting shields, helmets, and breastplates worn over red and black uniforms, and others in all-black but for swaying slashes of green.

With his scan of the lines, he could not help but ponder the words he would scrawl with charcoal on a torn, ink-dotted page—were there no keyholes and no grey or yellow uniforms fallen from the sky. Sol switched the spyglass back and urged weaknesses to reveal themselves before the front obscured them and everything else.

G lyn looked at the codes across the labels. Though created and maintained by him, they only deciphered panicked swearing through his brain.

"Hey, Sprout," Den whispered from the floor. He stood between the slimly parted doors, where hurried shadows broke from the hall. Glyn swung his head to the elf, then back to the labels like a thrown pendulum.

"You… I can't right now!" the young man exhaled, low and frantic. "Come up here if you wanna tell me something. Even if not, I'd get away from that hallway and hope no one saw you on that window!"

"Rather take my chances here than in there," Den muttered.

"Why? She's out. Maybe for good, if I-I…I dunno how I'm gonna—" Glyn sighed and dropped his elbows to the workbench. His forehead fell against his fists then quickly lifted away at a sharp sting—caused by residue along the jar in his grip. He placed it on the bench and grabbed his gloves.

"Out or otherwise, don't mean I wanna see 'er. Seen more than enough 'a her today."

"Why were you up there in the first place?" Glyn lined up a series of jars and bottles, blinked at them, then added another.

"Was up there for *you*!"

The young man hardly heard the elf through the landing of a large metal bowl. He steadied it and started measuring out components. "I can't think, and listen, and mix, and hear you over there. If the sight'a her bothers you, then just don't look behind me."

Den let his eyes drift up for an instant. He could see only tangled brown locks dangling from the rim of the tub. The rest of her form—limp within the stained shift and crossed with deep and shallow, clotted yet unhealed wounds—remained out of view. Despite that, the elf could picture the aftermath of what he witnessed. It hastened his scurry along the floor and climb to Glyn's workbench. The vapors wafting from the surface first sent the elf's sleeve across his mouth and nose. He then took the kerchief from his head and wrapped it around the lower portion of his face.

"Said that I was up there for *you*," Den reiterated in a muffled push. "Was tryin' to catch ya before the alarm. Last supply runs're goin'. Then it's siege code."

"Siege code? Already? It's just one approach. Doesn't even look that big for all the pressure they got on me."

"Ain't look that big 'cause it ain't that close and it ain't done comin'. Ain't just one either. More's movin' from the south. No alarm on that one yet. Bigger, more engines…type that'll make'a dent. Better hope them urkas get to 'em before we run outta sticks and stones and monsters."

The spoon of powder in Glyn's hand momentarily halted at the rim of the bowl. "Giles told you that?"

"Said they're waitin' on transports and greys still spread from that whole scavenger hunt. Lines're tied up guardin' those palaces when nothin's in sight'a 'em for miles. But the march from the south, saw that myself from the air. Came to let ya know, this ain't your standard pack'a stone-scratchers. If you're still a'any mind to be outta this place, now's the time, Sprout. 'Less ya wanna risk doin' it later with your tail gettin' stepped on. Or worse. Me, Earl, and Wob, we ain't gonna be far behind."

"You're leaving? But what about—"

"Feh, I ain't seen the brunt'a my payment yet. And I ain't waitin' to see who's left to give it or stop me from takin' it."

"Is that where you're going?"

The elf shrugged. "Depends who's got boots on it by the time I get there. But 'long as I gotta chance at gettin' somewhere, that's the place to try."

Glyn paused his mixing. "What about them?"

"Huh? Them who?"

The young man looked down at the deep green liquid in the bowl and picked up three long cloths. He let their ends soak within and carried the bowl over to Araina. "Her folk."

His answer earned a slow chuckle from Den. "That's a joke, right?"

"I dunno. Talking to her this morning had me thinking about a few things." Glyn wrung out one cloth, then another, and wrapped the wounds above Araina's elbows. He layered the last over the slices across her chest and carefully folded her arms to weigh it taut. "Maybe if we cross the right line and give 'em something useful…they'll let us over."

"Heh, you're funny, Sprout. While you're sayin' all that, think about what you're doin' and who you're doin' it to. Then think about why you're doin' it." Den looked over and quickly lowered his eyes again. "What *are* ya doin', Sprout?"

"Stuck with compresses. They're not leaving enough time for the way this is supposed to work. Hopefully it's enough. Don't know if it'll do anything to revive— Oh! That's right! Her throat! Bladgen squeezes the life outta her and just expects me to—"

"Listen to ya. Ya gonna go plead sanctuary from 'er folk when you're in the room where *that's* happenin'? And you're the one makin' it so they can do it over and over. Her folk're welcomin', but they ain't that welcomin'. It ain't like you and me here. They like 'er back where she's from."

"Well, how much do they need to know, far as the details? C'mon, you're good at this sorta thing. Just tell me what I'd need to say."

"This sorta thing's a bit more complicated than my sorta thing. Just come to the woods with me 'til this all dies down. Think'a all the other critters ya can practice bein'. I'll loop 'round and tell Giles where ya went 'fore walls start fallin'."

"I dunno. The thought of throwing all that work away." Glyn sighed. "Can't take the books unless I'm human."

"Always the tunnel." Den shrugged.

"Even then, there's the getting to it. Downstairs'll be upside-down if things're like you say."

"That's why ya gotta go before!" the elf urged, his voice rising from its covert volume.

Glyn looked down at the unconscious witch. He rubbed the back of his neck and leaned over to reposition her head, causing her throat to open and impelling a faint gurgle.

"Huh. Well, that's promising." He looked back to Den, whose revulsion was thoroughly detectable despite the cover of the kerchief. "What if she puts in a good word?"

"Don't look like she can give any now, good or bad. Even still, ya think she's gonna have many for ya if she gets outta this? Can't say I see either happenin', no matter what ya got in that bowl."

"She's been pretty nice about it so far. To me, anyway. Ah, those wings! Right outta her back like that! Did you see them?"

"Seen 'em plenty. Gotta wonder what's left of 'em under there."

"Whatever there is, they're going after it." Glyn sighed and returned to his workbench. Retrieving another bowl, he again began to measure contents from jars, then briefly stopped to wonder, "Maybe we just gotta make sure of it."

"Make sure'a what? They cut 'er wings off?"

"No! That she gets out of this alive. Or has a chance to. If Bladgen didn't turn around, if all that blood was still in her... What if... Maybe we just need to lean on the scales a little. Then she'll do the rest."

"Won't that catch up to ya, Sprout? Who's gonna bring *you* back to life?"

"It only needs to be enough so that whichever side tips it, they either don't know it was us...or they *really* know it was us."

"Huh? What're ya gettin' at?"

Glyn looked at the liquid in the bowl and added another spoon of powder as he calculated, "She's seen me transform. She knows that's me. Bosses don't. What if I...I bite a tear and free her hands once she's conscious again?"

"Guessin' ya mean when you're a 'possum. I know ya think she's sweet, but take it from me, you free that left hand'a hers, ya better clear the room 'fore she can use it. She's gotta streak in her you ain't seen. Witchy through an' through. Huh, come to think'a it, maybe lettin' that loose at the right time ain't the worst plan. Hmm. You still got 'er stuff?"

"I know where it is."

"Butter knife she had with 'er might be a startin' point. Gotta say, you're lucky 'er folk don't know your face. Can't say the same myself. Gonna take more than a little gesture or token to get me back in 'er favor, let alone theirs."

"So make it a big one." Glyn proceeded to funnel the contents of the bowl into a bottle.

"Heh, short a' bringin' 'er the keys to this place, doubt there's much I—" At Den's self-quashed musing, Glyn pointedly met his friend's little eyes. "Heh. There ya go again, Sprout. You and your jokes."

"You said it, not me."

"So? What's in just the sayin'? Ain't like I know where the things are."

"Bladgen's got a set on him. Another on Lealon. Then there's the antechamber. Key to every door in this wing and then some's in there."

"The antechamber? How'd ya know that?"

"I drop off and collect the bottles if things get busy."

"Plenty busy now. Can't ya make a run for some? Slip in an' grab'a key?"

"Now *you're* joking. You think they'll let me or anyone near that place if we're under siege code? Either way, keys're your idea. *Your* big gesture. I only wanna tip the scales, not knock 'em off the table."

Den squinted at his boots, then shot his head upright to request, "Hey, before you go tippin' scales or tossin' 'er stuff back, can ya grab me somethin' outta it?"

"What?"

"Need that ring or little star she was wearin'."

"What for?"

"May come in handy 'case I run into someone. Doubt he's gonna be in the mood to chat, but either a' those little things'll send the message."

"To who?"

"No one ya know. Drinkin' buddy'a mine."

"Earl?"

"No, it ain't Earl! I got somethin' to say to Earl, I chuck a rock at his head. I'm talkin' 'bout someone else. If he's anywhere, gotta feelin' it ain't too far away. Knowin' where could come in handy. Question is how much time I got 'tween him seein' me and him killin' me."

"Sounds like most of your drinking buddies."

"Heh, you ain't far off."

Bottle in hand, Glyn looked at the light beyond the doors—still in motion between passing forms. "I gotta get this down her throat. Even if I get her awake, her brain might be long gone. But if not, she's gonna make a noise when this stuff hits. They're gonna hear it and take her upstairs. Then I gotta get up to my room and figure some things out. I'll bring 'er stuff up there. Pick what you're gonna take, but leave me the blade. Hopefully that and her hand'll be enough."

"Don't need nothing bigger than I can throw. Gotta get somethin' else for now. See ya upstairs."

He removed the kerchief from his mouth and tied it back over his hair. With a drop from the workbench, he slipped out of the room.

The archers readied as the wake of fleshfalca took to the sky, soaring from the western rampart to the first of the Crest and Svet Hagen lines. As they crossed into range, so sounded the call to loose. The first archers drew and shot, sending all but ten to the ground. The seconds followed and halved the remaining birds. The thirds dropped only one before the rest descended to swoop. Suddenly one, then another, another, and the final fleshfalca plummeted to the ground—landing not a full chain from the feet of the infantry.

Dionis looked at the confused archers at her call. Though they had readied for the attack, the targeted birds dropped without a single arrow through their breasts. She fixed her view north to the sweep of trees, then looked back among her comrades to see if any had caught the slight southern push of the fleshfalcas' bodies. They only muttered among themselves.

Dionis called over her shoulder, "I need a falcon."

The branch below Sol's boots came into question sooner than anticipated. Its whining integrity was no better than the few remaining leaves providing his cover—a problem that reasserted itself when he heard a driven, rustling approach.

A perturbed though muted voice growled, "Honestly?! Here? And *how… This* is how you give away your position?"

"Dionis' third call was late. Those things only get faster and meaner when they get low," Sol glumly answered Imari.

"Get down here!"

"Can't. Good vantage." The bough creaked as he reset the crossbow's draw.

"At least that branch sounds like it's on my side."

"You forget we're on the same side, Imari? Like your Coven has? And I'll take my chances with it."

"*Are* we on the same side?" She revolved around the trunk to gain a more confrontational angle. "If so, you might want to explain what you think you're doing, apart from just wasting my time and ensuring my sanity's questioned?"

"So you sent my message?"

Imari tried to maintain a hushed tone as she rebuked, "With an addendum. At least you left me something to show it was actually *you* trying to command two armies, before disappearing while wounded, and then doing whatever this is. Would you get down here and listen to some sense, or at least how much trouble you're in?"

Sol's huff sent a pair of desiccated leaves flying from their spindly hold. He released the crossbow's draw, lowered himself through the moaning limbs, and dropped to the soil with a slight wince. "G'head. Quickly, please."

"What do you think this is going to achieve?"

"Came down here for consequences, not questions. Not very interested in either at the moment. Gotta keep my eyes east," he flatly informed.

"To do *what*?"

"Confirm keyholes." He turned to the other side of the trunk and squinted across the weeds. "Just gotta wait for that space between the last of the wakes and the lines crossing into range. Little less light would be preferable. 'Course that brings its own complications. But until then, let's see if Dionis can't snap to it. They can only hatch those beasts so fast. Based on the wake that just went out, I'd say they're running low. That usually ruffles Vexhi. And higher ground or not, I expect they're out of practice on defense. Their best work's always done on the field. You want to get any of this in a message? Send it to whoever has such a keen eye for short bolts on a full draw?"

"Why don't you tell them yourself? This is ridiculous! What happened to you, Ekwidou?"

The stony set of his jaw yielded nothing.

She sighed. "Listen, if you get out from whatever you're under, I'll see what I can do to get you in rank. If you're healed enough to be shooting fleshfalca, at this range, from the top of a tree, they'll take you. They just want to talk to you about what happened. By then, that curtain will be breached and the Vexhi will be out of their comfort. That means we can get you into yours. The southern approach is nearly at the range line and the recovery squad's at the ready. Come back with me now and you'll probably be—"

"Too fast, too messy, too long, too much to go wrong. *None* of that works with her still in there. Miles from it, yes. But not *in* there. Sounds like the Coven's willing to pull what they need out of the rubble 'long as they have the Hagen's numbers and arsenal to get to it—"

"I don't think you've really considered what you just suggested."

"Think you need to start considering it."

"They wouldn't risk her like that! Tanzan wouldn't—"

"Tanzan will say what he needs to, when he needs to, for a certain result. And he's not the only one," Sol hissed.

"This is only subdue and recover! Provided she's still—"

"She is."

"All they've been able to confirm is that Vexhi haven't progressed since they uncovered the last. Or at least not yet. What they must have already done to—"

"Will they confirm her location before they aim over the curtain or through it? Do you know their plan for that?"

"I'm sure they—"

"Then why haven't they loosed it!" Sol's view whipped through the trees toward a swell of fleshfalca shrieks. He loaded, cocked, then stayed, and finally grumbled, "That's more like it, Dionis." He then turned back to an increasingly bewildered Imari and growled, "Whatever their plan or lack thereof, I know they have their priorities. Based on what's lined up and how little they've told their scouts, I have doubts if they're still the same as mine. I'm not waiting to confirm it."

"Even *you* have to acknowledge there's no slipping in that thing. There's no knocking on the front gate. Look at it!"

"Have you looked at it? To keep that thing going, while they're spread out as they've been, they need ways out as much as we need them in. Just got to spot one and get to it."

"And the moat, Ekwidou? That's not your average motte to ascend or barbican link to cut. No one's tunneling through that for supplies, siege or otherwise. It's not as though we haven't been scouting this thing for weeks. Their lines are severed. That bridge is up. They're in there, we're out here, and there are few options after that."

"Too simple. Not enough for Machalka. Likes things stark, not simple," Sol muttered before assuring, "I'll take care of him once I'm in there. Be the second thing I do. Then have at it. Level it, raid it, whatever they want. But I'm not waiting on new orders. Keeping with my first."

"Solairous, listen to me. You are not the only one eager to see her out of there, but this isn't going to get that done. You can't just be out here complicating—"

"Anything else, Imari? Or you going to drag me across that field now? Afraid it's your only option. I'm not turning around and you can't send me tied around a bird's leg. I only move closer and I'm doing it before that front forms."

Imari looked away from his glower—all of it iron but for a wounding in his eyes. "You're running out of time for it and you better keep clear," she warned. "Because if you become a liability, they will not hesitate—"

"Won't be a problem. Mind passing on that last part in a message so they don't get too loose with the meaning of liability? If there's any ink to spare?"

"Not enough to make any sense of what you're saying."

"I know you'll try. Your folk like things wordy anyway."

"What do you want me to do with the response? Not that I don't have a few ideas…"

"If I'm still here for any of them, it won't matter."

Chapter Thirty-Three

Gestures and Tokens

Den found the strident southbound calls of fleshfalca preferable to the wretched din at his shoulder. A primal cacophony of pitiful moans, fleshy gags, and predatory snarling oozed from the ornate doors of Machalka's inner quarters. It kept the elf frozen and baffled on the windowsill and Pidgie barely clinging to the stone ledge below.

"Steady, buddy. We'll wrap this up quick. C'mon."

Despite the urging, the passenger pigeon would not budge.

"You kiddin' me? We ain't got time for your hysterics!"

Pidgie only blinked.

"Waspscum!" Den spat through a whisper, then thrust a finger at the bird's impassive face. "Don't even think'a leavin' without me!"

The threat gained nothing but another idle blink of Pidgie's gingery eyes. After a nasal huff, the thwarted elf nudged himself to the inner edge and dropped down into the antechamber.

The walls of polished stone and the curling bronze-framed doors still held their opulence through dust and shadow, and among scattered bottles and piles of cloth with curdled stains. Their odors only compounded the sensory agitation while the ongoing growling and squealing could not be outdone. It rolled over hurried steps and muffled responses, pleading, "Sire, you mustn't! Sire, please!"

The entreaties then descended into struggle, a spill of metal and glass, and further shouts. Footfalls hastened beyond the ornate doors and sent Den sprinting into the drapery along the wall. He suppressed a dust-choked gag and looked across the room to an inlaid cabinet on a gilded table.

More hurried footfalls scraped. The growling slowed and a muffled discussion followed—first tense, then placating, then defensive—then the doors parted suddenly. An alchemist marched through with his arms full of black-stained garments and a covered metal bowl. Faint prints of blood left his rushing boots. He blindly kicked one of the discarded bottles, sending it spinning, then rolling in Den's direction with a glassy grinding. After the alchemist's laboratory-bound exit, the antechamber fell silent.

"Ya better still be there," the elf hissed toward the window. "How would the General do this?"

He looked at the still-rocking bottle. Fighting the cringe from its residue, he hoisted it over his head and scurried across the floor. Just as he passed the chamber's center, a door creaked. Den almost slipped with his start, but planted the bottle and narrowed his body against the slim cover. More footfalls raced across the room, then came another door slam. Cued by the click of its latch, Den dashed the remaining stretch and climbed up the table leg.

The instant after his hands landed on the cabinet's lower trim, the snap of a lock from the far corner of the room sent him scampering again, this time past the table's edge and up the bronze scrollwork of the nearest doorframe. He slunk behind a finial as Bladgen and Lealon entered. Their smocks were disheveled and freshly stained. Bladgen's hood barely held to his sweat-soaked hair. He pushed it back and inquired, "What of the witch?"

"The compresses are proving effective enough, though not comparable. It will be some time before she can be re-tapped."

"That at least can wait. She speaking?"

"Not with much coherency or strength, though they're confident a few hours will remedy that."

"Check that the saws've been brought in and the teeth are honed. I'll draw it out as I choose, but I want to ensure I can do it quickly if needed. Or if they start throwing their pebbles out there."

"There have been more requests for birds."

"They've had the last of them down to the fledglings. They'll need to do their own work for a change. Tell them to make do with that mangy dove that haunts the rafters. It'll all be irrelevant soon enough."

Den sneered as he watched their exit. He jumped back down to the table and again gripped the trim of the cabinet doors. They budged but would not part.

"Feh! Where'm I gonna get the key to the keys?!" With his back to the cabinet's frame, he fixed the tip of his boots along the inner edge. "Damn Rainy. Shoulda just got on'a stinkin' ship when ya had the chance!" Through his pushing and sniping, he managed to strain the latch and created just enough clearance to permit his form.

He sighed among the swinging graze of metal and recalled Glyn's rushed description of cell keys being longer and thinner than door keys. After a fair bit of groping, he narrowed his options to four. Each was wedged and pushed between the gap at the bottom, except for the last, which he used to shim a more comfortable passage out of the cabinet. Cleared of its confines, he threaded the bows of two keys over his right arm, then did the same over his left. He dropped from the table and scurried back across the chamber in a clanging jumble.

On reaching the windowsill and finding Pidgie still barely anchored on the outer ledge, Den turned an ear to the primal gurgling resuming its swell. He furrowed his brow at it one last time and descended to Pidgie, who took to the sky with the elf just on his back.

The viridescent tint of the bandages was streaked with crimson dulling to rust. Araina looked past the wrappings above her elbows and over her chest to the same clumped-up version of her left fist. This time it was tethered to her right and hung before her hips. Her exposed wing scars went on throbbing through the torn fabric of the shift. She implored the emerging sensations to hush with a slow breath from her buzzing larynx, which was answered by a skittering of claws.

The opossum met her heavy-lidded eyes from his place on the window ledge. He turned back and dragged forward a bundle of black fabric. A nudge sent it to the stone with a muted thud. He followed it down, gripped it in his teeth, and pulled, then pushed it against the bars of the cell. Though it would not pass through the lower portion, it rested within the witch's reach.

The opossum slipped between the iron barrier and placed his paws upon Araina's joined wrists. He took up the binding strap between his teeth, and through rapid gnashing, split the leather. He blinked at her once, scurried from the cell, and climbed back out the window.

Araina only stared, mystified. She finally lifted and fully parted her wrists, sending the bitten strap to the floor. Her right hand trembled as it unraveled the swathe that kept her left. She spread her sallow, shaking fingers, flatted them, and looked upon the pale scar across her palm. The witch called up her light. The fragile luminous force kept her eyes for an instant and drew restless breaths. She clutched it back and cradled her hand into her center.

At the window, she found neither opossum nor a young man waiting to confirm or observe the results of his act. Were her mind not so addled, the witch wondered if his intent would have come clearer—whether it was a gift, investment, or simply something sown out of curiosity and in bait of chaos. Araina then turned to the bundle of cloth against the bars.

She moved to crawl and winced, only then recalling the slices across the bottom of her feet. Their lack of immediate mortal consequence left them untreated and unhealed. The cuts over her face and ear were similarly neglected. She unwrapped the compresses from her chest and elbows and found the wounds below. They were thick and swollen, but nearly closed. She relocated the bandages to her feet, securing the dampest section to the arches of her soles. Her attention then returned to the bundle before the bars.

The dull black fabric was irrepressibly familiar. Some dense shape waited within its hold. Araina lifted and passed it between the higher portion of the bars. She unbuckled the belt that held it tight. Her bodice and trousers unrolled and sent her seal ring and earrings chiming and briefly spinning upon the floor. She watched them cease, then looked at her dagger within the scabbard.

Even with it finally in her hands and in such a place, it seemed more useless than all other times she had worn or drawn it. The witch could not recall a single consequential thing she had accomplished with it except kindle mild approval when it caught superficial strikes, eased him to find sleep, and let her follow a path in search of sustenance—one that only led her to where she sat and stared at it. She removed it from its scabbard and saw a sliver of her reflection in the blade. As Araina recoiled from the sliced, haggard thing it revealed, she found the red wolf watching her beyond the bars.

She broke the long, sharp stillness to observe, "You are here now."

It said nothing, only sat, almost attentively.

The witch looked back at the dagger, then to the red wolf. "I think I know what you are."

It waited.

"You are doubt," she whispered. "And now that I've named you, and you say nothing, I would tell you that you can go. But you are loyal. That is in your form. And you are mine. And through doubt and loyalty, comes resilience. If she would not see the light she fed, it must have been that. That is what remains." Araina seethed out a shivering breath. "He saw it." A tear slipped and stung the slashes over her face. "Regardless of the light. In spite of it. He saw it. He saw it always. And alone. When I would not."

She hung her head. The red wolf moved its massive form into the cell as though the barrier did not exist. It sat behind her, rested its muzzle over her shoulder, and breathed one faint, whistling whine aside her sliced ear. Araina blindly reached, touched its smooth, hot coat, and dropped her hand back to the blade.

"If I move from here, it will be to let him know. Every step is toward that. Whether or not I see you. Whether or not you stay."

With a slow uncurl of her back, she looked over her lightened shoulder and found herself alone.

"Ｎone of them are right," Glyn repeated on emerging from under his bed with a stack of books. He shoved them in a satchel.

"Those're the longest they had in there!" the elf defended, staring dumbfounded at the quartet of keys on the nightstand.

Glyn fastened the bag, picked them up, and one by one set them down again. "Don't know what this one is, but it's a not a cell key. This one is to the second roost. This one to the lower corridor. And this one…I think this opens one of the stores outside the lab."

"After all that! None'a these get 'er anywhere?"

"Well, even if you had the cell key, the bolt to that room is held with a lock. Bet only Bladgen has that one now. Maybe Lealon. If your pickpocketing isn't too rusty, I'd try him first." Glyn opened the drawer of his nightstand and lifted a sealed message tucked within. "Can you get this to Giles when I'm clear? Tell him it's for Mom. Know he'll read it though."

"Alright, but ya owe me." Den resumed his huffing at the keys. "Thought the cell one'd be enough. Figure ya give 'er the butter knife, she could be out and ready for 'em. The whole point'a this was show 'er I'm tryin' to—" His scattered frustration fell below a sudden crash of stone. A faint tremor rolled across Glyn's tiny chamber.

"Sounds like they've moved into range," the young man starkly gathered and hurried his packing. "You said west? Blue glass?"

"Uh huh. Head to the coast route. I'll find ya on the way. If I get held up or ya snag a ride, ask 'bout a witches' library. But don't rush ahead or push through any hedges 'til I drop a message on the doorstep. Then ya just gotta hope Rainy lives long'a enough to… Waspscum! What's she supposed'a do with the key to a bunch'a fleshfalca nests!"

"Waspscum?"

Another crash and quake rolled across the room. Glyn steadied his focus.

"Well, they still open doors. One for the corridor might be useful. Someone has that, they can get outta this wing, siege code or not. Or they can get into it. Didn't ya say you knew someone out there? Isn't that why I saved this for ya?"

He pushed his charcoal robe aside and took Araina's copper star from his pocket. "That was gonna make one of your drinking buddies not kill ya or something?"

Den took the ribbon from Glyn's fingers.

"Eh, ran outta time for that. Busy gettin' useless keys! Ain't sure where to start lookin' for 'im. Not gonna happen now if that mess's started up…" The elf squinted at the copper star and listened to more crashes rolling across the wall. "Wait a sec'. They're strikin' 'cause they're outta fleshfalca. Giles said they'd been losin' 'em all to the west. By the trees— Ha! Gotta be! Always with the cover! That's the closest patch out there!" Den hopped off the nightstand and onto the bed. "Alright, catch ya up soon, Sprout. Oh, and stay away from Radomezen Port. But if ya end up there, don't say nothin' 'bout elves or witches!"

"Another one'a your drinking buddies?"

"Nah. Rum thief. Tell ya 'bout it on the road."

"Alright. Good luck."

"Back at ya. Heh, ya got that look Rainy had anytime we turned 'round a corner. Don't sweat it. Tunnel's gotta be clear by now. And if ya get caught behind the lines…just talk 'bout 'er, only without givin' too many details. Witch folk'll probably give ya cake while they question ya." Den wrapped the length of ribbon across his chest, bounced back to the nightstand, and claimed a key. "This one, right? Corridor?"

Glyn nodded.

Den tipped his chin, hopped to the end of the bed frame, and sprang up to the window. "See ya west, Sprout," he bade and dropped out of sight.

Sol collapsed against the tree trunk as though struck by the massive stones sent across the field. They chipped away at the drawbridge, curtain wall, and gatehouse before falling back into the moat or embedding themselves in the ground. With the counter of ballistae, onagers, and archers into the western and southern offensives, the front had taken the first of its forms.

He listened to the crashes and breathed the waft of burning oil, as though they would order him to turn, seek out Imari, and plead for a place—one that would not ultimately be sifting through rock, metal, ash, and bone. There came no worthy prompt among the quakes, fumes, and shouts—not before he felt a small strike against his bowed head. The copper star, ribbon-strung and now looped with a key, landed between his boots. Sol briskly grabbed it and lifted his view. The elf, on the back of the pigeon, looked down from their perch upon the creaking bough. Sol readied his crossbow.

"Easy, General! Listen!"

"W-where?! She alive?!" the soldier barked.

"Ya think I'd be here takin' the chance'a you shootin' me like a fish just to tell ya she's dead? ...Might be a couple'a bad swings away from getting her wings sawed off though."

Sol lowered the crossbow.

"See that key," Den directed and drove Pidgie to the lowest branch. "That'll get ya where they got 'er. Or 'least close to it. Alchemists' wing. No soldiers up there. Still a bunch'a bastards though. I'll link ya to the door. Up to you what ya do from there."

"You think I'm going to—"

"Don't flatter yourself, General. 'Case it ain't obvious, they got more pressin' business than ambushin' you and usin' me to do it, again. Hardly given ya a second thought in days, 'less ya count wonderin' why they've been losin' all their birds in one direction. I gotta swing back and grab'a letter just the same. Take it or leave it. Maybe Rainy'll hold 'er own. Tough to say at this point."

"Alright, lead!"

The elf and pigeon fluttered from their perch. Sol slung his crossbow, unsheathed his sword, and dashed below their path through the trees.

Dozens upon dozens of twisting yards on, Den and Pidgie landed beside the roots of an overturned stump, at which, Den directed, "Roll it that way."

Sol placed his boot on it and pushed, coaxing up a mechanical grinding as the stump rigidly completed a semi rotation. A short distance through the brush, a dirt and clay-covered hatch parted from the ground. Sol sped to it with his blade at the ready. He slipped the toe of his boot between the hatch's gap and kicked it open.

"Not so rough! It ain't gonna shut right if ya treat it like that," Den cautioned.

The soldier peered within and found only a flickering lantern waiting on the bottom of the brick-walled cavity.

"Should be plenty'a fuel left in that. Lucky for you, Sprout moves quick, 'part from just knowin' keys."

"Sprout?"

"Glyn. Ask Rainy. And tell 'er to put in'a good word for the kid when the time comes. Well, c'mon. Suddenly you ain't in a rush?"

"After you."

"Ya always gotta be so pushy, General? Last time I do you any favors."

Sol tightened his grip on the hilt and concurred with a deep nod.

Little of the threatening assurance was lost on the elf as he and the pigeon promptly flapped into the tunnel. With a final survey of the thinly wooded surroundings, the soldier dropped in after and pulled the hatch behind him.

Chapter Thirty-Four

The Witch and the Soldier

Araina leaned into the latest crash and its resulting quake and continued pressing her soles into the bandages. She raised her right foot to observe its progress. The fading traces of sunlight did little to help her evaluation. She ceased her squinting, rolled her eyes at her lapse, and lit up her palm to see the razor-forged slash had shrunk. As she spread her toes, its sting was all but gone. She returned her foot to the pile of cloth and went on squeezing out the lingering medicinal damp.

With her meager flicker of light still holding, she examined the cell's gate, lock, and hinges. Their joining rattled as another strike rang from below. She cocked an ear for the retaliation. When it rumbled forth, she cast her light into the lock plate. The thrust threw her back with a grunt. She recovered her breath and crawled to the gate. It was hardly dented. A brisk shake of the mechanism gained only an askew jittering—her light had done so little for all it had taken.

Through a ravenous hiss of air, she turned to the hazy dusk beyond the window and summoned up another spark. As she extended her hand beyond the bars and urged a new swell of light, the passage from her throat to her hand sharply echoed the cutting flow through her veins. She wondered whether the compresses had fallen short of mending damage so deep or if simply too much time was lost below binds. Without patience to await the cover of another strike, Araina thrust her light into the windowsill. The stone chipped at the corner, leaving only a fraction of the impact caused to tower fireplaces—certainly nothing amounting to a cavern-shaking cave-in. She glowered at her work and droned, "Has my suffering been insufficient as of late?" before catching a faint though frantic exchange nearing the door.

"You checked his quarters?"

"Yes, thrice. Not a sign."

Araina sturdied the scabbard and dagger at her hip, then tossed the shift—discarded for her bodice and trousers—back over her head.

"Has his brother been alerted?"

"They can't reach his position."

With her toes, she dragged the pile of bandages between her ankles and beneath the shift's hem. She folded her arms at her back and tensed her shoulders in imitation of the abhorrent, former binding.

"Has Bladgen been told?"

"No. He's with the Baron."

"You are absolutely useless, Peatrill."

"But I…"

The lock clicked and Araina let her body wilt into the corner. At the slide of the bolt and push of the door, Lealon briskly entered with Peatrill close behind. He moved to the bars, looked upon the witch, and scolded, "The order was to bind her in the front."

"I…I thought they had."

"Ridiculous. It never ends." Lealon snapped a ring of keys off his belt. The gate's lock stuttered before it gave. "Who locked her in last?"

"I don't know. I was working on the serum until I was ordered to find Glyn."

Peatrill and Lealon looked at one another, then the witch—utterly still and veiled by scattered waves of hair. Lealon opened the gate and another rolling crush of stone shook the walls.

A strong scent of burning oil and charred wood wafted from the window, prompting Peatrill to wonder, "Was that ours or theirs?"

"Ours. To the west. Working on lighting their engines."

"Why not save it for the south? West is full of Crest lines. They'll only snuff it."

"Not blazes like that. Won't be able to keep—"

Lealon, squinting across the ceiling, missed the sudden glow from the floor and the shock across Peatrill's face. The witch's light barreled into his jaw and knocked him back into the gate. The ring of keys spilt from his grip and into the cell. Araina weakly scrambled for them. Peatrill tried to intercept over Lealon's frantic agony. He garbled through a splutter of blood and bits of tooth while his cohort reduced him to a hurdle.

Araina narrowly hooked the ring of keys between her fingers as Peatrill dove for her legs. He caught the shift and dragged her down, knocking the ring from her hold. While she kicked at him and pushed for her left hand to fill with light, she slipped her right arm within the shift, unsheathed the dagger, and thrust the blade outward—cutting away the fabric and Peatrill's pull. She curled back and slashed for him. He stumbled to the bars, unscathed, but with enough of a retreat for the witch to conjure some illumination. It knocked the air from the alchemist's lungs and doubled him forward, then down.

Muffled howling rose with Lealon's crawling, retaliating charge across the floor. Araina drew up another meager spot of light and thrust it into his slack chin. He collapsed with a moist wail as she wobbled to her feet. The glow of a new sphere sent Lealon cringing and gasping more flecks of blood and jawbone. The witch spread her fingers to further light the cell. She kicked away the tangle of bandages, chewed binds, and the shredded shift until the keys revealed themselves with a clang. She sheathed her dagger to claim them, then passed the still-wheezing Peatrill and stepped over a moaning, shuddering Lealon.

Before peering beyond the door, she folded her light away and slipped her wrist through the ring of keys. The cries of the alchemists, laying in the wake of her paltry casting, were silenced by a pull of the door and slide of its bolt. Araina proceeded through the dim hallway.

When the grit below Sol's boots became a tacky cling, he raised the lantern and revealed thick mortaring stripes of oakum and pitch.

"Through the moat now," Den answered the soldier's unspoken curiosity.

"Hmm. Told ya so, Imari."

"Huh?"

"Nothing. What's at the end?"

"Lower stores. Used to be full'a food. Part'a the armory now. From the racket out there, might be a lotta in and out. Dunno how ya wanna handle that, General."

"Quietly."

"Ain't a bad idea. Ya go in swingin', might have a lot swingin' back. Though, movement was gettin' tight on the walls. Who's still lower'll depend on—" A massive tumbling across the brick cut Den's voice. It loosened a bellow of dust, which the elf coughed away to add, "...On what's goin' on by the time we get to the hatch. Huh. Big one."

"That the bridge?"

"Got the same view 'a the action as you, General."

"Would they've lowered for a charge already?" Sol clarified

"Goin' by the sound'a that, might'a had it lowered for 'em. Otherwise, they'll light it up first."

"Light up what?"

"The moat. Gettin' dark by now. Might not be far off."

"What do you mean light up the moat?"

"'Member that stuff ya saw at the lake? First spot of a urka, they're gonna light the moat with it. Push those things back into the field. Let 'em eat up the numbers 'fore any boots go 'cross that bridge." Den growled a sigh. "Waspscum! Sprout thinks I'm gonna find Giles in this mess? Gotta get better at knowin' when to say no."

Sol only furrowed his brow. The ground below his boots went gritty again.

"Alright, up ahead." Den tipped his chin. "If that somethin' was as big as it sounded, might be easy for ya to just slip in. Ain't much gonna be locked this low and this late."

With another lift of the lantern, Sol spied a wooden platform in the distance and a series of thick boards positioned over it. As he approached, dampened trampling shook dust into his hair and across slips of light. He lowered the lantern, stepped upon the platform, and listened to the overhead rumbling. A crawl of his fingers found neither hinges nor mechanism. The braced boards comprised little more than a thick lid waiting to be raised.

Though the rumbling continued, the trampling ceased. He looked at the elf and pigeon at his boots and swung his crossbow forward. He readied it and partially eased up the lid, then gestured for Den and Pidgie to ascend through the narrow clearance. They flapped up into the store above. A rolling crash of metal fell after. Sol nearly shot into a clamor of morning stars as they tumbled down and rolled across the platform.

"Ah! Den! You scared me to death!" a small voice cried from beyond the hatch.

"Shhh, take it easy, buddy. Just me"

"What're you doing down there? I-I was supposed'a bring those to Dad! How'm I gonna get them back up here! He's gonna kill me! He's waiting on them!"

"Hey, don't sweat it. We'll help ya out. Right, General?" Den asked into the tunnel. "Wanna give my buddy up here a hand?"

Through the gap above, Sol found the face of a wide-eyed boy no older than ten. He turned to the scattered morning stars at his boots, gathered them, and lifted their shafts up to the boy's reach.

"Thank you, General!"

"You got it," Sol answered, trying to ease forth a smile from the still-limited clearance of the hatch.

"Better get those out there, kiddo. They lower the bridge or somethin'?" Den inquired.

"Was almost knocked down!"

"Huh. Well, get those things where they gotta go, then hide. Got it?"

The boy puffed a wisp of his voice and tightened his grip around the morning stars. He sped between the maze of crates and out the door.

"Hope they ain't gonna have him swingin' one'a those before long," Den muttered.

Sol slid the hatch in full and pulled himself up into the tight storeroom. He slung his crossbow back, unsheathed his sword, and moved to the door. A hair-width parting revealed racing bodies clad in grey.

"If that bridge's goin' or gone down, and ya ain't got a green stripe or spot'a red on ya, they ain't gonna so much as see ya. What'd I say, General. No one's thinkin' 'bout ya," Den assured as Pidgie perched on Sol's shoulder. "Put that thing away and follow the madness goin' right. C'mon, some'a us got things to do."

Though his hand kept to the hilt, Sol sheathed his sword and pulled back the door. The elf and pigeon barely clung along his dash into the hallway.

B efore she could enter the newly discovered stairwell, nearing footfalls and lantern light forced Araina to retreat. She eased the door back, cupped her hands to mute its locking, then waited as a scraping ascent closed in. A futile rattle of the handle and a confusion-laced swear preceded a descent—telling of a keyless subordinate. She loudly clicked back the key. The footfalls paused, then rapidly reascended. A befuddled alchemist appeared through a push of the door. Araina summoned and sent her light into his ribs. He and his lantern fell to the stone with a cry and a crash. She shuffled past him into the stairwell, shutting away his moans like the others, and locked the door with a swift snap.

Unlit sconces, forgotten amidst the fray outside, held only faint reflections against the darkness. She squinted to gauge whether they would serve as adequate guidance while rationing the light at her palm, until their glass began to shudder in the iron frames. One by one, they teetered loose with a surrounding swell of force. The tremor traveled up Araina's wounded soles and tested her tenuous balance. She moved to steady herself on the wall, but a quake across the stairwell's core knocked away her reach. She tumbled down into shadow and shards of sconce glass.

The erupting wave almost threw Sol's grip from the corridor key. Den fought to keep leverage through Pidgie's startled flutter before the bird recovered on the arching doorframe.

"Curtain's breached," Sol inferred and turned the key. He pushed through the door and shut it just shy of pigeon's tail feathers.

"Alright, General, here's where we part ways. Last I know, they had 'er higher level. Might be in the lab again. Dunno. Just find stairs and go up. Sprout and me...*Glyn* and me, we tried to tip the scales for 'er. Just 'member what got ya this far. I'd move fast 'fore they—"

A syphoning whoosh of air pulled from the high windows and the night sky beyond flashed pale. All distant quaking, crashing, and shouting forces ceased while a silvery flare rippled across clouds of smoke.

"The moat?" Sol asked through a choke.

Between gags and through a dart of his tiny eyes, Den concluded, "...Either your friends got too close or those things'er risin'. Or both. Well, so long, General."

With a press of his knee to Pidgie's side, they flapped out the nearest window. Sol sped through the corridor before they cleared its ledge.

Araina lifted her head from the landing and faced darkness. On gaining her bearings, she understood the jangling ascent of keys. She scrambled upright and called up a tight spark. With the reveal of a door, she folded back its cast to grip the handle. Its rigid hold screamed that the ring of keys was gone from her wrist. Her hands groped for them across the stone while the approach moved from a faint chime to a clanging alarm. She rose, unsheathed her dagger, and fed another glow over her palm. Its weak flickering was worsened by the waver of her fingers, but it was enough to illuminate Bladgen.

Once the hovering flare and the sight of the witch filled his eyes, he bounded toward her. She thrust the light into him, inciting a growl and returning the stairwell to darkness. Araina slashed the dagger forward. Its edge fleetingly caught some friction of fabric and flesh and conjured a roar. She struggled to strike another single-handed blow while flitting her left palm to shake free more light.

In her blind swinging and descending advance, Bladgen was able to knock her to the wall. He caught her by the hair and dragged her into a backward bend. Araina flung the dagger to cut away her clutched locks, his hand, or both. She regained a trace of light. Its cast give Bladgen a view of the hilt in her grip. He lessened his clawing to reach for it. Though he was unable to gain a firm hold, Araina could not retain hers. The vying clash sent the dagger tumbling down the stairs, out of reach and nowhere in sight.

The witch contorted and tried to send her struggling light into Bladgen's face or center. It flew off, only tipping his wrist. The bruising impact was just enough to free her and permit a stumbled dash downward to the next landing. Araina groped for the handles of the double doors waiting there. Their parting gave a glimpse of the laboratory lit up beyond. She was dragged away, thrown to the stairs, and pinned under Bladgen's knee. His blood-coated hands thrust to her throat.

Even as the sliver of laboratory light lessened the stairwell's shadows, Araina lost all orientation. Her skull was ground against the stair's edge. Her wings below their scars were tamped under Bladgen's weight and rage. It sent a familiar panic over her senses. She was almost too ready for its drag, for all to go haloed, then grey, and then black. But then, it began to ebb. Bladgen's grip went weak, quivering, then limp. A drop of hot liquid landed below Araina's right eye. Another fell slightly lower, leaking from a bolt-driven puncture in the alchemist's temple. His body lolled down, across, and then beside her on the stairs.

Choking all the while, the witch shoved Bladgen's slack arms off her chest and his leg from across her hips. She rolled and raised herself on her elbows, gasping and searching to gain some anchoring in the sparse light. She found Sol— shadowed on the lower landing and staring from the flight of his crossbow. Their gazes fused and he sprang up the stairs.

The soldier sank to his knees. The witch's frozen face was smeared with blood as he smoothed and searched it with incredulity. He swept her up. Araina's body came to life and clung to his. Sol blinked at the scantly healed slashes that crossed her skin. A pained trace of his voice caught on his breath.

He swallowed thickly and could only ask, "Where's Machalka?"

She reluctantly slipped her arms from his center, and over a crackling hindrance in her throat, answered, "He doesn't matter. The touchpoints do." Her slick eyes shifted to the line of light from the laboratory. "Up there."

Sol reached at his belt and returned her misericorde—recovered from the bottom of the stairwell. He again moved his hand across her cheek and vowed, "You won't need it. I've got our path."

Araina slid the dagger into her scabbard. "It's this way."

∗ ∗ ∗

The witch and the soldier traversed the bodies of alchemists thrown to the reaches of the laboratory. Splayed limbs revealed traces of blue and grey pitted skin. Liquid putrescence soaked their smocks and leadened the fabric to define their contorted, broken shapes. At their hands, shards of glass lay in ashy scorch-marks and told of strange flame risen free, then extinguished. Other containers, overturned but intact, bled sharp, cold glints between the stretching windows.

The room's center was thickly dark. Within, a twitching mass was only just visible. The touchpoints were scattered near it, strewn on the stone amidst saws, blades, vessels, and black sediment spilled from toppled tables. Araina raised her quaking palm and strove to fill it with light. She and Sol watched the darkness stubbornly sweep back and define the waiting mass as a fleshy, hunched figure. Araina released a dire scratch of a gasp.

"There's Machalka."

At her telling, Sol swallowed away his stupor and raised his sword. He slid a boot across the stone, moving to cover the witch as she fought to keep and feed her light. Evoked by the mounting glow, the fleshy ball began to rise. It asserted itself as some bent and elongated version of the baron's body—a form vaguely holding its human limits and limbs within the stretched casing of a stained doublet and breeches. The mass went on uncurling itself. Its eyes, scantly held in the bald and sliding skin of its face, reflected back Araina's light with a predatory clamp.

It stooped to the floor. A slick scrape of metal preceded the emergence of a slim blade taken from the many scattered alchemists' tools. It resembled a flaying knife—one preposterously long—that also gleamed in Araina's waiting cast. With its rise, Sol steeled his grip and stance.

"I'll draw it away. You collect them. Stop for nothing. I've got you."

Before Araina could breathe a word, the figure charged. She flooded her palm and thrust her light over the cover of Sol's sword. The shine dissolved with the racing push.

"Drop!" the soldier shouted.

She barely cleared the swing of flaying blade as it crashed into Sol's sword.

"Go!" he hollered, his voice struggling with his parry.

The witch blindly dashed into the center of the room, pushing against the sound of clanging metal and Sol's exerted grunts behind her. She groped around the floor, pleading with her palm all the while. The tip of a touchpoint grazed her fingertips. Before she could grasp it, Sol roared, "Araina!"

The witch spun to see the flash of the blade. She freed her dagger and caught the strike. The figure reached for her throat with its grotesquely extended fingers.

Even with its single-handed hold, the ground of its blade into her dagger was staggering and relentless. It pushed her faltering stance across the litter of saws, bowls, and sediment.

Sol raced toward the witch's struggling. He swung and prompted the reaching form to spin and match the strike, and with such twisting force, it ripped the hilt from his hands. The soldier dodged and dove after his sword. The fleshy figure raised its blade and swept down again. The slash into Sol's center was narrowly stayed by Araina's dagger. Her desperate, resolute reach spared him a breath to reclaim his sword and footing.

The figure locked into her dagger's guard and tangled Araina into her own weakening hold. As Sol moved to sever the clash, the figure reversed with all its strength. The twist broke Araina's grip, but sent the flaying knife to fly away in kind. Any gain from the slip was lost when the lunge of Sol's sword met the witch's stumble. Its point sank into her side and only ceased as she caught herself ahead of its guard. Sol froze, seized in horror at their places.

"Don't stop," Araina pleaded.

She shoved the blade back, withdrawing the sword from her flesh, and fell to the floor as the figure again slashed for Sol. He barely caught the strike, then the next, and the next, and was unable to so much as call for Araina in the melee. With each parry and counter, the slide of his boots and his roaring became labored and unsteady. Araina held her bleeding side and crawled back to the clutter of tools and overturned tables. Just as Sol's breath ramped to struggling shouts, her reach met Yurkci.

She grasped it, dragged and turned her fingertips across its surface, then flattened it to her hand. Her throat filled, dense and stinging. Her palm went luminous and spun the figure away from Sol. Araina cast her light into the fleshy thing, knocking it into a twisting stagger. Sol thrust and swept his sword, catching it through the neck and splitting its stretched spine. Its pendulous head nearly ripped from its body before the whole of it tumbled to the stone. A puddle of black liquid oozed toward the soldier's boots. He leapt past it to the witch.

Though her side continued to spill, she searched along the floor and gathered up touchpoints. Four were dropped into Sol's quivering reach while she went on pushing her way through bowls and blades for the remaining three.

Araina came to her own dagger, but dropped it immediately and ripped Yurkci back from Sol's arms. She summoned another sphere of light as the soldier turned to the source of her horrified stare. A massive, ripping umbra streamed from the torn pile of the baron's flesh. Araina cast into its center, splattering it into voids. They clung to the wall before slowly worming back to rejoin.

With the last of the touchpoints gathered, Araina returned her dagger to its scabbard and struggled to her feet. Sol tried to aid her through his aghast survey of the vibrant darkness slithering around them. The witch called forth her still-razor-torn wings and moved her bloody hand from her ribs to pull him to the windows. She took Celuf from the scatter cradled in his arms and worked her fingers across its surface.

"Hold tight," she rasped and stepped onto the windowsill.

"To-to you? But your wings...your side. No. No, not both of us."

"I must get these in the ground. I need you with me."

The witch took the remaining touchpoints from his hold, freeing him to lock his arms around her waist. Araina stretched her hand over Celuf and a gale mounted from the windows. Leaning into the gust, she dropped off the ledge with Sol, into the glaring grey sky, and away from the continued convergence of umbras across the laboratory.

Her sliced wings would not stay taut over the rush. Her weakness and their combined weight sent them spiraling. The ground threw Sol's hold from Araina and scattered the touchpoints from hers. As they were lost to the weeds, umbras began to rise.

The witch shot them back with the faint sparks she could muster and continued her desperate crawling search. Sol slashed and separated them as they ceaselessly emerged and amassed at her back. She spied and gathered touchpoints, one by one. When her eyes came to the final one in the weeds, she bounded with the frail aid of her wings, fell to it, and reclaimed the whole of them.

Sol gave a guttural shout before his voice choked away. His form was scarcely visible through the swell of umbras. More continued to charge for her. She dashed away, broadened her wings, and rode along the air, barely keeping above the grass.

Depleted, and with slim gain through distance, she plunged back down, withdrew her wings, and clawed a crude circle of soil. The touchpoints were dropped and slid into the arrangement. Then her skin rapidly stiffened and chilled, her movements strained—an umbra had begun to syphon and thicken.

Araina thrust her hands from the binding necrosis, fighting to link the formation. She pulled, turned, and spread her fingertips. The wound in her side screamed through the invade of a densely leeching force. Though her joints defied her pleas for strength, a final desperate drag called forth the markings. A vacuous pressure clutched her throat. She choked it back and dropped her face to the arrangement. Through tiny, lung-strained traces of her voice, the evocation was sent over the risen surfaces.

"Aqzim, Yurkci inno, Ecivy vheto, Celuf, intot, Mtolin, yeon, Fiwrn, herlon, Weraln, seant Aqzim, Aqzim, Aqzim."

The earth-born forms bonded. Not an instant after its formation, the single mass vanished into the soil in a sudden dissolution. All that told of the sealing was a fierce though silent exhale. It swept from the dirt and thrust the witch back, upright to her knees. The umbra was ripped from her body and into the air, where it dissipated through the same sharp breath. A small illumination swelled below the skin of her throat. With its fade, Araina collapsed to the soil.

The exhale swept on, out across the field, over Sol's fallen form—tearing free and fraying the umbra held within. It carried out across what remained of the curtain wall and snuffed the glare from the moat. Further, it radiated across Vexhi, Svet Hagen, and Crest lines, rushing over all fighting and felled or gasping and writhing.

It pulled at the drape of Glyn's charcoal robe, sweeping with his northwestern trek. It fanned the passenger pigeon's feathers and dragged the ends of the tiny kerchief knotted over a pair of pointed ears. It moved through Zunera and her children, and Ceedly and her students, gathered below the clear glass dome, where their view of the stars seemed to suddenly sharpen. It rolled over the toil-born warmth of Sage's skin and halted his troubled examination of another blight-claimed root. When Tanzan met it from the wall of windows, he lowered his goblet and gaze from the portrait of Kerikan of the Moonserpents. The mist over his eyes cleared at the sound of footfalls beyond the study. Trinera slowly parted its doors.

Chapter Thirty-Five

Fortunate

The soldier briefly squinted at the octagonal slab and kept his hobbled pace. His view tore away and went on desperately darting across the expanse. When it fell upon a dark spot in the weeds, he briskly limped toward it.

Sol dropped and eased Araina from her collapse. The witch spilled slack into his arms. He brought her to his shoulder and tried to send away the rage of his pulse in a quest for hers. He closed his eyes and felt, and listened, then gripped.

"Araina." He sharply swallowed away the seize in his throat. "Araina. Please."

A quivering trail of warm air fell at his neck.

Sol answered it with a shuddering note and tightened her into his shoulder. He gathered her legs and lifted her from the ground.

Glyn fought the slide of his focus—again slipping to the climb of books—and set his eyes to the cake crumbs on his dish. He took another sip from the green glass teacup.

"Of course, if it were strictly based on aptitude, there's no question you'd still be there. Although, there's more than enough to which Ceedly must tend at any time."

Glyn nodded at Tanzan's ongoing explanation and returned the cup to the low table.

"And your access to things there or here would be equally limited, even bearing in mind what you've already achieved. Then there is the broader issue of hands. Our losses are felt harder here, even as they will boundlessly ripple. That was also a factor in the decision. I urge you to be mindful of that. These circumstances are not to be abused any more than they are to be neglected."

Glyn nodded again.

A gentle knock sounded from behind him. With Tanzan's prompt, Sage creaked the study doors forward. "Sorry. Held up at the kitchen again. Chaos down there, more so than usual."

"I'm glad you found your way through it." The warlock smiled. "Glyn, may I introduce Sage of the Phytemagsy. He heads the main conservatory. Since we've resumed our planning of traditional plots and foresting for this coming spring, it's a fortunate place for you to start learning the rhythm of life here. And in the more immediate future, you'll have a fruitful opportunity, pardon the pun, to lend a hand in preparation for the Pulchra Moriendi banquet. It's set for the evening after tomorrow, or was it…"

"The evening after tomorrow evening," Sage answered Tanzan's uncertainty. "The last of the scouts are due to arrive by then." Sage then turned to Glyn. "It'll also be a good way to work up an appetite for it. You don't happen to play an instrument, do you?"

Glyn shook his head.

"Too bad. Was hoping to find a fill-in for me on trubizar so I can get my turn to dance for a change. No matter. You'll have a chance to learn that too, if you'd like."

"Would this sort of work give much time for study…in the long term?" Glyn inquired.

"It *is* study, young man," Tanzan was quick to inform him. "It will have as much to offer as any book in this room or, for that matter, any that somehow found their way to you as an alchemist. The work in that conservatory and our soil is the reason why our books exist." The warlock rose from his armchair and turned to the desk by the wall of windows. "And, as I said, your access is to be very limited until further consideration. We are grateful for your efforts and honesty, but matters are still…raw."

Glyn kept silent and his glacial eyes low until Sage offered, "The value of the work is better shown than said. And it really is interesting. Hard but rewarding. I imagine it will have some overlaps with your previous wor—C'mon, I'll show you the way."

"Thank you," Glyn answered with a nod. "And thank you, si—Tanzan."

"You are welcome, young man. Make the most of it." Tanzan's view remained on the desk as the young men exited the study.

Sol watched the warbler creep along the wall remnant. The black and white maze of its plumage spurred him to wonder how it would appear in strokes of charcoal on pale parchment. The little bird fluttered off into the sky over the southern yard, stirred, along with Sol's attention, by the sweep of a skirt over grass.

"Why is it I can never get a clear answer on your whereabouts?" Imari plunked down his pack.

The soldier lifted his head and sat up. "That's on purpose. But apologies if you carried that all the way to the barracks and back."

"Carried it from there to here. Ended up mixed in with the others after I found it without you. Response is inside."

"Response? Oh." Sol exhaled.

"Supposed it's irrelevant now." Imari looked at the warbler as it returned to perch in the lone tree. "But while I'm out here, I might as well tell you that she's lucky you have the nerve to use novaculite that don't belong to you. Her side's closed up clean."

Sol moved to his feet. "Is she—"

"How are *you* feeling, by the way?"

"I... Mostly normal. Maybe a little off. Tired but restless. Come to think of it, queasy, a bit foggy..."

Imari smiled. "That sounds like the effects of something el—"

"Did you end up with one?"

"An umbra? No. Not I. Dionis did. Along with most of the lines nearest the wall. She's back on her feet now. Well, a foot and a crutch." She sighed. "The others are starting to turn around as well. Seems if they ended up with one right before the moat just...went out, they got through. And if they held on through the journey here, it's said they'll come around."

"I am sorry."

After a somber nod, Imari requested, "You'll have to tell me how you found it."

"Found what?"

"That keyhole of yours."

"I didn't. Just knew to look for one. I came close to... But then, something showed itself."

"Fortunate."

"Just the best option at the time." Sol thickly swallowed and reached into his belt pouch, semiconsciously checking its contents. He looked up from his daze. "Will they let me..."

"Hard to say. She's been moved to her room. It's quiet up there now. As long as you keep it that way, you can probably make an attempt. Mind your manners and don't tunnel in otherwise."

"Thank you, Imari." Sol moved past her, then quickly turned back. "How do I get to…"

"First door after that entrance. Fifth floor. Her room's second on the right."

"Thank you."

"Your pack!" She nodded to where it lay in the grass. "You leave it there, that's where it's staying. I'm through lugging it around."

Sol skidded back, scooped it up, and moved toward the keep a third time, calling once more over his shoulder, "Thank you, Imari."

The silver threads of the moonserpents' tails were a little too radiant against the violet, green, and grey yarns of the storm clouds. Araina squinted into the tapestry, wondering if she had ever paid it much notice in proper sunlight before faintly recalling how her daylight hours were spent at the southern yard. She settled back into the pillows, closed her eyes, and swallowed against the stubborn soreness across her larynx.

Though she vaguely heard footfalls, she didn't bother to part her eyelids. There was nothing left in her to observe yet another pitcher of water, cup of tea, or bowl of broth carried in her direction and ahead of cushioned questions and sanguine utterances—even as this approach sounded faster and denser. It crossed into the room, ceased, and slowed. Moments later, a lingering kiss upon her cheek called her eyes open. Sol knelt and rested his head before her. Araina weakly ran her fingers over his newly cropped hair.

"You," she exhaled, her eyes welling. "Oh, I thought you might've gone."

"Not far," he muttered into the featherbed before meeting her view. "They wouldn't let me camp in the infirmary."

He cupped her reaching fingers into his and bowed back down, feeling her slow breath at his brow for some silent, floating length of time. It ended when steps drew and stopped before the door.

"Sergeant Ekwidou," Trinera observed.

Sol hesitantly uncurled his fingers from Araina's and stood. "Ma'am."

"I expected I would find you here. I understand you requested we speak."

"I did, ma'am."

Araina's hand faintly crawled in search of his. Sol discreetly met her touch as Trinera stated, "We can speak in my study. She still needs her rest."

Araina muttered a stifled protest.

Sol knelt down and whispered, "Be back soon as I can."

"Sol... I need to tell you, I should've..." Her voice rasped away.

"I won't be far." He kissed her cheek again and stiltedly parted their hands, then followed Trinera out of the room.

Down flights and through hallways, the soldier was led to an opulently draped and furnished study—one with even more books than Tanzan's. Instead of the red tufted armchairs, a stretching table with ornately carved high-backed chairs waited in the center.

"Please," Trinera offered a seat with a fluid gesture. "Was there more you thought to tell?"

"Thank you, ma'am. No. And no. I only require a few answers."

"Oh? Regarding?"

"Regarding the offensive, ma'am."

Trinera sighed a short, impatient note. "Answers to the same questions you submitted following your return? You're speaking to the decision to proceed with—"

"To put her at risk as you had. To make no attempt to—"

"As you were aware, Sergeant, she was already under considerable risk. The sort we sought to prevent through our earlier decisions. Per our generals, there was no feasible alternative at the time. And per Svet Hagen command, neither the western nor southern approaches could be adjusted. Our arrangements did not permit that, among other things. That said, and as we've already expressed in many ways, we are immensely thankful for your...well, I suppose I will only say improvisation rather than insubordination. Considering the outcome, it was very fortunate."

"With respect, ma'am, that outcome was up to her, not fortune. To rely on all that and be just as willing to discard—"

"Before you continue, young man, I will remind you that you are still held in the highest estimation and have the utmost gratitude of the whole of our community, but you are not of it. You were appointed by it for a set task. One that you've fulfilled, and despite turns taken. Now, you remain welcome to stay and memorialize with us, but our wider decisions and methods are not—"

"After everything you ordered of me. After everything you told and asked of her. And what it *did*. You would've just taken all that, and—"

"Our decisions and methods are not yours to question. Further considering who and what you are, Sergeant, I fail to see why you would expect otherwise."

Sol met Trinera's austere, poised glare with loosely tempered ire. Its scarce guise of pained underpinnings inclined the high priestess to add, "Araina is safe. As are you. You've both filled your respective roles. There are no more expectations of you at this time. Nor answers waiting for you. And if you seek nothing else, I must insist that you leave me to other business. Much is in need of tending by us, now and as always."

Sol tightened his jaw. He gave a short bow and turned to exit.

"Solairous." Trinera caught him just shy of the doors. "Let it rest. And her. That door has a lock. I would rather not use it. Understood?"

He nodded and left the study.

Chapter Thirty-Six

Anchors and Harbors

Araina watched the song sparrows leap at the tips of the herbs. The bounty of their seeded heads scattered and was fast snapped up.

"Brought back to life just in time to go to seed. Like one big zeadase," she observed.

Sol only smiled and turned into the breeze. It swept more sienna and russet leaves between their feet and below the iron bench. He sniffed at the aroma on its edges. "What is that?"

"Walnut, maple, hare-print…. Whorl cake. For tomorrow night, I imagine. Be prepared to fight for a slice."

"I can smell why. No chestnut in it, right?"

Araina crinkled her nose and shook her head.

The scent thickened and layered with baking dough, released from the door leading to the kitchen. Out stepped a notably tall young man. She blinked back across the plots, and with a slow rise from the bench, breathed, "Oh, that's right…"

Glyn caught sight of the witch's mulberry dress and the bronze cast over her slow curls—only just recognizing her through the contrast of when he last saw her.

"That's Glyn, isn't it?" Sol asked on standing.

Araina nodded.

The young man defrosted and slowly approached through the plots. His smile and greeting were dually cautious. "…Good to see you, Rainy."

Sol furrowed his brow at the nearly forgotten sobriquet. He noticed no changes in the cordial softness over Araina's face.

"Good morning, Glyn. Sol, Glyn was—"

"Yes, so I've heard," the soldier answered. "I was told you're owed some thanks. From me included."

"Oh. Ar-are you the drinking buddy?"

Sol faintly fought the disruption to his countenance. Araina steadied herself on his arm and laughed thoroughly as her mending body would permit.

"Have either of you seen...or heard..." Glyn guardedly inquired.

"No." Araina's smile fast fell away. "Not since..." For a moment, she looked to Sol, whose eyes were fixed with a small impatient flicker. She spread and smoothed her fingers over his sleeve and asked, "Did you bring your books, Glyn?"

"Not mine anymore. Guess they never were."

"Just the same, books only get you started."

"Been told that. Well, I better get back to— Wait, Rainy! I never got to see..."

"It's not nearly as impressive in daylight. And it's sorting itself. I need some time."

"Alright. I'm not gonna forget though."

"I've no doubt of that."

"Good to meet you, Sol." Glyn dipped his head. "'Til next time, Rainy."

He turned and proceeded along the path to the conservatory.

With his parting and passing from earshot, Sol muttered, "Already? They've just let him in and..."

Araina lowered herself to the bench. "The amount of trouble an alchemist could cause here is...somewhat reduced. And he's a unique sort. Aptitude is never unwelcome among Crest. You now know the mountains they make of merit, for better or worse. I'm certain precautions are in order. He wouldn't be where he is otherwise. But I'm presuming that look you wore wasn't really for Glyn. Was it?"

"Don't know." Sol returned beside her. "Got plenty of looks to go around lately."

"He is the reason I'm still in one piece. Apart from you, as always and yet again."

"*You're* the reason you're still in one piece."

"You know it's not that simple." She sighed and looked across the plots. Her eyes went glassy. "I owe you that, Sol. I owe you everything, but I've owed you that for so long. Through so many failings, you still... In the willow swamp, I should've... I was the one who..."

Araina's thickening voice was stifled by Sol's drag of her curls. He cleared them off her neck, and from his belt pouch, retrieved her ribbon-strung copper star. Through his carefully tied restoration of it, the witch lifted her head and took it between her fingers. In her other hand, the corridor key was presented as Sol disclosed, "You're probably right about that look not being for Glyn. I forgot I told you the rest of it on the way back. Hoping it would wake you up. Nothing did. No matter how many times I said please."

Araina turned the key in her fingers. "That's when you last saw…"

"Not a trace since the other side of that door. Little while after that dropped on my head. That reminds me." Sol reached into the front of his jerkin and uncovered Araina's field book. "I confess I flipped through it. Was all I had to keep busy at times."

She slowly untied its woven cover. A sealed slip of parchment fell at their feet. "What's that?" she asked as he lifted it from the leaves.

"Imari must've put it there. Coven's response."

"Response to what? What's it say?"

"Doesn't matter." Sol tapped on the field book's pages. "That does."

Araina fanned the sketches of the harbor seals, luna moths, whelk shells, and the view from her bedroom window between her fingers.

"That's all waiting, isn't it?" he quietly asked.

As she came to his portrait, her breath thickened again. She worked to collect her voice. "And yet, I cannot picture…" She looked up and found him mirroring his depiction in her lap. "You've made the strangest, most fatal places less so through your very presence. Now, the most familiar place seems less so through the thought of your absence. What am I to do, Sol?"

The soldier leaned in and found her lips with his.

"As you've always done." He kissed her again. "Face it. I have to learn if I can do the same. And anywhere near as well."

Araina dropped into his shoulder and looked at the field book. She gripped the edge of his portrait and tore it from the bindings, then placed the book and its remaining pages back in his hand.

"Why would you— Araina, you just took my favorite page," he griped through a smile.

She leaned up and kissed it. "Sorry. Mine too."

Tanzan refilled the green glass teacup and conjured a breezy thanks from the witch. Her eyes wandered within the fading steam while her slow stroking of Usil's right ear remained unbroken.

"Do go on, my dear."

"Oh…but isn't it getting late?" Araina looked to him as he resettled in the armchair.

"Still not quite supper time. But if you wish to retire…"

"No, I'm alright. I just forgot you're no longer…that you are supposed to be this age."

"All hours, once again." Tanzan's smile broadened.

"If you don't mind me asking, what did it take to sort that quarrel?"

"A common concern. And even without it, I had time to remedy matters from my own end. It became necessary for me to seek distraction at times. Particularly when word from Ceedly and then Imari had their lulls. That being said, my dear, do go on."

"Forgive me, where did I leave off?"

"You said they turned to soil."

"Well, they…it…disappeared into it. Or became it. Though I could see so little. I saw them join and then disappear with the last of the evocation. Then I saw nothing until I saw the lamps in the infirmary."

"Our scouts've found not a trace."

"Should there've been any?"

"No. None." Tanzan sipped his tea. As Araina lifted her cup, he observed a fading tremor, only just evident in her knuckles. "You've certainly restored in leaps and bounds, my dear. I thought to suggest we postpone the banquet out of fear you'd not be well enough to—"

"I'm fine, truly, but I'd still rather not." The witch sipped then set her tea down. She rested her hand upon Usil's back. He stretched and settled at her feet, dragging white fur along the hem of her dress.

"Nonsense, Araina, you're the—"

"Please, Tanzan. Let it be a proper Pulchra Moriendi. Let nothing, recognition least of all, come at any expense of the fallen. And I'd rather not let a late night delay my return."

"Your return? Oh, of course. To the shore."

"Yes."

"So soon? But, my dear—"

"I must insist upon it this time. If you've any dire truths or secrets to share, I'm afraid you'll have to send them in a letter. If it outpaces me to the cottage, so be it," the witch declared with her eyes firmly fixed on the old warlock. He watched their maple glow hold the firelight and the shadows caught in the shrinking wounds on her face, then sighed in surrender.

"We will arrange transport then."

"Thank you, but that's unnecessary. I could do with a walk."

"Still? Are you certain?"

"Quite."

"Oh, my dear. When…when will we see you again?"

Araina leaned back in the armchair and stroked Usil's back with her foot, collecting more white fur on the wool of her sock. "For the solstice, I think. If the snow's not early and the path through Barrier's End has eased."

"Or sooner than the snow, perhaps?"

"Perhaps. If it's piled up, it'll at least be cause to learn the sea route and a test of how the sailboat fairs beyond the inlet."

Her softly suggested plan restored Tanzan's grin.

Sol watched the bonfire climb to the scattered stars and spread over the concentric crowd. At his back, the rich aromas of the banquet lingered in the empty and cavernous hall. Its nourishment was shown in the dynamic but finite bodies of those who mourned with calm smiles and vibrant interweaving dance. Cloaks and skirts twisted below line-strung, tinted bottles that held marked paper and beeswax set aflame. Music, all at once haunting and mirthful, guided hands to join and part and steps to cross and spin. The soldier let it fill his senses and blunt his questions a moment longer. He then turned back through the stained-glass framed doors.

He climbed five flights, walked to the second door on the right, and eased it open to look upon a sleeping Araina in the low cast of the bedside lamp. Though silent as he moved to the scoop seat and sat, his presence eased open her eyes. They stayed with his while he slipped free his boots, unfastened his belt and sword, and removed the tailored uniform jacket. At his approach, her fingers, all but covered by the gathered sleeve of her nightgown, uncurled and answered his reach. Sol lowered himself below the quilt.

Araina watched the faint lamplight in his dark eyes and rose to meet his lips with hers. Over and over they joined, taking and then being taken, until there was nothing that existed but senses of warmth, and density, and urgency. Sol's hands gripped and then traveled. Their coarseness smoothed along the skin of her neck, pushing and then fighting the fabric of the nightgown, down her shoulders, across her back. When they wandered to Araina's side, a cutting gasp slipped from her mouth, ran against his, and sliced through his brain.

He quickly withdrew his touch while she tightened hers, shuddering through her pain.

"…It's alright."

That same poorly suppressed sting below her voice moved from his memory and struck him again in the present. He opened his eyes and traced the raised skin of her face, seeing the slashes he met in the shadows of the stairwell.

"It's alright," Araina again promised while her fingers shook through their clutch of his tunic.

Sol searched her eyes and kissed her. He lingered upon the lush, agonizing loveliness he found waiting for him, then he left it and folded her into his chest. Araina briefly pressed her face to her askew sleeve. She let the fabric collect her gathering tears before burrowing herself into Sol's hold, where she remained until dawn bled through the window.

But for the ting of the buckle-fastened sheath, quiver, and crossbow strap, Sol and Araina walked in silence to the edge of the southern yard. When the wall remnants were only grey shapes at their backs, they stopped.

"You're sure that I can't—"

"You walk me to that seashore, I doubt my ability to let you leave it," she warned.

"Can't say there'd be much of a fight."

"I'd plant vineguards to ensure it just the same."

"You're returning today?"

"Yes. Just as soon as you've— And hopefully long before everyone's finish sleeping off last night."

Her answer birthed a small solace in Sol's voice. "Good."

Discarding the curiosity it spurred, Araina dropped her view to the grass and submitted, "Witches and soldiers."

"At times. But from witches and soldiers prevails you and I." His same stalwart tone roused her smile.

"I find the latter preferable. Though as far as its resilience, I'd love your certainty."

"Already have it. But this time, I could use assurance of something."

Sol reached into his long coat and pulled out her field book. From its pages, he presented a fold of paper. Araina slowly uncovered a map of the western coast of Drudgenwood. An inked circle marked the inlet that kept the cottage.

"Wanted to confirm that. I'd like to avoid going anywhere too far from it for too long," he stated.

Araina silently folded and returned the map before raising herself up to kiss him. He held it and her, nearly lifting her from the ground until they parted but for the grip of one another's hand. She let her arm drag back, waiting for his fingers to leave from hers—trying to avoid the sight of his steps with it. Instead she was grasped back and spun. Sol kissed her once more, then turned, almost thrusting her away, to march on without a word. Araina briskly pushed on opposite, if only to keep from looking back or crumbing to the ground.

Under the warm confines of a new cloak, the witch slipped down stairs, over landings, and into the great hall. She kept to its edge to lighten the sharp echo of her boots, which quickened on approaching the stained-glass framed doors. As she moved to part them, she nearly summoned up light—startled by an equally surprised Sage, who entered from the climbing sunlight.

"Good morning." He laughed away his alarm, then his smile fell away. "You're leaving."

"Sage…" The witch pulled her hood back. "I-I'm sorry. This just seemed—"

"I understand. Sorry as I am to see it, I'd been hoping for it. I only wish I would've had a chance to better live up to my offer from so many weeks ago. To give you something for the journey back."

He reached into his pocket and offered a cloth-wrapped seed cake and apple. Araina tried to hide her welling eyes behind her hair as she accepted and slipped them into her sling bag.

"Thank you. I've left a message upstairs, but I'm glad I got to say that to you. Thank you, Sage. Thank you endlessly."

He took her into a brief embrace. "You are welcome, Araina. Endlessly. So don't stay away too long."

With a nod, she returned to the cover of her hood. He let her continue down the stairs and beyond the gapped walls of the courtyard.

The trees kept their odd twists and the short days had begun their work on the weeds and leaves, but Barrier's End was something renewed. The rock-ridden mud and gravelly slopes that so hindered her path had gone mossy and smooth. Fewer boughs scattered the ground—no longer shed from weakened trunks. Those that still lay hosted polypores and served as hunting grounds for tiger beetles and vantage points for chipmunks, who scampered to investigate the passing witch.

The transformations fostered new passage, straight and swift. By early afternoon, it brought Araina to the old split that once swelled with swamp. The cut through the land only held a murky though free-flowing stream. The witch looked into it and removed her cloak. She waited a moment, her eyes crossing its edges for some sign of Lem. When none was found, she breathed forth her wings. A single sweep sustained her glide across the gap, which now called for little more than a leap.

On the opposite side, Araina withdrew the wings below her scars and returned the cloak to her shoulders. Behind the rustle of the fabric, an undeniable flapping asserted itself, then stopped—somewhere high and just to her left. She turned and looked into a twisted tree, spying a stacked silhouette between the golden leaves.

"Having trouble with your passenger pigeon again? If he's still being disobedient, I'd gladly take him into my care. I'm in need of a messenger bird and I'd rather not rely on Crest red-tails or kestrels."

"Whatcha' offerin'?" the elf inquired, his voice low.

"What *was* offered?" Araina then looked away from Den and Pidgie's forms before the sinking sunlight and went on, "What was your reward? The one you were so sure I couldn't offer against?"

"Bit late for that, ain't it, Rainy?"

The witch raised an eyebrow. "Perhaps. I ask because I'm curious of the value of a key now in my possession. And of this star around my neck. They've both found their way to me. And, so have you. I can only presume all of that was once held for a very high price."

Pidgie flapped down to the lowest limb of the tree, carrying himself and Den into clearer view. The elf languorously sighed through his nose.

"Last place I saw 'em. Place we lived 'fore Hagens burnt it to the ground. For nothin'. Like it was nothin'. Patch 'a woods. Was just startin' to grow back. Used to be ours. Was gonna be mine again. Ain't no seashore, but all I had of 'em. Little patch 'a trees."

Araina's eyes softened and lowered. "No, I certainly cannot offer against that. But if you ever dare to cross my path again, I could see about a patch of trees. I know I needn't tell you how to get there."

Den silently watched her return to the cover of her hood and carry on through the stretching shadows.

Just as the torchlight fell over the dirt road, Araina reached the outskirts of the slowly un-boarding and partially patched Drudgenwood market. Her steps halted once to refill her canteen at the fountain, and again, by the amber glow from Monworth's windows. All was still but for the leaves, windswept across the plank walk, until a rhythmic teetering of bottles broke over their scratch. A young blond man limped from the alley with a crate, held to his side with the remaining portion of his right arm.

"Lovely evening, miss," he greeted.

"Yes. Beautiful," Araina concurred with a smile.

"Stews on and it's quiet, if ya need rest for the night." He squinted into the shadows of her hood. "No one to give witches any trouble."

"Thank you. I haven't much further to go though. But, if you will and if she's working, please say hello to Margret."

"Sis? She's right inside." He gestured toward the entrance with his shoulder.

"I'm glad to know it." Araina's smile broadened. "I'll pay her a visit soon. Good evening to you."

"And to you, miss."

Araina turned, crossed the dirt road, and on, to the wooded border.

Her light rippled back from the estuary's pockets, briefly disrupting the congregation of horseshoe crabs and the overhead watch of a screech owl. She passed them and the last of the trees. When she entered the moon's cast, the witch called back her own with a fold of her fingers. The lunar shine fell across the rocks, reeds, and sand, and soon lit the walls of the round stone cottage. Near her sailboat, she dropped her bag and slipped her feet from her boots and socks. Her cloak was shed and lowered beside the pile.

She approached the rising tide. It met the hem of her dress and pulled her ankles into the sand. The racing breath of salt pushed her waves from her healing face and traded with the air in her lungs. The witch let it push, and hold, and harmonize. She turned back to the sand, where she retrieved all she wore and carried, then moved to the door. Her heartbeat rose along the joining of her fingers to the cold handle. Araina held its echo for a moment, eased the door forward, and reentered the cottage.

Acknowledgements

Sincere thanks to those who have formed this work in some way or simply did something to ensure it has made it this far. They include but are not limited to:

David Patterson
Zunera Tahir
Vanessa Maybeck
Caitlin O'Neil
Anthony Beller
Carol Claassen
Ian Hunter
Ali Jackson
Jasmin Robinson
Rhiannon Heim
Nancy Montefusco
Nicholas Montefusco
Sue Lilienthal
Emma Chasen
Marianne Chasen
Deborah Robinson
Ted Delaney
Janet Winberry
Melissa Norton
Michelle Zeman
Diana Florez
Kristen Crescenzo
Mike Grant

A very special thank you to Lauren Humphries-Brooks for her editing services, guidance, and incredible patience.